"Do not let your hearts be trou
In my father's house are many ı
told you. I am going there to prepare a place for you. And if I go and prepare a place for you, I will come back and take you to be with me that you may also be where I am."

John's Gospel quoting Jesus Christ
John 14: 1-3

"Therefore keep watch, because you do not know on what day your Lord will come. But understand this: If the owner of the house had known at what time of night the thief was coming, he would have kept watch and would not have let his house be broken into. So you also must be ready, because the Son of Man will come at an hour when you do not expect him."

Matthew's Gospel quoting Jesus Christ
Matthew 24: 42-44

"For God so loved the world that he gave his one and only Son, that whoever believes in him shall not perish but have eternal life. For God did not send his Son into the world to condemn the world, but to save the world through him."

John's Gospel quoting Jesus
John 3:16-17

THE UNEXPECTED HOUR

A Journey of Tragedy, Faith, & Love

Rob Michie

"The Unexpected Hour"
Global Publishing House
www.globalpublishinghouse.com

© 2015-2018 Rob Michie. All rights reserved. Copyright under Berne Convention.

This publication is designed to provide accurate and authoritative information in regard to the subject matter. It is sold with the understanding that the publisher is not engaged in rendering legal, accounting, or any other professional service. If legal advice or other expert assistance is required, the services of a competent professional person should be sought.

No part of this book may, including but not limited to, be reproduced, scanned, distributed or posted in any printed or electronic form including social media sites and private media rooms, or posted in any format on any website without prior written permission; all usage without permission is in violation of federal copyright and trademark laws and international agreements. Further – to all educational institutions, profit and non-profit organizations; purchasing of this product does not entitle any usage – including but not limited to formulation of class curriculums, no usage is implied or otherwise without prior written permission. Contact our office for all usage permissions.

All characters in this book are created in the author's imagination and bear no resemblance to anyone living or dead. Any resemblance to persons living or dead with a similar name, feature, professions, or life, is purely coincidental.

Scripture in italics taken from the
HOLY BIBLE, NEW INTERNATIONAL VERSION
© 1973, 1978, 1984 by International Bible Society. All rights reserved. Excerpts herein used by permission of Zondervan Publishing House.

For all those who possess a discerning mind and a loving heart.

Also, for Sue, my wife, who has provided love and editing.

And, for my children, Karen, Ken, Deidre and Scott, who keep me laughing and dreaming.

And, for my Mother and Father, who first brought me into the Word.

Table of Contents

Acknowledgements — 9

Foreword — 11

Part One — 15

Tragedy

Part Two — 67

Beliefs

Part Three — 222

The Savior

Part Four — 355

The Return

Part Five — 439

Looking Ahead

ACKNOWLEDGEMENTS

I owe considerable thanks to Zondervan Publishing House for their wonderful NIV Study Bible, which has been a constant companion throughout the writing of this book. Without their excellent Bible I would not have been able to write this story with the necessary scriptural references. I applaud them for spreading the gospel in the manner they do. Thank you, thank you!

Thanks to James P. Gills and Tom Woodward for their book titled *Darwinism under the Microscope*, copyrighted 2002, and published by Creation House. This book inspired me to coin the phrase *Divine Design* to explain the origin of humankind. Thanks to Jerry Quain of Creation House for providing a copy of this book.

Special thanks go to my wife for putting up with my absences while I wrote. She has been my constant companion in our travels throughout the world. Thanks too for her editing.

Thanks to Karen, my daughter, and to her husband, Nick, for their editing and technical assistance. Both improved my writing in form and content.

Thanks to my sons Ken and Scott, and to friends who spent time with me in Alaska floating the fascinating Branch River.

Thanks to my daughter Deidre and my son Ken for doing work for the Lord. Your dedication inspires me.

Thanks to my father who survived a prison camp in World War II and went on to be my dad and someone I always have held in high regard. He is in heaven and I look forward to seeing him again. Thanks too, to my mother who has always been an example of a loving Christian. She continues to be in my prayers as she gracefully walks with the Lord on a daily basis.

Thanks too, for the scholarly advice and Christian wisdom from one of my close church ministers, Doug Dornhecker. His service to the Lord and his love for all of God's children provides a shining example of faith and love.

This publication would not have made it to completion without the help of my publisher, Paula T. Webb. She tirelessly edited the book and improved upon its content with constructive suggestions. She guided me through the publication process for which I will be forever grateful.

Most of all, thanks to my Lord and Savior for calling me to His service!

Foreword

In my latest faith-based book, Michael Channing, a successful entrepreneur, is a fictional character in a drama that unfolds following a family tragedy. Like many of us, Michael faces a fork in the road of life. There is no going on as before, and choices need to be made while dealing with the pain in his heart.

Like Michael, my life, and, no doubt your life, has led to forks in the road. In those times when we must face choices, those choices define who we become. Notably, the collective results of those choices define our lives in the end.

Michael's path leads him to deal methodically with deep depression and his personal beliefs and expectations. Just as Michael progresses in a thorough search for answers and directions, we, in our own way, follow a self-directed path. It is a path that needs to be based on fundamental beliefs and actions aligned with those beliefs.

In many respects, this process of self-determination based on our beliefs is what should focus our actions towards becoming the person we aspire to become. Properly aimed, it is what will reconcile us through love to the one who created us in the first place.

A little of my background would be appropriate at this point. After graduating with an engineering degree from Texas Tech University, Rob married his high school sweetheart, Sue, from Arlington, Virginia. In 1975 following five years of military service at bases in Texas and Alaska, I found myself starting a civilian life in the Pacific Northwest. I had a new job in a different region of the country, and I was waiting to buy a home so my wife and children could join me. Ultimately, over the years we relocated a few times. Each time we attended local churches and encouraged our four children to attend church and participate in church programs. We wanted our children to know God. It was during those years that I first began thinking about God's plan for me and my family, because raising four children in a Christian environment was first and foremost in those early years.

My professional work as an engineer, financial manager, and ultimately as a timber company executive allowed me the luxury of an early retirement with time to concentrate on serving the Lord in church, in our local community, and in state prisons. Parallel to this volunteer work I became fascinated with God's plan for humankind. Since 1975, I have read and studied biblical prophecy, and have reinforced my faith with extensive travels throughout the world to explore my understanding of God's plan to bring Heaven to Earth. I have even been blessed to have traveled to where the apostle John stood when he received the Revelation on Patmos Island in the Mediterranean.

Yet, as my family and I progressed through the years that followed, it became evident that many relatives, friends and neighbors did not feel the same draw to God. They simply did not know God well. We respected their personal choices and hoped they would find God.

Ultimately, this gave rise to the belief that everyone needs to have a comprehensive explanation of God and His plan for us. This book is an attempt to provide everyone a chance to take a parable-type journey searching for the answers to the universal questions about faith in God and His Son Jesus.

In this book, I explore the importance of faith in God's plan and the likelihood that Christ's return will occur in the next 20 years. I hope that it inspires you to draw your own conclusions about the future.

Enjoy the journey!

And may the peace of God always rest upon you!

Rob Michie

Part One

TRAGEDY

1

Mercer Island, Washington

The phone rang at 11:11pm. It was Adrian, his son-in-law, on the other end of the line and he sounded frightful. He spoke in broken sentences separated by sobs and tears.

"Lisa and Catherine are gone...," he said. "Michael, I can't believe it. They are gone...," he said again. "A drunk driver headed in the same direction, southbound on I-405 crossed two lanes of traffic and hit Lisa's car on the driver's side. Lisa apparently lost control of the car. The car swerved off the interstate hitting the guard rail at 50-60 miles per hour. Michael, they say the car flipped on its side before hitting another barrier. They have been taken to the nearest hospital."

"Oh my God! Who told you this?" Michael inquired.

"The State Police are here to take me to the hospital where they are. They got a call on the way here that Lisa and poor little Catherine were dead on arrival. Michael, will you come to the hospital?' Adrian responded.

"Oh, my God, Adrian, of course." Michael started shaking. He got the name of the hospital and replied, "I'll be there as soon as I can. Oh, my God."

That was five months ago and the time since that late-night telephone call seemed like a blur. Michael Channing, a successful entrepreneur, had lost his own wife, Mary, two years earlier to pancreatic cancer. In this unexpected hour, he now had to bear the burden of having lost his only daughter and his only grandchild.

Adrian Defoe, Michael's son-in-law, had not fared any better in those five months since the tragic accident. Working as a 35-year-old aerospace engineer for the largest aerospace company in the country, Adrian had been grieving through the memorial service, the funeral, and every day since. Work was an escape for Adrian, but it did not shield him from the depression of such a loss. Returning home each evening to an empty house only paralleled the emptiness in his heart.

Adrian became lonely during those five ensuing months. His parents lived on the east coast but he spoke to them frequently on the phone receiving some reassurance about a brighter future ahead. Work friends rallied to help him with work projects. Working on the avionics of the world's largest commercial aircraft required all of his attention at work, however, his now empty home, especially weekends at home, presented him with time to contemplate his losses, and his were many.

Adrian and Lisa had met at a University of Washington Husky football game 14 years earlier. Each of them showed up with dates who happened to be good friends and who arranged a double-date for the game and a party afterwards. It was at that party that Adrian and Lisa struck up a conversation that led to dates on their own. Following graduation they got engaged and a spectacular wedding followed a year and a half later. That was 11 years ago. After working in the Seattle area for the next eight years Lisa and Adrian were ready to have children. That decision was followed with the pride of their lives in the form of a cute little girl named Catherine Mary Defoe.

Catherine was a good baby. Other than waking her parents up during the night for the first nine months and two bouts of ear infections, she was as sweet a baby and toddler as any parent could hope to have. She walked when she was 11 months old and at two years old seemed very content to tell anyone just how much she knew whether she was asked or not. She was very normal, and she was loved as much as a child should be loved.

For Lisa and Catherine to be gone just did not seem right and it ripped at Adrian's heart. He questioned God. He cried. He sobbed. Not in public, not with someone, but he did all those things at night and at odd times on weekends. He did them alone. He grieved!

If Adrian was struggling with grief as any husband and father would, Michael would have to be considered a complete "basket case." Having to endure these two most recent losses, on top of his wife's passing just over two years ago was more than he could handle. He had work with which to contend, but his professional circumstance was unusual.

Michael Channing was one of those rare visionaries in the technological world of computer science. He could see things no one else could see and combined with an extraordinary ability to pick equity investments it made him a very wealthy man.

With a Bachelor's degree in Industrial Engineering from Texas Tech University, a Master's degree in Computer Science from M.I.T., and an M.B.A. degree from Harvard he was recruited heavily by the high-paying tech world. He came to Redmond, Washington and excelled at every challenge he undertook.

Seven years prior he had left his employer to pursue the development of an artificially-intelligent software diagnostic system to be used by large-scale enterprise developers. In layman's terms, he was developing an application that operates like a full-time dedicated doctor/specialist/pharmacist/hospital that would operate for patients. It would identify current and potential problems in a software system and take action to cure them immediately. Basically, it would solve problems before they showed up and it would even suggest improvements to the system that might not have been identified by anyone.

Michael was so far along in the development of this system he called PROPHET that his previous employer made him an offer he could not refuse. The offer was for the acquisition of all rights to his software application package plus a three-year commitment to finalize the development and sales strategy of the package. Sales for the system were conservatively estimated to be more than a billion dollars.

For Michael's agreement he would be paid $50 million for signing and $40 million at the end of each of the following three years. The offer totaled $170 million dollars. He signed the deal two and a half years ago, and it was not a month after signing the agreement that Mary was diagnosed with terminal pancreatic cancer. All the retirement planning was gone! That too had been an unexpected hour. It changed everything for him.

Michael was fulfilling his business obligation to this lucrative agreement, all the while dealing with Mary's last days. However, his system was so well developed the company was able to step up the time-frame it planned to deliver the product to the marketplace. Michael only needed to be available on a part-time basis for three more months.

The memorial service for Mary had been a sight to behold. She had touched so many people's lives. Over 450 people showed up for the service. Although he attended church a few times each year, Michael wondered just how many folks would have shown up for his service if it had been him who had died. For certain, most of those who would have shown up would have done so in support of Mary, not him.

Now, after having attended the services for Lisa and Catherine, Michael felt as though he had lost everything. Like Adrian, Michael was okay at work, but the nights, the evenings, and the weekends were torturous. Work was to end in three months and he felt his life should be at its end when he leaves work for the final time. He simply longed to rejoin Mary!

All the ideas and all the plans that he and Mary had made were all for naught. They had laid awake some nights talking about how life would change when he retired. Mary was pretty happy the ways things were and really was never interested in following their financial fortunes. To her the present was everything. As long as travelling did not interrupt her schedule too much she looked forward to doing the travelling they had only dreamed about. He had wanted to take Mary to Paris and show her the City of Lights. Michael loved to fish and had always thought about building a wooden boat. Maybe having a small house on a lake in eastern Washington would promote both dreams. That had sounded wonderful to her!

All for naught! His motivation was gone.

2

King Salmon, Alaska

Their flight landed in the afternoon at the King Salmon Airport, a facility used by the U.S. Air Force as a forward fighter intercept base and a radar search location. Earlier they had taken a flight from Seattle's Sea-Tac airport to Anchorage where they made a connection. It was the last week of June and the plane was packed with fisherman and military folks. The commercial salmon season was looking good for a big run of sockeye salmon. Gillnetters were loaded and ready as were the shuttle boats and the canneries.

Michael and Adrian had scheduled this fishing trip a year ago and they decided it might be best for them to just do it. Neither was as excited about the idea as they would have been had circumstances been different. Michael had done the same trip a half dozen times but this was a first for Adrian. Adrian, however, was an avid fly fisherman and frequented southwest Montana to fish for brown trout on an annual basis. Except for this year!

The plan was to fish a half day the next morning on the Nak Nak River. A few kings (Chinook salmon) were running the healthy waters through King Salmon. These are waters flowing out of the

Katmai National Park, including waters running from the famous Brooks River where brown bears are commonly photographed fishing for salmon that pass over the falls on their way to spawning tributaries.

The second part of the trip plan was to float a four-man raft 40 miles down the Branch River. This would require a float plane ride in and ride out five days later.

Michael and Adrian stayed in a rustic lodge near the Nak Nak River. After getting the necessary license and tags at the local hardware store they met their guide, Jeremy, at dinner and decided to meet at the dock at 5:00 a.m. the following morning. The tide would be favorable for the four hour morning fish run. Along with the fishing, Michael had planned a surprise for Adrian in the afternoon.

So it was, at 5:00 a.m. the three of them left the dock and headed downriver in Jeremy's boat. Fishing with 40-pound test was not something Adrian had done, but he caught on quickly. He liked the thought of catching fish big enough to test that kind of line strength.

Sure enough, after about half an hour of dragging wobbly lures around, Michael's pole bent down hard. Jeremy had fished with Michael for the past couple of years and respected his ability to handle a pole. He knew Michael had a good idea as to what to do, so he kept quiet and let him play the fish expertly. Once the fish got tired after about 15 minutes, Jeremy guided the boat close enough to net it. The fish weighed 26 pounds.

The next hour was slow. Other boats caught a fish here and there, but Michael and Adrian did not get any action. Adrian was beginning to wonder if salmon fishing was all it was cracked up to be. Jeremy had both fisherman reel in; he ran the boat upriver around a bend to the right where a large rock protrudes into the river.

Jeremy took each lure and placed a drop of his special recipe on each one. He rubbed it around with his forefinger and said they were good to go. It wasn't five minutes until Adrian's pole bent straight down. Fifteen minutes later, after chasing the fish all over the river and figuring it had gotten off twice, the fish rolled onto its side next to the boat. Jeremy netted it perfectly. It weighed in at 32 pounds.

Back at the dock Jeremy recommended a place to have the fish cut, wrapped and frozen for the trip back home in five days. Michael settled up with Jeremy giving him a nice tip and promising to schedule another trip in one of the next two years.

After leaving the fish with the folks who would package it, Michael and Adrian got an early lunch and crashed for an hour of sleep. There is not a lot to do in King Salmon that is not fish related that time of year, but there is one thing Michael had always wanted to do but simply had not gotten around to doing.

Keep in mind, it does not get dark in King Salmon until after 11:00 p.m. in the summer due to the northern latitudes. So when Michael arranged for an afternoon excursion flight to Brooks River Falls, it left plenty of time to do that and return for dinner with the float plane pilot.

They arrived at Brooks River in time to see that several brown bears had staked out a claim for the fishing that day and perhaps the days ahead. Once the sockeye salmon enter the Brooks the word travels fast and the number of bears multiplies. At any rate, there were plenty of bears around to give all the human visitors a thrill.

It was the mama bears with cubs that captured the attention of everyone. Seeing the cubs stand on their hind legs and looking all about was a special sight in nature. The cubs were just like little kids.

Climbing into the float plane for the return trip to King Salmon, Adrian commented. "Michael, I know I have seen photos taken at this very spot. I did not expect to ever be here. Thanks for the side trip. I'll never forget it!"

Flying back to King Salmon Michael pointed out the immensity of the landscape in all directions. Looking north he pointed in the direction they would be flying the next day to reach the lake where they would begin their 40-mile float trip. After seeing the bears at Brooks River, Adrian may have had misgivings for signing up for the trip, but if he did, he didn't show it.

The next morning they had breakfast in the lodge and checked out. The air charter outfit sent a driver to pick them up. Once at the river's edge they helped the crew load their gear along with a raft, oars and safety vests. They were flying in a DeHaviland Beaver, one of the safest float planes being flown in the Alaskan bush.

Their flight took them north of King Salmon. As they gained altitude it was easy to see Bristol Bay to the west and the Katmai Mountains to the east. As they continued north rolling tundra passed beneath them as did many unnamed small lakes. In the distance they could see large expanses of water. Adrian began to wonder just how far they were going into this untamed wilderness.

The pilot motioned that he was flying west of the drop-off spot. He wanted them to see the pick-up point, a small gravel bar, so they would better recognize it five days later and not float on by. Adrian, seated in the back thought: sure thing, one gravel bar looks like scores of others!

From the pick-up point the pilot flew low and right up the river they were going to float. One raft was seen in the lower section and two were spotted in the upper section as they made their way to the outlet of Nonvianuk Lake.

Adrian thought: well, at least there are others doing this trip!

The landing was awesome for Adrian, who had never flown in a float plane. The plane skimmed over the lake water and nosed toward the south edge of the outlet. Just before hitting the beach the pilot cut the engine and in one swift move left the cockpit area, jumped to the pontoon on his side and stepped in the water at the lake's edge. He slowed the aircraft's movement, spun the plane around 180 degrees and lodged it on the gravel bar using a rope attached to one pontoon and tying the other end to a nearby willow.

Once ashore they unloaded their gear and piled it on a dry spot near the beach. After a quick goodbye the pilot was in the plane and speeding across the lake before they could get more than one picture of the departure. Michael had a big grin on his face. Adrian wasn't so sure about being left way out in the middle of nowhere with an inflatable rubber raft as the only means of transportation back to a civilized spot, but he certainly wasn't going to show anything but delight.

Michael had mentioned the possibility of encountering bears. It had been a discussion point from the first mention of the trip. Michael had told Adrian that he had seen bears each and every time he had done this particular float. It was one of the reasons he enjoyed the trip so much. It was such a completely different environment from where he worked, that it was one of those things that helped him stay balanced. He felt like there was something bigger about the world and life than the "normal" world where he spent most of his time. Adrian understood, but still wanted to know more about the bears.

On previous trips Michael had brought a rifle or a large revolver. When it was easy to transport rifles through airports, Michael brought a Winchester 30.06 with special "hot loads" of 200-grain cartridges. Later he brought a .357 magnum revolver, but even that had become a hassle to get on the airline. So, for this trip he brought bear repellent. They read the directions and each packed a canister where they could get to it easily.

After setting up camp, which consisted of a four-person tent with waterproof fly, they stepped down to the water's edge. Michael said, "Conditions look good for fishing. The river has dropped more than normal because the weather has been unseasonably warm for most of the month. The snow melt from the mountains has largely pushed through and the river is clear. Even the forecast is for cloudy but fair weather. For the next few days conditions look very favorable."

Adrian, said, "Well, how about if we do some fishing. Trout for dinner sounds good to me."

It did not take but two casts with a spinning rod to hook a nice 1 ½ pound trout - dinner would be easy. Adrian quickly moved to his fly rod using a sinking line and a newly purchased wet fly he had picked up in a local fly fishing store back home.

For the next hour and a half all you could hear from the two of them was "fish on" as they both enjoyed a tranquil time of catch-and-release fishing. Dinner was caught at the end. Adrian did the cooking and Michael cleaned the dishes and cook site to minimize the presence of food scent in the area.

Although the two were concerned about bears it was the mosquitoes that were the real threat to enjoying this serene place. They weren't particularly large, nor were they as ferocious as, say, Florida mosquitoes, but they were *so* numerous and *so* persistent. They were everywhere! This is the reason so few folks are here, Adrian thought.

Michael had warned Adrian, but you simply have to see it to believe it. Michael had insisted they both bring plenty of bug spray with a high percentage of DEET content and to bring head nets. To be without these, would be asking for insanity to set in.

As they sat around the fire, they finally couldn't stand it any longer and climbed into the spacious tent they brought. After swatting the mosquitoes inside and accepting the tedious buzz on the tent walls outside, they settled into their sleeping bags.

After a while Michael asked Adrian how things had been going since the last time they had talked. Adrian said he was still grieving and that he had almost called Michael to back out of the Alaskan trip. Michael asked, "Why?"

"Well, I didn't feel I really deserved to go on this trip. I still feel empty, and in some ways I feel guilty for what happened. Perhaps, I'll know one day that it is okay to carry on with life. All of this was so unexpected," Adrian replied.

Then he added, "How long did it take you to move on after Mary passed away?"

"Can't really say I've moved on!" Michael responded. "I've thought about this a great deal in the last two years. You know Adrian, you and I are a lot alike. We both loved our wives more than we even knew. We both loved little Catherine more so, and we both can't see clear of our loss. Simply speaking, that loss stays with us, and it could be that way forever. What I've concluded, is that if I'm to move on, it will not be by reducing the load of my loss, but by learning how to carry it with me as I move on. In general terms, Adrian, I think we have to deal with this loss by not expecting it to go away, but by being glad for the time we had with our loved ones and by being able to carry them with us in our hearts. I know I have to quit feeling sorry for myself. I need to cherish the love that still burns in my heart for three people who have been closest to me in my life, and then I have to do what I can do to carry on their legacy, as well as my own."

Adrian replied, "Michael, you have been dealing with loss longer than I have, so I respect what you say and I believe you are right about learning to carry the burden of loss as you described it. I appreciate hearing that. Also, I am a bit surprised you think we are alike! I have always looked up to you for your love of family, your professional success, and the integrity with which you do everything you do. Thanks for being a good father-in-law and, oh, yeah, for flying me into this mosquito-infested fishing paradise! Ha ha!"

Michael responded quietly, "Adrian, you know what first impressed me about your marriage to my daughter? It was that you and Lisa were able to develop common goals as a family, and you worked so well together in operating as a family. Mary and I had separate agendas throughout much of our married life. Early on, even before we were engaged, I insisted that my work was my passion and Mary always accepted that. She never complained about my work and she was always supportive of what I did. Likewise, she was insistent from the beginning that she wanted church and her belief in God to come first, including her charity work. I admired that in her and accepted it fully. On the other hand, you and Lisa had more of a common purpose. You always placed work high on your priority list, but you lived your life hand-in-hand with Lisa when it came to church and family obligations. I admire that trait in you!"

Adrian said, "Thank you! Wow, you have a very discerning mind. That is a trait I greatly admire in you. We are all different in how we handle relationships, but love remains the single thing that holds us together." Michael agreed.

Soon they drifted off to sleep.

3

Branch River, Southwest Alaska

The following day was spent at Nonvianuk Lake. And, Nonvianuk Lake was huge. It appeared to be about 14 miles east to west and perhaps four to five miles north to south. Michael and Adrian camped on the far west end of the lake where the river exited to the west. East of the lake were the coastal mountains, including periodically active volcanoes like Mt. Redoubt.

To the north about 10 miles was another large lake called Kukaklek. Flowing from that lake to the southwest was a large outlet river that merged with the one from Nonvianuk. Together these two rivers meandered through lowlands of tundra, small hills and vast areas of wetlands which headed toward the commercial fishing mecca of Bristol Bay. And, all of these lands have served as spawning grounds for salmon for millennia.

Across from the campsite being used by Michael and Adrian, on the north side of the river outlet was an old fishing camp named Hammersley Camp. Although used by fly-in fishing guides sporadically it was vacant today, making the whole area rather serene. Adrian awoke first the next morning, and could hear loons on the lake calling to each other. With the stillness in the foggy air and an equal stillness on the water the loons made a beautiful sound. Only the gravel-washing sound of the river accompanied the loons. Oh, of course, the mosquitoes were also ever-present.

The next day was a day for the books as far as fishing goes. After rigging the raft with all their gear, they fished the shoreline and even ventured out in the lake to fish the center channel of the river. Lots of catch-and-release activity!

Afterwards, they paddled to shore to check air pressure in the raft and to see that all their gear was well stowed. Then they headed downstream. Michael handled the steering from the rear of the raft and Adrian sat upfront and helped power the nose of the raft in the direction Michael called out. They quickly clicked as a team and deftly handled the raft as it swiftly headed down stream.

Not half a mile downstream they spotted a mama bear with two cubs on the south bank. As if choreographed, the two cubs stood on their hind legs and watched them as Michael steered slightly to the far bank. This was a sight to remember!

They found ways to pull the raft in behind some of the center channel islands. They quickly found fish in eddies at the downstream end of these islands, and the challenge was to do this swiftly so as to avoid leaving Adrian on the island as the raft pivoted away downstream with no means to reverse its course upstream. They learned *quickly* and never missed!

Having avoided this threat, they would carefully secure the raft before either one of them exited the craft. Fishing these areas produced some excellent trout and they marveled at the abundance of fish in the river. The water was cold and perfectly clear. The fish were hungry and anxiously awaited the feast of salmon eggs soon to be their summer diet.

Michael proved to be very well equipped to maneuver the ungainly raft and Adrian was an excellent oarsman up front. In slower water they would drift through large holes where inevitably one of them would hook a nice four to five pound fish and fight it some distance downstream before they drew it near the boat where they could release it.

By afternoon they had floated 10 miles downstream from where they had started. They pitched camp at a spot less than a mile from the confluence with the river flowing from Kukaklek Lake. The area was timbered and it had been difficult to find a good landing from which to off-load. In fact, they had been lucky to find one.

After building a warming fire and eating a quick dinner they once again found themselves inside the tent and shielded from the mosquitoes. After recounting the superb fishing of the day, Adrian asked Michael, "What are you planning to do six months from now when your contract ends at work?"

Michael smiled and said, "You know, Adrian, I haven't quite decided. But I am close. Mary had the foresight to leave me a note to be opened after she passed away. She wrote it when we decided to bring in Hospice to work with us. As you know they are wonderful folks, and I do not know how I could have made it through that time without them. Of course, Lisa and Catherine brought a smile to Mary's face every day when they would show up. Still the Hospice folks were there in the afternoon and at night when Mary experienced some of the worst effects of the cancer."

Michael continued, "At any rate I did not get around to reading Mary's note until a week or so after the memorial service. I haven't told anyone about the note, and I must admit her note has caused me to rethink some things in my life. Basically, after saying how wonderful our marriage had been and how wonderfully we had honored our commitments to each other, she wanted to 'cross the line' on our agreement for her to not press her religion on me. She asked that I read and contemplate two Bible verses. The first is from Luke, Chapter 16 verses 19-31. The second is from Matthew; Chapter 16 verses 24-28."

Adrian said, "I have to admit I can't quote chapter and verse even though I attended many Bible study groups and many sermons with your daughter. So, refresh my recollection on those two."

"Adrian, you are a saint in your walk with Christ. I am a novice comparatively. Like I said the other evening, work and family have been my life. Anyway, the first passage has to do with a rich man named Lazarus."

Adrian interrupted and said, "I know that story. The rich man dies and goes to hell where he wishes to warn his family of the consequences of his life, including ignoring the sick man at his front gate."

"Well done Adrian", commented Michael. "The poignant part of the second passage is *'what good will it be for a man if he gains the whole world, yet forfeits his soul?'* It goes on to talk about the forthcoming return of Christ and the judgment that follows."

"Okay" said Adrian, "I've heard that one a few times, as well. So what was Mary telling you when she included them in her note?"

"I feel conflicted," Michael replied. "That's the bottom line. Mary is simply warning me about where I place my priorities. She knows it isn't so much the money as it is the devotion to work at the expense of more important things. She is calling me to rethink my priorities."

"So what are you going to do about it?" Adrian challenged.

"If ever anyone had a chance to refocus their life, I have that opportunity. I don't want to miss it. With my contract ending in six months I could take on another project, build another company and build a better 'mousetrap' in the technology sector. God knows I have plenty of offers out there to do just that. But, no! Mary's life and her note have sent me in a different direction. I want to discover what she discovered about God and his plan for all of us. I firmly believe in God and I want to believe Jesus Christ is part of that plan."

"Wow, how do you propose to do that?" Adrian urged him on.

"Early thoughts are this. I want to put a very small team together of people who want to take 'a journey of discovery' with me. The idea being that the team would scour past and present facts that provide evidence to God's plan for humanity, including physical evidence, prophetic evidence, historical evidence, etc. Then based on those findings, make our own projection of God's plan."

"Holy smokes!" exclaimed Adrian. "Who has the time and the resources to do all that? I thought we're supposed to live in faith, do what is right, and just let the small stuff take care of the big stuff."

"Well, stated Adrian," Michael replied. "That is why I need you to be on the team. I need someone who is well based in the fundamentals to help me drill out what is important and what is not."

"Like I said, holy smokes! Hey, I have a job already; at least until the next corporate decision forces my job to move. I appreciate the thought of including me, but I'm not qualified for that and, besides I need to rebuild my life."

Michael paused, "Listen, Adrian, I am going to set up a Foundation to do this work. The paperwork is already being drafted and I expect to sign all the necessary papers when we get back. I am going to fully fund the Foundation upfront and I am prepared to make you an offer that I do not think you can refuse."

"I could use some good news, so try me." Adrian replied.

"What is your current salary?"

"I make $93,000 per year."

Michael paused, "With benefits that is roughly $125,000 per year. Right?

"Yeah, that probably is close."

"For the job I have in mind for you, the Foundation will double your current pay. That is $125,000 per year and you buy your own benefits, that way I keep the accounting for payroll simple. Secondly, you sign up for two years and I commit the Foundation to a two-year employment contract. Third, at the end of the two years you will receive a $200,000 guaranteed bonus. Fourth, all your travel expenses, which may be extensive, will be paid by the Foundation."

"What is the name of this Foundation?" Adrian asked.

"It is going to be the 'Mary J. Channing Foundation.' It is being set up as a non-profit foundation for the advancement of Christian studies. It will accept donations and provide charitable funds as they become available. I will be Chairman of the Board, CEO, and President. If you accept, you will be the Vice President of Christian Studies. I expect to have two other employees. One administrator and one financial/travel specialist. Oh, the Foundation will soon receive from me $10,000,000 contribution as seed-money."

Puzzled, Adrian said, "Wow. Michael, this is a bit overwhelming. I still don't know why me?"

Michael responded, "In the early years of developing and operating my company, I searched for the best people I could find. I am pleased to tell anyone that the five code writers I hired are as good as any in the world. They are from all over. One lady is from Israel, two of the men are from Romania, one man is from Turkey and the other is from Boston. I paid them well, gave them a huge bonus when we sold, and now they are doing great things for the company that purchased mine. In some respects, I feel like their father. A proud one at that!"

He continued, "Adrian, you made my daughter so happy. You have been a great husband and father and son-in-law. I know your astuteness and your willingness to speak your mind. I want to go on this journey with you at my side. After two years, you can leave if you like. I will respect any decision you make at that time, but please consider this offer."

"Thank you for your faith in me and let me think about it. I'll give you a decision right after we get back to Seattle."

Michael simply said, "Fine."

The next three days passed with the two of them simply rafting and fishing. Neither spoke of the job offer Michael had laid on Adrian. They simply were sport fishermen enjoying the scenic Alaskan wilderness. Michael remembered back to the first time he had been on this same river. It had been in 1985. A particularly dry year that year he and his dad had to pull their raft through many of the low lying stretches of river that lay ahead of them in what is called "the braids."

The first day when Michael and Adrian hit the confluence of the two rivers their speed picked up noticeably. They easily covered 13-14 miles finding themselves at less than 250 feet of elevation. Having started at the lake where the elevation was nearly 650 feet they knew they had definitely dropped elevation. More tundra was evident on the sides of the river and more wetlands were ahead as they entered the "braids."

By the end of the second day their progress slowed going downstream. They stopped often to fish in the "braids," and the fishing was good. Paddling into some of the side channels they found resident northern pike anxious to strike anything that moved. Adrian tied on a large lure that closely resembled a mouse. He quietly tossed it onto the edge of the bank. He slowly and gently would work the fake mouse into the water and start wiggling it so that ripples in the water would send out the alluring signal that dinner was served. When lucky, a northern pike would rise from the depths and make a beeline for the lure. After an exciting thrashing of the poor mouse the hooked pike was less exciting to reel to the boat and neither of the two ever volunteered to unhook the tooth-laden fish by hand. Only with long nosed pliers in hand did the fish get the release it awaited.

The "braids" are an incredible feature to this wonderful river. Waterways meander in every direction tirelessly progressing toward the salt water of Bristol Bay. Michael recalled to Adrian his first trip years prior when the area was full of beavers. Lodges the size of medium sized homes frequented the journey through this area. He remembered tying off the raft with his dad and the two of them climbing to the top of the largest lodge in the region. It was over 20 feet high. From the top they could see the dammed area behind the dam and it looked like an Olympic sized pool. The lodges now were not as frequent or as majestic as Michael remembered. Beaver trapping and more severe winter ice break-ups had reduced the virgin nature of this river area to something not as glamorous as he thought it once was.

Still the fishing was good. On many of the small river islands they stopped and used fly rods to catch grayling. These fish with their abnormally large dorsal fin weighed in at one to two pounds. During a cadis fly hatch like the one Adrian and Michael were now experiencing, the grayling fishing was unbelievable. It was mesmerizing to simply watch the fish rise to the flies as they landed on the water's surface. The fish were simply gorging themselves on this week long event. At least the caddisfly's did not bite like the mosquitoes!

The last day of rafting was a long arduous day of slow moving water. More times than they could count they had to get out of the raft and pull it through a shallow pool and back into deeper and faster moving water. They were exhausted at the day's end.

They did have some excitement, however. First, it wasn't 30 minutes into their morning float down river where there was fog hanging above the river that they saw a bull moose cross just ahead. He was a huge, massive animal – and this bull had a rack over five feet tip-to-tip.

After beaching the raft, the two of them headed up the bank to get a better look at the magnificent animal. After following the animal and getting closer Michael stopped and realized that if the moose turned and charged there was really nowhere to get away safely. As a result, he stopped, took a quick photo, and led Adrian back to the raft.

Later at a good spot for lunch, they heard splashing along the river's edge. Sure enough the sockeye salmon had made their way into the lower reaches of the river and were headed to the spawning grounds upstream. They tossed a few lures in front of where they stood but to no avail. Adrian got out a bright pink egg pattern fly and tossed that out. It wasn't long and they had a fish on. With Michael's help they landed the fish and were now set for a delicious dinner on this their last night of their float trip.

The next day they packed up all their gear at the pick-up site and piled it up on the gravel bar ready to load it on the float plane scheduled to pick them up at noon. While waiting they explored the area nearby finding a great spot to look in the deep water by the bank. Countless numbers of sockeye were passing along that bank. It was a steady parade of four- to six-pound fish headed up river. They were no longer the bright shiny salt water fish from Bristol Bay. They had turned varying shades of red. The fresh water at the mouth of the Branch River had started them turning. They were going to continue that transformation to a deep red before they spawned and died.

Adrian and Michael were amazed at the incredible cycle of life these fish lead. Their determination to find the same stream of water from which they were born is a special event in nature. It makes you believe in a wise and loving Creator!

It was 1:00 p.m. before Michael and Adrian heard the steady sound of the Beaver's prop overhead. Neither of them admitted they were getting somewhat anxious about the possibility of being forgotten. If either of them had thought that, those thoughts vanished with the anticipation of returning to King Salmon and a hot shower.

The pilot made short work of landing, beaching the aircraft, loading it and taking off again for King Salmon. He never mentioned being late and no one else brought up the point. In 30 minutes Michael and Adrian were standing at the dock on the edge of the Nak Nak River. A van was available for stowing their personal gear as they helped off load the raft, oars, and life vests. The emergency repair kit for the raft had been with them and all parties were glad it was not needed.

Michael had arranged for the two of them to return to the same lodge where they had stayed before the float trip. That way they could wash up, get a clean set of clothes on, and enjoy a relaxing dinner and night's sleep before catching the morning flight to Anchorage and on to Seattle.

It was at dinner when Adrian brought up the job offer. "Do you really believe I am the person you want to partner with in running your foundation?"

Michael said, "Two points, Adrian. One, we would not be partners. I will be the President, CEO and Chairman of the Board. Your job will be the senior employee of the foundation. You will be a Vice President. Second point, there is no one I know, nor do I think I can find anyone better suited to do what I have envisioned for the job, than you. This trip has reaffirmed that to me."

"Again, all I can say is wow! Do you mind if I could ask a few more questions," Adrian inquired.

"I would be disappointed if you didn't."

"What do you hope to get out of the study work you want us to do together?"

"Good question", Michael smiled. "Let's see. I want to understand God's plan for humanity as best He wants us to know it, and I want to feel God's love and sense of purpose in my life. Essentially, I need to discover God through study, prayer and listening to others, so that I can come to realize the potential of my spirit, like Mary did years ago. And, lastly I hope this journey does some of the same things for my favorite son-in-law."

"That is a lot to ask for in two years," Adrian replied.

"Yes, and I hope we can do it quicker than that, so we can get a clear direction on what to do after that. You would be my travel guy, Adrian. I will send you to the far reaches of the world, if necessary, to meet knowledgeable people who can help us do what we are setting out to do. So be prepared to travel a lot if you take me up on my offer!"

"I love to travel Michael, so that is not an issue for the two years we are talking about. What do you see the other two positions doing?"

Michael said, "I plan to bring my long-time administrator, Nancy Wilson, into the position of Chief Administrator. She is married with grandkids, and expecting to retire in two years. Nancy is on board with what the foundation will do and she will be a great asset to all of us. She is very sharp and she will keep things in line on the home front while we do what we need to do. I expect her to sit in on all our meetings and I promise you she will contribute to everything we accomplish."

"The other position is one that will work for Nancy in the beginning. The position is for someone who is a good administrator and is particularly good at travel planning and can coordinate financial matters with our CPA and our attorney. As this person grows in the job I would expect them to become our Chief Financial Officer. So, this might be hard to fill as the pay is not for a CFO, but I want someone with good administrative and financial potential."

"Are you open to a suggestion?" Adrian queried.

"Of course, who do you have in mind?"

Adrian cleared his throat and said, "Do you recall Lisa's best friend from high school and college days? Matter of fact, she was Lisa's Maid of Honor."

Michael said, "Do you mean Rachel Madison?"

"Yes, I do."

"Why her?" Michael questioned.

"Well, it is really quite simple and a natural fit. Rachel knows you and she knows me. She works for a travel agency in Redmond. She is bright and I believe she has an accounting degree from the University of Washington. She recently broke up with a boyfriend who simply did not want to ever get married. I believe she is looking for a new job that has more potential. She is a strong believer in God, like Lisa, and she is very active in her local church. I think she would jump at the chance to do this job if she were offered it."

Michael thought for a minute and added," I know Lisa thought highly of her and if she has the basic skills to help us from day one then she could grow as we all grow. The idea has potential. I like it. She is a friend of the family, lives nearby and could easily relate to the work we have in mind here. Okay! See, you are already coming up with good ideas."

Michael added, "Okay, I will think about Rachel. However, I am not going to do anything on this until I get your answer. So you think about your decision and let me know when you've decided."

"Michael, I have thought about it ever since you first mentioned the offer. I can't get the whole thing out of my mind. I need this just like you need this. So, I am going to do something, which for me is rash, and say 'yes' I will work for you and your Foundation. I will need a few weeks to give my employer notice and help with any transition."

"Thank you. I can't describe how happy it makes me feel to have you taking this journey with me. I trust it will be a life changing journey for the two of us. Congratulations young man! Oh, go ahead and talk to Rachel about the job in the next week or so. If you are still convinced she would be good for the job and she is interested, then have her meet with us for an interview."

4

Bellevue, Washington

After the exhilarating Alaskan adventure, both Michael and Adrian returned to work. Adrian gave notice at his workplace and agreed to finish his work with the company at the end of the month. He met with Rachel who was truly elated over the prospects of a job offer with the Foundation. She looked forward to the upcoming interview with Michael.

Michael had six months to go on his employment contract. His development team had performed well while he was gone, and they remained ahead of schedule for the release of the newest version of their diagnostic program. Basically, the release was waiting on marketing to finish the promotional campaign. All this meant that Michael was free to work 50% of the time or less, forward. That worked well since he now had a more important project on his plate. The Mary J. Channing Foundation!

First, the legal papers needed a final review. This was done at the office of Michael's longtime friend and attorney, Braxton Miller.

The conversation with his attorney was an interesting one as Michael described the recruitment of Adrian and the plans he had for the foundation. Braxton was expecting more of a charitable purpose to the foundation than the study nature Michael had in mind upfront. Of course, Michael anticipated a charity side later on and he told Braxton so.

Still Braxton asked, "Michael, you are a very good friend and I would appreciate it if you would indulge me as to why you want to take on such a daunting task at this stage of your life. You have earned some easy living after all the years you put in at work and the tragedy you have endured with family losses."

"Braxton, I simply want to go where Mary has gone, and I know I have to do this to even have a chance to get there. It's that simple."

"I wish you well, Michael, and I am always here to help you if you need me. May God bless your endeavor and may He open your heart to the light of his way."

"Such an eloquent man you are, Braxton. You should have been an orator or perhaps a politician." Michael quipped.

"An orator would have been nice, but a politician, no thank you. I would like to think I have far too much integrity for that calling!"

Later that same day, Michael met his financial advisor at the brokerage house where he held his investments. The financial advisor, like Braxton, was a friend. His name was Allen Cooper and they had been working together closely over the past six years. Michael's portfolio would make most financial advisors giddy over the prospects of numerous large transactions. Unfortunately for Allen, Michael seemed to know more about investing than anyone in the building. His strategy was a simple one. He prided himself in never owning more than ten stocks at any time. He stuck to that principle, as well as picking his own stocks. Allen executed the transactions Michael wanted and that was about all Allen did.

Over the years that Michael had worked with Allen, no one represented in that office had ever generated a larger percentage return on their investments than Michael. His picks were uncanny. He targeted large companies solely and he picked the right ones. He concentrated on the tech sector because of his work but he bought some key stocks very early on and only added to those investments over the years. Michael may have made nearly as much money through investments as he did from his work and the sale of his company.

Today, Michael did something a little different. He told Allen to sell one of his ten stocks and to transfer $10 million dollars to the Mary J. Channing Foundation. He provided the bank routing number and the account number.

Allen had learned well over the years not to question Michael's requests. For this sale transaction, both Michael and Allen knew the commission on the deal would yield Allen a nice commission.

Allen simply said, "The transaction will be completed tomorrow." After a pause, "Is there anything else I can do for you today?"

Michael liked his financial transactions to be quick and simple. He did not engage in small talk during money matters. Afterwards he was just as friendly as anyone. However, when Allen asked "How was the fishing trip with your son-in-law," they talked for nearly 30 minutes. Their conversation sounded like a couple of loggers talking about a weekend trip to fish for steelhead on the Bogachiel River near Forks, Washington. Whether Allen really was interested in fishing, he did a masterful job of seeming enthralled.

Next, Michael called his C.P.A., Joyce Hillary. She had an office in downtown Seattle and did taxes for many of the "big hitters" in town. She was good at what she did and her fees showed it. Michael told her about the Foundation and promised to send a copy of the legal documents as soon as they were available. She said she had an assistant who specialized in non-profits, if that was okay. Michael consented.

Later, Michael met with an office equipment company and arranged to have two bedrooms in his home outfitted as offices. As expected, he ordered the most up-to-date communications equipment to go along with the high-end furniture. One office would be for Adrian and the other would be for Nancy and the administrator, perhaps Rachel. To him, this made perfect sense since his home was paid for and there was no reason not to use the space. His five bedrooms, plus his own office were more than enough space to convert to meet the needs of the Foundation. There was no sense in paying for office space, especially if it turned out there would not be a longer term need for the Foundation.

Prior to heading home Michael called and arranged to see his local minister at the church he and Mary attended. Reverend Osgood was waiting for Michael when he arrived.

"Hello, my friend, I have not seen you for far too long. How are you?" the Reverend asked.

Michael enjoyed the company of the older man as he seemed to always be at peace with the world. Reverend Osgood never was stressed or in too much of a rush. He was a contented man.

"I am fine Reverend and I owe you my apology for not being more attentive to services here."

"Well, you have had more tragedy in your family than any man should have to endure. I understand your need to take care of things you feel need taking care of." Once again, the old man was as considerate as anyone could be. He added, "What can I do for you?"

Michael told the Reverend of his plans for a Foundation and its purpose. The Reverend listened for the better part of a half-hour without saying much. He nodded and seemed reaffirming in all that Michael revealed. Finally, Michael stopped and asked what the Reverend thought.

"Well, Michael, you are preparing for a great quest. Many have tried to understand God's plan and, yes, I fully believe He has one. I am one who believes with child-like faith. I do not need to know His plan. I reckon Mary was a bit like me, in that way. I know that the journey you describe, if well-travelled, may lead you to a stronger faith. So, I endorse your idea with one recommendation. Yet…"

"And what might that be?" Michael inquired.

"How do I best convey this? Michael, your process of discovery is based on study, listening and discerning as I understand it. What is missing in all that is your direct invitation for God to walk with you. It requires prayer to communicate with God and to involve Him in all you do. Involving Him may reveal things to you that no one else has seen or understood. Remember, 'ask and you shall receive'."

Instantly Michael knew the reverend was right. "Reverend, I don't know if I am really good at this or not. I may need help with this."

"Listen, Michael, you've been coming to church irregularly over the past six years. I believe you have faith in God. I know you say prayers at every service you attend. So, to do what I am suggesting is nothing more than having a conversation with God as you go along in the process of searching. Make God a partner in your search for answers. Talk to Him like you would talk to Mary. Praise Him, give Him thanks, and ask Him to help."

"Reverend, would you consider being my spiritual adviser as I work to add prayer to our whole process? I do have a basic faith in God, and, yes I am willing to talk to God through prayer."

"Michael, let's start right now, right here. Grab my hands. Dear Father in heaven, behold your child Michael. At this moment we acknowledge your sacred name and we glorify you above all else. We thank you for the blessings of this life and we thank you for watching over us in times of grief. We ask that you be with Michael as he journeys through the months ahead to better understand your plan for us. May you be present when he calls your name and may you be with him and those with whom he works, so that they may do your will. Amen."

"Thanks Reverend."

"God bless you and I hope to see you often."

Michael left the church feeling different. This wasn't the "hurry up and leave for the next thing on the day's agenda" feeling he normally experienced. He knew prayer was missing from his whole process. As a matter of fact, God was missing from the process. He felt guilt for committing the mistake, but it was something he could correct with the support of the Reverend and Adrian, who he knew would be happy to see prayer interjected into the process.

After he arrived home from work Adrian called Michael. He asked Michael when he would be available to meet with Rachel. Michael suggested Rachel meet with the two them for dinner tomorrow or the next evening. He suggested a restaurant in Redmond and asked Adrian to make the reservation for 7:00 p.m.

The next evening Adrian came to Michael's home well in advance of their dinner engagement with Rachel. Michael brought Adrian up to speed on what had transpired. Adrian was pleasantly surprised at just how much Michael was able to get accomplished in a short period of time. In fact, it was something of a wake-up on just how intense this whole process was going to be. It scared him, but then again it bolstered his faith that in working under Michael they may, in fact, accomplish what they were setting out to do.

Adrian explained how his conversation with Rachel had gone. He said she had called him twice since his call to her to inquire about the Foundation's work and exactly what would be expected of her. Adrian was obviously very impressed by both Rachel's enthusiasm for the Foundation's work and her penetrating questions.

"I think she's smart and I know she feels she has much more potential than her current job allows her to use. She is ready to be challenged, that's for sure. The timeline of two years seemed to be fine as it is long enough to find out if it is the kind of work she would like to continue doing versus moving on to something else."

"Would you hire her?" Michael asked.

"Absolutely, she has the motivation and the skills we need. The timing is perfect."

"Well, then this should be easy. We should simply let her interview us as we enjoy a delightful meal, and then offer her the job at dessert, as long as no red flags come popping out of the conversation. Agreed?"

"Agreed."

The evening turned out to be a delight for everyone. Rachel showed up slightly nervous but extremely well prepared with resume in hand and a smile on her face. She was professional throughout the meal, although a little taken back that more questions were not being asked of her. Her questions regarding the Foundation, the position she would assume, the timeline of guaranteed employment, and the nature of her duties and Nancy's showed that she had thought through things about as well as she could.

Interestingly, she never inquired as to how much she would be paid. Curious from Michael's perspective, but nevertheless polite and astutely keeping us mindful that the job needed to fit for her before pay was discussed. When dessert arrived Michael asked Rachel if she had any more questions. Her reply was right on! "What is the next step in your hiring process?" she asked.

Michael looked at Adrian and got an almost imperceptible nod. Michael looked back at Rachel and said, "We would like to make you an offer to come to work for the Foundation as soon as is reasonable. Based on what you told Adrian about your current pay and your resume credentials we are prepared to offer you a two-year employment contract that will pay you $100,000 per year assuming you use part of that for your own benefits, like healthcare. At the end of the two-year contract term, assuming you stay that period, you will receive an additional $100,000 as a bonus. You will be the Financial Manager for the Foundation and you will manage Foundation finances, accounting, travel services, and assist in our study work sessions to the fullest extent possible."

Rachel's eyes got noticeably larger, but she remained quiet.

Michael continued, "You should also know that as of today the Foundation has funds totaling $10 million. There are no debt obligations, but that will change slightly as some business and travel expenses will be forthcoming. You will have access to a lawyer on retainer, likewise an assistant C.P.A. Your office will be on the first floor of my home and you will share that office with Nancy Wilson, our part-time Chief Administrator. I will work from my office on the second floor. I hope this helps show you just how much we need you. Any questions?"

Holding back her jubilation, Rachel asked, "What do you see happening in two years?"

"As far as your contract goes, it expires. I see two possibilities when we get to that point on the calendar. One is that we may deem it best to close down entirely; in which case we would all be out of a job. The second, and this is the preferred option, is that we continue on with some study work and some charity work. I structured the offer to you and the offer to Adrian based on the first scenario. If we go down the second road we will decide what the best fit is for all parties when it comes to pay and benefit packages. Anything else?

"No, I don't believe so." Rachel replied.

"Well, do you accept the offer?" Michael pressed.

"Absolutely! I am really excited! When can I start?"

"As soon as you feel it works for your current boss. I will have our lawyer draft your employment contract and get it to you within a few days. Sign it and send it to me."

"Okay, I will give my two week notice tomorrow." Added Rachel.

"Rachel, you are joining a small but dynamic team, and together we are going to do great things. Thank you for your decision to join us."

Adrian added, "Rachel you are joining a largely family effort here. You lost your closest friend recently. Michael and I lost our families. We are ready to carry that grief with us, as Michael likes to refer to our plight, and we need to carry on with life and do something for ourselves and for those whom we have lost. This is an opportunity I can't pass up, and I am so glad you are on board with us."

Rachel was in tears now and it was time to leave. So Rachel and Adrian left Michael with the bill and headed in different directions with the understanding they would all get together a week from Saturday to plan the next steps.

5

Mercer Island, Washington

Michael's home had been built seven years earlier. Located on the northeastern side of the island, the half-acre lot is 120 feet wide with low-bank waterfront access. It was built for Mary and Michael, who wanted a Cape Cod-style home. During Michael's years in Boston, he had become infatuated with homes on Cape Cod. This was his dream house and Mary couldn't help but love it. With just over 7,000 square feet of space, the home easily accommodated five bedrooms and four bathrooms. The last appraised value of the home exceeded $6 million.

The view from the numerous decks and lake-facing windows was spectacular. The skyline of Bellevue glistened at night, and, when it wasn't raining or cloudy, sunrises and sunsets were special all around. Constant lake activity with sailboats kept the scene in a constant state of change.

Besides modifying two bedrooms for offices, Michael now took advantage of the time he had to clear out most of the basement area. He made a realistic sweep of the house, boxed all the unused and excess items he and Mary had collected over the years and donated them to the Salvation Army. Then he had a local contractor remodel a large portion of the basement. Now it became a fully operational conference room with extensive wall space to display their plans and project status info. A large LED "smart" television was mounted to the wall for teleconferencing. Adrian would be checking in frequently from his travels and Michael wanted the capability for his team members to use this method of communicating whenever they needed it. Large screen viewing of football, baseball and soccer games also would be a bonus.

Multiple telephone lines and two computer work stations were installed to provide the ability to work from the conference room. A large map of the world was framed and hanging on another wall to locate destinations and time zones. Rachel brought with her, seemingly, a ton of travel documents she had collected over the past few years at the travel office. Her boss at the travel agency had regretted seeing Rachel leave, but was happy for the opportunity she was getting. Michael also made it clear that the Foundation would carry an account with the travel agency where Rachel had worked to provide travel service for the Foundation staff.

It was July when all four team members sat down in the conference room for the first time to a business meeting. Nancy was recording all formal meetings of the group and this was the first of what would turn out to be many. Most would be scheduled but often the ad hoc nature of their meetings would require many unscheduled ones. Therefore, Nancy would record them to preserve a record. Only the major ones would be transcribed with copies sent to all parties.

On this occasion Michael began the meeting. He was elated to have chosen this endeavor and was pleased to be taking with him people he respected and loved. He said he needed to apologize for one thing at the very beginning.

"In describing to each of you the nature of this endeavor and the process we would use to achieve our goal, I now realize I left out one important member of this team and one very important procedural step."

The other three looked at each other and wondered what in the world Michael was thinking now. Adrian spoke up and said "What's up?"

Michael described his meeting with Reverend Osgood. He recounted the Reverend's comments about including God in the process and, specifically, about using prayer as a means of conversing with God and involving God in the entire endeavor upon which they are embarking. He concluded by saying, "I am ashamed of not starting with that as part our process. I am ashamed that I thought we could achieve the understanding we seek on our own. I am committed to correcting that at this very point in time. I am not as far along in my walk with God as each of you. I hope you will forgive me for that and help me commit to involving God as a member of this team. The very least we can do is to start each meeting with a prayer and ask God to be with us, reveal to us what we seek, and encourage us on how to use that knowledge."

Each member of the team spoke from the heart and expressed an expectation that God should be involved in all they do. Each committed to help one another maintain that focus and encourage prayer as part of their daily routine. Adrian ended his comments by asking the group to join hands. Each said aloud their own prayer.

"Thank you", said Michael adding, "Lord God, help me do thy will."

Next, Michael asked that each person comment on the reasons they wanted to be a part of the foundation. He started.

"While Adrian and I spent time fishing in Alaska, I shared with him the contents of a very personal note Mary wrote to me prior to her passing." Michael went on to tell Nancy and Rachel the same story he had told Adrian. At the end both women had tears in their eyes.

Nancy, said, "That note is so typical of Mary. She had so many ways of touching the lives of people in a soft and gentle manner."

Michael replied, "Well, it hit me like a 2x4 to the backside."

Rachel laughed, "Yeah, she generally got the last word in one way or another. Furthermore, it always came with a smile!"

Michael continued, "As a non-regular churchgoer, I want to search for God's plan in whatever form He has represented it to us. We are blessed with so much history and so many people believing we are in the 'end times' that I want to capture the best look at God's plan for humanity. I know we will not get all the answers, but I want to know all that He allows us to know."

"Just as I need to understand God's plan to have my faith ratified, I believe there are millions like me who can be reconciled to our faith if they can see God's purpose and his plan more clearly. Not everyone is like Mary. She simply knew the validity of her faith from early on in her life. She always maintained a child-like faith in Jesus and God. Yet, for me and many others it would help to have a clearer vision of whatever insight God has given us in order to be as fully committed as Mary. I think she knew that was the case, and that may be what inspired her to write her note to me."

Rachel quickly spoke up, "I think she wanted to warn you. We only have so much time in this world, and we need to accept God's love. When we do, we'll share it with others. She wanted you to know God like she did, so she can see you in the future."

"Well spoken, Rachel. Well spoken," thanked Michael.

Adrian added, "I have thought about Mary's note ever since you told me about it. The note spoke to me like it did to you, Michael. It is a love note, and I can't tell you how much it has meant to me that you would share it. I think there are a lot of people who need to get a note like that one from Mary."

Nancy joined in, "Michael, Mary's note is a blessing to each one of us. We all knew her. We all saw her reflect God's love to anyone who crossed her path. Her grace and caring touch were infectious. As Adrian just said, we should all be thankful that you shared her note with us."

"Okay, I've said enough. Adrian, why don't you tell us why you want to be a part of this journey?" Michael questioned.

"*First*, to be honest I am still grieving. I need to learn to carry the load of that grief and I feel this is the best opportunity I have to get closer to God in the process. My faith, like Lisa's, has been solid since childhood. But that faith has been tested severely with the loss of Lisa and Catherine. Like Michael, I need a deeper relationship with God. I think this will help."

"*Secondly*, I will admit that the financial package and a two year commitment fit perfectly for my situation. After two years, I may return to the aerospace industry, and I may relocate if necessary. I will wait and see how things turn out."

"*Third*, I think I can work with anyone for two years, but after that I am not so sure, especially, a father-in-law!" Everyone had a good laugh.

"Okay, we know who the light-hearted one will be around here." Michael quipped. "How about you, Nancy?"

"Well, it looks like I will be the mother hen of the group, and that suits me just fine. So, why am I here? I simply could not pass on the offer Michael made. I have worked for you, Michael, how long now?"

"Twelve years, I believe."

"That long! Not many people can say that. I have seen a few come and go, and, yet, I remain. Anyway, my reasons are less faith-based and more family-based. Don't get me wrong however. I am totally intrigued by all this advanced study work we are going to do. I am just a bit set in my ways when it comes to religion. I go to church and I love it. No need to complicate matters, I say. Yet, I know there are a great many folks who don't go to church and I think if this work gets some of them to go then it is all for a good cause."

She continued, "My family means everything to me. Next is Michael. He has taken good care of me over all these years and I think I have taken pretty good care of him. We've settled onto a good agreement for my work at the Foundation. I had planned to work till I hit 65, and that is a little over four years from now. This job will let me retire in two years, so I am thrilled. Also, according to Michael I will be working 30 hours per week on average instead of the 40+ I have been working. All this means more time with my two grandkids. All in all I am thrilled to be here."

"Okay, Rachel, you're up," Michael said.

"On the personal side of the decision to accept Michael's offer to work for the Foundation, I will say like Adrian, I miss Lisa and little Catherine more than you can imagine. Lisa was my best friend and I am struggling with not getting to talk to her. Catherine was like a niece to me." Rachel started to cry. Nancy passed her tissues.

"Sorry about that. I too need to deal with grief. Let's see, on a personal note I have been ready for a job change for the past year. I want to do more in the finance field and this offered opportunity in that area. Yet, perhaps the main reason for choosing this job opportunity is that I can use the spiritual growth that promises to come from this much research into the Bible and what it says about our future. I expect my faith to grow immeasurably over the next two years. Thank you for inviting me in to this exciting project. I feel overwhelmed and under-qualified to contribute, but I will do my best to do what I can to help."

Michael waited to see if anyone wanted to add anything. He asked Rachel to say a prayer before they broke for a catered lunch. She agreed.

After their lunch Michael gathered the four of them at the conference table to begin a discussion of what questions they wanted to research in the course of their studies. He let the three others stay at the conference table while he went to his office upstairs.

An hour later he checked back with the group and they said they still needed another hour. He left and returned again in another hour.

Adrian said, "We are finished and we have five questions to consider. First, we believe the Bible is the logical place to start and we believe the plan details are an accumulation of chapters and verses throughout the old and new testaments. So -

1. *What does the Old Testament say about God's Plan?*
2. *What does the New Testament say about God's plan?*
3. *What do experts say?*
4. *What do other religions say about God's plan?*
5. *Where is information available other than the Bible?*

Michael, this last question is a catch-all question that encompassed many ideas we floated to each other."

"Okay, if I understand correctly, most if not all of your questions are process questions. Maybe the order could change a bit, but essentially the questions are where we would search to find the answer to the question of what is God's plan for mankind? Am I right?"

"Essentially, yes."

Michael walked around the table and sat down. "Although these are all very good points that need to be covered in what we will do, they are too process oriented. Let me take you through some of my thoughts."

"I told Rachel and Adrian we were wasting our time and that you had the answer before you even asked us the question," Nancy spoke up.

"No, I worked on the answer while you were doing the same thing. I just felt it was important that you withstood the process of tackling the question on your own. Remember I have had a little more time than the rest of you to think about how we might tackle this big issue."

"See I told you he had already worked it out," Nancy tossed out.

"Okay, perhaps it wasn't entirely fair, but remember you three are well ahead of me in the 'faith' department, and I have some serious catching up to do."

Adrian prodded, "Show us what you are thinking."

"My pleasure! I see four questions sequentially leading to our fundamental conclusion on what is God's plan for mankind."

"First, *we need to deal with the whole issue of whether God exists, and, if so is he known to us, and, if so, is he believable?*"

"Second, *if God is knowable and believable, were we created by God suddenly as the story in Genesis infers or did we evolve over an extended period of time as science seems to conclude?*"

"Third, *if we believe there is a Jewish/Christian God, did He send Jesus as a prophet or as His divine Son?*"

"Fourth, *is there a plan for Jesus' return? If so, what does that plan look like?*"

"Wow, I like it already," Adrian applauded. It is a series of fundamentals that form a kind of decision tree leading to a conclusion where all the assumptions and the facts are right there for the sake of understanding, contending, perfecting and so on. I do like it." Then he added, "Michael, don't you think on question number two that we need to add a theory or at least a supposition on why mankind is here, or in other words, what is God's purpose in having mankind?"

"I agree fully. If we are, in fact, created in God's image, then what was God's purpose in doing that? Okay, that is a good upgrade. In fact, I want all of you to challenge these questions as we go along. I expect we will change or expand these as new thoughts and concepts are discovered. So feel free to suggest changes.

"I'm glad I signed up for two years, but I doubt I'll see all this concluded in those two years." She paused thinking about what she just said, "Although, the more I think about it, I would not ever bet against Michael," Nancy surmised.

"I need to digest this for a while, but on first blush, I like what I see. You definitely must have thought on this for more than a couple of hours," Rachel said.

"Yes, Rachel, I have. Matter of fact, I started on this right after Adrian said he was on board."

"Thought so," Rachel added. "So where do we need to start?"

"Rachel, you and Nancy need to concentrate on getting the administration of the Foundation up and running. I will tackle the first question. Adrian, I want you to take on the second question and I want Rachel to assist on your question. It will be necessary to do some travelling to finish the work on your question. I have some contacts I want you to interview and they are not close by. Nancy, as time is available I want you to do some research on the third question. I will help after I finish work on the first. The fourth question will take us a long time to answer as we'll have to do the process work you three captured in your questions. That too may require some travelling, as well as some serious Bible study."

"Let's meet weekly as a group and, of course, as needed otherwise," Michael said as their meeting concluded.

6

Mercer Island, Washington

The following week the group reconvened in the basement of Michael's home for their next meeting. Following a prayer the discussion got lively.

Adrian immediately asked why the group was not planning to undergo a comparative study of religions if they were tackling such basic questions as does God exist, where did mankind originate, and what might be the purpose of humankind's creation.

Michael nodded to Rachel and Nancy signaling they should comment on Adrian's question. Rachel spoke first, "The way I see it is that we are not here to evaluate other religions. We are Christians and we should be building a case for Christianity in this work we do. God respects each person in this world and expects each one of us to make up our own mind about what we believe. We are building a case for Jesus and His Father. We are not here to tear away at someone else's belief."

"If so, why are we spending time in Question #1 on answering the question whether God exists? Shouldn't that be an assumption?" Adrian challenged.

Nancy responded saying, "But that is part of the decision tree you mentioned last week, Adrian. You were right in calling what we are doing a decision tree. In our case the basis for Christianity starts with the fundamental assumption that God exists and that He is knowable and believable to us. I think Michael was right to include that question as the first one in our case for Christianity."

Adrian laughed and said, "I see you two ladies spent some time doing your homework for this session. I concede to what you both say and I admit I really did not want to add more to what already is an enormous undertaking. I just wanted to test the waters with my question to see if we all felt it was okay to not compare Christianity with other religions. What have you got to say Michael?"

"I am in the presence of some very special and intelligent people. You three are going to be a pleasure to work with through this entire adventure. I think I am going to learn a lot."

Michael went on to say, "I was going to have a comparative study question, like what Adrian just mentioned in the middle of our list of questions. However, for the very reasons you three discussed I left it out. Mary always told me that Christianity was built on love. Therefore, to enter into anything approaching disparaging comments about another religion would be contrary to that principle and would, as Nancy so aptly pointed out, cause us to invest an enormous amount of time and effort for what I believe would yield little or no return. We should leave the comparative work to others. Mary was a Christian through and through, and what she had is what I want. I do not need to search out opposing views on the fundamentals of religions to get there. With that said what other questions have you wrestled with over the past week?

Adrian asked, "What level of detail are we going to want to answer the questions we are tackling? For example, Michael, you are handling the first question that builds a case for God's existence, and our ability to know and believe Him."

"I am not sure how much detail will be needed. Perhaps, the answer is to have enough to make the case for a normal young adult to admit that it is hard to argue against the conclusion. We need to focus more on the true fundamental logic for Christianity rather than focusing on historical facts. We should make the case simple where it is simple and more in-depth where it needs to be."

"Since I have the first question, let me give you an example of what I mean. God either exists or He (I use He because all ancient writings refer to God as He) does not exist. I plan to build a case for His existence based on physical logic/evidence, personal witness from Moses and others, Jesus' accounts, and intuitive reasoning. The line of logic for answering this first question will be solid enough to show that the Christian God in which we believe does exist. The logic will refute the atheist's belief that no God exists. Likewise, it will prove that our God is knowable refuting the agnostic that says God is not knowable."

Michael concluded by saying, "We need to go far enough with a detailed study to make our case credible to a normal person, but no further. Some will never believe."

"I like it," said Adrian. "Now help me understand where you see us going with the second question?" queried Adrian.

"Well, one of the first arguments against the book of Genesis is that it says Adam was the first man and Eve was the first woman having been born in the garden 6,000 to 7,000 years ago. This contradicts scientific evidence of human beings existing over a time period much greater than the Genesis story. Some plausible reconciliation of this is necessary for us to move forward with the Jewish/Christian story from the Bible. We need to find that explanation, so we can move ahead to the written word of prophets and the life of Jesus. To get a start on all that, I have in mind for you, Adrian, to travel abroad.

There is far more to see and experience, as it relates to your question, abroad than there is in the USA."

"What do you have in mind, if I may ask?"

Michael paused, "Well, I have been making a number of phone calls to faculty members back in Boston. It helps to have a list of professors and graduates from the universities I attended in Boston. There is a wealth of experienced folks out there who are very good about helping out fellow graduates or past students. I have used these connections for years in my business and our work here will allow me to do more connecting with folks from disciplines I never thought I would need."

"Anyway Adrian," Michael continued, "I want you to visit a couple of the best museums in the world. I want you to go to Africa, Croatia, Athens, Paris and London first. Africa, and specifically Ethiopia, is where most believe mankind originated. Croatia has a small but fine museum depicting human ascent in a simple evolutionary display. In Athens I want you to test your early conclusions with a friend of mine. Likewise, in Germany I want you to meet another special person. Lastly, the Louvre Museum and the British Museum are must-sees to get a cross section look at mankind's journey through the ages. Also, I want you to see the Darwin Institute in London and challenge your creation thinking. I would send you to Cairo if I thought it was safe, but it may not be as safe as you might want, so you might need to skip that one. I'll leave that decision to you."

Adrian retorted, "That sounds like an around the world trip. Is all that travel necessary?"

"Yes, you will soon have more frequent flyer miles than you know what to do with!" Adrian, Ethiopia is a must for your project. Discoveries there by the French and others record the earliest origins of man. I've already lined you up to visit one of the principal French archeologists working in Ethiopia to tour you through the ancient sites where their research has produced evidence of these findings."

"Then I want you to see a little known museum in northern Croatia near the Slovenian border. The director there is known world-wide for his depth of knowledge on the physical evolution of man through the millennia. You should read selected works by Charles Darwin before going on the trip. You'll be surprised to see that he never mentions the word "evolution" in his principle work. He does use the word "evolved" once or twice, if I remember correctly. Then, while you're in Paris I would like you to take a side trip south to see the reproduced cave paintings at Lascaux. These are wall paintings that are believed to originate in the Paleolithic period. They, along with what you see in the two major European museums, should give you a good understanding of the development of man's ability to generate art, tools and pottery in the years predating Adam's birth. As such, you need to explain man's development to do these things either in opposition to the Bible's timing of man's creation or in harmony with it. This will be your greatest challenge in answering question #2."

"Well Michael, I like the locations you have in mind, but finding the answer will take a whole lot of help from above. I'll pray on it and work out the details of travel with Rachel. What do you have in mind for Rachel to do on Question #2?" Adrian asked.

"Rachel, when you have time I would like you to work with Nancy to begin researching work that has been done on the early chapters of the book of Genesis. That should include a timeline of key events from Adam to Jesus," Michael suggested. "Likewise, I may need you to assist Adrian on some of his research."

"Sounds good," Rachel replied.

"Nancy, as time is available for you to do some research, I would like you to begin cataloging the key prophetic messages from the Old Testament that might in some way give us insight into God's forewarning of events to come. That way once we begin a serious look at the Bible we can begin with your list and address what is and what is not relevant to God's plan. Don't make too many close calls on what should be included. When in doubt leave it in."

"Sounds good! I love the Old Testament and I will enjoy that," Nancy said.

Rachel chimed in, "Just to be clear on where we are headed, Michael could you elaborate on question #4 so we get a sense of what the conclusion of our work might reveal?"

"Okay, assuming we work through the first three questions and convincingly believe Jesus is the Messiah and believe God's plan is unfolding toward the Second Coming of Christ, then we would want to take it to its logical conclusion as to who, what, where, how and when that takes place," Michael surmised.

Adrian jumped in saying, "Importantly, in doing what you just outlined, I believe we have to remember that there is much that we do not know and will never know in our lifetimes that occurred before mankind came into existence. Likewise there is, no doubt, an unknowable future for mankind in the spiritual sense that will carry on after Jesus returns, and of that, I have little to no chance to know what to expect. A spiritual life in the New Jerusalem world is something I believe we can only imagine, and we would be presumptuous to think we can conclude much about that. So, I think Michael is right we should concentrate on what we can learn about God's plan leading to the Second Coming. Coming up with the 'when' could be very interesting indeed."

Michael added, "Well stated, Adrian. What you just said should give us boundaries on where we spend our time and effort. What happened before Adam and Eve may well add context to what we will see as God's plan for mankind, and to the extent it does then we will consider it. That's why you will be looking into question #2 on evolution versus creation. However, what truly happened between God and Lucifer, for example, is something I doubt we will ever understand with any real depth. Therefore, God's motives for mankind may not be perfectly known, and as you so poignantly said, we may not understand God's plan after the Second Coming. There are biblical references to the millennium that follows the Second Coming, but looking into that in detail is for future consideration. We have enough to do with the boundaries you stated. Rachel, does that help?"

"I am really glad we took the time to address all this now. I was concerned about doing something this complex and not really knowing the boundaries that we all need to have in mind. I could see some of us following a course off into 'never-never land' and getting totally lost."

Nancy piped up, "Don't worry, Rachel, Michael is never afraid to guide his team back on course if we start to stray. Just keep asking questions and all will be fine. When I get lost I just walk into his office and say I'm confused, and I always walk out knowing right where I need to be."

Part Two

Beliefs

7

Seattle, Washington

Rachel drove her five year old Honda CRV and Michael was her only passenger. Cruising the 520 bridge through the light mist of the day into the north Seattle area Rachel soon found a parking space on the University of Washington campus. The two had an appointment with the highly regarded sociologist Raymond Devane. Michael's $10,000 donation to Professor Devane's research work guaranteed them his undivided attention for a couple of hours this afternoon.

Professor Devane's disheveled look and too small office fit the image of a man buried in his work with little time to organize much of anything. However, Michael had researched enough to know this man was highly regarded as knowing more than most about the nature of those who oppose church and religion.

"Hello Professor, it is a pleasure to finally meet you. Let me introduce you to Rachel Madison. We both work for the foundation I mentioned."

"Yes, Michael and Rachel, thank you so much for your donation. Funds are always needed to make it possible for researchers like myself to carry on with our work. Please have a seat and tell me a little about your foundation and how I can be of help today."

Rachel presented written material on the foundation, answered a few questions and then deferred to Michael as to why they were here.

"Professor we understand that Washington State leads the nation or is close to leading in the percentage of residents who prefer to claim no religion. Can you please tell us what your research tells us about why so many are either atheist, agnostic or unchurched?"

Rachel was prepared to take notes, but also recorded the interview to be sure she captured the whole conversation. The professor did not mind having the conversation recorded as long as the use of the recording was for Foundation work only.

This would prove to be invaluable going forward as the entire team found the conversation to be fascinating. Over the next few months the tape would be played back many times as the group wrestled not only with answers to the first question, but also with how they might relate the findings of their research to such a large group of potential Christians.

Having largely lived his life as an agnostic, Michael knew better than any of the team that not everyone should have to endure one or more tragedies before waking up to search for a deeper meaning in life, and, specifically, one with God. He hoped that what they learned today might truly help them to understand ways to lead others to Christ.

The Professor started by saying, "My own research mirrors the conclusions of other academic researchers. It simply reflects the fact that the tenets of why we as humans choose to be atheistic, agnostic or unchurched is exacerbated in areas where individualism is more pronounced. Not surprisingly, that includes the Pacific Northwest region of America where the pioneers of the 1800's left the civilized eastern regions of our country and moved as far west as they possibly could."

"Okay, take us through each of the two or three types of unbelievers and help us understand why they believe the way they do." Michael added.

"I am not sure it is quite so simple as to put 'non-believers' into two or three separate buckets, as you characterize it. However, let me attempt to do that for you," the Professor said in an accommodating manner.

Professor Devane replied, "The atheist is a person who fundamentally does not believe in the existence of God. Period!"

He continued, "The atheist distrusts any evidence validating the existence of a God or gods. For example, as a group they point to the evolution of life and the vast amount of evidence confirming something other than the godly creation of mankind. They point to the nearly infinite size and age of the physical universe. They point to the lack of physical evidence in the universe that God exists today, much less ever did. Finally, they simply believe that, in fact, all evidence points to the very natural conclusion that there simply is no God."

"Although my research shows that over a quarter of the residents in Washington have no religion, I would say that the percentage of those who are purely atheists is likely to be less than 5% of the total population. Many more are agnostic or secular. Both claim no religion, and I would surmise that 20% of the resident population is either avowed agnostic or secular."

"Notably, the agnostic group is the fastest growing group of the three. You may not want to hear that, but I see this as an indisputable fact. Furthermore, I see this as a widespread occurrence nationwide."

Michael interjected the question, "Why is this group growing so rapidly?"

"Michael, the agnostic is one who finds God to be at least unknowable. The agnostic will acknowledge that God may exist, and that fundamentally differentiates this group from the atheists. Rachel is younger than you. Right?"

Michael replied, "Of course."

"Okay, Rachel, how many of your closest friends and acquaintances go to church?"

"Not many. I see a few at church, but at least three-quarters do not attend," Rachel responded.

"Exactly" replied the Professor. "Many of the young adults in our area do not have any friends attending any religious institution. This is a generational issue that began with the "baby-boomer" generation and continues to today."

"The traditional Christian church institutions in America have seen marked reductions in attendance. Evangelical churches have drawn some away from the traditional churches but still church attendance is becoming less relevant to younger folks entering our working population."

"There are five major causes for this trend. First, traditional churches are increasingly seen as ritualistic antiques. By that, I mean the music lags by one or two generations. The liturgy language lags, as well. It is deemed outdated by younger folks and is repeated over and over week after week. Hence, when you go into a traditional church you see a whole lot of 'gray hair.'

"Second, family dynamics for young adults have changed. Far more families embody two working adults. Weekends necessitate chores and some well-deserved leisure time. In many cases that leaves no time for church. Basically, we are seeing many families where church attendance is not a priority."

"Third, young families are less traditional in their make-up. Some are heterosexual couples who are unmarried with or without children. Some are homosexual couples with or without children. Single adults have fewer friends attending church and along with the non-traditional families I just mentioned, many do not feel comfortable with church teachings."

"Fourth, there are so many competitive things to do that are fun and relaxing, that church does not compete well for a busy person's time. Young people like being outdoors when it is conducive to doing so. Some feel the outdoors is their church after being cramped up all week in a building or a rigorous job environment. Some young people move often and don't feel they want to be tied down to a fixed church knowing a relocation is likely. Likewise, there are clubs, gyms, classes, and countless other opportunities for a person to become involved. Many of which are simply seen as being more fun!"

"Last, for some the church is seen as hypocritical. Churches ask for money all the time. They spend lots of money on brick projects, salaries, landscaping, hierarchy, organs, and electric bills, etc. They spend far less on outreach needs in the community. People see this and they question the whole concept of the church. Supporting this trend is the fact that although fewer people in Washington belong to a church, they give immense amounts of time and money to other charitable causes."

After a short break for Professor Devane to deal with an urgent administrative matter, Michael asked, "With the growth of the agnostics in Washington State, what is the percentage of our population that claims to be identified with a religion?"

"In the U.S. it varies dramatically by state. For example, in Texas roughly 85% of the population claims a religious identity. Here in Washington that percentage is under 70%. Now let me add an important note. I believe that some of the higher percentage states are questionable. In many areas of the country people claim a church affiliation, yet that identity may well be more for social reasons than religious reasons. I firmly believe our national identity is less than most studies show for this very reason."

Michael asked, "If Washington State, therefore, has 31% of its population not claiming a religion where do you see that percentage in say 10 years?"

Professor Devane searched one of his desk drawers and brought out a graph he had developed. "Michael, I could easily see the percentage grow to 40%, 10 years from now."

"In other words, 4 out of 10 residents in Washington will fail to claim a religious identity 10 years from now based on current trends."

"Yes, I believe it will be very near that. The percentage of young families with low religious identity will grow and the percentage of older folks claiming religious identity will shrink. Likewise, I expect other states to experience a 5-10% point growth, as well."

After further discussion Michael was ready to leave. "Well, Professor, I believe that concludes our questions, and we want to thank you for taking the time to see us on such short notice. I trust if we have an additional question or two we might indulge your response by e-mail?"

"Most certainly. If I can be of further assistance, please do not hesitate to contact me. I wish you the best on your endeavors. It has been a pleasure meeting you both."

On their way home Rachel thanked Michael for including her on this interview. She made the comment that she had no idea that so many people lived their lives with no religious identity.

Michael commented, "Well, I must admit I have been one of those people, Rachel. Although I attended church on a somewhat irregular basis, I must admit my heart was never quite with it. I'm afraid I should have been counted in that group of agnostics."

"Yes, but you are doing something about those feelings."

"Only because my family losses have caused me to wake up and see the light. It should not have taken multiple tragedies to get me where I am today. I have a lot of time to make-up for and I can only have faith that God will forgive me and help me to help others."

"Michael, I am sure God is smiling on you. He has already forgiven you for the past. Now, let's finish what we have started and see where God leads us. If we trust in Him he will make sure we are doing it right."

"Okay, thanks for your faith. Let's get Adrian off on his trip and then we can talk more on this whole interview."

"Oh, by the way, Michael, I worked with Nancy and we prepared an update to our financials. Last month we made more money on our investments than we spent."

"We'll up our spending as time goes on. Thanks for the update though," replied Michael.

8

Dubai, United Arab Emirates

Having just endured a 14-hour flight from Seattle to Dubai, Adrian slept 12 hours straight in his high-rise hotel room. To be fair, Adrian had excellent service aboard the flight and he now found himself halfway around the world. It was the longest flight he had ever taken and he was farther from home than ever before. Yet, there was a certain air of excitement in being in this strange part of the world.

With a day to rest before making the next leg of his journey, Adrian went to the dining room for the morning buffet breakfast. The faces and dress of the patrons and the wait staff confirmed he was on foreign soil. The meal provided choices fit for the likes of a Hollywood movie set in Saudi Arabia.
Adrian sampled most of the offerings and found them all to his liking.

He had planned to spend the day resting and planning in his hotel room. However, he could not resist the temptation to see the city sights of the most modern city in the world. He scheduled a two hour tour offered in the reception area. After a quick change of clothes he was back waiting for the private van scheduled for the tour.

Joining his tour bus was a young couple from the U.K. and an older couple from Vancouver, British Columbia. This was their first trip to Dubai as well.

The first stop was an incredible mosque. Adrian was pretty sure he had seen the mosque the night before while riding into the city. At that time the mosque was draped in a beautiful green glow of light. Even in the daylight it glistened like someone might see in a modern religious art magazine. It was as impressive on the inside as it was on the outside.

The highlight of the tour was seeing the world's tallest building. It is the Burj Khalifa and was opened in January 2010. The massive building stands over 2,700 feet in height, nearly a thousand feet taller than the new tower in New York that replaced the two Trade Center Towers taken down in 2011.

The tour bus operator allowed the group to walk around the building. They saw large pools with water fountains, streets with rows of palm trees wrapped in white lights highlighting the grand boulevards that encircle the area of man-made lakes and parks that accompany the giant building. Of course, nearby is the world's largest shopping mall, perfectly placed for those who are either natural residents or well-to-do visitors.

The other highlight was to drive out to one of the manmade islands in the nearby gulf. The one Adrian saw was shaped like a palm tree with individual waterfront homes placed on each palm on the tree. Fascinating, yet almost an anachronism when compared to the dry desert only a few miles away. This was not simply a large oasis along the seashore. No this is an area that emits the very real presence of wealth; and yet, it seemed to be out of place by lacking any sort of tie to the natural landscape surrounding it. Odd but impressive nonetheless!

Adrian returned to his hotel room after the tour and began planning for his journey to Addis Ababa, Ethiopia. He felt rested but his head and the clock where not yet in sync. He expected it might take a few days to work through that.

Poor Rachel had worked countless hours on Adrian's schedule. Michael and Adrian re-routed the trip more than once. Fortunately, all the visas needed covered the time in each country and flight schedules were the primary hassle for the trip.

For Adrian, he was glad to be underway on this first of who knows how many stops. No trip could be much longer since this one was to make an around-the-world circuit. His excitement surpassed his apprehension as he had a chance of a lifetime to see things most could only read about.

Adrian was still amazed at the process he and Michael had gone through to reach this point. He thought back over a month and a half when he expected to visit a few notable museums where he could compile the information he needed. Yet, it was not going to be that easy.

Previous to this trip, Michael and Adrian had spent a valuable day in Tempe, Arizona with Professor Harold Wilson from Arizona State University. Professor Wilson is the noted head of ASU's Human Origin Institute. His work has taken him across the globe to key locations where notable evidence of human origin exist. Through his advice and contacts Adrian was now headed on a trip to meet some of the leading experts in the world.

Michael's grant of $25,000 sparked considerable interest and cooperation on the professor's behalf. He was very willing to make several key contacts to assist Adrian in getting first class cooperation with key people in key places.

As a Christian, Professor Wilson made it clear that his work on human origin has always been based on genetic history and scientific fact leading back to the very roots of our specie. He saw no conflict with his work and his faith. In fact, he stated that the more he learns about our origin the more he is impressed with the awesome God that created us.

When Adrian and Michael asked the Professor how he reconciled the difference between the Genesis story of godly creation with Adam and the ancient findings he and others are finding across the globe, he had replied, "You need to find that answer on your own. When you do, call me and tell me what you discovered. I will then share my beliefs on the matter. But you need to struggle with this for a while before you can truly understand the origin of man. I have no doubt you will come to the same conclusion I did years ago when I sought an answer to the very same question."

The next day Adrian took a private car to the capital of United Emirates and caught a flight at the airport to Bole International Airport just outside Addis Ababa, the capital of Ethiopia. This airport is located east of the downtown area of Addis Ababa, and provides good access via a ring road to Highway 4 leading southeast of the city.

Just over 150 kilometers east of the city is the small town of Awash. Beyond the town to the north is the lower reaches of the Awash River area, and nearby is an archaeological site called Middle Awash valley.

To the northeast is the region in the neighboring country of Djibouti. It is in the northern part of this country that the Red Sea meets the Gulf of Aden and the Indian Ocean. Across a narrow span of water 30 kilometers wide, one can cross from Africa to Yemen and the Arabian Peninsula. This is the likely migration route chosen by people in ancient times who wanted to travel to Asia or Europe.

Adrian spent the night in one of the few motels in Awash. The town is rather non-descript and offered few choices, but the motel was definitely better than a tent. The next morning Adrian was met by a French scientist named Jacque Piquet from the Ethiopian National

Museum - Jacque had worked with Professor Wilson years ago and was happy to see another American in these parts.

Jacque worked with a number of the collections in the museum and had been in Ethiopia for seven years. The Museum was opened in 1944 and exhibits of cultural artifacts accompany many of the archaeological objects stored at the museum. A new building opened in 1966 and contains some of the oldest remains related to mankind. In fact, the earliest hominid, "Lucy", is currently housed there. She is 3 ½ feet in height and her weight is estimated to have been about 64 pounds. Her bones were discovered in 1974 and she is believed to have lived 3.2 million years ago. Interestingly, Lucy's name is used in a notable Beatles song!

The Awash River is one of the largest rivers in Ethiopia. It is comprised of three primary regions. These regions comprise about six percent of the total land base in the country. Each region is characterized by its unique flora and fauna. As you might expect each area has its own climatic conditions.

The Middle Awash Valley is the most notable region due to its famous archeological sites and findings. Fossils spanning a period over five million years have been recovered in the region. Specifically, the region has produced significant hominid (human-related) fossils.

Jacque took Adrian to the site of the famous Lucy find. Lucy, or 'Dinknesh' as she is called in Ethiopia, was discovered at this site in 1974. Once they arrived at the site Jacque explained, "Over 50 bone fragments were recovered here making it one of the most complete skeletons found to date. The skeletal remains are estimated to be over 3 million years old."

Adrian got a personal description from Jacque of how the dig was conducted and how the fossils were carbon-dated. Further, having a quality national museum in place has secured the care and proper protection of these fossils to this day.

Jacque continued, "Other archeological sites in the area have produced similar findings. In fact, in the same region the oldest hominid fossil was discovered in 2001. Additional remains were discovered in 2004. These fossils are estimated to be in excess of 5 million years old."

Adrian asked what other human-related species had been located in the vicinity. Jacque said, "Other fossil finds include fragments from a homo-erectus in 2002. This finding is estimated to be one million years old. Also, in 2003 fossils from homo-sapiens were recovered. UNESCO (*United Nations Educational, Scientific and Cultural Organization is a specialized agency of the United Nations based in Paris*) has recognized the region as a world heritage site for its historical and archeological significance.

Adrian, being from the Pacific Northwest where green is the everyday color, kept his opinions of what he saw to himself. Although this may have been a pastoral setting a million years ago and human-like ancestors may have thrived on living here, still the place looked a lot more like the southern part of Utah or central Nevada. It was pretty arid for as far as the eye could see. On the other hand, Adrian was impressed to be in an area known as the birthplace of early humans. It might be hard to imagine with so little food available today, but at some point in the ancient past this is where humankind's gene pool began.

Jacque was like a father showing a young boy around a candy store. He was as excited as he must have been when he first came to this country and found the remnants of ancient peoples.

Jacque explained, "There are other sites in the region, particularly south of Addis Ababa that have revealed large numbers of Stone Age artifacts. The river had done its work over many centuries in uncovering all types of stone artifacts. Many of these are on display in the National Museum we visited the day before."

When asked about the Homo sapiens fossil finds Jacque explained, "Many of the finds are older than the Homo sapiens of today. The species of note in these finds is the ancient homo-sapiens species which is an intermediate species between homo-erectus and modern homo-sapiens. The ancient homo-sapiens species is believed to have lived approximately a half-million years ago."

Adrian was learning far more about ancient human origin than he had expected. It was becoming increasingly clear that in the minds of scientists around the world that the human species was much older than it was thought to be.

Later in the afternoon Jacque took Adrian to a high lookout point where they could view the vast region of highly arid land through the middle and lower valleys. As Adrian looked across the landscape all he could see were rifts and brown arid soils. This was not a very hospitable place.

However, as he had surmised, Jacque painted a very different picture for him on what they were seeing. He explained, "Five million years ago this was a fertile and rich region. Chimpanzee and human lineages had split by then. Human-like species were present in the area. In time they developed the ability to create stone tools and fire-baked clay objects."

He went on to describe an environment much different from what Adrian was seeing. In those times the region was wet and the land was covered with forested areas and woodland grasses.

They talked of what life may have been like for the human-like people who inhabited the area. Jacque speculated, saying all the evidence points to an environment where a fairly large number of human-like people could have resided year-round. At this latitude there would not have been a significant reason to migrate to other areas. It would have been a question of food supply.

Jacque did say that because of the proximity to the Arabian Peninsula that a natural migration route would have passed directly through this area. He felt that as the modern homo-sapiens species evolved there is little doubt this region saw heavy migration movements to the east and to the north.

Jacque also pointed out the large rifts in the landscape that influenced the river course as well as the soil composition. He noted that the region also has had a history of volcanic activity that may have influenced life throughout the general vicinity.

As the sun began to lower itself to the horizon behind the two of them, they decided to head back to town and enjoy the best fare the hotel could offer. Jacque was an interesting and astute fellow, but Adrian could not imagine anyone wanting to spend so much time in such a dusty and foreign environment. Jacque explained that he doesn't see the country as it *is*. His job is to see it as it *was*.

After a shower and a clean set of clothes Adrian met Jacques in the hotel lounge. First class this wasn't. But after the day they had had, it looked just fine. Adrian and Jacque shared a bottle of French wine that Jacque so adeptly had brought along from his personal home supply. Most of the discussion at the dinner table revolved around the Foundation, families, World Cup soccer, favorite sights to see in and around Paris, and Jacque's friend Harold Wilson.

9

Mercer Island, Washington

"I take it Adrian made it to Dubai?" Michael asked.

"So far he is doing well. He sent an e-mail from the hotel in Dubai saying he was headed out to Awash Landing. He seems to be on schedule," commented Rachel.

"Thanks for all the work you put into making this global adventure a reality for Adrian. He is going to see so much, and it will help us all to hear about what he sees, hears and does. I bet he returns with a few good tales to tell too," Michael quipped.

"I think I am glad Adrian is making the trip and not me. I'm not sure I could handle that much globe-trotting," Rachel commented.

"I bet you would prefer the beach on some south Pacific island," Michael fired back.

"You've got that right. I prefer a flight that simply gets me to where I can lay back and relax," she closed her eyes and dreamed of a sunset over the ocean.

"Okay, enough day-dreaming, let's discuss what we heard from Professor Devane," said Michael, bringing the discussion back to the topic at hand. "I have a frozen pizza to cook for lunch, if that is okay with you. I think this will be a long discussion."

"Fine by me. I enjoyed my weekend by going up to Snoqualmie Falls. It gave me a good chance to think and make a few notes"

"Good for you, Rachel. I spent the weekend reading. Why don't you start first and give me your thoughts on whether God exists, and, if so, whether He is known and/or believable. I think that is how we phrased the first question."

"May I tape this conversation since I know you will want me to draft a copy of what is said today?"

"Yes ma'am!" Michael chuckled at Rachel's ability to know what he would like before spelling it out.

"Okay, my first thoughts on the matter resulted in a complete mental block. I actually had to hike the nearby trails for an hour and say a prayer before I could focus on the question. Initially my thoughts did not have anything to do with Professor Devane. In fact, my first thoughts were whether this question could be answered absent knowing what Adrian is working on. I mean, I was stumped with trying to contemplate God's existence not knowing whether we are created or evolved."

Michael commented, "Interesting, keep going."

"This was a 'chicken or the egg' issue for me. Then I recalled our group discussion when we agreed on the order of questions. Basically, if we did not believe God existed we did not need to go any further in the whole project. We all would just go home and do something else."

"So I recalled a conversation I had with a classmate at University of Washington. Her name is Sara and she lived on the same dorm floor as Lisa and me. She is Jewish and we would periodically share religious views to better understand each other's beliefs."

"When we discussed whether there really is a God her views were like mine. God's existence is self-evident. Sitting there at Snoqualmie Falls this past weekend, I was looking at what the Creator had formed. The surrounding trees and mountains were evidence that God had shaped them with His own hands. The chipmunk that tried to steal my sandwich was created by God and the raven that wanted my last cookie left at the picnic site as I walked around the Falls also was created by God. All this cleared my mind. Once I did that I could focus on why I believe it is self-evident that God not only exists, but that he is knowable and believable."

"You are on a roll, so keep going," Michael laughed.

"So, we know there is a portion of the population that do not believe in God. This group of atheists have made a conscious choice for various reasons. Fortunately, this is only 5% of the population according to Professor Devan's research. Furthermore, unless the fundamental reasons for this disbelief are challenged it seems very unlikely that this group will convert to believers. A hard heart and a hard mind make it difficult to be reasoned with. Love, in fact, may be the only means by which they may see the light."

"The agnostic group, although considerably larger than the atheistic group, still must contend with a hardened mind. Their hearts are open to love and this is evidenced by their charitable nature. This fact makes it clear that given enough reason they may open both their hearts and their minds to God. It is their minds that are inquisitive, yet they are not able to clearly see God for all the negativism they see in church history, culture and actions. Of course, all these negative factors are human driven and not God driven."

"So I say all one has to do is look around to know that God exists."

"Now, the second part of our question is whether or not God is knowable and/or believable. Honestly, I am with Nancy on this one. I do not pretend to be a learned theologian or a religious scientist, if there even is such a thing. I simply have faith in God based on the 'word' I read in the Bible and what I observe in the world. That is not to say I understand all there is to know about the 'nature' of God, but it is something in which I can firmly place my faith, much like a child places faith in his or her parents."

"Michael, I am at the end of my notes and that's all I got!"

"Splendid, Rachel. I must say, I am impressed. I am glad you recorded that because we all need to hear it. Let's take a break and move outside to the deck. The fog has lifted and the lake view is spectacular."

"Sounds good"

A short while later they reconvened on the deck. The views across Lake Washington were superb. The temperatures were ideal which made it very comfortable to be outdoors.

Michael started by saying, "Rachel, how would you feel about flying to Paris to meet Adrian and join him both in Paris and London. After listening to your thoughtful comments my expectations were confirmed. You are adding an in-depth perspective to this work that Adrian and I cannot bring to realization on the subject matter. Perhaps it is a woman's view or just another approach, but whatever it is we need your perspective not only on question one but on each one of these."

Michael continued, "I am also seeing why Lisa considered you her best friend. She spoke so highly of you, but I guess I never got to know you all that well."

"Michael, you said something about me going to Paris? Were you serious?"

"By all means. I know Adrian is going to be tired of traveling by the time he gets to Paris. A few days off there to see the sights would be good for both of you. Plus it would be a good time for you to tell him just what you told me minutes ago. He can bring you up to date on where he is on his project and you can pass my comments on as well. Have you ever been to Paris or London?"

"No, it has been a dream to go. I just, well, never took the time or felt I had the money."

"Well, welcome to an expense-paid trip to the *City of Lights* and the *City on the Thames*. I'll notify Adrian and I can't imagine he'll have any objections. Once I've done that you can make all the necessary travel arrangements."

"Okay, I'm in and thanks. I'll stay up with the other things going on in the office so nothing is left hanging while I am gone."

"I'm not worried," quipped Michael.

Michael moved on to the question at hand, "Okay, does God exist? Here is my take on the matter. First, I agree wholeheartedly that God's existence should be self-evident to any reasonable observer of the world we live in. Yet, because the Genesis Chapter One creation story may be just a story, some people discount the whole notion that God exists. Some need proof."

"For those that are avowed atheists, I hold little hope that reason and observation will prevail in convincing them that God exists. Your idea that love is the only thing that might open the door to their heart is something I had not thought about, but I like it and think it should be the central theme in our approach to them. This is what Jesus did!"

"For the agnostic folks out there we agree there is more room to reason. This is where I think we have an opportunity to make some progress. If we can find a good way to show the many reasons why God is part of their lives, then perhaps we can open the door to not only their minds but also to their hearts. Some relevant education and reasoning along with love may help some of them decide to open their hearts to God."

"Rachel, I have read a lot lately about the nature of human beings, basically focusing on the second part of the question Adrian is working with. It is the one we asked Adrian to look at dealing with God's purpose for us as human beings. I want to take some time with you next week and go through some of the thoughts I have collected on this matter and ask you to share those with Adrian while you are in Europe."

"Okay, I hope I am up to the task," Rachel replied, cringing a bit.

"Well, I am ahead of myself, so let me get on with some thoughts on how we might help others reason why God exists. Understand that not everyone has the same comfort of faith as you do, Rachel."

"Yeah, Nancy and I were a pretty easy sell early in life," Rachel snickered.

"Rachel, there are a lot of folks out there like me who thought the whole religious thing was more ritual than anything else. Maybe I was a lot like Thomas - that is the doubting Thomas of the disciples. I needed more proof but, of course, I was too busy to look in the right places for it."

Rachel quickly asked, "I understand that, but how would we go about educating folks as to why they should believe God exists other than love them and hope one day they open their heart to God?"

"Okay, how about outlining to them four key facts. First, if we put ourselves in relationship to the universe we will understand the immensity of God's creation. For example, if we put the earth's history in the time perspective of a single year where the earth begins on January 1st and today is December 31st, the first living things on earth arrive on July 1; insects and trees show up in November. Reptiles, birds, dinosaurs, birds, flowering plants, apes, cats, dogs, and primates all show up on December 30. Humans show up on December 31st."

"Furthermore, if we look at December 31st in that same year we see that Adam, Jesus, and all of us arrived in the last minute. All of this is with the perspective that our planet is somewhere around 4 ½ billion years old. Now if that was all we had to offer as evidence of God's existence then I would say we have a tough road to convince very many of the agnostics. So why don't we take a break and have lunch and I'll pick up from here after we finish?"

"Sounds good!"

After lunch they picked up where they had left off. Michael continued, "Besides this incredible earth that we are a part of, there is a universe out there that dwarfs our concept of time and space. To date, we have yet to discover any recognizable living form anywhere in the vastness of space. It is as though the entire universe is there for our benefit to marvel at the awesome creative ability of God. However, the farther we travel in space and the more we look into space the more we see of the Creator's work. Look at what the Hubbell telescope has shown us so far, and imagine what the James Webb Space Telescope will show us. God the Creator is the only rational conclusion! Still, that will not convince the skeptics."

"So what other evidence do we have to convince the skeptics? Well, there is the Bible, a collection of books written by numerous authors over a span of approximately 1,500 years, starting with the book of Genesis and ending with the book of Revelation. The Bible serves as a holy book to believers and it provides historical, cultural, spiritual, poetic, songful, praiseful, instructional, prophetic and spoken words of, and about, God and His people on earth. Furthermore, it provides witnessed accounts of God's only Son and His ministry on earth. No account bears the truth and word of God like the Bible."

"Finally, the life of Jesus Christ is a testament to the Father. All that He did and said, He did with and through the Father, the one and only God Almighty. His sacrificial death reconciled forever all who believe in the Son. With an extensive accounting of the miracles Jesus performed in his ministry we have a perfect example of God in human form based in love and mercy. Beyond the Word and the acts of love and sacrifice shown by God's only Son, we have countless testimonials of miraculous things happening to disciples of Jesus and many more of His saints – which can be substantiated to, and still happen, to current day. The collection of all these is boundless."

"In closing on this subject, I realize still that there are those skeptics who even in light of the foregoing evidence still waver in their belief that God is knowable. To those I say take a hard look at the next question in this line of reasoning. Take a look at the forthcoming section on God's purpose for the human race. After reading the answer to that question, it seems unlikely anyone would take their choice in beliefs lightly. Essentially, their eternal life depends on it!"

"Wow, thanks for the lesson in spiritual living. Before long Reverend Osgood is going to ask you to preach on Sunday," Rachel chuckled.

"I seriously doubt that is going to happen. I am afraid half the congregation would get up and leave before he finished my introduction," Michael laughed as well.

"Michael", said Rachel, "if there was a way to get folks exposed to what we are discussing in a reasonable amount of time, I think we could get the attention of a lot of people. It is just that so many folks are rushing around and doing this and that. No one seems to have the time to do that kind of soul searching on their own."

"Rachel, we need to ponder on that very point. I've been thinking all along about how we might develop an interactive means that exposes folks to our approach and conclusions in a fun 21st Century interactive means. I know we can do that if we make it a priority. Let's attack that very issue when we are close to wrapping up our study. Basically, it would be a focus item for Phase Two when we are implementing the best ways to help others going forward with the Foundation's resources."

"Okay, I suppose you would like me to transcribe this session, also?"

"Yes, please. Let's follow up next week. We can close off our work on Question One and I want to make some comments on Question Two. I would like you to take those to Adrian when you head to meet him in Paris."

Michael continued, "Adrian is a busy man these days. I think he is sort of enjoying this adventure of his. However, he will be pretty tired by the time you see him."

"Have you been to Paris before?" Rachel asked.

"Years ago I took Mary with me on a business trip. I was doing some classified systems security work for the Defense Department and I needed to do some work in Brussels for NATO. Mary joined me in Paris afterward and we did all the tourist things. Mary loved the river cruise on the Seine right at dusk. The lights of the Eiffel Tower would come on while we were cruising, and we would pass under those amazingly beautiful bridges on the Seine separating the west bank from the east bank. Later the cruise rounded Notre Dame Cathedral and Mary would get a bit chilly with the river breeze. It was great! You should do that and think of Mary when you do."

"It is on the list, talk to you later," Rachel returned to her office to return a couple of phone calls. She couldn't help but wonder how

Adrian might take the idea of her joining him for the last two stops of his trip.

10

Athens, Greece

Adrian's flight landed at Eleftherios-Venizelos International Airport just outside of Athens after a long trip. Based on his recent diet and his extended day of travel Adrian was feeling rather ill. He was having severe stomach cramps and had rumblings in his digestive tract. Thus far, the 'cipro' medication his doctor had given him 'just in-case' was working.

Once he found his baggage he arranged for a taxi to take him to his hotel. He had a two-night stay reserved and he was glad. Tomorrow was to be a free day to sight-see or recover his wits about himself after the long trip he had just traveled.

He decided to schedule a half-day tour through the hotel concierge for the following afternoon. That provided him time to sleep in and recover from whatever bug he had gotten. Besides he could cancel the tour if he did not feel up to it.

Adrian wanted to see the Acropolis, of course. In fact, he wanted to walk to the top and walk back. The hotel concierge assured him that was planned for the tour as well. The only scheduled event for this stop on his global circuit was to meet with a professor named Nick Dawson from Harvard University. Michael had known Nick in graduate school and was aware Nick specialized in DNA tracking for ancient fossils. Since Nick had recently retired and was to be in Athens with his wife, Michael arranged for Adrian to meet with Nick the second day Adrian would be in town. They were to have lunch together before Adrian caught his next flight to Zagreb, Croatia.

After getting settled in the hotel, Adrian took a warm shower and rested just over an hour. He got up and went down to the hotel restaurant for a cup of soup, lots of crackers and a light salad with no dressing. He headed upstairs and made a telephone call to Professor Dawson. Nick answered the phone and they agreed on to a 10:00 a.m. get-together the day after next with an early lunch. Adrian explained that he had a 4:30 p.m. flight to catch following their visit.

Adrian checked his e-mail from the room, and lo and behold he had good news from Rachel. She was planning to join him in Paris if he thought that would be okay. Knowing the schedule he had in Paris and London was the most relaxed of the trip he was elated with the idea. This would give the two of them a chance to get caught up on what was happening on both fronts, his travels, and what was going on back home.

He immediately fired off a response saying he thought the idea was a great one. He noted that he really could use some time with another team member to talk about all he was seeing and learning, and he appreciated Michael suggesting Rachel come. In his response he also updated Michael, Nancy, and Rachel on what he had accomplished in Ethiopia, and that he had made contact with Nick for their scheduled meeting the day after next. After a bit of additional reading on the theory of evolution of the human species, Adrian found himself totally exhausted. He was drained physically and it took no time for him to fall asleep.

The next morning he arose feeling better, but for safe measure he took one more 'cipro.' He dressed and headed downstairs. He wasn't hungry so he picked up a brochure on Athens and headed out for a walk. It was noticeably cooler here than in Ethiopia but still it was warm.

He walked a few blocks and found a good viewpoint overlooking the city. The first sight that struck him was the Acropolis - such a dominant citadel in the middle of the city. According to the brochure he had picked up, the city's population was around 800,000. It looked to be much larger and, in fact, the brochure also said the greater Athens vicinity included a total population of 3 to 4 million depending on where you drew the line. That seemed more like it based on what Adrian could see.

He walked back to the hotel and had a very light brunch in the restaurant before heading back to his room. He checked e-mail again and read for an hour, getting prepped for his meeting the following day. He then washed a few items, as well.

At 1:00 p.m. the tour bus picked up Adrian and the driver made one last pick-up before doing a general city tour. Obviously, the Acropolis would come toward the end of the tour. You know, save the best for last!

The tour bus driver kept the group entertained as well as informed. He was a comedian want-to-be. He drove by an old church and said that some time back they had a sign out front that said in Greek *"Don't let worry kill you, let the church help!"* He commented that the sign came down after a short while. He also noted there had been a convent in town that had a sign on the wall that read *"No Trespassing – Violators will be prosecuted to the full extent of the law"* signed by the Sisters of Mercy. It too was eventually changed.

The tour included a good thumbnail history lesson. The group learned that Athens was one of the oldest cities with a history dating as far back as 3,400 years. The city is noted for being the cradle of western civilization and the birthplace of democracy. From one vantage point the group could see the massive harbor of Piraeus where many cruise liners and merchant ships share port facilities. In town he saw numerous monuments from Roman, Ottoman and Byzantine eras.

The tour drove by the National Archeological Museum with artifacts dating back 7,000 years. Although he knew the collection inside must be very special, after having been to Ethiopia and seeing what he had seen, Adrian really wasn't sorry that the tour didn't include a long guided tour of the museum's contents.

As the tour headed to the Acropolis Adrian was excited. Along the way the group heard about the first Olympics held in Athens in 1896 and the more recent Olympics of 2004 held in Athens. As they drove, Adrian did not really listen very carefully to the Olympic talk. He was fascinated by each view of the Acropolis. It stood resolutely in the middle of the city area and it captured one's attention. Certainly, those who lived here found the sight so natural that they paid little or no attention to it. Yet, for a newcomer the sight was absolutely majestic and captivating.

Finally, the tour bus stopped in a crowded area and off-loaded everyone. A local guide met the group and escorted everyone to the top. The climb was gentle enough for most everyone and the view from the top was incredible. The city lies below and all around.

The Pantheon centers one's attention at this UNESCO-deemed World Heritage Site. However, panels surrounding the upper fascia of the Pantheon are missing. Many are found in the British National Museum in London to the dismay of the Greeks and others who would rather see the structure adorned with those panels. Walking around the never-ending restoration work on the Acropolis, Adrian was touched by the absolute majestic feel of this place. No other place in any city could be so prominent, he thought.

After a short return trip, Adrian left the hotel lobby and found a nearby store to purchase a few postcards and a small gift for Rachel. He walked around the neighborhood and returned to the hotel. He spent the evening in his room reading a book Michael had sent. He did get out to buy a couple of souvlaki skewers in a local deli he had spotted on his walk. Along with a bottle of stomach-settling soda, the skewers proved to be enough for the evening. But it was the book that Michael had sent that held his attention. He read late into the evening.

After sleeping in late in anticipation of a long day, Adrian purchased some fruit and another soda at the hotel restaurant. He read awhile, packed his suitcase, checked out of his room and left his bag with the bellman. He planned to return for the bag and catch a cab to the airport after his luncheon with Nick.

Nick arrived on time and after introductions he asked what kind of Greek food would Adrian like. Adrian, embarrassingly explained his current sensitivities and suggested a mild chicken pita sandwich with a light Greek salad. Nick said he knew the place that matched what Adrian wanted and off they went.

"Tell me, I understand Michael has retired and he is involved in non-profit foundation work. You and he are starting a new foundation, if I have it correct," Nick inquired.

"You do know Michael lost his wife a couple of years ago and more recently he lost his daughter and his granddaughter in a terrible car accident?"

"Yes, I know about Michael's losses. Also, I know you lost your wife, Lisa and your daughter?"

Adrian sighed and stared out the car window at nothing in particular, "Yes that is true."

"I am terribly sorry for your loss. I've never lost a child and I cannot imagine living with that pain."

"Michael and I have our good days and our bad days," Adrian responded. Nick sensed that Adrian didn't want to discuss the tragedy further and politely changed the subject.

"Adrian, I'm not sure what Michael has told you, but he and I have been friends since our college days. We've stayed in touch about once a year with Christmas cards and the odd phone conversation once in a while. Even so, I was surprised to hear that you and he had taken on such a magnanimous and forbidding task as to start a non-profit foundation to further Christian beliefs and actions."

"Michael is the one who took the initiative," Adrian replied. "His family losses are what prompted him to do it. I'm blessed to be a part of it and together we hope to strengthen our own beliefs, as well as help others with their beliefs."

"Okay, here we are at the restaurant that I've been drawn to whenever I've been in Athens. They will prepare exactly what you want, and we can have a private table reserved where we can talk. Michael said you have some questions for me. Let's go inside."

Adrian followed Michael into the restaurant and was immediately overwhelmed with the distinct aroma of Mediterranean food and a surprising number of patrons for such an early hour. He took in the ambience as he followed Nick to the reserved table set away from the noise in a side wing of the restaurant.

Nick asked Adrian if he would join him in a Greek tradition. He asked if Adrian would share a small glass of Ouzo with him. He explained that the drink is traditionally a means of bringing spirit to the occasion. Adrian accepted and thought perhaps the alcohol would kill any remnant that survived the 'cipro.'

"Adrian, what questions do you and Michael have for me?"

"First, Nick, you are most kind to have taken us up on this meeting. I know you are on vacation and this is taking you away from your wife. I apologize for not expressing my thanks earlier. I haven't been myself since Lisa and Catherine died."

After a short pause Adrian continued, "Nick, we are working to prepare a clear path for people, us included, to understand God's plan for mankind. My current focus is to sort out the rationale between those who believe in a creation theory and those who believe in evolution. Then we hope to gain as best an understanding as we can on why mankind is here."

"Wow, Michael does not shy away from the big questions, does he? Tell me the context with which these answers need to fit into the larger scope of your project."

"First, we are dealing with the issue of whether God exists; and, if so, is he known and believable? Next, we are dealing with the two questions of interest that Michael thought you might comment on. The first is about whether humans were created or evolved? The second is about God's purpose in bringing humankind into existence. These are followed by two more questions. First, did God send Jesus as a prophet and/or as a messiah? This is followed by detailing God's plan as best we might know it, including when Jesus might return."

"Wow, Michael is not slowing down in his retirement," Nick smiled. "Okay, thanks, now just one more question to you before I give you my answer to the two questions you asked of me. Tell me, what you have found so far in your readings and your experience in Ethiopia?"

"To be honest, I have not even begun to explore God's purpose for humanity," Adrian admitted.

"Good, because I cannot help you on the second part and I would only preach my own beliefs, as unsubstantiated as they are," firmly stated by Nick.

"I understand, Nick, and I did not expect you to want to answer that question. So let us concentrate on the first question. Were humans created or evolved?"

"Nick, as much as I might like to believe the Genesis story of human creation I am afraid that the scientific evidence is overwhelmingly in favor of the fact that our human species, at least physically and likely mentally, originated much farther back in time than the Genesis story would lead you to believe. The Ethiopian findings seem to be very conclusive to the scientific community that our species evolved hundreds of thousands of years ago, if not earlier. Also, there is evidence that our species inter-bred with other species after we came into being."

"Well said. Adrian, the amount of evidence is staggering and we are adding to it nearly every day."

The ouzo showed up at the table and this was cause for a moment of toasting and enjoying a taste of Greece. The oil of anise in the drink gave it a unique flavor. Using a shot glass, Adrian found that the drink went down smoothly. Now they were getting into the Greek spirit. However, if he consumed too much "spirit" Adrian realized he would likely miss his afternoon flight.

"Adrian, you are right about the fact that our species has been around longer than many people thought. But, let me add to the evidence you have seen and then let's talk about your question in a broader sense."

"While in Ethiopia, you saw the result of many archeological digs happening over many years aimed at uncovering human-like species and a few that have actually produced evidence of homo-sapiens. You saw evidence of ancient species like hominids and homo-erectus and what we call ancient homo-sapiens. Many of these discoveries lead us correctly to believe that these species have a history dating back millions of years. Now, if we talk strictly about the early discoveries of homo-sapiens we still go back in time, but to date, we only go back a bit over 300,000 years. Keep in mind this is all on a planet that is billions of years old."

"Our DNA work throughout the world shows some very interesting things relevant to your question. We have followed the 'Y' chromosome in men as far back as 338,000 years in one of the most recent studies. Likewise, we have traced the human woman back over 140,000 years. Each new discovery edges the dates farther into history, so we may not yet have found the 'Adam' and 'Eve' of genetic history. But, certainly we are well beyond the 'Genesis' Adam and Eve of six or so thousand years ago. Most of these finds center around various areas within Africa, but there is evidence also of inter-breeding with Neanderthals in the Middle East and even with other species as far away as Southeast Asia."

"Geneticists are likely to continue finding the links to human species aimed at building a family tree for mankind. I doubt I will see it completed in my lifetime, but given enough time and resources to do the research the picture will get much clearer."

The meal arrived and Adrian was pleased. He could get to like Greek food pretty quickly, he thought. The Ouzo was not bad either.

Nick continued, "Adrian, I want to be sure you keep all this in the proper context. What you have seen and heard is all about the physical makeup and history of the human species. I believe your question, however, needs to be about finding the origin of our species."

Adrian responded, "Why is that?"

"Well, there is confusion around what I call 'old-school' evolution and Darwinism. I think you need to realize there exists a major debate in the scientific community as to whether Darwin-type evolution is the origin of humankind or whether another answer to the origin question is better."

Adrian responded, "Nick, Michael sent me a book on this subject and I read a portion of it yesterday. I was fascinated by the fact that this debate you refer to between those who believe in Darwin's theory and those who believe in 'intelligent design' is becoming prominent in the scientific world. Would you elaborate on this debate for me?"

"Adrian, the reason I had Michael send you the book is for you to realize the importance of the scientific questions associated with your question. Evolution has come to represent Darwinism and scientists who support it are being challenged by others who say the science is faulty. In the last two decades science has confirmed the origin of the human species to be much more complex than Darwin ever imagined. It has led many scientists to join in a movement calling for 'intelligent design' to be at the core of human origin, not rudimentary evolution."

Continuing, Nick stated, "Adrian, for me 'old school' evolution relates to the recognition that there are many things that differentiate humans from one another. Prolonged exposure to different climates, different diets, different levels of sunlight, and different interbreeding, just to mention a few, all lead to diversity within any species."

"In other words, our environment and the intellectual way we adapt to it has helped us develop into the species at the top of the food chain. However, this 'old school' approach has been replaced by Darwinism, which tends to lead one to disbelieve God created all things."

"Science has progressed a lot since Darwin did his research. No one can blame Darwin for concluding what he did with what information he had at the time. However, our research capabilities are so good we can now see things Darwin never saw or heard. Decide for yourself, but I believe we have already proven that the human race did not have a simple single-cell origin but rather a complex one engineered by God! I simply see no other explanation!"

"Wow, thank you, Nick. So should our question be 'what is the origin of the human species?'"

"Yes, I believe it should," Nick replied. "Adrian, let me be very clear in saying that all the work on the origin of the human race has been aimed at understanding the family tree and its timetable, as it relates to the physical characteristics of the species. All this work is based on the skeletal remains of people we know to have existed many years ago. We can try to estimate their capabilities based on what we find buried with them, but it is very difficult to determine their mental aptitude, their level of consciousness, and their spiritual capacities. Some will say the body has evolved in many ways and it is no more than a vessel. Therefore, this leads to the possibility that we are evolved physically and mentally. Later we may have evolved spiritually. Maybe Adam and Eve were the first humans to have a conscience and a soul. Yet, this is hard to validate scientifically."

"Wow, I never actually considered that. Is this a belief you've held for some time?" Adrian asked.

"To be honest, Adrian, I have always held a faith in God as Creator and as Our Father. Professionally, I kept my belief to myself. My work was not faith-based work. It was scientific-based, and I only share my faith-based views with those who ask. So, no, I have never published my thoughts on the matter, but I hope if spelling this out it helps you put your questions and your answers in a better perspective."

Nick continued, "I believe God is the Creator of all we see. Therefore, we are created. That does not discount the fact that in God's creation of humankind he did not mold us through an 'old school' physical evolution to where we are today. He may, in fact, have molded our mental and spiritual attributes, as well. So I believe we have been created and molded like clay in at least a physical sense and likely in a mental and spiritual sense as well.

"Nick, I cannot tell you just how much I appreciate what you have told me. I am blessed to have had this lunch with you, as I say again, especially since you and your wife are on vacation. Is what you have told me something Michael and I can use in answering our question?"

"By all means. Tell Michael he owes me though!"

"I certainly will!"

They ended the lunch, Adrian paid the bill, and Nick drove Adrian back to his hotel. After good byes, Adrian retrieved his luggage at his hotel, caught a cab and headed to the airport. He was excited with what he had just learned. It certainly helped reconcile one of the biggest stumbling blocks for people in search of answers. Adrian couldn't wait to see Rachel and the rest of the team to tell them what he had learned today, as well as what he had learned throughout the trip.

11

Zagreb, Croatia

Adrian's flight into Zagreb was on time, but after making a connection along the way it was dark upon arrival. Adrian did not seem to mind as he was on a mental and emotional high following his luncheon with retired Professor Nick Dawson.

He stopped at an ATM to get some local currency, caught a van shuttle to his downtown hotel, and slept like there was no tomorrow. The next day was a free day and he knew exactly what he wanted to do with it if he was up to it physically. Fortunately, his bout with traveler's illness was over and he felt strong when he awoke. He called the hotel concierge desk to arrange for a private car for the following day. That would be his workday at Croatia's well known Neanderthal museum. With those arrangements made, he quickly dressed and headed out to catch a cab.

The cab took him a short distance to the city bus station; there he caught a bus at 9:00 a.m. and it took him south. The bus ride was just under two hours. He exited the bus at Croatia's *Plitvice National Park*. Nick Dawson had been to the park years ago and had told him not to miss the opportunity to see this sensational park. He suggested Adrian spend a full day hiking around the perimeter of the countless waterfalls in the park.

And the day was perfect to do so. Skies were overcast keeping it from being too hot for hiking. It had rained twice in the past week keeping the water levels high in the lakes. This would make for excellent runoffs over the falls.

Adrian had brought along a camera which was small and light. He had a pair of boots for hiking that he knew he needed when in Ethiopia and he was glad to have them since the rains would yield plenty of mud along the pathways. Surprisingly, there were busloads of Japanese tourists and many of them were wearing flip-flops.

Nick had given him a map of the park and explained how to get around, so after paying his entrance fee he caught a ride on one of the many trams in the park and immediately headed for the upper end of the falls. Getting off the tram, he used the convenient restroom and passed through one turnstile checkpoint and headed out on the trail. For the next four hours he passed numerous waterfalls, many of which were approached using wooden plank walkways. In fact, other than the main shoreline trails, all of the scenic waterfalls could be seen up close from the amazing array of wooden pathways. And as a group of soggy tourists hurried past Adrian, barely taking in the sites, he was especially thankful for his waterproof jacket. The falls released so much spray it felt as though it were raining.

Adrian pulled out his map and reviewed his options. The park was definitely large enough to keep a hiker challenged for an entire day. The waterfalls were the main attraction and they were spaced reasonably apart for a good hiker. In areas where there is some distance between the falls the park provided boats to ferry hikers from one spot to another.

Adrian enjoyed his walk, which allowed him time for reflection and the opportunity to really enjoy the park highlights. He opted to take one boat ride to shorten his walk so he could return to Zagreb in a timely manner. After five hours and countless pictures, Adrian found himself back at the main entrance feeling hungry and renewed. He stopped at the small food court at the park for a quick snack before heading to the bus stop.

At the bus stop Adrian discovered he had just missed a bus by about 10 minutes. Fortunately, a van stopped and picked up a full load of passengers from the bus stop headed back to Zagreb. The van driver charged the normal bus fare plus was willing to deliver each passenger to either the bus station or any major hotel in town. Adrian eagerly jumped in and it turned out to save him time and money to do so.

Catching the last hour of the hotel restaurant being open, Adrian had a quick meal, took a shower and headed to bed. He wanted to get up early so he could e-mail his trip status report back to the office on Mercer Island. Staying busy helped Adrian deal with the constant reminders of his family loss. However, the images of Lisa and Catherine that continually paraded through his mind made it hard to fall asleep. On this particular night a worn-out body helped.

Adrian was up by 7:00 a.m. He dressed and had a full breakfast in the hotel. When he had completed his report and e-mailed it, he focused his attention on the day's meeting at the museum. He carefully thought through what he might get out of the meeting today. Being not quite sure what that might be, he stared out his window looking toward the main downtown area. He could see a city center museum that he would later find is named the Mimara museum. Not that the museum meant much to him; and, in fact, he really wasn't all that keen about museums in the first place, but he was aware that a lot of people like them.

It gave him pause that perhaps today's visit should not be solely about broadening his view on evolution, but perhaps he needed to also re-think about how museums attract people. After all, at some point the Foundation may well want to publicize its findings and promote a greater understanding of God's plan. With that in mind, he gathered his stuff to catch the private car that would take him a fair distance out of town to see another museum and meet another expert.

After an hour and a half of driving in the direction of Slovenia, the driver pulled up in front of the Muzej Hrapinskih Neandertalaca. This museum is located very near the town of Krapina. Adrian asked the driver to return in three hours. Then he walked past a group of school kids who were obviously having fun on a school field trip, and he started looking for an office.

Upon announcing who he was and that he had an appointment with the Director, the lady at the ticket desk proceeded to escort him to an office area in the back. They passed by more kids lined up in seats waiting for a 16-minute introductory film. Teachers were scurrying around the kids trying to maintain some semblance of order.

The director, Petar Jagic, arose from his desk when Adrian entered the office and they exchanged pleasantries for a few moments. Then the director asked Adrian to join him in the conference room. He offered Adrian coffee but Adrian took water instead.

The Director has been director of the museum for 31 years. He worked here while attending college in Zagreb and had family connections throughout the local region. He is an active member of the Croatian Geological Society and his love for what he does was evident after only a few minutes of conversation.

"Adrian, is there anything you would like me to do for you before we tour the museum and take a short walk to the discovery site we have on the premises?"

"Director, if it is possible, I would like to reserve time at the end of the tour to raise a few questions. I think we would both be better served if we do things in that order, if that is agreeable to you and your schedule?"

"By all means. Your Michael Channing has made a sizable contribution to our meager museum and I am most happy to do as you request."

As the Director and Adrian walked beyond the children who were now giggling and shuffling around, to the dismay of their teachers, they entered a darkened area designed to assist the viewer in going back in time. The exhibit was essentially a virtual cave designed to have you walk through ages past and relate to the variety of human-like species.

Starting with Stone Age people, the exhibit characterizes many of the better known human-like species leading up to today's homo-sapiens with timelines provided along the way. Appropriately-sized representations of the various species are depicted along the route and the visitor has a sense of passing from one era to another as you walk the route.

Admittedly, the displays were more of the 1970's variety. With a limited budget and being a long way from much of a population base, it was understandable that the museum was not what you might call modern. Yet, the message of evolution was inferred, if not intended. Adrian doubted if any of the kids about to pass through this walk of time would argue against some form of evolutionary change leading to modern humans.

After a thorough review of the contents on display in the main building, Adrian and Petar walked out to the nearby excavation site on the Husnjakovo hill. This is where Neanderthal people lived over 100,000 years ago, and it is believed they are ancestors of some percentage of modern-day Europeans. Returning to the conference room Petar provided sandwiches and wine for lunch. The wine was a nice touch and Adrian appreciated something to eat before making the long drive back to Zagreb.

Adrian addressed Petar with his first question, "Petar, is there substantial evidence that Neanderthals inter-bred with homo-sapiens?"

Petar responded quickly saying, "Absolutely, the DNA evidence of today is very conclusive on that point. The only question remaining is how long ago did that first occur?"

"I take it, that like with other archeological findings, we keep discovering fossils that date back farther in time? So, relative to our species, we can expect to continue to find more evidence of interactions with other species?" asked Adrian.

"That is a pretty fair conclusion. You saw evidence of that trend, no doubt, in the Ethiopian work that is ongoing today?"

Adrian nodded in agreement and continued, "Petar, what do the kids who come here think about what they see?"

"It is funny that you ask. I would say they laugh a lot and tell each other that their great-great-great grandparents looked like monkeys. Surprisingly, they are okay with that. Sure they laugh, but they recognize that their parents look larger and different so why not recognize that the people of the world change in different ways. Just as Europeans look different from Chinese, and so forth, confirms to them that change is normal."

Adrian agreed with Petar on his point. In his mind he questioned whether there would be a place for a modern museum of this type in the future for the Foundation. He asked, "One last question, Petar, do people come back more than once to experience what you have here?"

Petar smiled, "We do have a long list of faithful patrons who support this museum, and they are extremely important to the survival of the museum. Tourists come once and we seldom see them return. Our entrance fee is cheap to tourists, but the trip to get here and return requires the better part of a day. Kids from the region come with their class once or twice in their schooling. Occasionally, they return to work on a high school or college paper. To be perfectly honest Adrian, unless the museum gets a major facelift with modern technology we will be faced with a declining base of visitors. There is simply so much information available at a young person's fingertips that they do not need to come here. If we improve our website we run the risk of losing more and more of the young folks who say to themselves, why go to the museum when we can take a virtual tour thru the internet. Unfortunately, that is reality. We are not well located to weather the change ahead, I am afraid."

"Petar, I wish you well. It is time for me to go. I appreciate your hospitality and I hope you fare better than you think you might!"

On Adrian's return trip to Zagreb he couldn't help thinking Petar was right about the poor prospects for the future for museums like his. It was becoming a Neanderthal in its own right. Upon returning to his hotel he stopped by the hotel concierge desk and thanked them for arranging the private car. He also asked for a recommendation for a good local restaurant for dinner. After being cooped up in the car for a good part of the day, Adrian was looking forward to stretching his legs, so he informed the hotel concierge he wanted to walk a ways to get there.

With directions in hand, Adrian returned to his room, showered and then strolled through the downtown area. He passed the museum he had seen out his hotel window. He continued on through areas of open, outside seating where throngs of folks were having a beer, a glass of wine, or a coffee. It did not appear that many local folks actually ate dinner out. Tourists, on the other hand were more noticeable as they seemed to be the only ones actually having dinner.

After crossing the city tram tracks he crossed through Bana Jelacic Square where he briefly stopped to take in the statue of Josip Jelacic Buzimski. As he strolled through the Dolac market area, with its notable red umbrellas, he strolled up Tkalclcava to the hotel concierge-recommended restaurant. Adrian ordered what the waiter recommended, and all he asked was that he be served the best and most popular local dish. He drank a wonderful local Rizling (Croatian for Riesling) wine with his meal, and afterwards he thought to himself that was one of the best meals he had ever eaten.

The waiter explained that the dish he ordered was cooked in the traditional way within a clay pot that covers the dish and tenderizes the meat. It was a beef dish marinated in a red sauce, but all Adrian knew was that the meal was heavenly. His only regret was that he didn't have someone along with whom to enjoy the meal and the wine. After two glasses of wine and a full meal, Adrian took his time walking back to the hotel. He wished he could spend more time in this country. He wished he could travel to Dubrovnik and spend time in that walled city on the Adriatic, but that would have to wait for another day.

Returning to his room Adrian checked his schedule and realized he needed to catch an early train. He had his train ticket to Vienna and simply needed to catch a cab to the train station in time to catch the train and find his cabin and seat.

12

Mercer Island, Washington

While Adrian travelled around the Mediterranean region, Nancy worked on the Bible's genealogy from Adam to Jesus. She had a meeting with Michael to share her initial results.

"Michael, you asked me to research the time-line from Adam to Jesus using only the Bible as a source. I've done that, but I was awfully tempted to use one of those search engines you are always referring to and let it do the work for me."

"Nancy, doing it that way would not be any fun! You need to struggle some to be able to believe that you found the right family tree. You can check it after we have a chance to look at your independent work."

"Well, my grandson probably could do this better than I can, but I've given it a good try."

"Okay, take me through what you found."

"Very well. To be perfectly honest this started out to be boring, but as I went through it I found it to be sort of interesting."

"That is why I wanted you to do it and not me," Michael smiled.

"You should not do that to an old lady."

"Nancy, you are as young at heart as anyone I know. I love that about you. So tell me where you are on this?"

Nancy explained that she had simply taken the Book of Genesis literally and walked through Chapter 5 where Moses outlines the lineage from Adam to Noah. Then she took the lineage from Noah's son Shem to Abraham as outlined in Chapter 11. This provided an ancient account in years of the family tree from Adam to Abraham.

With all this information at hand, she said it took a while to boil down the years between birth and first born male child to get the right time period for each generation. She shared the partial family tree that she generated in the process.

Name	**Years Lived**	**Bore**
Adam	130	Seth
Seth	105	Enosh
Enosh	90	Kenan
Kenan	70	Mahalalel
Mahalalel	65	Jared
Jared	162	Enoch
Enoch	65	Methuselah
Methuselah	187	Lamech
Lamech	182	Noah
Noah	502	Shem
Shem	100	Arphaxad
Arphaxad	35	Shelah
Shelah	30	Eber
Eber	34	Peleg
Peleg	30	Reu

Reu	32	Serug
Serug	30	Nahor
Nahor	29	Terah
Terah	70	Abram
Abraham		

"The total years from Adam's birth to Abraham's birth is 1,948 years. I suppose these may be Hebrew calendar years, but I may be wrong," Nancy noted.

"Okay, what about the period between Abraham's birth and Jesus' birth?"

Nancy paused, "Well, Michael, this is where I went to the footnotes. Someone much smarter than me had put together a timeline in the front of my Bible saying Abraham was born in 2,166 BCE *(Before Common Era/Before Christian Era)*. So, Michael, I used that date and simply listed the family tree from Abraham to Jesus in the order it is written in the book of Matthew. Here is the list."

Abraham
Issac
Jacob
Judah
Perez
Hezron
Ram
Amminadab
Nahshon
Salmon
Boaz
Obed
Jesse
David
Solomon
Rehoboam
Abijah

Asa
Jehoshaphat
JehoramUzziah
Jotham
Ahaz
Hezekiah
ManaAmonJosiah
Jeconi
Shealtiel
Zerubbabel
Abiud
Eliakim
Azor
Zadok
Akim
Eliud
Eleazar
Matthan
Jacob
Joseph
Jesus

"If Abraham was born in 2,166 BCE, then all we need is Jesus' birthdate to finalize the family tree. Mind you this is the male lineage and not the maternal lineage the Jewish folks like to use. At any rate, we need to know when Jesus was born. The Bible I used says Jesus was born in either 5 or 6 BCE. If that is accurate, then the time from Abraham's birth to Jesus' birth is 2,161 years. Added to the 1,948 years from Adam to Abraham, we get a total of 4,064 years from Adam's birth to Jesus' birth. This means I think we need to work through Jesus' birthdate a little because I understand that there is a real debate on His birthdate and His date of death. I'll be happy to work on that, if you like."

Michael followed up saying, "Yes, please see what you can find out on the birthdate debate and let's consider this enough to make our own assessment. It can be an assumption in our future work if appropriate. And thank you for this work. Please give me a copy of what you have and let me review it. I can do some Internet search work for us and see how this compares. This is a good start and I'll check it over."

A few days after Nancy had given Michael her preliminary written report, Michael asked her to join him to discuss a specific attribute of her report. "Nancy, I am fascinated by one aspect of your report. It has to do with Jesus' birthdate and the date he was crucified. I looked up the topic on-line and I remain surprised that with all the dates we seem to have before and after Jesus, there is not a consensus on when Jesus actually lived."

"Michael, actually, like a lot of folks, I assumed the calendar of years started with His birth or His death. But that isn't even the case."

"Nancy, you did a good job of relating the story of Jesus' birth as it is outlined in Luke: Chapter 2. In that chapter, Luke clearly states that Caesar Augustus, who was Emperor of Rome from 31 BC to 14 AD, issued a decree to have a census taken of the Roman Empire. This had to be a daunting task!"

"At any rate, Luke goes on to tell us that the first of two censuses were taken while Quirinius was governor of Syria. My Bible's study notes indicate that was between 6 and 4 BC. The second census was apparently held between 6 and 9 AD."

Michael went on, "Then, as you note, Luke: Chapter 3 tells us that Jesus was 'about 30 years old when he began His ministry.' So, if Luke is correct, then Jesus may have been born between 4 and 6 BC, and started his ministry between 24 and 26 AD. If He ministered approximately four years, we are saying His death occurred between 28 and 30 AD. Is that a fair representation of what you found?"

Nancy, responded, "Yes it is. Along with that, Luke's genealogy in Chapter 1 is different from Matthew's. I pointed that out in the report, and I thought it might be a good idea for me to talk with Reverend Osgood about why this is. He might be able to help us."

"Nancy, you have a good idea there. You do that and I'll continue looking into this whole timeline. I'd like to have this done before Adrian returns as I know we will have lots to do when he gets back. Thanks, let's talk in a few days."

13

Vienna, Austria

Before his flight from Zagreb landed, Adrian reread his notes from Michael. At this point in his trip Michael had wanted Adrian to shift his focus for the next two stops, away from the "origin of man" issue to what might better be called the "nature of man."

The itineraries for both this stop and Paris would focus on viewing artwork that dated back thousands of years. The point of this was to reconcile the physical and mental attributes associated with the development of our species. Basically, Michael wanted Adrian to describe the types of artwork that existed thousands of years ago and what that artwork means in terms of human capacity versus what could be considered primitive animal capacity.

Adrian was the least excited about this part of the trip. To be honest with himself, he'd been dreading it a little. He was happy when he learned Rachel would be joining him to help out in this area and hoped that she, at least, had a better appreciation for art. He'd never taken art history or, really any type of art classes. In fact, he counted himself a failure at stick-figure drawings. He double checked his camera to ensure he had plenty of space to take pictures. They were sure to need them since his explanations might be lacking.

Fortunately, the schedule for this first stop was to visit only one museum and focus on one piece of art. That should be tolerable he thought.

Upon landing at the airport in Vienna, Adrian caught a taxi for his 20-minute ride to his hotel. He had asked the driver, who spoke excellent English, to drive by and point out some of the major sights along the way.

Adrian's hotel was well located in the main part of the city directly on the Danube River. Most captivating on his trip in was the sight of St. Stephen's Cathedral. The driver noted that the cathedral was the primary church of the Roman Catholic Archdiocese of Vienna, and it served as the seat for the Archbishop of Vienna.

Having served as the most important church in Austria for nearly 700 years, St. Stephen's Cathedral is a majestic sight to see. The construction is a combination of Gothic and Romanesque. Above all else it has a spectacular multi-colored tile roof. A double headed eagle formed in the tile adorns the roof and sets it off as one of the most unique churches in the world.

The city of Vienna itself is full of great architecture and a delight to tour. Still, the cathedral tugged at Adrian and he asked the driver to circle the church again. This time the driver pointed out the relief sculpture of Christ in the Garden of Gethsemane. What a marvelous depiction Adrian thought. He wondered if one day he might visit that very special garden and pray where Jesus prayed.

Before he got to his hotel he asked the driver why some people call the city Vienna while others call it Wien. The driver did not know exactly, but said tourists like to call the city Vienna and the locals call it Wien.

It all seemed strange to Adrian that so many European cities have a long-standing tradition of calling their cities one thing while an English version is entirely different. Italy is full of cities like that. Roma versus Rome. Firenze versus Florence. Venezia versus Venice. Even his next stop in Munich is locally called Munchen. Why don't we all call it what the locals call it!!! It is not that difficult, Adrian thought.

After getting to the hotel Adrian unpacked, showered and had a light dinner in the hotel restaurant. Afterwards, he stepped out the front door and crossed over the boulevard to the riverside. It was getting dark and he could see riverboats tied up along the shore in both directions. He expected some of the riverboats had stopped in Vienna as they headed down rivers from as far away as Amsterdam. He thought a river cruise on the Danube might be a nice vacation someday.

The next morning Adrian woke up, dressed and had a nice breakfast in the hotel restaurant. He was in fact getting tired of eating out all the time. A hard-boiled egg, a bowl of cereal with blueberries, and a fresh glass of orange juice at home sounded pretty good. Adrian did not want to start counting the days till he got home, but he was beginning to get travel weary. Plus, his heart was not into this particular stop and he found his mind wandering. He was not as focused as he had been and he felt bad about that. He really wanted to be focused the entire trip, but it was not happening.

Catching up with Adrian was the fact that he desperately missed Lisa and Catherine. Although it had been months since the funeral, the loss of his wife and daughter was beginning to hit him again. He had cried the night before and asked God to help him with the pain. He asked God to hug Lisa and Catherine since he couldn't. He just felt so alone. Still he had a job to do and it was one he really wanted to do well. He checked his bag with the bell captain and caught a taxi to his only meeting point in Vienna. It was the Museum of Natural History. The local name is the Naturhistorisches Museum Wien.

At the museum he met Josef Rattenberg, one of the official guides of the museum. Michael again had made a modest contribution to the museum to ensure that Adrian would get first-class treatment for his short visit. Lunch was included and he had the services of Josef for several hours.

Of principal interest was The Venus of Willendorf. Perhaps the earliest sculpted image of a human being, it represents an amazing image of a woman carved out of limestone. Josef took Adrian straight to the display. Adrian took several photos from different angles before Joseph briefed Adrian on the discovery.

Joseph explained that in 1908 an archaeologist named Josef Szombathy found the artifact in the town of Willendorf, Austria. He said that the material used was a type of limestone not found in the local region and, therefore, it has been concluded that the carving must have been made elsewhere and brought to the location where it was discovered. When it was discovered, early tests indicated the carving was 12,000 to 17,000 years old, making it close in age to the Lascaux paintings in France. However, more current estimates place the age at 24,000 to 26,000 years old.

The carving is less than five inches in height and depicts a large-bodied woman with over-sized breasts and torso. Clearly the artifact shows the ability of the carver to create a clear representation of the human species. In answer to Adrian's question about the accuracy of dating this piece of art, Josef went into a technical discussion of multiple studies performed to establish the date of origin. Over the last 40 years, he said all the studies performed were in the same rough time-frames in terms of origins. Clearly, he and all members of the museum staff were of the steadfast belief that the Venus of Willendorf was well over 20,000 years old.

Adrian had seen what he came to see. Yes, the human species seemed to have the wherewithal to create art well before Adam was said to have been born. How that reconciles with evolution theory was the question. Adrian recalled his conversation with Nick in Athens. The evidence here seemed to suggest humanity had grown to a higher form mentally over time, just as it had changed physically over an extended time period.

Josef was kind to show Adrian around the older artifacts on display in the museum. Many of them dating back to prehistoric times. Afterwards, the two had lunch in the cafeteria. Adrian thanked Josef for the visit and returned to the hotel.

Since it was still early in the afternoon, Adrian took the time to write up some of his conclusions from the trip thus far. He wanted to send them to Michael so the team could respond with any questions that might need answering while he was still in Munich, Paris, or London.

His summary to Michael made the case that the preponderance of evidence is that mankind has a long history of growth and adaptation. Furthermore, all the evidence that he had seen and all the scientists whom he had spoken with are faced with an overwhelming prevalence of evidence that mankind dates back hundreds of thousands of years. Therefore, unless something striking shows up he would have to conclude that mankind has grown and adapted physically and mentally over a period of time far exceeding the genealogical date of Adam's birth (i.e. roughly 6,000 years ago – according to Genesis). He knew from discussions with Michael that Nancy's genealogy work would spell out the date for a biblical birth of Adam, and that date would be about 6,000 years ago or roughly 4,000 BCE.

Adrian went on to note that the question he has been endeavoring to research should be changed from one focused on evolution versus creation theory, to one that asks what is the origin of humankind. He said all he can conclude for certain is that humankind has grown and adapted physically and mentally over hundreds of thousands of years. Period!

Importantly, he went on to note that he fully believed God created the human species and that growth and adaptation have been with the species from its origin. Still he wondered if this was the kind of evolution Darwin had in mind.

Adrian ended his report by saying he was still processing all this and was looking forward to discussing it with Rachel and the rest of the group. The next morning Adrian e-mailed his report to Michael, and then headed to the airport to catch a flight to Munich, Germany.

14

Mercer Island, Washington

Michael, Nancy, and Rachel met in the conference room. This was their weekly meeting to discuss all aspects of the Foundation and the work they were doing to find answers to their four major questions. Michael opened the meeting with a prayer.

Nancy started by saying she was prepared to give an update on her work regarding Jesus' genealogy and biblical timelines. However, she had asked Reverend Osgood to join the meeting to help her with what she had to present. Since the good reverend didn't need to sit in on other business she asked him to come for the second hour of the meeting.

Michael and Rachel thought that was just fine and they proceeded to discuss current issues. Michael gave a brief rundown on the status of Adrian's trip. He told them that Adrian's meeting in Athens had led him to make a change to their second question. It needed to be restated so as to ask 'what is the origin of the human species'. Michael said he expected Adrian would use Rachel as a sounding board when they meet next week in Paris to test his conclusions.

Rachel said she had all the arrangements in place for her trip and she was looking forward to the opportunity to help Adrian with his work. Seeing Paris for the first time was a pretty big deal too.

Michael noted that Adrian was getting tired of the travel schedule and with her arrival it might serve them both well to spend a couple of days seeing the sights in the city. Rachel had no problems with the boss granting some downtime for the two of them to see Paris.

Rachel gave an update on the prior month's financials. Amazingly, the Foundation's investment portfolio had far exceeded the month's expenditures. In fact, year-to-date the Foundation's financial position had increased thirty eight percent, excluding Michael's personal contributions.

Michael's reaction was not quite as jubilant as Rachel was expecting, but she quickly found out why. "I have several ideas swimming around in my head," Michael said. "Future projects that the Foundation could undertake, but they will require significantly more money than we currently have."

Curious, Rachel asked what Michael had in mind.

"I foresee a major construction project down the line as well as a substantial missionary support effort to help us spread the message."

Rachel asked if there was something she could do to help. Michael responded that when she gets back from her Europe trip that there was one item he needed help doing. He explained he would eventually need a set of first-class materials to present to individuals and groups for fundraising.

Rachel volunteered to start thinking about putting these materials together even though it would be some time before the materials would be needed. Nancy volunteered to help and Rachel agreed she could use the help. Michael consented and thought the idea was in good hands.

After a short break Reverend Osgood rang the doorbell and was greeted by Nancy who escorted him to the kitchen where she got the Reverend a cup of tea and a biscuit.

Greeting the Reverend, Michael said "Welcome, John, it's kind of you to join us today."

"Nancy has graciously asked that I help the Foundation with some work on a topic with which I am very familiar. You know, Michael, I was a student once. In fact, I studied religious history to get my Master's Degree before attending seminary. When Nancy asked me to help I pulled out my thesis and checked to see if things I wrote about are, in fact, still relevant."

"What was your thesis titled, if I may ask," Michael inquired.

"*The Life and Times of Abraham*, if I recall correctly."

Nancy handed each person a nicely bound notebook. "I would like to introduce the subject matter I've discussed with John and then let him walk you through the answers we have prepared."

"Sounds good Nancy," Michael replied.

"Okay, to get started the two questions you asked for me to look into have to do with biblical history. The first was to outline the genealogy of Jesus as noted in the Bible. The second was to put together a timeline of key biblical events leading up to the life of Jesus. Let's take the genealogy question first and follow that with the timeline."

"There are two genealogical family trees depicting Jesus' ancestors in the Bible. One is found in the book of Matthew and the other in the book of Luke. Although they are similar from Abraham to David, there are notable differences from David to Jesus. Matthew traces the line from Jesus' father, Joseph, using only heirs to the throne of David. Whereas, Luke's version is predicated on following the blood line through Mary back to David and ultimately to Abraham."

Nancy continued, "It was at this point I needed help and recruited Reverend Osgood to clarify the matter. Reverend John would you please help me out here."

"I'd be delighted to render what help I can. First, relative to the genealogy report Nancy prepared for you before she came to talk with me, I found the work she did on identifying the 1,948 years from Adam to Abram's birth to be on target. That covers nearly two millennium of biblical time and we can come back to that work and add in some important events if we have time. But for now let us look at the timeline from Abraham to Jesus where we simply do not have the detail dates to comfortably say when Abraham was born. We can say it was 1,948 years after Adam was born. But that is all we can say with any certainty and biblical backing."

"Therefore, I suggest you resist the urge to pick a date from one editor using his or her educated guess. Instead, I would use the ancient Hebrew calendar as the best alternative to set a timeline. The Hebrews used a calendar system to record dates and special holidays that begins with the creation from Genesis."

"Whether we believe as the Jewish people do that creation occurred in the beginning of year one or not, it is relevant that they start with Adam and proceed through the generation time-wise as Nancy did believing Abram was born 1,948 year later."

"Their tradition continues today in counting the current year as 5776. Therefore, Abraham was born in 1813 BCE using the Gregorian calendar nearly everyone uses today."

"When I did my thesis work I discovered widespread disagreement as to when Abram was born and when he died. His life span is spelled out in Genesis Chapter 25 as being 175 years. Theories on his birthdate range over 200 years."

"Lastly, if you choose to use the Hebrew calendar as I just did to pinpoint a date you will find other important biblical dates. For example, the flood that destroyed much of the known world in and around Mesopotamia would have occurred 1,656 years after Adam's birth or 2104 BCE. Likewise, the Tower of Babel would have been destroyed in 1998 BCE."

Rachel asked, "Did you have a chance to evaluate what Nancy concluded on Jesus' birthdate, his date of death, or his second coming?"

"Rachel, I did look into those issues briefly. I must admit I did not do so aggressively. Please understand that early in my faith journey the words in scripture that Jesus spoke saying 'you will neither know the hour or the day' meant I should not attempt to figure that out. Also, I am driven by Jesus' warning that we must come to Him in faith much like children. For me that is easy. For others, like you Michael, their faith breeds an appetite to learn more of God's plan for them and the world."

"That said, relative to his birth date and the date of death, I can tell you the consensus of those who study biblical dates generally believe Jesus was born in the time of the first Roman census or more precisely between 6 and 4 BCE."

"Jesus' death occurred after he had spent the necessary time to become a Jewish rabbi. Typically, that required reaching the age of thirty. Since Jesus taught for approximately three and a half years he could have been thirty three or thirty four at the time of His death. That would place His death between 27 AD and 30 AD."

"However, I do know there are many theories out there placing different dates on his death. The earliest date I've seen is 27 AD and the latest date is 40 AD and that would be predicated on the biblical reference to Joseph taking Mary and Jesus to the second census later in 6 or 7 AD."

"Well folks, that is about all I can help you with today. I need to return to the parish, but if there is anything else I can help you through let me know. God bless you for the journey you are taking. It is a road not well travelled by very many. I wish you the best."

Michael, Rachel and Nancy each thanked the Reverend before he left.

Once they all returned to the conference room, Rachel said, "Wow, I get so much out of these sessions."

Nancy added," I am glad I thought to ask him for help."

Michael paused as they awaited his reaction. Then he spoke, "For all the years I attended church for Mary's sake I regret not listening closer to what that man had to say. He is so honest and so wise in the way of the Lord. Now I want more of what he has in his soul. There is a certain peace within him. It is a kind of certainty about where he is headed when Peter opens the heavenly gates for him to enter. Wow is right!"

"Okay, where do we go with this from here?"

Nancy piped up. "I think I want the preliminary report I gave you back. I took pretty good notes today and from the earlier meeting I had with John this week. I would like to incorporate his suggestions and finalize the report."

"Rachel, do you have anything you want to add," Michael asked.

"No, that sounds good to me."

Michael added, "Nancy, it is still over a week before Adrian and Rachel get back. I trust that gives you enough time to rework what you have and get it ready for all of us to discuss. In addition, I would like to have a separate copy of John's comments in response to Rachel's question. He verified that we will never know the exact date of the greatest sacrifice in the history of the world. That is astonishing! Also, we can't even pinpoint the exact year Jesus was born. Amazing! It has been a long week, why don't you take tomorrow off?"

Nancy jumped on that offer. "Michael, you need to get out more often. Tomorrow is Saturday and I don't think either Rachel or I were planning to work tomorrow anyway."

Rachel jumped in saying, "That's right, I am flying to Paris next week and I have to figure out what to wear. I might be shopping tomorrow. So, I'm not planning to be here."

Nancy couldn't resist, "I've got grandkids coming over, so that is where I'll be."

Michael sighed, "Wow, you are right I need to get out more. One day just sort of runs into the next. You two do what you have planned. I think I'll drive over to Leavenworth and get some good German food. I can't let Adrian be the only one eating sauerbraten."

15

Munich, Germany

Adrian's flight to Munich was smooth and relatively short in duration. Shortly after getting his single bag Adrian was on the "S" train to Munich's city central. He stepped off the train and immediately was impressed with the size of the station. The station was huge - he had to walk through the underground lower shopping areas to get to the main train station. Once there, he found more than 20 sets of tracks that confronted him along with the main departure board listing train destinations throughout western and central Europe. The scene was awesome with passengers departing and arriving and crossing everywhere.

He noted countless eateries scattered throughout the terminal in case he needed a quick meal any time of day. He knew his hotel was nearby and that proved true as he left the station and crossed the Bayerstrasse. The hotel actually faced the train station and was within short walking distance.

His room was on the 10th floor and had a nice view toward the ever-busy train station. Back home there was no station approaching the size or configuration like the station he had just come through. All the commuters seemed to be tuned into which track went where. An active taxi stand with two dozen awaiting vehicles stood ready to carry those who needed to travel a bit farther.

After a shower Adrian picked up the phone and called the local number Michael had given him. Joel Goldstein answered the phone and was happy to hear from Adrian.

"Did you have a good flight in from Wien?" Joel asked.

Adrian understood Wien to be the European version of Vienna and responded, "I certainly did and I look forward to seeing you day after tomorrow. Where should we meet?"

Joel asked, "Are you available for the whole day or only part of the day?"

"Joel, I am available for the entire day if you have the time."

"Adrian, do you have some good walking shoes with you and would you be interested in taking a hike with me. We can talk while we hike if you are up to that."

"Yes, I have walking boots with me and I have a small backpack as well."

"Splendid! Here is what I have in mind. We can meet at your hotel early, catch a train headed south to Garmish, catch another small train toward the Zugspitze (*the tallest mountain in Germany*), hike around Eibsee Lake, have an early dinner at a lakeside hotel and then take a train back to Munich. That should give us plenty of time to talk and enjoy some of our beautiful Bavarian Alps country."

"I cannot think of anything better, and if I read the weather report correctly, day after tomorrow should be cool and clear."

"It certainly looks that way, but do bring a hat and a light jacket just in case the mountain surprises us with a shower or two. By the way,

I am sorry I had a previously scheduled event lined up for tomorrow. Do you have plans or are you open to suggestions?"

"Joel, I knew you would be busy, so I simply plan to do some sightseeing. Any suggestion would be welcomed."

"Well, since you are here to discuss Jewish history and religion, I suggest you take a morning train to Dachau and take what we call *'The Walk of Remembrance'*. It will take you on the same route that incoming Jewish prisoners had to take to get to the German concentration camp operated by the SS. Trains leave every 30 minutes and if you go early enough you will be back in the city for lunch at the train station. Then you can catch an "S" Train to the main square in town."

"I like it and that is what I will do. One question?"

"What is that?"

"Would you mind if I record our conversation on the hike? I simply will not be able to take notes and I would not be pleased with myself if I missed what you have to say."

"I totally understand and I see no problem as long as you do not publish my comments with my name. What I will have to say will be of no surprise to anyone, however, I still am cautious as I have had a bad experience or two. So tell Michael to feel free to use anything I say, just don't tag my name with anything you publish."

"We will honor your request. Thank you for that and I will look forward to seeing you at say 7:00 a.m. in the hotel lobby day after tomorrow."

"Sounds great! I know the hotel well and I will be there. Good night."

"Good night, Joel."

Adrian was pleased with how the conversation went and he was excited about the prospect of getting to do some hiking. Also, the idea of visiting Dachau the next day on his own seemed appropriate. He was very interested in walking from the train station in Dachau on the same route where thousands of Jews had walked to the town's concentration camp.

After the call Adrian headed across the street and found a place that served hot and tasty pizza with a nice garden salad. Afterwards, he sent an e-mail via the room's internet connection to Michael updating him on the plans for the next two days. He took a hot shower and dropped off to sleep in short order.

The next morning Adrian got up, dressed and headed across the street to the train station. He purchased his round-trip ticket from the sales office and found that he had a bit of a long walk to his assigned platform. It seemed the local trains were placed on outside tracks while all the long distance trains were placed front and center.

With a fresh croissant in a bag along with some German cheese and a bottle of orange juice he was on board and seated when the train departed for Dachau. He was already liking train travel in Europe. It seemed so efficient and you could sit and work quietly or just stare at the landscape as it flashed by the window.

After arriving in Dachau, Adrian exited the train and began looking for a map showing the route of the walk Joel mentioned. Before spotting the map Adrian could not help noticing the pictures of SS officers off-loading rail cars packed with Jewish prisoners. These prisoners were herded down a nearby street to the concentration camp where the SS did all it could to keep local residents in the dark about what was really going on at the camp.

Along the route that seemed to be two or three kilometers long there were plaques with photos and accompanying explanations providing a realistic depiction of the way men, women and children were targeted for extermination. The photos inside the camp and the short films scattered about the Visitors Center portrayed the stark horror of gas chambers and furnaces. They reminded Adrian of just how much hatred some people can have for others. Not what God intended, for sure!

After a two-hour stay Adrian left and solemnly walked back to the train station. After a 20-minute wait he was headed back to the city. Joel was right to suggest the visit and the walk. While tomorrow's walk was going to be a lovely walk in nature this was the opposite experience. It was one most people would rather forget, but one that should not be forgotten by anyone.

After a quick lunch at the train station in Munich, Adrian caught the local train to Marienplatz in the old city center. He joined others in the square waiting to see the famous Glockenspiel ring in a new hour. It is located in the old Rathaus building that serves as City Hall. The chiming and performance was great. Afterwards he headed over to the traditional tourist-plagued beer house called the Hof Brau Haus. He had a beer, listened to Bavarian music and marveled at the mix of tourists who were there from all corners of the world.

Adrian took the train back to the main station and got lost in its lower reaches as he attempted to get back to the doorway he had entered earlier. He did find a grocery store in the maze underground and purchased a variety of odds and ends to comprise his dinner for the evening.

Once he found a way out of the building he recognized that he was a short block away from the street that passed in front of his hotel. Walking two blocks he entered the hotel and found his room. After a good shower he relaxed watching news on the television, eating his dinner and making a few notes about his visit to Dachau.

After a somewhat restless night's sleep, Adrian met Joel in the hotel lobby at the agreed upon time. Joel was in his fifties and appeared to be in excellent physical condition. He was dressed for hiking and carried himself as though he was a well accomplished outdoorsman.

Before stopping to get properly introduced to one another, the two quickly headed over to the train station, purchased tickets to Garmish, grabbed a few breakfast items at two different stands and headed to their platform. They boarded the train, found an empty compartment and settled in for the 80-minute ride.

Adrian sighed, "I am not used to the whole train travel thing. I must admit I like it, however."

"I assume you travel primarily by car in the U.S.?" Joel asked.

"As a matter of fact, I do. Most Americans do. A number of the larger cities along the east coast of the U.S. have good rail service, but not like Europe."

"In Europe we tax oil very high and our rail transportation is subsidized by the government to the extent it is economical to use the rail and bus services over having to always drive. I believe the economics are reversed in America and that explains the difference."

"Joel, I suspect you are correct. We like our independent automobile transportation to a fault. Congestion on highways is a huge problem for us in and around the larger metropolitan areas. Plus, we don't get to sit back and take in the scenery when we are all driving."

"Well, today you will get a good look at one of our prettiest regions. Have you ever been to Bavaria?"

"No, this is my first trip to Europe."

"Adrian, I don't know if Michael told you about how we met."

"Well, he told me he met you at Harvard and that you two have stayed in touch over the years."

"How is Michael? I know he lost his wife a couple of years ago."

"Joel, Michael lost his wife and has struggled emotionally as anyone would. He had a great deal of work on his hands having sold his software company. Furthermore, you may not know, but he recently lost his daughter, my wife, and our daughter in a terrible car wreck. All this has weighed on Michael, and for that matter, me as well. Both Michael and I are working to establish and grow a non-profit foundation in his wife's name."

"I knew about Michael's wife but not about your family's most recent loss. My God, I am so sorry for you both."

"Thank you Joel. I know Michael does not like to talk about it a lot, so I imagine he left it to me to tell you. It is difficult, but we are trying our best to move on. Since Michael established the non-profit foundation, I have been working for Michael. In fact, all this work is a blessing for the both of us."

After the two sat staring out the train window for a couple of minutes, Joel proceeded, "Michael called and said he would like to arrange a meeting with his son-in-law so we could discuss the Jewish faith. I was raised in a very devout Jewish family adhering to all the traditions of the faith. As a matter of fact, my grandfather was a Jewish rabbi. Sadly, he and my grandmother were murdered in the Holocaust. Michael wanted me to speak to you about Jewish faith because it is the root from which Christianity has sprung. Jesus was a Jewish rabbi and Michael hoped that in talking together you might come to better understand your faith as a Christian."

"Not having much exposure to the Jewish faith I need to learn the fundamentals, and, as you said, garner from that a proper understanding of Christianity. So any insight you can pass along will be welcomed. With Michael's help I have prepared a number of questions for you that I would like to get responses about."

"Adrian, that sounds perfect. Our walk this morning will allow us the opportunity to do that. It will take two to three hours to circle the lake depending how many stops we make and how quick we walk. I think you will love the views from the far side of the lake when we can see the Zugspitze, as long as the clouds don't obscure the view."

For the next hour the two got to know each other better and Adrian felt really comfortable with Joel. Having spent a lot of his trip time with professors and museum curators, it was nice to spend time with a smart and very well-balanced person. Joel talked about World Cup soccer, his family, his work as a businessman, and international developments. Adrian could see how Michael had easily struck up a close friendship with Joel.

As they departed the train from Munich, Joel led Adrian directly to a small office serving as the ticket office for the local cog-wheel train that goes to the Zugspitze. Joel said that although he had enough food for the two of them to have a light snack on their walk, he recommended that after their walk they stop at a lakeside hotel for a proper lunch. They simply needed to complete the walk by 1:15 p.m. since the restaurant in the hotel stopped serving lunch at 2:00 p.m.

The train finally stopped at the lakeside village of Eibsee on its way to the Zugspitze, having made a few stops along the way. It was a gorgeous morning with only a few autumn clouds hanging near the top of this 9,718-foot tall mountain. This is the tallest peak in Germany and it is one massive rock with near vertical rocky peaks. Adrian thought the ride up the mountain would be a real kick, but that would have to wait until he could return to this spectacular place. Adrian knew this must be a crowded place in the summer, however, in the early fall this was a place to behold. It was spectacular on a clear day like this and uncluttered with tourists.

Once in Eibsee, they left the train and walked down to the lake. Joel opened his pack and withdrew two sets of hiking poles. Adrian graciously accepted the offer to use a pair. They adjusted the poles, checked their gear, water supply, and then set off in a clockwise direction around the lake. The view of the mountain faded away as they drew nearer to the lake and headed along the forested lakeside. Adrian could see across the lake and imagined that the view looking back across the lake from there would provide an excellent view of the mountain and the massive glacier residing across the top.

"Joel, before we get into the subject of the day could you explain why Garmish has two names on every sign?"

"Sorry for not clarifying that when we got into town. The actual name of the town is Garmish-Partenkirchen. Today's town is the combination of two towns. Partenkirchen is the oldest part and has its founding during the life of Jesus, as it was a Roman settlement first. Today the two towns are one with each part having its own unique characteristics. The old part is a bit staid, and the new part is definitely more youthful and party-like. In the winter the Garmish crowd here is all about mountain skiing as you might imagine."

"Do you come here often?"

"I am not a skier, but I do like to walk this lake once a year."

"So, is this your first walk here this year?" Adrian asked.

"No, I came here with my wife just before the tourist season kicked in. It rained that day and we wore raingear all day. It was pleasant enough, however. Today is more special than you might know. This weather is about as pretty as it gets. You are very fortunate."

After a few more minutes of walking Joel stopped for a short break and asked Adrian for his first question.

Adrian responded, "If I may, let me explain why I have these questions for you so you may understand the context in which I ask them."

"That would be helpful. Additionally, personally I would like to understand how Michael got into this venture. While in college we were very ambitious and very secular-minded (*non-spiritual*). I never knew a side to Michael that was so religious-oriented."

"Joel, Michael has changed since his wife's death. The change may have begun when she became critically ill. He went from denial to accepting her fate in the months leading up to her death. Following that he buried himself in his work for over a year. This was followed by the loss of the remainder of his immediate family. He changed. He wanted to embrace the faith that Mary had, and in order to do that he needed to intellectually rationalize his way into that type of deep faith. He has a very demanding set of standards to meet in order to commit himself to a belief, and he is in the process of doing that. He is literally changing before my very eyes. And, he has put $10 million into an effort to help him in his faith journey; he wants to use his experience and resources to help others to find their faith."

"That explains a lot. Thank you. What can I possibly do to help?"

"Here is the recorder I asked you about. Simply put it in your shirt pocket and it will record for the next three hours. Don't let it keep you from saying anything you want to say. The recording will go directly to Michael along with a transcribed copy."

Adrian continued, "Joel, we are not doing any work in comparative religion in our quest. We do, however, have a need to better understand the fundamentals of the Jewish religion since Christianity was spawned from it 2,000 years ago. So to help understand Judaism we have prepared five questions for you. The first question simply asks you to explain Judaism in your own terms?"

"Adrian, I will do my best to answer each question. No doubt there are others that know far more on this subject matter than I do. So, I am honored to be asked."

Joel began, "Judaism is not simply a race of people nor is it simply a religion. Religion is more of a component of Judaism as opposed to Judaism being a component of the world's many religious groups. Likewise, Judaism is not restricted to the race of Hebrew people. It is more like many Hebrew people are part of the faith group that adheres to the tenets of the Jewish faith."

After a pause Joel asked, "Before I go on, does that make sense?"

"Joel, I got it."

"Okay, so what is really included under the term Judaism? Or said another way, what does it mean to be a Jew? Keep in mind there are more Jews in Israel who are secular-minded than there are Jews who practice the faith of Judaism. Likely, this is true in the U.S. and any other country where large numbers of people of Jewish decent currently reside. Again speaking for myself, I am a Jew raised in a family with an extensive historic Jewish family tree. I practice some of the Jewish traditions. I love the Jewish culture. I have an ethnic heritage as a Jew. I have a dual loyalty to Germany where I live and to the homeland of the Jewish people, Israel. Yet, I am a secular person in many respects. I do not attend a synagogue. I do not speak Yiddish. My children don't even know any Yiddish words."

They walked a few minutes without saying anything. The lake was calm and Adrian was looking forward to getting to the far side to see the Zugspitze reflected in the water.

Adrian, said, "Okay that was the easy question. The next one is tougher."

"I'm ready! I get the idea though you don't want a simple 'yes' or 'no' answer." Joel chuckled.

"These are pretty open-ended questions, so I think a longer answer will be appropriate. Good try though."

Adrian continued, "How do Jewish people state their faith, and how would you list these fundamental beliefs if they are not outlined in a creed?"

"Talking about an open ended question!" Joel quipped. "Adrian and Michael, if you are listening, there is no official Jewish Creed like there is for Christianity. There is, however, what are called the thirteen principles of faith. I had to memorize these as a child, so I think I can recite each one to you. Now there may well be slightly different versions of the thirteen, but these are the ones I learned growing up. I'll try and elaborate on each briefly."

"The *first* is a fundamental belief that God does exist. To the Jew this is self-evident. We say just look around. Look to the sky. To us, it is what you Americans call 'a no brainer'."

"The *second* belief is that God is one and unique. For thousands of years most people thought that if there was such a thing as a god there had to be more than one. Many civilizations held beliefs in many different gods. Not the Jews. Our heritage was built on one and only one god. Additionally, Jews believe that God is unique. There is only one God and no one is like our one God."

"The *third* belief is that God does not dwell in a body. Jews do not represent God physically as you and I see each other as physical beings. There are scriptural references to God walking or placing a hand, but these are considered to be figurative writings only."

"The *fourth* belief is that God is eternal. There is no beginning nor is there an end to God. Essentially, time does not apply to God's existence. Time does apply to God's creations however."

"The *fifth* belief is that prayer is to be directed only to God. Simply and clearly prayer is not to be made to anyone or anything except to God. Period!"

"The *sixth* relates to the prophetic messages in the Old Testament. It basically states that the recorded statements from the prophets are true."

"The *seventh* belief is like the sixth, but this one is specific in saying that Moses was a prophet, and he, in fact, was the greatest of the prophets."

"The *eighth* belief holds that God delivered to Moses the first five books of the Bible, called the Torah."

"The *ninth* belief is that there will be no other Torah."

"The *tenth* belief is a frightful one for everyone. It says that God knows the thoughts and deeds of all people."

"The *eleventh* is that God will punish the wicked and reward the good. The book of Genesis repeatedly provides examples of this."

"The *twelfth* says the Messiah will come. This is in reference to the savoir who reconciles the good and the evil that resides in the world."

"And finally the *thirteenth* says the dead will be resurrected. This relates to the final judgment of each person."

"Adrian, you can see just how well I listened in class as a youngster. I haven't had to recite those beliefs for a very long time. They are pretty basic and there is a lot of history that goes with them, but I think I got the essentials across in my answer. You could ask any rabbi to check them over if you care to double-check my answers."

As they rounded the end of the lake Adrian could see several small rocky islands nearby. Adrian felt they added character to the lake. Lots of trees were grown in the area and someone had done a recent thinning of smaller trees. Likely, some firewood was removed to space the bigger trees and to remove less vigorous trees. They stopped at a bench and paused to have a snack before proceeding.

"Do you have areas like this back home where you can hike in the woods?" Joel asked.

"We certainly do. In fact two years ago a friend and I hiked just over 90 miles in 10 days on what is known as the Wonderland Trail. It is a trail that circles Mt. Rainier, and like the Zugspitze, Mt. Rainier has glaciers on all sides."

"How tall is this Mt. Rainier?" Joel inquired.

"Well, if I remember correctly it is just over 14,000 feet above sea level."

"Wow, that's more like Europe's Mt. Blanc."

"Yes, I believe you are right."

"Adrian, we best continue on. I do not want you to miss lunch at the hotel. If you like fish you must try the locally caught lake trout from this very lake. It is quite unique and it has an excellent flavor. Many folks come here to enjoy this local fish. Also, I know you have more questions. I hope we can get them all answered so we can quietly enjoy a bottle of German beer with lunch."

"Sounds good! Carrying on, the third question basically asks you to describe God as those of the Jewish faith see him."

"Wow, the questions just get better and better. I can see Michael behind these. He is the most brilliant man I met in college. He impressed me with his fundamental thinking ability, because he could see a path through to a solution in a complex environment far better than anyone I have ever met. I have no doubt his company was a tremendous success."

"You got that right!"

"Sorry for the diversion, Adrian. You want to know how Jews see God. Well, much of our belief relates to God's basic nature so my answer may be slightly repetitive."

"That's okay. It will help us take what you say and let the answers you provide sink in. So, answer any way you want."

"Well, our view of God always starts with the fact that God exists. We do not believe God is divisible. He is one. He is complete.

Christianity differs in its belief in a holy trinity. Oh sorry, I did not mean to start a comparative discussion. We also see God as being omnipresent. That is, God is everywhere. God can do anything and God knows all."

"Another point you may find interesting is that the Jewish belief of God is that God keeps justice and mercy in perfect balance. There is no need for reconciliation through a third party. This too is an important difference with other religions, including Christianity."

"Adrian, based on what I know of your travels and your work preceding your visit here, this next point may be of some interest. In Jewish belief God is an active partner in the creation of each person. Besides the mother and father who form the person physically, the Jewish belief is that God provides each person their soul, personality and intelligence."

"Joel, I understand the logic behind God supplying each person with a soul and I have become enamored by the fact that in that belief lies the very essence of our special creation by God. To me it is one of the fundamental reconciling concepts that God has provided each of us with something special in the form of a soul. Perhaps this is what we should recognize when we say that we are formed in God's image."

"Interesting, Adrian! I like what you said. I believe the Jewish belief structure supports your position in the fact that humankind is made in God's image - by virtue of a soul. The Jewish faith, however, does not recognize any evolution concept. Even our calendar starts with creation occurring nearly 6,000 years ago, not millions or billions of years ago."

"Joel, I appreciate you explaining your belief that God gives us our intelligence and our personality. I had never heard that before today."

"Adrian, you can make from it what you wish. On that note, I think I have answered your third question as well as I am able."

At this point the two were on the side of the lake where they could clearly see the Zugspitze. It was majestic. The sun shown in its reflection off the massive glaciers near the summit with the lake reflecting a perfect image of the mountain. The view was stunning. And, they both took in the beauty in their own quiet way.

As they left the viewpoint Adrian asked the fourth question. "Joel how would you describe the Jewish belief in a messiah?"

"You do realize I am not a rabbi, I trust."

"Michael wants your answer, not that of a rabbi. He knows you and has great faith in you."

"Thank you. The Jewish word 'mashiach' comes to mind. Some people outside the faith think it is the Jewish equivalent of the Christian savior. Oh no, there I go again making a comparative remark. Anyway, the Jewish messiah is not a savior. He is not of God. He is a human being who will come on the scene as a great military leader from the linage of David. He will be strong in Jewish tradition and be charismatic in many ways. He will be an anointed king in the end times."

Joel continued, "Interestingly the concept of a messiah is not literally mentioned anywhere in the Torah. All references come later through the prophets."

"Joel, is there a mention of when the messiah comes in Jewish tradition?"

"It is regarded as an end-time event. Most Jewish scholars agree that the date is one only known to God, and God will make it happen when the time is right. Some scholars, however, contend the year 6,000 on the Jewish calendar will be the time the messiah comes and he will lead the Hebrew people into the so-called millennium. If those scholars are correct, then we are 223 years away from that happening as we are in year 5,777 currently on the Jewish calendar."

"Part of that belief is that the messiah will follow a time of war and suffering. He will bring a peaceful and prosperous co-existence to Israel. Some believe that the world will become enamored with the Jewish faith and many will be converted."

"Joel, I take it that the Jewish faith does not recognize Jesus as the messiah in any way, shape, or form."

"Adrian, that is, basically true of the mainline Jewish tradition. Jesus did not meet the description of the messiah. However, he was a great rabbi and a great prophet. Now let me also say that outside the mainline members of the Jewish faith there is a growing number of Messianic Jews who *do* believe Jesus was and is the savior we call the messiah. However, their numbers remain low comparatively."

"Okay, we are down to the final question. Are you ready?"

"Fire away! Let's do this thing! Isn't that the right slang response in America?"

Adrian laughed, "Okay, I get the point. I appreciate your sense of humor. The fifth question is what does the Jewish faith consider to be the nature of human beings? In other words, how do you see the words play when it is said that Adam and Eve were made in God's image. Is our nature as humans bent toward being fundamentally good or bad?"

"Again this is a 'wow' question. Besides not being a rabbi, I am neither a philosopher nor a psychologist

"That's okay, I'm not either," Adrian replied.

"Okay, I'll make a couple of points on this one. First, the 'image' issue is one we touched on earlier. I like your point of concentrating on the fact that God gave us our soul and leaving the issue of the intellect and personality alone. The soul is what is given and is what is saved. That then is enough to make us made in God's image. The part about whether we are wired to be good or bad is a fascinating one that we really haven't touched on yet. It is important to have this discussion because there are fundamental beliefs imbedded here that you need to know."

"Many Jewish rabbis adhere to the belief that God has given each person two inclinations. One is called 'yetzer tov' and it masters the will to do what is good. The other is called 'yetzer ra' and it constantly draws us to do what is selfish."

"The inclination to do good is what many of us call our conscience. This is our moral compass trying to convince us to constantly do what is right. Jewish tradition says a person is endowed with this inclination on their 13th birthday. This coincides with when a person is responsible for abiding by the Commandments."

"The inclination to do what is selfish means putting ourselves ahead of others, including God. It is what drives us to meet all our physical needs. It leads us to do those things without regard for any moral consequence. It is not considered evil necessarily because it does drive us to meet certain vital needs in our lives like working to provide shelter, food and medicine. But carried to excess it can cause many wrongful acts to be committed."

"Essentially, this concept of two inclinations playing out in a person's life is essentially what drives us to understand the free will each of us has in our lives. How we address our individual circumstance and how we lean toward one inclination or the other is what makes our individual lives so interesting."

Joel added, "I believe God makes no mistakes. He does not make bad people."

Adrian responded, "I wholeheartedly agree. He gives us the choice and it is up to us to make the right choice."

"Agreed. Adrian, I can see the hotel, and I am pretty well tapped out of information. Are you ready for a beer or a glass of wine?" Joel handed the recorder to Adrian.

"Thank you so very much. I've learned a lot today that is spot on relevant to our project. Your answers are appreciated more than you will ever know. I would like a beer first and then wine with the meal. I've loved the hike and we could not have had a better day."

Following dinner they caught trains retracing the morning route. In Munich they bid farewell and Adrian returned to the hotel for a good night's rest.

16

Mercer Island, Washington

Nancy arrived in the conference room first. She had her coffee mug full of fresh brew and was ready for another challenge at work. Time was flying in her mind and she was enjoying being part of a Christian team dedicated to doing all the things they were doing. She was fresh from a weekend spent with her grandkids and felt that life couldn't get much better.

Rachel showed up next. "What's up? I don't see you dressed like a Parisian. Didn't you say you were headed out shopping for trip clothing?"

Rachel responded, "Nancy, I figured I wouldn't know what to look for, so I stayed home and packed what I have and it will have to do."

"What time is your flight today?"

"It leaves from SeaTac *(Seattle-Tacoma International Airport)* at six o'clock."

Michael walked in and overheard the last part of their conversation. "So, when does your flight arrive in Paris?"

"Well, the plane lands in London at Heathrow Airport, and I change to an Air France flight that gets into Paris at four in the afternoon. I should be at the hotel about dinner time."

"Have you got room in your bag for an old lady? I would love to go!" Nancy smiled.

"I am afraid there is absolutely no room in my bag."

Michael piped up and said "Okay let's cover what we need to cover and get Rachel on the road."

"Thanks boss, but I planned to stay till early afternoon. I'm packed and everything is in the car. I'm ready to go."

"Okay, Rachel, would you lead us in prayer?"

The group rotated giving a prayer at their meetings, from one week to the next. Everyone did something different and it was all good.

Rachel asked if she could cover a point as it related to timelines.

"I have been reading my Bible and I recently read a passage that struck me as something important, yet something I had never heard mentioned in church or Sunday school. I believe it is very relevant to what we are doing in trying to understand God's plan. The passage is from Second Peter: Chapter 3 starting with verse 8. First, let me put the Chapter and verses in context with what is said before and after these special verses."

"Chapter 3 is about the 'day of the Lord' in the end times. Peter warns us that there will be scoffers who believe there is no coming of the Lord and that all is as it has been. Therefore, hearts will be turned to evil ways. Then Peter warns us not to forget one thing. He says *With the Lord a day is like a thousand years, and a thousand years are like a day.*"

"Peter goes on to reassure us that the Lord is not slow to keep his promise. He simply wants no one to perish. He wants everyone to repent. Then he tells us that since everything will be destroyed in the end we should turn to holy and godly lives."

"I found this verse to be inspiring. I was having difficulty in grasping the concept of a destructive end times like what we are going to study when we get to the book of Revelation. But here Peter puts it in context of a patient God waiting for souls to turn to righteousness and godliness."

"Furthermore, my mind has expanded to be better able me to look at thousands of years of history and then put it in God's concept of mere days. In a way, it has helped me think that Jesus was here two days ago rather than 2,000 years ago."

After a pause Rachel continued, "I don't know if this helps either of you as much as it does me, but I thought it might."

Nancy asked for the scriptures again and said she needed to read them and digest them for a while. Still, she agreed this was a different way of looking at time.

Michael started to say something but paused. After a moment he commented, "Rachel you did strike upon something that is important. The scripture you mention is nearly at the end of the Bible. Perhaps Peter was inspired by the Holy Spirit to reassure us that God is in control and all things important will occur in His time. The passage is a wonderful suggestion for us to have patience. I too hope it is as applicable today as it was to the early Christians who expected the messiah to return and lead Israel, if not the world, into peace and prosperity. That did not happen and Peter's words are a testament to God's desire to have patience while believing in a life of daily holiness."

Michael continued, "I will say that this passage from Peter sparked a particular interest in my mind. If taken as it is written and not getting too wrapped up in the exact number of years we've seen in

Nancy's genealogy report, I wonder if God planned the time from Adam to Abraham to be 'two days' or in *our* perception of time 2,000 years. Carrying on, God may have seen the time from Abraham to Jesus as two days and the time from Jesus to today as two days. If so, that would leave a single day of 1,000 years left in God's week, which coincidentally may be what the Book of Revelation written by John refers to as the millennium. This might be more than a coincidence!"

"That is an amazing thought," Rachel said as she sat with a look of wonderment.

Michael went on, "Anyway, I think we should keep Peter's words in front of us as we complete our work on understanding God's plan. Rachel, please see that you relay this discussion to Adrian when you see him. Thank you so very much for pointing out this scripture. I feel like God is working through each of us prodding us forward. I hope I am right!"

"Rachel, I'm amazed at how much we have learned from scripture. Each of us has experienced an amazing amount of growth in such a short period of time. We are all blessed beyond words from this journey we are taking together."

Nancy added, "Michael, I feel the same. I'm captivated by what we are doing. And Michael, thank you again for inviting us along on this journey. We will never be able to repay you for this opportunity."

Michael commented, "Both of you, along with Adrian, are my family now. You are making me a better person. I feel closer to each of you than you can imagine. I am beginning to get a feel of what I saw in Mary, and it leads me to believe that what she had as a Christian is there for the taking. I am not quite there yet, but I feel I am getting closer. Much of that progress is due to the three of you."

Michael continued, "I will tell you that Adrian is coming up with some great stuff. He continues to write reports on the progress he is making. So far, he has made all the connections we arranged for him and the material he is gathering is on target. I expect that we should wrap up our work on questions one and two shortly after he and Rachel get back."

"Adrian's contact in Germany is an old Harvard classmate of mine. Joel and I were close friends in graduate school and although we've periodically written one another we really haven't spoken since school. Fortunately, he turned out to be as sharp as I remembered. Joel provided some real life insight as to how Judaism sees God, and Adrian said it has truly expanded his mind. Likewise, Rachel, you expanded ours today with insight from Peter."

After a break the three found themselves ready to carry on with the meeting.

Michael said "Do either of you have anything else that needs to be discussed today? We won't meet for two weeks as Rachel and Adrian get back after our scheduled time next week."

Neither Rachel nor Nancy had anything left to cover so Michael led into a discussion he wanted to have regarding some scriptural readings he just completed.

"I believe I mentioned a short while back that I had read a book of the Bible written by King Solomon titled Song of Songs. It is the book written in prose and highlights the foolishness in much of what we do. Do you happen to recall that discussion?" Nancy and Rachel both responded that they remembered it well.

Michael continued, "Solomon had his hand in two other books of the Bible. One is the book of Proverbs that encourages prudence and discretion while living a godly life. Fearing God's revenge for failure to follow the commandments should motivate a person to live in the law. Solomon basically says that a commitment to righteousness when combined with wisdom leads one to a contented and blessed life."

"The other book I want to mention has had a profound impact on me as I grapple with gaining a clearer understanding of God's purpose for humankind. The book is titled Ecclesiastes. In this book, much like in the book *Song of Songs*, Solomon looks back upon his life and he marvels at the foolishness in much of what he pursued throughout his life. He blatantly chastises himself for all the frivolous endeavors he sought to please his personal wants."

"In Chapter 2 he recounts many of these endeavors that brought him wealth, possessions, property, and women. Then he states that although he had met every need, everything was meaningless. It was a 'chasing of the wind' in his mind. He felt that nothing was gained by doing all these things."

"Basically, Solomon tells us that he hated his life because what he had done was meaningless in the eyes of God. All the pain and grief that went into meeting all his needs was wasted in frivolous ways. He says *'better a poor but wise youth than an old but foolish king who no longer knows how to take warning.'* He describes how God has created everything and man cannot take any of that with him when he dies. Since we came from dust and we are to return to dust we should make it our priority to focus on our relationship with God. God loved us as He created us and we need to simply love Him and love the creation He made for us."

Michael was getting emotional at this point, "Unfortunately, I see a great deal of Solomon in myself. I don't believe I have been entirely self-centered, but I certainly haven't done much to be friends with God and to strengthen that relationship. Basically, I feel that I did a poor job of prioritizing in my life rather than enjoying and adjusting to my relationship with my Creator. I feel I have been selfish and haven't recognized God for who He is."

Rachel responded, "Michael, what you just said came from your heart and I can see why you feel the way you do. But keep in mind when the rest of us hear what Solomon says in those scriptural readings, we all feel somewhat convicted by our own sins. Yet, it is not too late for us to strive to learn from Solomon and the other biblical writers. We have an opportunity to improve and become more like Jesus. Said another way, we all are blessed with time to become more like Mary."

Nancy seconded what Rachel had just said.

"Thank you, Rachel. I still feel somewhat ashamed. However, what you say is what I need to focus on going forward. Thank you."

The meeting ended with lots of 'well wishing' to Rachel for her trip to Paris and London. She smiled as she left the conference room stopping to pick up a few things in the office before heading to the airport.

17

Paris, France

Rachel's flight to Paris arrived late in the afternoon. She was tired from the long flights and yet, was excited to see Paris for the first time. She did not appreciate the fact that the airport was well out of town and a 30-minute taxi ride was needed to get to the heart of the city. And, although Rachel had taken two years of French in high school she was reticent to use what little French she remembered.

As is the case in most European capitals Rachel was relieved to discover that the taxi driver spoke broken but quite understandable English. Having reserved rooms for Adrian and herself at a small hotel near the Eiffel tower, she was prepared with a 3x5 index card with the hotel name and street address in case.

Entering the city center Rachel smiled while gazing out the taxi window. She was in Paris! She had wanted to see Paris ever since taking those language classes in school, but never saw herself actually doing it. She sat in the backseat of the taxi mesmerized by the architectural beauty of the city.

Soon, there it was, the Eiffel tower. She could not see the base of the massive steel structure but there was no doubt it was *'the tower.'* It stood alone as Paris' most iconic structure in a city with many competing sights.

The driver asked to see the card with the address again as the hotel was not one with which he was familiar. The address was on a small street in an area where some streets are narrow or blocked on certain market days. Still the driver found the hotel, and upon arriving helped Rachel with her bag.

After paying the driver with Euros she obtained at one of the many ATMs at the airport she walked into the quaint and very French hotel. One receptionist sat behind a single desk near the doorway and after checking in Rachel was told her room was on the third floor. She could use either the single elevator or the stairway.

She asked if Adrian had checked in yet and the clerk said that he had checked in a couple of hours earlier. Furthermore, the clerk said Adrian had gone out for a walk leaving a message for Rachel. The message welcomed Rachel to Paris and gave his room number which happened to be on the same floor as hers. The note said he would stop by her room at 7:30 p.m. to see if she was up to going out to dinner.

With her bag in hand she entered the smallest elevator she had ever encountered and pressed the button for the third floor. Her room was a third of the size she expected, but at least it had its own bathroom. Otherwise, the space was cramped. Since this was home for three nights she hung up a few clothes, selected what to wear for dinner, took a shower and laid on the bed to read a magazine she had brought from home.

At 7:30 p.m., Rachel awoke to knocking at her door. She looked at the clock and discovered she had been asleep for over an hour. Opening the door she saw Adrian was excited to see her and eager to go to dinner. On the other hand, Adrian saw a haggard-looking Rachel who looked like she had just returned from the dead. Rachel was duly embarrassed and begged for 30 more minutes to get herself pulled together. Adrian said he would be back then.

At 8:00 p.m. Adrian knocked on Rachel's door and a totally different looking Rachel appeared. She apologized for the wait and said she was excited to see Adrian and have a chance to hear about the adventures he had already experienced.

Adrian was stunned by her transformation. Although dressed casual, she had the look of someone who had lived in Paris. A very smart look indeed, he thought.

They left the hotel and walked less than half a block to a restaurant that has seating both outside as well as inside. The evening was very pleasant, so they chose an outdoor table near a street called the Rue Cler. This was a popular market and shop area with a few hotels but mainly shops and small markets selling fresh produce, meats, chocolates, wines, and such sundries.

The restaurant is one recommended in a popular travel book written by a well-known European travel expert who lives just a short way north of Seattle. Prices were reasonable for good meals and the customers are both local and tourist.

Adrian ordered a carafe of wine as they looked over the menu. It was interesting to see what others seated around them had ordered and then to find it on the menu. They placed their respective orders, sipped wine, and looked at each other. Rachel couldn't help but think what a lousy first impression she had made when Adrian initially came to get her. She had looked in the mirror immediately after he left to return later, and she had to admit she looked hideous.

Adrian had already moved on, thinking just how good Rachel looked at the small table they were sharing. He also thought how great it is to be with someone he knew after constantly having been with people he was meeting for the first time. Adrian felt really glad to be with Rachel.

Rachel broke the silence, "I am really sorry about being asleep when you came to get me. I looked awful, I know."

"Forget it. Although that image of you will haunt me forever." He laughed. "I have had my share of jet lag on this trip, and so I avoid mirrors after a long flight. You just need a good night's sleep after this and you'll be fine. Trust me, I know." Adrian continued, "Tell me about your trip."

Rachel gave a thumbnail version of her flights and asked about Adrian's travels. He responded, "We'll have time for that tomorrow. It has been a long and grueling trip, but a fantastic trip in many ways. We need to talk through what I've seen and learned, but that can wait until tomorrow. Tonight we should talk through our schedule and just enjoy dinner."

"Sounds good to me."

Adrian complimented Rachel on the work she had done for him in setting up all the travel arrangements for his trip. He said things had gone like clockwork and he was especially glad to have some time off tomorrow with her in Paris. He said the schedule for the two of them tomorrow was to sight-see and update each other.

He didn't really want to go to a museum anyway. "The Louvre can wait a day for us to venture in," he said. They agreed on a plan to see the Louvre on the second full day of their stay in Paris.

On the day following, the Louvre visit they were booked to take the train to Sarlat where they had reservations for two nights at a local hotel. They were to pick up a rental car for the day in Sarlat and drive to see the caves at Lascaux. The day after that they planned to return to Paris by train for a one night stay at the airport. The airport made sense since the flight the following day was an early one.

Once their meals arrived Adrian asked Rachel what she wanted to see in the city. Her response was, "Everything!"

After thinking about the question she said, "I really want to go to the Eiffel tower and get some photos there. We could go up to one of the higher platforms and take pictures. I also want to see the Arc de Triumph. A cruise on the Seine would be nice as well as a visit to Notre Dame. You may not like this, but I love the impressionist paintings from France, especially Claude Monet. So, going to the Museum d'Orsay is on my list. Of course, walking down the Champs Elysees is on my list. I don't need to shop or anything, but I do want to be there and see it all."

Adrian was defeated, "Okay, sounds like we'll have to break that list down into two days. My only request is to do the Museum you mentioned the same day that we return from Sarlat. I really don't want to do that one tomorrow."

"That's okay, we can do that." replied Rachel.

"So, how should we proceed tomorrow?" Adrian responded after having succeeded in getting the only concession he needed.

"How about if we get some breakfast food from a local store in the morning and walk over to the Eiffel tower and have a picnic there. Then we can get in the early lines to take the elevator up the tower to the platform just below the top. From there, let's take the underground Metro to the Arc de Triomphe and then walk down the Champs Elysees. In the afternoon we can go to Notre Dame and maybe Sainte-Chapelle."

Adrian was impressed, "Sounds good to me. You've done your homework, I see. We can update each other in the process I presume?"

"I think so," Rachel replied thinking the updating could be done anytime. She thought, hey, we are in Paris, so let's see Paris. She had definitely done more studying on Paris than Adrian had even thought about.

They returned to the hotel, bid each other good night, and headed to their respective rooms to get as much sleep as they could. Rachel was feeling the effects of being nine time zones away from home, and although Adrian had been on European time for a while now he too was still feeling travel weary.

The next morning Adrian and Rachel left the hotel at 9:00 a.m. and stopped at a small local grocery store. Each found fruit, a bread roll and juice for a picnic breakfast. They headed toward Parc Champs de Mars. It is the large rectangular park stretching between the military school building called Ecole Militaire and the Eiffel tower.

As soon as they entered the park grounds they saw a poorly dressed man hustle towards them picking something up from the ground. Looking at what he had found he smiled and walked directly to Adrian saying in broken English "Look at this gold ring I just found. It is worth a lot of money. Would you please buy this, so I can have money to buy food."

Adrian glanced at it and asked how much for the ring. "Whatever you can spare," replied the man. Adrian asked to see the ring and after holding it briefly he handed it back to the man and said "thank you, but no thanks." The man persisted and asked for only five Euros, but again Adrian passed and he hurried Rachel along.

"What was that all about? Looked like a pretty good deal for five euro."

"Rachel, it's a scam to get money. The guy is pawning off gold colored aluminum rings like you might find on a cheap curtain holder or something. The ring is weightless and worthless."

"I felt sorry for the guy, but I guess we are in the city and we look like gullible tourists with money."

"Yeah, so much for being preyed upon!" Adrian quipped.

"Oh, that is a sick joke," Rachel replied.

They found a quiet place on the park grounds, sat on a plastic ground cover Adrian had brought, and enjoyed their breakfast. Rachel updated Adrian on the genealogy work Nancy had done and the discussions at the most recent staff meeting. Both enjoyed the view, took some photos and watched as the tourists begin to show up. Rachel had read up on the tower and passed on some facts. She told Adrian that the tower was just over 1,000 feet in height and when it was completed it was the tallest man-made structure in the world - and it retained that status for 41 years till the Chrysler building in New York City became the tallest. Furthermore, the French built the tower as the centerpiece for the 1889 World's Fair.

Adrian said, "I am impressed, but I don't think Michael is keeping you busy enough while I am away in places like the Ethiopian desert."

"No, we women are good 'multi-taskers' while you guys don't appreciate the gift we have and you simply won't admit you can't do as many things as we can."

"Wow, I struck a sore point there, didn't I?"

"All in good fun."

They got in line for tickets to take the elevator up. After seeing the prices, Rachel was thinking they should just go to the second platform up. Adrian, said no, we are going to the top. So up they went. It was a beautiful fall day with a light wind from the northeast. They got great photos of the city below. Adrian got someone to take a photo of the two of them with the wind blowing Rachel's hair and the Arc de Triomphe in the background. It was one they would cherish for a long time.

From the Eiffel tower they headed back toward their hotel where they walked past an entrance to the underground Metro stop. They each bought a strip of ten one-way tickets, checked a route map, entered the escalators heading down, followed signs to the appropriate platform and only waited three minutes for the train heading in the right direction. After two train changes they came up from the underground on a long escalator ride and, lo and behold, they looked around to see the Arc de Triomphe across the roadway that encircles it. What a shock!

Now they were at the west-end of the Champs-Elysess. Crossing the street they stood below the two hundred year old massive archway that had been built to commemorate Napoleon's many victories. They took the elevator up to the top and marveled at the wide road that circles the Arc.

Of particular note and fascination was watching how cars maneuver through the many lanes to and from the dozen roads that radiate from the circle. One would think there would be a car crash every few minutes, but there does seem to be some order to the constant counter-clockwise progression of vehicles. Adrian was fixated on the spectacle when Rachel prodded him onto the elevator so they could keep moving.

They re-crossed the circle street underground as they had done coming over. It would have been total chaos above if there were cross-walks up there. Walking down the Champs-Elysess on the north side took them along a broad walkway, crowded like you would not believe with stores, restaurants, car dealers, a hotel or two, night clubs, clothing shops, and so forth. After getting a good hike in, Rachel and Adrian came to the Place de la Concorde. This is where many years ago they held public executions using the guillotine. Today two lovely fountains and an Egyptian obelisk stand in this very central spot in Paris.

After a few more photos they crossed over to the Jardin Des Tuileries. Here they found one of the few shady spots available and took a long water break. This too gave Adrian time to talk through the stops he made in Ethiopia, Athens, and Croatia. He explained that in his mind, if we talk about time as we know it, there is no question that the human species emerged more than 100,000 years ago.

He went on to explain to Rachel that evolution does not win out over creation, however, and explained to Rachel why that is. He detailed why their second question should start with the question of what is the 'origin' of the human species.

"Michael told Nancy and me that you had concluded that our second question should be re-stated. He said the question is not the right one to ask, and that he was excited you had come to that conclusion."

"Rachel, the whole trip was worth it for this very point. I am a stronger believer in God today because I can see that what God did for us was to give us a soul, a spirit that cannot be seen. That is what makes us different from members of our species who preceded Adam and Eve. That is what makes us created in God's image."

"Keep in mind that image is not so much about our physical nature as we know it. We do not know precisely what God looks like. In fact, He may exist in a spiritual body only. There is biblical reference to His hand, eyes, and back, making it likely He does, in fact, have a visible form. Likely, we will one day be with God in a spiritual body form like His with our own soul continuing to guide us to do what is right."

"Rachel, God also clearly gave Adam and Eve the means to know right from wrong when they ate from the tree of knowledge. In turn, our predecessors could do what is wrong or what is right. In other words, we were left with free will. Again, that may have made us different from those in our species that preceded Adam. So, yes, we have changed physically over many years, but we were created with a spirit and a conscience. Hence, we can say we were formed physically and born spiritually, perhaps simultaneously or at a separate time. That doesn't really matter."

Rachel asked, "What about Eve being created from Adam's rib?"

"Good question. Just as Moses wrote that the world was created in six days, he wrote of Eve's existence to have been directly from

Adam. Think about the understanding level of people living thousands of years ago. They could not comprehend what we can today. They did not need to be baffled with facts they could not understand. They only needed to understand that God made them special and they would be favored by God."

Rachel responded saying, "Okay, I can buy your rationale Adrian. In fact, your explanation is one I have never heard before. I have to believe Michael is on board with it, and I think most people are longing to hear your explanation to the long running argument about evolution versus creation. Cool!"

"Rachel, before we get to London I want you to read parts of the book Michael sent me. Here is my copy with the sections marked that I think you should read. For now, let's go into the Louvre since we are right here and get tickets for tomorrow. Also, there is a cafeteria at the Louvre that is supposed to be good. We can have lunch before heading to the Notre Dame Cathedral."

"I think that will be just fine," Rachel agreed.

After buying tickets they went to the cafeteria and sat down for lunch. Adrian volunteered to say a short prayer to say just how blessed he was to have Rachel alongside for the rest of the trip. At lunch Rachel asked why Michael wanted Adrian to look at artwork in Vienna, and now in France? She had not totally connected the dots on this point and thought Adrian's explanation would help her with their visit to the Louvre, the Lascaux, and the London Museum of Natural History.

He explained, "One of the thoughts Michael and I had regarding this whole evolutionary thing, was whether humans showed signs of artistic intellect prior to the genealogical age of Adam which is approximately 6,000 years ago. Interestingly, Judaism has a fundamental belief that Adam and Eve were endowed with intellect and personality along with two inclinations. One to do good and one to do what is wrong. We want to test the intellect component of that belief and form our own opinion."

"What have you found so far?"

"Interestingly, my visit to Vienna made it clear that the human species clearly was developing artistic intellect more than 6,000 years ago. One sculpture I saw is a very good artistic representation of a woman, and it is over 20,000 years old. Likewise, two days from now we are going to travel south to a town called Sarlat. There we will see a reproduction of art that is over 15,000 years old. From these visits I suspect we will conclude that there exists artistic evidence that proves that the human species was growing intellectually prior to Adam and Eve."

"Sounds good to me. I'm excited that your trip has been so productive thus far."

"In London we only have one appointment with a gentleman who will be helpful in testing our progress. He is a leading expert in human origins and we will learn a lot in a short time that day as to whether what we've just shared stands up to the kind of rigors he works with in the scientific community."

"So, other than that one appointment, we will be free?"

"I trust you have a list of what to see?"

"I have more than a list. I have two tickets to one of London's best plays courtesy of Michael."

"What a great boss! Rachel, when I went over this trip itinerary with Michael, he told me to add in extra days here and in London. Now I understand why."

Rachel, laughed and said, "Michael told me you were crazy. He said you would be really tired coming into the final two stops. He wanted you to slow down."

"Well, I am glad he added the days and that he sent you over too."

Rachel smiled, "I never would have thought about being here. Of course, I've seen lots of brochures and lots of travel reservations, but for me this is a dream come true. I still wake up in the morning and marvel at having a job like this."

"Me too!"

They left the Louvre and headed toward Notre Dame. When they arrived at Pont Neuf they crossed the bridge and now stood on Ile de la Cite, the founding spot of Paris. They wound their way to the Sainte-Chapelle and went in to visit.

What a gorgeous chapel! They read a brochure stating that the chapel had been built in the 13th century or better known as the Royal Medieval period. The chapel was magnificent!

Next they went to Notre Dame. This is such a big cathedral in comparison with Saint-Chapelle. It was built in 1345 with French Gothic architecture. The main spire can be seen from many locations in the city due to a spire that reaches 300 feet. The rose window is spectacular, as well.

The two spent an hour inside and out before heading back to the hotel. They rested a while after taking showers. As a surprise to Rachel, Adrian had managed to get a reservation at a small French restaurant not far from the hotel. The hotel clerk highly recommended it and even agreed to make the reservation. The restaurant only holds eight to ten tables depending on party sizes. Having had an earlier cancellation Adrian got a reservation that normally takes two weeks advance notice to get. He thought Rachel would enjoy such an evening.

Rachel enjoyed the surprise dinner and now felt well entrenched in good Parisian culinary delights. They did not speak of work matters, but rather topics of personal interest. Rachel inquired about how Adrian was holding up with the grieving she knew he still was processing, and Adrian inquired about what Rachel was up to since her break-up with her boyfriend. It was a healthy time for a good heart-to-heart for both of them. The wine was really good as was the entire meal.

The next morning showed signs of being a good day. Although it was cooler than the preceding day a light jacket was all that was needed in the morning. They caught the Metro to the Louvre where they had a light breakfast before heading in to the galleries.

The Louvre is located on the right bank of the Seine River and located in a huge building that dates back to the 12th century. It was originally built as a fortress, and when Louis the XIV moved to Versailles in 1692, he left behind much of the royal art collection to be displayed.

Since Adrian knew his day was going to include another museum he was on the anxious side to move along and not linger too long. Rachel served as a brake on his desire to speed along. She was fascinated by all the exhibits. They took time to go through the excellent gallery on Egyptian antiquities. Adrian thought this display had to be one of the best outside of Cairo. Still, after going through the Egyptian exhibit there really was not much there older than 6,000 years. At least nothing like what he had seen in Vienna.

Finally they made their way to the paintings. Now the pace slowed and Adrian kept finding himself having to go backwards to find Rachel and be certain they didn't get separated. Once Adrian found the Mona Lisa by Leonardo da Vinci even he slowed down. The painting is so real. It seems to depict the very nature of the person posing for the portrait, not just the image.

As they moved along, Adrian found one sculpture that dated back to 2,500 BC, but failed to find any art from an earlier period. Based on his experience in Ethiopia he knew there were many collections throughout the world that have findings of Stone Age implements. These, however, show a certain degree of intellectual development, but they don't show enough to say there had been significant intellectual development before Adam. Tomorrow's trip south to visit Lascaux may add to what he saw in the "Venus" while in Vienna.

While Rachel could have spent days walking through the Louvre, Adrian was inclined to stay more on task. He proposed they leave the Louvre for the smaller museum, the Museum d'Orsay, then head over to see the Basilica of the Sacre Coeur. Rachel was excited to take in as many sites as she could and quickly agreed.

On the opposite side of the river, the Museum d'Orsay is a converted old railway station. Here, Rachel found an entire collection devoted to Claude Monet. Two of her favorites were on display. The first is called Le Bassin aux Nympheas, Harmonie - a colorful impressionism at its best portraying a walkway bridge over a stream with colorful vegetation in abundance. The second is called En Norvegienne - this portrays three women dressed in their finery floating in a boat on the water.

After visiting several of the other impressionists' works Rachel was ready to go to the Sacre Coeur with a chance to see the sunset from its steps. Again they used the Metro, but this time the crowds had increased. It took longer to maneuver through each station to get to the right platform. Then each train seemed to be loaded more than the previous one. Still they made it in time to catch the funicular that carried them to the top of Montmartre Hill.

Just as they had hoped the sun was well above the horizon and they had plenty of time to look inside and outside the basilica. They were on the steps when the sun went down over the city. It was one of the best sunsets they had ever witnessed...another moment to remember!

After catching a quick bite to eat in the area of the Basilica they were on the Metro and off to a stop near Pont Alexandre III. Once they arrived at the bridge named after Alexandre III they stopped to marvel at the beauty of the bridge. It is ornately decorated and is definitely one of the prettiest bridges in the world. In fact, when they walked to the center of the bridge and looked over the side

Adrian held up his arms and loudly declared that he was claiming this bridge as his own. Rachel was pleased no one was listening.

They retraced their steps to the right bank and took steps down to the river. There they bought tickets for the evening river cruise. A large sightseeing boat leaves the dock every half hour and they waited only 20 minutes to board the next one. Having been one of the first to get on they ran to get seats on the upper deck in the front row. Once the boat left the dock it seemed to be only half full. It was, however, getting darker. They were glad to have jackets along to protect them as the boat turned into the wind.

Over the course of little over an hour, the boat made its way first toward the Eiffel tower and then back past Notre dame before returning to the dock. Getting darker by the minute they saw the lights come on the Eiffel tower as they approached it. The journey put an exclamation point on the saying that Paris is the city of light. It truly is!

As Rachel got colder Adrian held her hands to provide some warmth. He asked if she wanted to go in where it would be warmer. She said no and just moved closer to Adrian to get out of the wind. Once they docked they got off the boat and walked all the way back to the hotel. It had been a good day. They said good night after coordinating their checkout time and retired to their respective rooms. Both were tired and they knew they had a fairly long journey south the next day.

18

Sarlat, France

Rachel and Adrian checked out of the Paris hotel early and caught a taxi to the Gare Montparnesse. At this train station they were able to use their reservation to board a high speed TGV train, headed to Bordeaux in southwestern France. They switched trains to a local train headed first to Bergerac and then on to their destination of Sarlat.

Sarlat is one of France's best examples of 14th century architecture. It is a medieval town originally formed around a Benedictine abbey, located in a region called Perigord Noir and may one day be granted status as a UNESCO World Heritage site.

The town's population is near the 10,000 mark, and is a very popular destination for western European tourists in the summer months, due to the plentiful sights to see in town and in the local surrounding area.

Adrian and Rachel booked a two-night stay in Sarlat to enable them to have a full day to see the Lascaux caves located a short distance to the northeast. They reserved a car for the following day to give them the flexibility to go and return at their discretion. Besides, they did not know of any public transportation to the caves; and driving in a foreign country would, unquestionably, make it more of an adventure anyway.

After disembarking from the train and not seeing a taxi they decided to simply roll their bags the three or four blocks to the hotel where they had reservations. It was a little on the warm side, but they made the walk without incident. As they rolled their luggage along the sidewalks the town's architecture began to make them think they had gone back in time. Soon they felt like they were in a storybook setting.

The hotel looked as old as the rest of the town from the outside, but inside it was beautifully decorated and maintained. Small tour groups frequented the hotel since it was well located near the city center and apparently had a good dinner plan.

Their rooms, like the main floor, were well maintained. They were small, quaint, and perfectly functional. After taking time to get settled, Adrian suggested they take a walk into the city center. Rachel agreed as long as they returned in plenty of time for a shower before making their way to the scheduled 8:00 p.m. meal in the hotel's dining room.

Before leaving the hotel they did a little exploring around the upper floors of the hotel. The staircase led to various nooks and crannies at each turn. At one spot they found a small balcony open at the corner of the building. It was not connected to any particular room and if you stretched your neck just right you had a magnificent view out over tiled rooftops into the city. Adrian took a cute picture of Rachel making a funny face with all these 14th century buildings in the background.

Except for the modern dress of pedestrians, the walk through town was like a walk into medieval times. Many buildings had the old fashioned signs hanging over doorways. Buildings were positioned somewhat randomly and at strange angles. Cobblestones gave a real feel of older times. Rachel took lots of pictures of buildings and simply couldn't get enough of the town.

It was getting darker as the two headed back to the hotel. They showered, met downstairs and were escorted to a very elegant table for two. After making their selections from the menu they ordered a bottle of Bordeaux.

"It is nice to be able to relax after putting in another day of travel." Adrian said.

"This is so cool. Paris is the city I have always wanted to see and it is just as great as I expected, but Sarlat is right out of some fairy tale. It is remarkable how they have managed to keep it from become commercialized in the 21st century. Good for the French and good for those of us who get to experience it," said Rachel.

"You are so right. After seeing a relatively poor country like Ethiopia where many people live in poverty, and then seeing large European cities like Athens, Zagreb, Vienna, Munich and Paris this is much more charming. Although I did get to see some beautiful areas in the Alps. Matter of fact, that area was stunning."

"Tell me more about the excursion you had with Michael's friend, Joel. I believe he is of Jewish decent and he got you to go hiking near Garmish."

"Well yesterday I told you about the five questions I had prepared for him. He answered all five and I have the answers recorded. You will have to read them once they've been transcribed. But let me tell you what I saw on that hiking excursion."

With a bottle of good French wine on the table their conversation took them to Garmish and Lake Eibsee. Adrian told Rachel that one day he would love to take her to where he and Joel hiked and to possibly take the train up onto the Zugspitze. Adrian enjoyed telling the story of that day's adventure and Rachel loved hearing it.

"You know I could really enjoy hiking the lake you describe. We should do that when this project is finished. As a matter of fact, I would love to see the Swiss Alps as well, and perhaps see that fairy tale castle King Ludwig of Bavaria built in the mountains. You know the Disneyland-looking one."

Adrian had the answer, "You must mean Neuschwanstein."

"That's it!" exclaimed Rachel who was getting pretty happy after two glasses of wine.

When dinner was over Adrian walked Rachel to her room and gave her a friendly good night kiss on the lips. Rachel returned the kiss and closed the door with a giddy smile on her face.

The next morning no mention of a kiss was made or expected, and their relationship through the day remained friendly although more business-like than the previous day. Obviously, both parties were contemplating how they felt about the kisses they shared. Was it the wine or something deeper?

After a nice continental breakfast, they walked to the edge of town where the car rental place was located. Getting a nice compact car seemed practical along with a local map showing their starting point and their targeted destination. Soon they were winding their way on roads headed to the northeast. Adrian drove while Rachel navigated and helped read road signs.

The countryside was scenic and it didn't take long to see a sign that said turn left onto the next road for Lascaux. Once at the parking lot they saw many chartered buses. Lots of tourists were standing in groups; most had a camera hanging around their neck.

Once tickets were purchased for the guided tour of the caves they had a 20-minute wait for the next English speaking tour. They shared a bottle of juice and walked around the gift shop until it was time to queue up for their tour. With a dozen visitors in the group, the guide explained the original caves were not open to the public due to the damage caused by the heightened temperature and humidity caused by people constantly passing through the caves. The guide also explained that the caves they would tour were a near-perfect replica located just 200 meters from the original caves. The construction of these caves was within a few millimeters of the actual caves and almost exact reproductions of the original paintings were on the walls. Rachel was disappointed they were not going to see the actual caves, however, after the guide's explanation, she understood the need for it. Furthermore, after seeing the parking lot full of buses and lots of tourists standing around waiting to see the caves she was completely okay with the idea.

They entered the caves called Lascaux II, which is a reproduction of two of the five caves originally discovered in 1940 by a boy named Marcel Ravidat. The caves contain some of the best Upper Paleolithic art dating back 15,000 to 20,000 years ago. Most of the paintings are representations of large animals that resided in the area. What surprised Rachel was the manner in which the painter or painters used the stone wall reliefs in a way that gave the colorful paintings a three-dimensional look. For example, a bulge in the cave's side walls was used to depict the body of a horse in one painting and a bull in another. In other words, these were not stickman drawings. Someone with a relatively high intellectual level painted these walls.

Rachel seemed far more impressed by the paintings than Adrian. However, they were beginning to realize that probably would be the case in most any art exhibit. Adrian appreciated what Rachel said about a high level of art intellect being involved in creating these paintings. That confirmed his conclusion from Vienna that humans showed improved intellect from their origin and leading to the time of Adam.

After the tour Rachel purchased a number of post cards of the cave paintings to take back home to show Michael and Nancy. She ended up buying more than a dozen.

They drove back to Sarlat and returned the rental car. Walking back to the hotel Rachel said, "I am so impressed with the quality of the paintings, especially being as old as they are. It seems the people living here in that era had an advanced capacity to represent what was important to them. These are not lines and patterns. These are actual images made into three-dimensional reliefs. I am impressed, and if the work to determine the age of the paintings is correct, then your observation in Vienna is fully supported by what we saw at Lascaux."

Adrian added, "Rachel, I do not know if there is a chance that the whole carbon dating process scientists used to date these paintings could be false. I do know that if there was valid concern regarding the dates then there would be widespread material saying so. I don't see that, however. What I do see is further refinement in dating these paintings. The latest study dated the paintings 17,300 years old."

"Well, there we go. I think we have what we need here. Your conclusion stands and, until something comes up to refute it, I suggest we continue on the assumption it is correct."

"I agree."

They repeated dinner at the hotel that night. Eight o'clock for dinner seemed late for both of them, however, 'when in France do as the French do'. The main entrée was local fish from the Dordogne River. Looked and tasted like trout. It was superb. The white wine was slightly sweet, but excellent with the fish.

The next day they retraced their train trip back to Paris and checked into a hotel at the airport. Their early flight to London the following day necessitated either a very early get-up or the stay at the airport. The convenience of the airport stay made the decision easy.

19

London, England

Adrian and Rachel landed at Heathrow Airport just after noon. Adrian was very appreciative of the short flight. The weather was excellent and they enjoyed seeing the white cliffs of Dover as they crossed the English Channel. Heathrow was busy, as planes and people from all around the world make their way in and out of Heathrow.

With luggage in hand they caught the express train to Paddington Station where a taxi took them to their hotel. They checked in, dropped off their bags, and walked to a local pub recommended by the concierge in the hotel. A meal of fish and chips with a beer was spot on for Adrian. Rachel ordered a pear cider and a mixed salad.

"This is your last stop on an around-the-world adventure for you. I bet you are ready to get home after all the hotels and such. We both know how much you love museums." Rachel laughed. "Think you can handle this last go at a museum or two?"

"Rachel, part of me has been wanting to get home for a couple of weeks as I have found this trip to be exhausting. In many ways I wish Lisa were here. I still miss her so much. Lisa would have loved seeing Paris and London. And yet Rachel, as conflicted as I may sound, I am really glad you are here. I had such a good time in France. Michael has been very considerate allowing for some personal time here at the end of the trip. I must say I feel refreshed by our visit to France. I am actually looking forward to being in London with you."

"Adrian, I am a little conflicted also. I lost my best friend and I really do wish she could have been here instead of me. My emotions are running in different directions these days."

"Rachel, let me make myself as clear as I can. I will always love Lisa. No one should expect otherwise. However, I am feeling a strong sense of love for you now that we are working together and doing things together. I want to be a part of your life more each day."

"Well, Adrian, I am feeling the same about you. I want to spend more time together and see where this leads us. Coming here I didn't know if I would cramp your style since you had your own routine prior to my arrival. Being here has made my heart skip a beat every now and then."

Adrian blushed and said, "Wow, let's take it slow and as you said, see where this takes us."

Rachel paused and then continued, "Okay, so what is our schedule in London?"

"Well, we have a free afternoon and evening today. Tomorrow we have a full day at the London Museum of Natural History. The day after is free and the day following we fly home. Now, as far as the free time goes I was counting on you to tell me what we are doing."

Rachel smiled, "You are getting to know me pretty well. I do have a few ideas. But first, I want you to tell me what are we doing tomorrow?"

"We are meeting a gentleman named Harold Brookings. He is head of the Darwin Centre at the museum. Michael sent him a large donation contingent on him giving us the middle part of a day to ask questions concerning the origin of man. He accepted the money and agreed."

"Adrian, I remember handling a money wire request for £7,000 from Michael for this. At first, I did not understand exactly why we were doing it. Now I get it." Rachel interjected.

"I planned for a discussion of two to three hours with lunch in the middle," Adrian asserted. "Now I do want to ask one thing of you. Please don't mention our discussion about how we interpret what God means when He says we are made in his image. Our purpose in this meeting is to clarify and expand our understanding of the human family tree. I would like you to record the discussion so we can transcribe it later at home. Also, feel free to ask questions to clarify anything you don't understand."

"I'll have to ask lots of questions if that is what you expect from me. I haven't been staying up on evolution or human origin like you have. Yet, what I read in the book Michael gave me got me to thinking that Darwin might well have not had the right information to draw the conclusions he made."

"Seriously, ask about anything. Rachel, I have the same concern about Darwinism, but let's listen to what they have to say. They may avoid the controversy all together." Adrian reassured.

"After the meeting how about if we go over and ride the London Eye or take a sightseeing cruise on the Thames."

"I don't really care which one we do."

Rachel saw how to handle this, "Okay, let's do both!"

"For some reason I thought you would say that."

They walked through a neighboring park before catching the Underground to Leicester Square where they purchased tickets from the discount booth for a London play that night. They hurried to the hotel to change clothes and dashed to the theater district, grabbing a quick bite to eat along the way. They made the opening curtain in plenty of time, and they both loved the play!

Following a continental breakfast at the hotel the following morning, they took a taxi to the Museum of Natural History where they asked for Harold Brookings. A receptionist escorted them to a lovely small conference room where coffee, tea, and crumpets were waiting.

Harold Brookings entered the room with another gentleman who was introduced as the Director of the Museum – he immediately proceeded to pour out praises for the new donation made by an American foundation he had never heard of before.

Adrian explained the newness of the Foundation, how appreciative the Chairman was to make the donation, and how appreciative he and Rachel were to be so well received today. The Director left the room having made his formal thank you and Harold smiled. "Large donations get the attention of the Director."

"It is the same way anywhere. Money does have a way, doesn't it?"

"For us the reality is that without large donations like yours this museum could not operate. In many ways it is our life blood. We are grateful for the donation and we are also pleased you are here asking us questions of a profound nature. We are happy to oblige and I trust we can help you in some small way."

"Harold, I believe I sent you an advanced copy of the questions we would like you to address. Did you receive it?"

"Yes, thank you. Having these in advance gave me time to pull together materials I think you will find interesting. I have made copies for you both, so you don't need to take notes unless you want to do so."

Adrian replied, "I've asked Rachel to take notes on questions and answers that come up in discussion. I believe she would like to record the discussion. I trust that is okay?"

"Absolutely, anything we can do to help."

"Great! Let's start with the first question. What are the major events or biological progressions leading to the human race?"

Harold responded, "You made the right choice to come to the Darwin Centre. We have a number of world acclaimed scientists and researchers here who have helped us build quite a basis of understanding on this question. Please refer to your copy of my notes on this one."

"We believe humans, that is Homo sapiens, first appeared in the Paleolithic Period nearly 200,000 years ago. We have not found any credible evidence yet that our species existed before that time. However we continue to look and one day we may be able to push it back."

"The ancestors leading up to our species takes us to a number of different species identified by DNA research. 5,000,000-7,000,000 years ago we believe there may have been chimpanzee ancestors. We see that connection disappear about 5,000,000 years ago, however. This is when our genus Homo became a biological category absent the chimpanzee DNA."

"If we look at how many species of the Homo genus we have found living over 1,000,000 years ago we can list at least a half dozen. Again, these do not include the Homo sapiens. These were not humans. Here is a short list showing when they existed and where."

Homo rudolfensis	*1,900,000 million years ago - Kenya*
Homo habilis	*2,300,000 years ago - Africa*
Homo gautengensus	*2,000,000 years ago - South Africa*
Homo erectus	*1,800,000 years ago - Africa, China, India*
Homo ergaster	*1,900,000 years ago - Indonesia*
Homo antecessor	*1,200,000 years ago - Spain*

"Do you have any questions so far?"

Rachel asked, "Do any of these species exist today?"

"The answer is no, and your question is a perfect lead-in to what follows." Harold was obviously impressed with Rachel's question. "This list of species and a more lengthy list of additional recent ones combine to form our ancestral family under the same genus. Many may have been distant cousins but nevertheless they have been part of the family."

"Let me mention one other species before we concentrate on Homo sapiens. Neanderthals had a significant presence in Europe and western Asia. They were in existence in these areas 400,000 years ago up until about 30,000 year ago. According to genetic research, there was some inter-breeding with early humans that occurred about the time our current species left Africa 45,000 to 80,000 years ago. Further proof of this is that most non-African Homo sapiens have between 1% and 4% of their DNA from Neanderthal DNA. The Neanderthal species became extinct as the Homo sapiens population grew much faster. It is likely that the growth rate of the Homo sapiens caused the demise of the Neanderthals some 30,000 years ago."

Adrian commented, "I saw a good depiction of what you have described at a museum north of Zagreb, Croatia."

"Yes, I know of it. We have contemplated developing a modern interactive exhibit to allow visitors to experience what we are discussing. We think such an exhibit would be well received."

Pausing a second, Harold nodded to the receptionist standing near the door, "If we could break for a few minutes I can have lunch brought in. Would that be all right?"

"Certainly," Adrian and Rachel replied in unison.

After a 20-minute lunch break, Harold carried on. "Okay, let's concentrate on the Homo sapiens specie which is to say the human race. Do you know what sapiens means in Latin?" Neither Adrian nor Rachel said anything. "Well, it stands for wise or intelligent. Recent genetic reconstruction work focusing on mitochondrial DNA has produced some interesting findings. Essentially, the research shows that all humans have DNA from a woman who lived in East Africa 160,000 years ago. She has been named Mitochondrial Eve. Equally interesting is that DNA testing for the Y-chromosome in men can be traced back to a man living in Africa at least 140,000 years ago. He is happily named Y-chromosome Adam."

After some lengthy discussion on these points Adrian inquired, "Do we think research will yield evidence of our species possibly dating even further back in time?"

"Adrian, chances are fair that will occur. Whether or not the time difference is material is becoming less probable since we have the methods down pretty well today. But *yes* I believe if we can keep the field researchers in the field, and keep in mind that requires money, we will have a few more major finds that push dates back."

"Harold, would you explain for us the development of humans relative to the development of intellect and artistic expression?"

"Certainly research from around the world, in general, has found evidence of tool work and artwork dating back 50,000 years. One of the best artwork examples is the Venus of Willendorf in Austria. Clearly that piece alone tells us humans produced artwork around 25,000 years ago."

"Tools themselves date back even further. There are many findings of tools that can be traced hundreds of thousands of years. Tool work, however, did not come to much use until the human race began a rapid intellectual development that spurred on the dominance of the specie starting about 50,000 years ago."

"Thank you for that Harold. Rachel do you have any additional questions?"

Knowing she was risking a delay in getting to do some sightseeing this afternoon she spoke up saying, "Just one and I am afraid it may require a lengthy answer. Harold, I have learned so very much today and our discussions have been great, but there is one important thing I seem to be missing. Adrian, do tell me if this question is common knowledge to you and we won't waste Harold's time answering it. Basically, I do not understand how new species form. You have mentioned many timelines as to when one species and then another of the Homo genus first came into being. Yet, I do not understand biologically how that happened?"

Adrian immediately spoke up saying that as long as Harold had time they would very much like to hear the answer to Rachel's question as this was a perplexing hole in their understanding of evolution.

Harold apologized for the oversight in not including that in the discussion, but that it would require a good half-hour to adequately give a full explanation to Rachel's question. Everyone agreed to proceed and Harold encouraged them to record the conversation since he did not have the necessary notes to provide them.

After a short pause, Harold said, "Your fundamental question is how do species form? Correct?"

Rachel responded, "Yes."

"Rachel, keep in mind there is, in our mind, a natural selection process that has that has taken place over millions of years. The early stages of life are believed to have been single cell organisms.

Through the evolutionary process these organisms mutated over time adapting to their environment. A natural selection process took place where the stronger organisms survived and weaker ones did not. In turn, the stronger organisms became more complex and adaptable. They, in turn generated an array of new species."

"This matter is referred to as 'speciation' and there has been a lot of research done on the subject and much work continues today. Of course, I would be remiss if I did not mention that this scientific approach began with Charles Darwin and continues today with current genetics research."

"In 1859 Charles Darwin published his book entitled *"Origins of the Species."* In it, he states that there is a process in nature that he entitled natural selection. It refers to a very natural process by which new species gradually form over time. Essentially, he believed the evidence he had seen pointed to new lineages forming from their ancestors over time. Darwin believed that a species could essentially split in two, or that a new population could adapt to different conditions in which it lived, so as to form a new distinct species of its own."

"Without genetics at the time, all this was incredibly controversial. This ground-breaking concept stirred up emotions on all sides of the many debates that followed. Darwin's theory was followed by concepts of mutation, whereby a species introduced to new genetic material could adapt; forming a new and different species. Other concepts followed basing species change on heredity and other factors."

"Then in the 1930s, mathematical models of genetic populations highlighted the need for more genetic understanding of the evolutionary process. These models were instrumental in getting the scientific community energized to follow genetics ancestrally to better understand the dynamics of change in species degradation and formation."

"Subsequently a concept surfaced stating that once conditions were in place for members of a species that prevent them from reproducing within their own species, they may then begin to reproduce with others resulting in a mutation of the DNA and a new hybrid species. About this time scientists also found that geographic influences were part of the evolutionary process in speciation. Basically, when populations are separated they will diverge from their previous population and begin to become different in appearance and DNA. Likewise, when one population is mixed with another, genetic change will occur over time."

"Other factors are now being discovered as having long term effects on species. Certainly, by the 1990s the concept that adaptation to the environment was another factor in biodiversity of species. Sexual selection and random drift have been introduced as factors supporting genetic change, as well. All of this has led to a worldwide effort to further our understanding of the evolution of the human species. I think I can conclude that science has made an undeniable case for evolution. Yet, I do not believe we can adequately detail all the factors built into the formation of any one species. For that we have a ways to go."

Rachel thanked Harold for an explanation she could mostly understand. Adrian seconded the comment. They carried on with their discussion for another 15 minutes, which at that point, Adrian felt all their questions had been adequately answered. He commented, "Well Harold, we will be returning to Seattle in a couple of days. Can you give us a good recommendation for a pub in the vicinity?"

"I like the pub right down the street to the right as you come out the front door. Turn right at the next corner and the entrance will be right there."

"How convenient!" Rachel and Adrian said their good byes and left the building.

They walked quietly to the pub and sat for a few minutes. Each ordered a beverage and a small salad. After ordering, Adrian told Rachel, "That was a lot to absorb. Wow! I am overloaded with information. However, this trip would not have been complete if we had not been able to have someone walk us through what we just heard. Thanks go to Michael for seeing that this stop was included in the itinerary. I was afraid we would get a hard sales pitch on Darwinism. This overview was fine and it fit well with everything I expected. Your question at the end, Rachel, was spot-on. Thanks for asking it."

Rachel said, "Adrian, we just had an interesting two and a half hours with Harold. I feel so humbled to have sat in on the meeting. I've wrestled with the issue of where is God in all of this evolution talk. I gained a lot of knowledge, but it didn't feel quite right."

"Rachel, here are my thoughts. Darwinism professes that humans and other living creatures have developed over long periods of continuous evolution. Yet, some fossil findings indicate new types of creatures have suddenly appeared with no trace of ancestors. The relatively recent Cambrian Sea findings in Canada and similar findings in the Yunnan Province in China tell us there are species with no known record of ancestors, thereby leading many to believe some, if not all, species were created."

Adrian went on, "In the last 20 years with publications like Michael Behe's *"Darwin's Black Box: The Biochemical Challenge to Evolution,"* Darwin's theory has come under serious attack. Many scientists now proclaim that today's science has discredited the fundamental theory of Darwin and replaced it with a theory called 'Intelligent Design'. Essentially, the scientists say that the complexity of all living cells is far more elaborate than anyone could have imagined. Only with today's technology are we coming to understand this fact. There is no way Darwin could have imagined, much less seen, the beauty and complexity we can see today."

"Unfortunately, 'Intelligent Design' still leaves open the question as to the *source* of that intelligence. Hence, I do not particularly care for the term 'Intelligent Design'. Personally, I accept the fact that humans have adapted to their environment over time. We do not all look alike. We do not all act alike. I do not believe we are the result of chance or the result of evolution from some simplistic form of life. I do believe we are complex in our physical make-up and in our mental and spiritual design. Therefore, based on what I believe from Christ's teachings, the origin of humankind is "*Divine Design.*" In other words, God created us along with all things."

"I like the Divine Design concept. Did you come up with that name?" Rachel asked.

"After talking with Nick Dawson in Athens I coined the name and I continue to like it. It brings God first and foremost into the design of our species and all others."

"Adrian, you are right. I have no doubt that as we finalize our answers we will have grown in faith more than we can imagine and that we will have been given a glimpse at God's intent for mankind. Look at what we just learned. How can anyone not see the work of God in all that has been created? I am all in for what you call 'Divine Design'. I have to believe Michael and Nancy will be on board, as well. Let's raise a banner that says 'We believe in Divine Design'."

"I agree!" They sat quietly reflecting on all that had transpired.

Finally, Adrian said, "We are now on free time, what do you want to do first?"

Rachel replied, "Well, let's see, we have a date for the play tonight so I don't have time for more than one thing. You know I'll need time to get ready for the play, so let's go ride the London Eye and then head back to the hotel. Does that sound okay?"

"Absolutely!"

They enjoyed the London Eye even though they had a long wait to get on. Rachel took lots of photos. She got a particularly good one of Adrian while they were high on the ride. Big Ben and the Parliament building were in the background and Adrian had a big grin on his face.

Following the ride, they caught a taxi and returned to the hotel. Adrian used the tablet and the hotel's internet connection to send an e-mail detailing the day's meeting. Later Adrian and Rachel took the Underground to the theater district, found a friendly restaurant for a quick dinner, and headed to the play. The play was great and Rachel could not be more pleased that Adrian would do this. He actually seemed to enjoy it. It was chilly leaving the theater and Adrian kept his arm around Rachel most of the way back to the hotel. They kissed good night at Rachel's room and then Adrian headed to his room.

The next day was filled with tourist activities. They saw the Crown jewels at the Tower of London, took a boat cruise on the Thames, had another pub meal, and generally enjoyed each other's company. Rachel did get to see the British Museum in the afternoon, and knowing Adrian's impatience at museums Rachel suggested they meet at the exit in an hour.

While Rachel headed to the art exhibits Adrian went straight to find the oldest artifacts he could find. He found a small section of old stuff. Fortunately, each piece had a card beside it telling the approximate date of origin. He found a couple of sculpted figurines from the 7th century BC. He found hand axes from 100,000 to 300,000 B.C. He found arrowheads, blades including sickle blades, an ax head, and hide scrappers from the Neolithic period of 6,900-3,800 B.C. Adrian was happy to have found something useful to their research and headed for the exit a few minutes early. Rachel, however, was 10 minutes late which conjured up memories of similar wait times while shopping with Lisa.

A part of Adrian felt guilty that he was enjoying his time with Rachel. But he knew Lisa wouldn't want him moping around forever. She'd be mad at him for wasting a second of this amazing thing called life. After another deep breath Adrian mentally wiped away the pain of the past and looked with renewed interest at the present. Here was Rachel with a shopping bag and a big smile. Rachel was breathing hard from the sprint, "So sorry! The line in the gift shop was long and I had to have the print of the most amazing picture I have ever seen." Adrian smiled and asked to see it.

Their last visit was to see Buckingham Palace. The Queen was in Scotland, but they still could not tour inside for some reason, so they walked around the fenced perimeter of the property taking pictures. Rachel drug Adrian in the gift shop for a souvenir. Adrian was afraid he might knock over some expensive piece of china so he took a picture of Rachel in the shop and headed outside to find a bench. A short time later Rachel came out with her souvenir and one for Nancy.

They strolled across a nearby park, then sat and talked awhile before catching a taxi to Harrod's department store, a landmark Rachel wanted to visit. In fact, Rachel simply had to see the store. Prices seemed pretty high to Adrian and he could not find anything he wanted. Meanwhile, Rachel was checking out clothes and all the styles the store carried. She found a nice blouse she wanted and Adrian took it from her, paid for it, and presented it to her as a gift. She was elated.

With bags in hand they caught another taxi to their hotel. Later, they walked to a nearby pub recommended by the fellow at the front desk. It was a perfect way to finish their visit to London, as they both liked the atmosphere of the British pubs. Rachel liked the pear cider and although not a big beer drinker, Adrian enjoyed the occasional glass of fine ale. They shared an order of fish and chips, the perfect meal for this pub experience.

There was a soccer game on the television in the pub and half the patrons were really into the game. Roars would go up any time something exciting happened, which added to the atmosphere. They soon found themselves cheering on Manchester United along with the locals. They had a blast!

The next morning Adrian and Rachel met for breakfast. They finished packing, checked out and took a taxi to Paddington Station reversing their incoming route to Heathrow. They were ready for the flight home. At least Adrian was. Rachel could have kept travelling!

After a wait in Heathrow's enormous waiting area, their boarding gate flashed on the overhead screen near where they had been sitting. They picked up their carry-on bags and headed to the gate. The flight to Seattle was long, but they passed the time quite pleasantly talking about the trip, reading, and napping. Once they arrived at the airport in Seattle they kissed goodbye and went off on their respective shuttles to nearby car lots. Both were a little sad to part company. They had enjoyed their time together more than they had admitted to one another.

20

Mercer Island, Washington

Michael had notified Nancy, Rachel and Adrian that he would like a staff meeting in the conference room at noon the day after the London flight returned to Seattle. His message said lunch would be provided and the meeting should not last longer than a couple of hours.

Michael was the last to get to the meeting although he showed up five minutes early. He was pleased to see everyone made it okay. After a prayer that he led, Michael said he was running somewhat late because he had been packing a suitcase. Everyone was wondering where he was going, but no one asked.

"Welcome home Adrian. I see that Rachel was able to find you and, no doubt, rescue you from the rigors of an around-the-world business trip."

"Well, Adrian did look a little worked over after all he had done getting to Paris," said Rachel."

"I pity you, child. Having to go to Paris and London on business," Nancy laughed.

"It was a business trip. Although I must admit Michael did allow a few days in the trip schedule to have some fun. It was a fantastic trip and thank you, Michael, for trusting me to do the research."

"From the reports it sounds like you two got the job done in fine fashion. I must admit I am impressed from what I've seen so far. If the final reports are near what I've seen in your preliminary notes I think we will all be very happy where we stand on answering the first two questions."

"Just for the record, I want to read Adrian's answer to Question #2. He wrote, 'Based on the preponderance of evidence available today the only rational explanation for the origin of humankind is Divine Design. This is predicated on the deficiency of Darwin's evolutionary theory that human origin evolved naturally from a single cell and the overwhelming evidence that humankind originated suddenly in a complex form'."

Adrian jumped in, "Michael, I cannot believe how much I have seen, done, and heard in the past three weeks. It is somewhat mind-boggling."

"Well, that is what we wanted, isn't it? Answering Question #2 is about as difficult as it gets, and you not only did that, you showed that the answer to a complex 'either/or' question can lead to a simple revelation. I love it!"

Michael continued, "Listen, I don't want you to do too much today after such a long trip. So let me tell you what I would like you to do over the next three weeks."

Rachel said, "Okay, but what is this about you packing for a trip? I don't remember you mentioning that before I left here."

"I've decided to take three weeks off."

Nancy jumped in, "You two have no idea how much Michael has done while you were gone. I'm surprised he didn't have a heart attack as hard as he has been pushing himself."

"Wow, I had no idea!" Rachel said.

"It is not like I am sick or anything. I have put a fair amount of pressure on myself to finalize my tenure agreement and wrap up my business while walking every step of the way with you in Europe, finishing up the conclusions on Question # 1, and then to begin looking ahead to Question #3. Anyway, I am flying to Texas tonight to see my brother and his family and to attend an awards ceremony at Texas Tech where I am being recognized as a Distinguished Engineer. From there I plan to spend 10 days in New England and travel around. Most people who know me don't know I spent an entire summer along the Maine coastline north of Bar Harbor. I was a camp counselor for young, underprivileged boys. I loved it and I am going back to see the area. The camp was located on Dyer Island as I recall. It was a great experience for me as a young man."

"From Maine I'll drive to Vermont and work my way back to Boston, where I will meet an old friend. He is a retired professor who has been my mentor ever since I took one of his classes. I have a meeting scheduled with him and plan to use him as an unbiased sounding board regarding our questions and answers. I think he will be impressed, but I want his honest opinion. Nancy has all my work on Question #1 and anyone can call me if you need to discuss any part of it. Also, she will forward the final report to me several days prior to my return to Boston at the end of my trip."

"So, I would like you three to take a day off tomorrow and then come in and organize all the information we have gathered to tackle these answers. Then e-mail them to me. I'll be in New England where I can get copies made of them. Do whatever it takes to cover every single fact that supports or doesn't support our conclusion. I want you to catalog the materials you are using in terms of where, when, and from whom you got the information. Organize all the material logically so anyone can follow the paper trail. I want you to work together and I want you to unanimously agree to everything, no matter how many nights you have to spend here."

"When I receive the report I will take a full day and study it very closely. I will then forward it to my old professor to read before the meeting. My hope is that we can have an in-depth conversation regarding his thoughts on our research. He will know if we are on target or if we have any holes that need to be filled. Basically, I want to get an editorial opinion from him. He has agreed to all this, and in fact, he is looking forward to it."

After a pause Michael went on, "I'll return with notes from the meeting, and then we can finalize answers to Questions #1 and #2. Is this okay with everyone?"

Everyone agreed this was a good plan.

"I have one last request for today before we break. I would like each of us to take a few minutes and explain where we are on our walk with Christ. Periodically, we need to have the chance to explain what is going well in our walk, as well as what we are struggling with. I'll be happy to start."

Everyone was fine with the suggestion and Michael paused for a short while before starting.

"I have had so many things revealed to me in the last few months while on this journey with you I may have forgotten to look to God as much as I should. I know He is there, but all too often I put myself first and I try to do something. I am coming to the realization that I need to listen to God more than I have. For example, when I received some of your e-mails or faxes I have been hurrying through them and trying to draw my own conclusions when I should slow down and pray about them. I really need to slow down and listen more. I need to develop the ability to have a conversation with God and to listen to God's response. My vacation is an effort to get away, slow down and listen better."

Nancy said, "That reminds me of something. I tend to get up in the middle of the night most nights to go to the bathroom. Often I stay up a short while and walk around the house talking to the Lord. My husband heard me one time and thought I was crazy, but you know it is so peaceful at night when it is just you and God. I know my walk with God is in good hands as long as I can talk to him."

Adrian was next, "Outside of family I have never been so close to anyone like I am to you three." When he said this he was looking straight at Rachel and Michael noticed. "My family losses have devastated me and I still need time to grieve." He looked at Rachel again. "But I know there is nothing I would rather be doing than working with you three. In fact, I feel like I am working with you three and God. I've never been so close to God. When I stood on the hill in Ethiopia and starred out over the Middle Awash region knowing that humankind may have had its beginning near this spot I was humbled. I kept asking myself 'who gets to do what I am doing?' I felt closer to God there than I ever have in church. It was strange to be where God's creative forces produced our species. Thank you Michael for that."

Rachel spoke last. "Ever since I was a little girl I felt like I was on a long walk with God. I know I can talk to God anytime. He does not always answer me when I expect Him to answer, but I trust He will answer me when the time is right. Taking this job was the same way. I knew He wanted me to be here and I am blessed to be here. So, I say thanks be to God every day."

Rachel went on, "I too still have some grief to deal with, though I know it can't compare to Adrian's." She gave him a sympathetic smile. "My faith in the fact that Lisa and Catherine are in God's hands, makes it bearable. I will always carry a scar in my heart, but it is most important that we all stay together in God's hands."

After a quiet moment, Michael thanked everyone for being so open and trusting. He said he would be leaving soon and that Adrian and

Rachel should do the same and get some rest. He knew Nancy would handle matters just fine for the rest of the day.

Adrian walked Rachel to her car. "I had a really good time in Paris and London with you. I'm very glad you came. I don't want you to think otherwise because of what I said in the meeting. I still need some time to work through my grief. I know you understand, but once I'm in a better place I'd really like to see you socially if you are up to it."

Rachel smiled, "I do understand. I want the time to be right too."

Adrian was surprised how good it felt to hear Rachel say she was on the same page. "Have a nice day off tomorrow, I'll see you here the day after tomorrow."

21

Boston, Massachusetts

While Adrian, Rachel and Nancy compiled the report on the first two questions, Michael was able to enjoy his time in Texas again. His brother's family was doing well. Seeing the interaction between his brother, his brother's wife, and their grown children was refreshing. It was nice being part of a family again. He had missed that.

The Texas Tech visit was healthy for Michael as well. Having been a faithful contributor to the University and to the Alumni Association ever since he turned 30, he still felt a strong connection to the University. It was nice that the University recognized not only his financial contributions but also his dynamic contributions to his profession by selecting him as one of the University's Distinguished Graduates.

Michael enjoyed catching up with the many changes to the campus. He was invited to join the University President at a Red Raider football game. He loved Red Raider football almost as much as he enjoyed watching the Seattle Seahawks.

Following Michael's 10-day stay in Texas he flew to Boston. There he spent half a day at Harvard and a half day at M.I.T. Just walking through their buildings and grounds at both universities brought back fond memories of his time in Boston. Michael's hotel was near Copley Square which he knew well. The square has history, he would often say. The square was formerly called Art Square and has its roots in the early era of local art in Boston. Later, the name was changed. John Copley, a colony artist, was honored in the renaming. A statue of John Copley is prominently positioned in the park and has been there since 2002.

The park is popular and centrally located. Surrounding it is the 1877 Trinity Church, the 1895 Public Library, and the impressive 1975 John Hancock Tower. In 1990, the city allowed a farmer's market to set up business in the park and many locals come there to shop. Additionally, the park is host to the iconic sculptures of the "tortoise and the hare."

Spending some quiet downtime in the park had always been a favorite of Michael's. While sitting on one of the park benches he made a phone call to his longtime professor/mentor, Thomas Carr. While a student at Harvard, Professor Carr took a particular liking to Michael and seemed to possess a sixth sense of the fact that Michael would one day be extraordinarily successful in some endeavor, professional or otherwise. Professor Carr simply felt there was something special about Michael.

They talked for 10 minutes. Michael told Thomas that the report they had previously discussed would be e-mailed in about a week. Thomas acknowledged that he would read it as soon as it arrived and that he looked forward to seeing Michael when he returned from his touring in 10 days. Then they could discuss the report. With plans set for meeting Thomas, Michael was prepared to depart Boston the following day. After picking up his rental car the next morning, Michael headed north to Maine. He looked forward to seeing the area around Bar Harbor. He had such good memories of the area.

The drive north past Portland, Maine was a pretty drive. He arrived in Bar Harbor and checked into his hotel for three nights. The following day he spent going to one of his favorite locations in the area, Acadia National Park. The views from higher up in the park were impressive. Michael loved the sea views from there. Back in town later in the afternoon, he found an art shop with a small but idyllic painting of the same scene he had enjoyed that morning. He bought it to take home.

The next day Michael drove north along the coast to a small town named Millbridge. Just outside of town he found the small dock where in his youth he was ferried to and from Dyer Island while serving as a camp counselor at a boy's camp. He could look out to the east and see the lobster fishermen working the same waters he crossed as a high school senior working his first job. He chose not to spend time searching out the status of the camp and to leave that for another day. He simply headed south.

Back in Bar Harbor, Michael walked around town and the harbor area. It brought back good memories from when he was 17 years old and watching a big dance hall filled with pretty girls. Quite an experience for someone marooned on an island with a bunch of boys half his age. Bar Harbor was and is a great place.

Leaving Maine the next day, Michael drove to the White Mountains of New Hampshire and then to a farmhouse in central Vermont. There are a number of farmhouses set up nicely for short or long guest stays. Wanting some peace and quiet Michael had reserved a four-night stay at one. He simply wanted time to read, pray and think, and this was the perfect spot.

Basically, Michael was certain the team back home was going to produce a first-class report answering the first two questions. He'd deliberately gotten a cabin with no internet so he could fully unplug. Once he arrived at the hotel in southern New Hampshire, where he planned to stay on his way back to Boston, he would download the file.

It wasn't the report that led him to stay four nights in Vermont. It was what he knew would not be in the report that had him here. He wanted to spend time alone in a peaceful setting and pray about what would be missing. That something had to do with the second question. He just knew the others would not address it, and he felt it had to be addressed. The others were just too busy to catch it.

Michael had decided not to make an issue of the expected omission. He wanted to answer this one on his own, because it would be fundamental to his transformation as a follower of Jesus. He needed to wrestle with this straightforward question. Pray about it and come to a conclusion that he would truly believe. The question, though simple, was quite large:

"Why is humanity here?"

God clearly wanted humanity here, but why?

Michael struggled with the question for the better part of the first full day on the farm. He joined a few others for meals but did not choose to join in any group events. He had told the owners that he wanted to be alone while at the farm. They were fine with the request and said that he was not the first to make such a request.

Michael must have scribbled two dozen purpose statements and then tossed all of them. He was pretty despondent by the second full day. In fact, he needed a break and went for a walk. The wind had picked up and leaves were falling at a rapid rate. This too was a sight he cherished. He never could get enough of a New England fall day.

Back in Washington State on the west side of the Cascade Mountains the trees are for the most part conifers, which are evergreens. In their own right, conifers are magnificent trees that provide a green blanket across the landscape. Yet, the colors and the leaves blowing in the winds of New England are truly special. Michael reveled in the scene around him. Later that evening Michal turned to the Bible he brought. He surrendered to prayer, as well.

He realized he could not adequately answer this very basic question. Why did God create humanity?

After breakfast on his last full day at the farm he took another walk. He tried to listen to the true meaning of the bible passages he had read the day before. The Adam and Eve story leads one to believe that God's purpose was to have mankind be obedient and to live in harmony with nature. However, that didn't work out so well when Eve ate from the tree of life and later Cain killed Abel.

As time moved on God saw that mankind needed to be dispersed during the time of Babel. Then, Noah comes along as being the only obedient one God could find. The flood wipes out nearly all the population seemingly due to their lack of obedience. This is followed by God providing commandments to Moses. Obedience continued to be the central purpose most people saw and most failed to achieve.

Finally, God sends us Jesus and the message changes. Not only is obedience asked of mankind, but we are asked to believe in Jesus as the Son of God. Jesus calls us to honor the commandments and to extend the love we have for God to others. In his life, Jesus serves as a perfect example of doing these two things. The messages of hope, faith and love that Jesus brought to us is paired with a prophetic message of judgment preceded by tribulation. All of which signals an end to the times we are living in and a new era thereafter.

All this got Michael excited and he hurried back to the cottage where he was staying to get some paper to write his thoughts down. He was worried his train of thought would vanish, so he hurried even faster. Once there, he was winded and he wrote a two-sentence purpose statement.

The first read:

"God's purpose for mankind is for us to use our God-given gifts in a way that reflects Jesus' love to the Father and to others, so that

through God's grace and Jesus' sacrifice we can be adopted into eternal life with God."

He also liked his short version:

"Be like Jesus."

Having written these two purpose statements, Michael felt relieved. The long version includes the fundamental fact that life is somewhat like an initiation test. Those who pass have eternal life in heaven with Jesus. Those who don't will have their souls sent elsewhere.

The short version focuses on one simple, but powerful, concept that either you are driven to be like Jesus or you are not. Those who are, will learn from the word in the Bible. They will want to be close to Jesus in prayer. They will behave as Jesus did and they will receive the blessings from God as Jesus does, because Jesus has reconciled all who believe in him through his sacrifice on the cross.

Writing this on one piece of paper, Michael placed the paper in his briefcase. He felt better. He believed the purpose statement represented what God wants from us. In doing those things our faith will grow and our love for God and others will drive how we live. The statements themselves may not be all that profound, he thought, but to Michael they were just what he needed.

After a great night's sleep, Michael drove down a crowded but scenic Interstate 89. He spent the night in New Hampshire reading the material sent from his group in Washington State. As expected, the report was excellent and covered all but the one relevant issue. That was the one he had wrestled with for the last four days. He forwarded the information to Thomas.

After New Hampshire, it was back to Boston where the following day he met Thomas for lunch. Thomas shared his surprise that, after retiring, he was taking on a non-profit foundation, especially one with such a daunting task as outlined in its charter. Michael explained his motives.

The conversation turned to the report. Thomas was impressed by the thoroughness of the research and agreed with the conclusions, particularly the part where the origin of humankind was determined to be from Divine Design. Although Thomas stated that more research in the area of Divine Design was needed, he did not discount the work done to date. Lastly, he offered a few modifications, all minor, and Michael noted the changes on a list he had started in New Hampshire. As they wrapped up their discussion on the report, Michael changed the direction of the conversation.

"Thomas, I have one last issue for you to consider."

"Of course, anything."

Michael explained what he had done in Vermont and passed the paper to Thomas to read.

"Well, well, you are getting into religious philosophy here. This must be like the million dollar question, isn't it?"

"Can't do this project without addressing it, Thomas."

"Well, I can buy the short version, but I realize it is because the phrase is like something from Madison Avenue advertising. The long one certainly makes one think a good deal more, I must say. I would have to digest the long one before I could say I like it, but that is possibly because it immediately forces me to look at my life and ask if I am going to be adopted when the time comes to pass judgment on my soul. Yes, the long one is provocative and it may be a very good one at that. What more can I say?"

"Thomas, thank you. I have thoroughly enjoyed our time together. You must know what a help you have been to me over the years as a mentor. Thank you so much and do say 'hello' to Helen."

Thomas smiled, "May God be with you, Michael!

Michael slept well that night. He felt ready to return home.

22

Seattle, Washington

Returning from his trip, Michael had some financial matters he wanted to settle quickly. Joyce Hillary's office was a plush one with a magnificent view of Elliott Bay. Located on Second Avenue in a modern high-rise it possessed one of the more spectacular views in the city. The westerly exposure provided a view of the Olympic Mountains as well as much of the Puget Sound region. Due west are the Straits of Juan de Fuca, named for an early explorer of the region, and to the northwest lay the San Juan Islands and the large Canadian island called Vancouver Island which is home of the British Columbian provincial seat of Victoria.

Joyce, having served as Michael's CPA and primary tax advisor along with Allen Cooper, Michael's Investment Advisor, were the closest confidants Michael had on financial matters. Joyce had helped Michael with financial advice ever since Michael moved to the area. Mary never wanted anything to do with finances. Mary had lived a life conservatively relative to the wealth they had as a couple and she simply left financial matters to Michael.

As the leading financial and tax advisor in Seattle, Joyce had a client list that would startle most financial advisors. Many of the top 100 wealthiest families in the United States used her services in one way or another. Her reputation blossomed when it became known that she advised two of the top 10 wealthiest persons in the United States. With the high-tech industry having a substantial presence in Seattle, this was a place, along with Silicon Valley where visionaries rose to the top of that industry.

"What a surprise to hear from you Michael," Joyce exclaimed.

"It has been all too long since we last met. I appreciate your thoughtful letter of condolence. Family matters have been a priority in recent months," Michael replied.

"Mary was a delight to have around and I miss our annual get together. She was so charming and so genuine. Although we were not close, I always enjoyed her quiet presence and her incredible devotion to family, church and community. You were so blessed to find her when you did, and I know she was an inspiration to you in all those hectic years you spent working and raising that precious daughter of yours. My deepest condolences will always be with you. I hope you know that Michael."

"Thank you and of course I know that. Mary trusted all that you have done for us and she was always grateful for the fact that she could concentrate her time and talent on the things she loved."

"It has been my pleasure. Michael, what can I do to be of assistance to you?"

"Joyce, I need to update you on my status and get some advice on proceeding."

"Certainly, anything!"

"As you know, Joyce, I have founded a non-profit foundation in Mary's name. You helped me with the initial contribution I made to the Foundation."

"Rachel and I have met a couple of times and she has kept me apprised of the Foundation's finances and we are current with our necessary filings. I am impressed with the investments the foundation has made and the returns you have earned. Well done!"

"Joyce, we have done a lot of research in the past months and my inspiration to press on with this project has grown to where I am interested in donating more of my personal holdings. Mary has inspired me more after her passing than I can tell you. God has been right there, as well, encouraging me to press on."

"Well, if I understand the finances correctly, your foundation has more funds on hand today than it did when you made the donation to kick it off. Your investments continue to out-perform most any of the market indices and you have earned more than you have spent. If I may ask, where do you see the foundation going and what kind of additional investment do you have in mind?"

"Now that I am retired, the Foundation is my work. I am fully absorbed by what our group is doing. We have perhaps a year of work in front of us to establish a fairly comprehensive understanding of what God has in mind for the human race. I want to share this work with others to help them see for themselves how wonderful and complete God's plan is. Furthermore, I am equally becoming focused on the need for the Foundation to respond to the needs in our community to help those who need help just as Mary did in her way."

"Okay Michael what do you want to do financially to help in this endeavor?"

"Joyce, I want to sell enough stock from my personal account to enable me to contribute another $6,000,000 to the Foundation, contribute $2,000,000 to my church, and pay my capital gain taxes.

I am expecting you to tell me that would require a sale upwards of $10,000,000 in securities."

"Michael, you are one of my favorite clients. You so often have the answer to your own questions. Depending on the tax basis of the assets you sell and the holding time you have on those assets the tax may be slightly less, but if you plan to cash out up to $10,000,000 you will have the cash to contribute and cover your tax liability. Have Allen forward me any transactions he completes on your behalf so I can properly adjust your quarterly tax advances. Also, you should be careful to avoid transactions involving investments held under 12 months because those will be taxed at your ordinary tax rate, which is way too high for you to consider doing unless there are extenuating circumstances of which I am not aware."

"All good points. I'll look at my portfolio and set some ideas in motion to make this happen during the first quarter of the upcoming year."

"Sounds even better. That way we can spread the quarterly advances out over the year. My guess is that you will have all that sorted out by the time you get across Lake Washington if not by the time you leave the building!"

"Joyce, you know me too well. If I may, let me be frank about a change that is taking place in me."

"By all means."

"During my working years I treated my growing portfolio as a measure of my success. Now that I have far more than I could ever imagine spending I am drawing closer to Mary's vision and work of helping others. In some ways I view some of what I have done as folly. I only hope that I have the time to make up for my blindness to the world around me and my myopic view of things centered on my work. Perhaps I can follow Mary's lead and do some good in the world with the resources given to me. I know that when I die I cannot take anything with me, so why should I not take charge now and invest more of what I have in something extraordinary?"

"Michael, have you set aside a trust for family members?"

"Yes, Braxton helped with my trust, but that trust represents less than 10% of my net worth. Even with this decision today, I still have more than 80% of my net worth to direct. I hope to direct most of that to the Foundation."

"Michael, you are a wonderful person and it is not too late to deal with this issue of wealth disbursement. I have several clients dealing with the same issue. You are blessed in that you see where you want your wealth to go. Many others in your position do not deal with this issue well. Stay focused on this issue and let me know when you want to make future moves. Do keep me in the loop."

"Thanks, Joyce, I will do that. Meanwhile, I will talk with Allen and have Rachel handle the funds on the foundation side of this new transaction."

On his drive across the I-90 Bridge, Michael phoned Allen Cooper, his investment manager.

"This is Allen. How can I help you?"

"Allen, this is Michael. Have you got a couple of minutes to talk?"

"Absolutely, what can I do for you?"

"Allen, I want you to sell my stake in the airline sector in January. Four years ago we invested $3,000,000 and my last check indicated the current value is closer to $10,000,000."

"Okay, yes, I am looking at your account and you are correct. May I ask how you want to use the funds?"

"Certainly! When the sale is completed I want you to hold $2,000,000 in cash for disbursement towards next year's tax advances. I will disburse the balance in two checks. I will want a check on the account for $6,000,000 to the Foundation and a check to my church for $2,000,000."

"Well, that's quite a way to start off the New Year."

"Allen, please keep Joyce aware of each of these transactions once they are all completed. I just left her office so she is expecting to hear from you in January."

"Sounds good, and you enjoy the holidays."

"You too!"

Michael drove to Mercer Island after making a short call to see if Reverend John Osgood would be available. He drove straight to the church and found the Reverend working on next Sunday's sermon."

"John, how are you?"

"Well, let's see. The pulse is still there and I am able to get out of my chair to shake your hand. So things are pretty good. What brings you to church today? I know you just got back from an extended trip to see family and friends."

"John, I wanted to see you and talk if you have the time."

"I have a couple coming in about an hour to talk about having their wedding at the church. I've given Sunday's sermon nine times in the past 30 years so updating it is pretty easy. Let's talk."

"Thank you. As you know the Foundation work is going well and I am more enthused than ever with the whole experience. But I know that Mary would want me to be attentive to the needs of our church and the community as well. So I am here to tell you that I would like to make a donation in January to the church for three purposes."

"Michael, you certainly have my attention. I am gratified to know that you see your service to the Lord includes working in community with the broader church. Mary was so giving in so many ways. We do miss her, Michael. Thank you for thinking of us."

"John, just as you have helped us with the Foundation, on behalf of Mary's memory I want to make three contributions. First, I am aware that you plan to initiate a campaign next year to raise $1,000,000 dollars for church renovations. I am pledging half that amount to be paid to the church next month. The gift will be anonymous."

"Oh, my gracious, you have no idea what a gift from heaven that is for this church. Bless you, Michael"

"John, the second and third donations to the church deal with community ecumenical work done by churches in the area. Our church has always been involved in helping regional needs through the involvement of church members like Mary. The outreach committee here has been so faithful in helping with community needs. Mary loved the work the committee does and I want to donate $250,000 to the committee to use as it sees fit and another $250,000 specifically split between safe houses for battered women/children and the prison ministry that Peter Hammond from our church volunteers with. These are also to be anonymous."

"Wow, our stewardship goals in that area have now far exceeded what we could have wished for. I am overwhelmed."

"John, the third donation I wish to make is targeted at the regional call to provide emergency food and shelter assistance to those in need. The example is the Oso landslide in 2014 when so many lost loved ones and their homes. As I understand it, the ecumenical council addressing this need is seeking $1,000,000 to start the program with equipment needs as well as food and other supplies. I would like to donate that $1,000,000 this project through the church as long as the outreach committee here believes the participating churches can cover the ongoing cost of the program. This too will be anonymous."

"My head is spinning. I came to work today not knowing what the day would bring and you have brought news that will bless so many. Michael, you have no idea how much of a blessing this is."

"I know now better than ever that what I have is God's, not mine. So let's praise the Lord!"

"All that is true, but good works are done by those who reflect the love that God has for all. We need angels on earth to do God's work. Today you are one of God's angels on earth. I will honor your request to remain anonymous and our staff will do its best to honor it, but I cannot guarantee that someone might say something out-of-school."

"I understand, John. My interest is seeing that folks focus on God's benevolence not the person whose hands it passes through. I am simply one of God's children who has been sufficiently blessed to be able to do these things. Hopefully, I am able to do more in the future."

"Michael, you have come so far so quickly. I am mystified!"

"John, my actions simply need to follow my new found priorities. I have a new-found faith in God and it obligates me to do some things differently. I am listening to not only my mind but now even more so to my heart. I hope I can use that to manifest some good in the world. I see a need to help spread the gospel in the world and to help in some small way those in need."

"Michael, I can't tell you how that makes my spirit glow in happiness for you. May God continue to bless you in your walk with our Lord. Let me know if I can help."

"I certainly will. Okay, I have taken up enough of your time. I will have a check made out to the church for $2,000,000 delivered to the church in January with instructions for dispensation as we have discussed. Is that okay?"

"I will not say a word to anyone until the check arrives with instructions. God bless you Michael. May God guide you in your walk with our Lord!"

23

Mercer Island, Washington

It had been just over three weeks since Michael left on his trip to Texas and the northeast. He had gotten a good taste of cold weather and now found himself at home in the wetter climate of the coastal northwest region of the country. Temperatures were moderate and the breaks between southwesterly rains passing through the region also provided some sunshine. Michael loved the year-round green provided by the evergreen firs growing up and down the area west of the Cascade Mountains.

Well rested from his trip, Michael smiled to himself as his crew of three scurried around getting prepared for the afternoon meeting he had called. Lunch had been catered and the four of them spent the time catching up on personal matters.

Michael noticed a glint in the eyes of Rachel and Adrian although there was no mention of the two of them having actually done anything together. Michael was a little curious, but he was not going to bring up the subject. Nancy went on about how her grandkids were in full Christmas mode. The 10 days were going to be fun and somewhat hectic. All seemed to be just as it should be. Following a rather lengthy opening prayer, Michael's first order of business as the meeting came to order was to discuss holiday plans. He made it clear that he was overwhelmed as to how well the team had performed in the past six months. The results were better than he had hoped for and that was a rare statement from Michael when it came to business matters.

He told everyone that he expected the office to be closed from Christmas Eve till the day after New Year's Day. The smiles around the table made it clear that everyone was ready for a break and that Michael's pronouncement was well received.

"What are you going to do this Christmas?" was the question from Nancy.

"After visiting my brother's family in Texas, they asked if I would like to join them for Christmas. So that is where I'll be."

"Sounds great! Being with family is what you should do. I am glad you are going back to be with them," Rachel added.

"Okay, let's talk about the material you sent to New England. I read the material while in New Hampshire and returned to Boston to meet with my old professor friend who also had read the copy you sent."

"We have not been so patient about hearing back from you on the results, Michael," Adrian chimed in. "In fact, we all lost some sleep preparing the reports and then we've lost more sleep waiting to hear how it went."

"Well, do understand professors take their sweet time reviewing anything, and in this case two professors went through it in detail. My friend had a colleague review both reports as he felt he lacked the best skill to evaluate the details. Anyway, don't worry a second longer. They found the work we have done to be some of the best work they have read reconciling the whole religious issue of faith and science. Both felt that although the actual research work done was short of what they would expect to see in a graduate dissertation, the contacts made with notable scientists more than made up for that deficit. Essentially, you researched the researchers, and they were duly impressed by your reports on both Question #1 and Question #2. I did return with the notes they made. I would ask you to consider their comments and modify your write-ups appropriately."

"Wow, you don't know what a relief that is to all three of us. We put so much time and sweat into doing the best job we could and it is an enormous relief to hear that the premise of what we did is on target. These were not easy questions to answer and to know we did it is amazing," Rachel exclaimed.

"Do understand, Rachel, not everyone will agree with our conclusions. The Christian literalists will still say the world was created in six days. The literalists will still say Adam and Eve were the first humans and they were born 6,000 years ago. So we need to understand that where our view concludes that science and creation are compatible in terms of Divine Design, in fact, it still will offend some people. But as my old prof commented, 'it wasn't long ago that most people thought the world was flat'."

Adrian asked, "Did Thomas feel we had missed any important facet to our Divine Design conclusion?"

"Yes, in fact, let me get my notes on what he said." Michael searched his papers and withdrew a sheet of paper with his handwriting all over it. "Okay, this is what I was looking for. I am so glad you asked your question, Adrian."

"Thomas had one point, but he did not see this as a major issue in our findings. He said that the Divine Design of the human species should clearly state that it includes the body, mind and soul of a person. He felt it would be consistent with our other findings."

Michael asked, "Can we include this in our work to state that this is an important facet of Divine Design?"

After a short discussion the group agreed. Following that decision Adrian asked, "I suppose they had few if any issues with our conclusions related to atheists and agnostics?"

Michael answered, "They were both pleased we spent the time talking to our friend at the University of Washington. One of them had read articles written by Professor Devane and knew he was highly regarded in that area. So, I felt they agreed with our work." Not hearing any other questions, Michael continued, "I suggest you take the next few days before our Christmas break and update your reports on Questions #1 & #2. Is that reasonable?"

"Shouldn't be a problem," Adrian stated. Everyone agreed.

"Okay, good! But let me say that we are not done with Question #2. Adrian's work was focused on answering the complex and controversial issue as to the origin of humankind. Our simple answer is that as humans our origin rests in Divine Design. However, when we outlined this question we added another part to the question."

"Yes, I remember," Adrian jumped in. "We asked, why were we created?"

"Precisely! After I read your reports, I did not pass that question to them as I knew you had not answered it, but they were insightful enough to ask why we were not addressing that question. I told them that we would."

"Oh my gosh, we were so immersed in the evolution and origin debate that we failed to address that part of the question," Rachel gasped.

"Not to worry! Your work thus far is excellent, and, in fact, we may not be able to give a proper answer to this question until we are done with the next two questions," Michael told the group.

"I think we will be better prepared to answer this part of Question #2 after we've done more of the Bible work that is coming up," Adrian replied.

"I think it would be better if we took a stab at answering this question now and then challenging the answer we come up with later," Nancy countered.

"I like that idea. I think we can give it a good go!" Adrian quipped.

"Me too," Rachel assured.

"Okay, let's take a run at it right now," Michael stated.

Everyone agreed. They took a short break and reconvened. Rachel led the group in prayer seeking wisdom through the written word. Michael wanted to lead off as he had put a sleepless night or two arranging his thoughts on this matter.

"I believe we outlined our first question on whether God is believable correctly. Our second question is in two parts. First, as Adrian has suggested, we should be asking 'what is the origin of the human species'? Having answered the first part, we need to ask 'why were we brought into this world?' That makes me think that having two questions blended into what we call Question #2 means they are closely related. Hence, the answer to why we are here is partly buried in what God has told us about our creation and partly buried in what God has not told us."

"Let me first address what God has not told us. God has not told us the full account of His creation of the heavens. Moses tells us that God created the heavens and the earth. But how little is it that we understand the heavens? How little is it that we know of the 'fallen angel' who becomes Satan?" He continued:

> *"We do know that Jesus calls us to faith like a child, realizing that without a full understanding of heaven and what has*

transpired over time in heaven we must rely on faith and trust in the Lord for our salvation.

- *We know that God created us in His image. We've determined that is largely a spiritual likeness as opposed to a physical likeness. In Vermont I came to the realization that God simply wants us to be like His Son Jesus. He wants us to love the Father as the Creator and to love others as we love ourselves. If this is correct, then God does have a very explicit purpose in creating us.*

- *To carry that further, think about the reasons God would have created us to have the same spiritual likeness as He. This is crucial to understanding why He created us.*

- *With all the hosts in heaven there was no one like us. The angels in heaven were created in heaven. We, on the other hand, were created outside of heaven and given great latitude to behave righteously or to do evil.*

- *It is our soul's determination that renders good works leading to the pleasing of God. This spiritual freedom which we cherish can please our Creator. On the other hand, if this freedom causes us to sin we distance ourselves from God and He is displeased with us."*

- *Basically, we are a unique creation. We are the very center of God's creation in the world He created for us. It is our choice whether we serve Him and those around us.*

- *Beyond all that transpires on earth God has a definite time clock running when He will bring an end to the world as we know it and bring all who have His Godly heart and all who love His Son into a new kingdom.*

- *Basically, God created us to love as He loves. He had to sacrifice His only Son in the process to reconcile our sinful nature, but He knows the love in a person's heart and He*

> *intends to make a place in heaven for all those souls who possess a loving soul."*

Finishing his thoughts, "This is the short answer as to why we were created. The rest is mystery."

"Wow, you have spent some time on this one!" Adrian said.

"No kidding. I am glad I had the recorder running," Nancy added.

"Thank you for covering that," Rachel had a tear rolling down one cheek and she fought to keep it from being more.

"As they say in the news business, I think that sums it up pretty well. Print it and let's move on," Adrian smiled.

"Okay, enough of that," Michael responded. "Let's get that copied so we all have a copy and let's keep the subject open as we go along. Anyone should feel free to add comments. We can review the whole matter months down the road."

"What I do want to run by you three is a schedule for our first session on the prophets. I would like to start with Moses and go through the first five books of the Bible looking for evidence that God sent Jesus as a savior/messiah or a prophet. This will cause us to cover much of the Bible and will further our understanding of God's plan for us."

"I would like us to go to different locations for these sessions if that is okay?"

Everyone agreed.

Part Three

The Savior

24

Mercer Island, Washington

It was a full week before the team convened for their next staff meeting. Michael had warned everyone that it would be a long day and to be prepared to review anything on their minds about their progress to date on Questions #1 and #2, and then to be ready to launch into a discussion of Question #3.

After a warm opening prayer by Michael, he commented that he wanted to go around the table and see what insights, questions or suggestions anyone wanted to share - and said he wanted to start first.

"So many thoughts and emotions have spun around in my head in recent weeks. For that matter, the same can be said for the entire time since we've come together as a team. I would like to share two thoughts today. First, I must admit that I was a secular person most of my life. I was not what you would call religious or even well-churched. In other words, I was thinking more about the world around me and less about my beliefs in God, and, amazingly, I was proud of that. Other than my love of family and friends I was independent. I liked the autonomy of being a person whose only real accountability was to myself, my family, and a few friends. My work was my primary focus and I felt in total control over my life."

"Then following the horrific family loss that Adrian and I experienced, I have gone through a lot of soul searching. Part of me wanted to pull away and retreat into the secularism I have always known. Yet, part of me wanted to follow the love of my life to a reconciliation with God, and a transformation to being more like my wife, and, hence, more like Jesus, because I have seen Jesus through the life and work of Mary."

"This is a long way of saying that I think we need to hit secularism head-on. No softball tosses from what we are seeing and believing. I believe secularism is a choice just like Christianity is a choice. Furthermore, that choice has consequences and it is important that we make people think of those consequences. Society in today's modern world makes it too easy to not think of the consequences of being secular. And as Christians we are too accommodating."

"I would like us to adopt a statement on secularism. The only accountability in secularism is to oneself. In Christianity one has to accept the fact that he or she is accountable to Christ Jesus. Entrusted in that belief in Jesus is the promise of eternal life to those who accept His sacrifice on the cross as the reconciling act to God. Therefore, each person must chose to be accountable to God through their belief in Christ or to be accountable to themselves. Therefore, step up and pick one!"

"I have been faced with that call to pick one and I now stand with Christ. I plan to live my life in a way that is a testament to that decision. I plan to one day join Mary in heaven and thank her for showing me the wayward path of my past and the blessings of following Jesus. This she always did through love."

Rachel asked if Michael would remain seated and then asked Nancy and Adrian to join her. She stood and placed her hand on Michael. Nancy and Adrian did the same. Rachel proceeded to say a beautiful prayer over Michael. It ended with Michael in tears. The group took a short break and then returned.

"Wow," Michael continued, "thank you all. I needed to say that and I appreciate your prayer more than you will ever know. Let me continue on to the second point. Relative to our conclusions on the fact that man was created in God's 'image,' I know we all accepted the important point that this may well pertain more to the fact that man and woman are endowed with a soul than to any similarity in appearance."

"I simply want it noted that in Exodus we are given a few words about God's appearance that we should acknowledge. These are God's words in Exodus 33: 21-23:"

'Then the Lord said to Moses, There is a place near me where you may stand on a rock. When my glory passes by, I will put you in a cleft in the rock, and cover you with my hand until I have passed by. Then I will remove my hand and you will see my back; but my face must not be seen.'

"When I recently read this scripture I came to believe that it is likely that in some way we may have a similar outward appearance to God. Also, it may indicate that we share similarities in design. Since God is in spiritual form it seems reasonable to think we will be in spiritual form later. Then I searched scripture for a better understanding. I found a few readings that made me think even more that we may look like God."

"I found in the Book of John, Chapter 12:44-45 it says:"

'Then Jesus cried out, 'When a man believes in me he does not believe in me only, but in the one who sent me. When he looks at me, he sees the one who sent me.'

"Then in Acts 17:29-31, Paul tells us:"

'Therefore since we are God's offspring, we should not think that the divine being is like gold or silver or stone- an image made by man's design and skill. In the past God overlooked such ignorance, but now he commands all people everywhere to repent. For he has set a day when he will judge the world with justice by the man he has appointed. He has given proof of this to all men by raising him from the dead.'

"In 2 Corinthians 4:4 Paul tells us:"

'The god of this age has blinded the minds of unbelievers, so that they cannot see the light of the gospel of the glory of Christ, who is the image of God.'

"I simply believe we should acknowledge these scriptures in our work dealing with mankind's creation 'in God's image.'"

Adrian said, "Sounds good to me and it fits perfectly well in our work. In fact, it helps us relate to God to have that similarity to God."

"Okay who wishes to go next?"

Adrian stepped in and said, "Wow, I don't have anything quite so deep as what we just heard from Michael, but I do have a couple of things to bring up. First, I find myself missing something I need and perhaps most of us need. That is, after all the work we've done to date and all the places we have visited to gain knowledge about mankind's creation, we have not gone to the Holy Land. I feel like I am missing a key component of what I must do to put the work we've done into its proper perspective. I feel it is difficult for us to talk about Jesus in such depth without going and seeing firsthand the place he lived, taught, and died. I don't know how the rest of you feel, but I really need to go on a pilgrimage to better put what I read into context."

Rachel added, "I have always wanted to go to the Holy Land, but it seemed so far away and I simply could not afford it. I agree with Adrian. I feel the need to go. I would love to see us all go."

Nancy quietly said, "I am an old lady and I don't travel so well these days. Besides, I am so firm in my faith I absolutely do not need to go there. I have read many books and I feel like I have been many times. Still, I think you three need to go. I can hold down the fort while you go, if Michael is in favor of the trip."

Michael smiled, "I have always known that a trip to Israel was going to happen. It is a question of when is the best time. I think Nancy is right in that the three of us should go together. But I firmly believe we need more study time of the Old Testament and, perhaps the Gospels before we go. It will mean more if we push through the study work first. So, if you are okay with the idea I'll promise a trip to the Holy Land in a few months."

"I can wait." said Adrian.

"Me too," added Rachel.

Adrian continued, "My second point comes from some of my readings in the Bible. I love the gospel of John. It really touches me and I am drawn to it. I believe we need to incorporate the first 31 verses of Chapter 14 in our work around the purpose of humanity. If you will indulge me I would like to read the passage and see if you agree it should be part of our purpose statement for God's creation of humanity."

Encouraged, Michael responded "By all means."

"This of John's gospel is at the end of the 'Last Supper' and shortly after Judas Iscariot left the room. It reads:"

'Do not let your hearts be troubled. Trust in God, trust also in me. In my Father's house are many rooms; if it were not so, I would have told you. I am going there to prepare a place for you. And if I go

and prepare a place for you, I will come back and take you to be with me that you also may be where I am. You know the way to the place where I am going.'

"Thomas said to him,

'Lord, we don't know where you are going, so how can we know the way?' Jesus answered, *'I am the way and the truth and the life. No one comes to the Father except through me. If you really knew me, you would know my Father as well. From now on, you know him and you have seen him'."*

"Phillip said,

'Lord, show us the Father and that will be enough for us'."

"Jesus answered:

'Don't you know me, Phillip, even after I have been among you such a long time? Anyone who has seen me has seen the Father. How can you say, 'Show us the Father? Don't you believe that I am in the Father, and that the Father is in me? The words I say to you are not just my own. Rather, it is the Father, living in me, who is doing his work. Believe me when I say that I am in the Father and the Father is in me; or at least believe on the evidence of the miracles themselves. I tell you the truth, anyone who has faith in me will do what I have been doing. He will do even greater things than these, because I am going to the Father. And I will do whatever you ask in my name, so that the Son may bring glory to the Father. You may ask me for anything in my name, and I will do it'. If you love me, you will obey what I command. And I will ask the Father, and he will give you another Counselor to be with you forever – The Spirit of truth. The world cannot accept him, because it neither sees him nor knows him. But you know him, for he lives with you and will be in you. I will not leave you as orphans, I will come to you. Before long, the world will not see me anymore, but you will see me. Because I live in you, you also will live. On that day you will realize that I am in the Father, and you are in me, and I am in you. Whoever

has my commands and obeys them, he is the one who loves me. He who loves me will be loved by my Father, and I too will love him and show myself to him."

"Then Judas (not Judas Iscariot) said,

'But, Lord, why do you intend to show yourself to us and not to the world?"

"Jesus replied,

'If anyone loves me he will obey my teaching. My Father will love him, and we will come to him and make our home with him. He who does not love me will not obey my teaching. These words you hear are not my own; they belong to the Father who sent me. All this I have spoken while still with you. But the Counselor, the Holy Spirit, whom the Father will send in my name, will teach you all things and will remind you of everything I have said to you. Peace I leave with you; my peace I give you. I do not give to you as the world gives. Do not let your hearts be troubled and do not be afraid. You heard me say, I am going away and I am coming back to you. If you loved me, you would be glad that I am going to the Father, for the Father is greater than I. I have told you now before it happens, so that when it does happen you will believe. I will not speak with you much longer, for the prince of this world is coming. He has no hold on me, but the world must learn that I love the Father and that I do exactly what my Father has commanded me. Come now let us leave'."

Michael jumped in, "Yes, yes, by all means! Please give this passage prominent standing in our references to God's purpose for His creation of us. It is a beautiful link to our whole approach to understanding God's grander plan. Thank you, Adrian."

Rachel said, "If I may, I would like to highlight some key passages from the Book of Genesis that I want to be sure are tied to God's purpose for mankind. These highlight fundamental things God expects us to do. Many of these are things mankind has done but they have long term environmental consequences that I believe are important to all of us living on earth."

"Please continue, Rachel," Michael encouraged.

"The verses in Chapter 1 of Genesis starting at verse 26 through verse 30 are filled with the expectations God had when He created man. They include an acknowledgement that man would be the ruler of the earth. Man should be fruitful and increase in number. Man should fill the earth and subdue it. Man should rule over the animals on the land and the fish in the sea. Man should use the green plants to produce food. Like I said, these expectations are part of God's purpose for mankind and I don't want us to miss the obvious when we present deeper reasons for us being here."

"Your comments are well founded and something we should definitely include," Michael confirmed.

Adrian added, "Michael, I think Rachel makes a strong point that from an environmental standpoint we need to emphasize mankind's responsibility to be stewards of the earth's resources. I would like to see Rachel bring some of our current issues to light as we frame a reasonable environmental expectation paralleling words like 'subduing' the earth."

"Sounds good to me. What do you think Rachel?"

"I would like to take on that challenge. Thanks."

Michael looked at Nancy, "Okay, any thoughts?"

"Well, well, I don't have anything profound to add. Listening to all the information the three of you have brought up, there is one small thing in the back of my mind. I can't help it, but I have to believe there was a strong sense of family in God's plan. Perhaps it is the underlying reason for creating others in His image."

"See, I ask myself how lonely would it be to be a God with all-seeing and all-knowing powers if there were no family to share it with. You all know I am really enjoying my days with my grandkids. I often think just how lonely it would be to not have any family. A son would be nice compared to being alone, but having a whole bunch of youngsters around is better. Anyway, I can't help but believe we are God's family and He wants us to revere Him as the Grandpa of the family. Just a thought!"

"Oh, my, gosh! What a great idea. I love it!" Rachel exclaimed.

"Me too," Adrian added.

"Nancy, you have a unique way of bringing things into a real-life perspective. I love you for that! Thanks, let's find a place for that," Michael added.

The group broke for lunch with Nancy and Rachel heading to the kitchen to make soup and sandwiches. Meanwhile, Michael asked Adrian to join him in the living room. He wanted some private time to discuss a personal matter.

Michael started, "Adrian, when you returned from your long trip you seemed to have a glint in your eye for Rachel. I haven't seen that since I returned from my trip. Is everything okay between you two?"

Adrian responded, "Wow, I did not know it showed. Michael, since returning to Seattle and getting back to my house I have been struck by the grief I can't quite shake. I see things of Lisa's and Catherine's and I just want to cry. I had this feeling a time or two on the trip, but being on the move all the time kept me from dwelling too much on what I am missing. Rachel has been very sweet and understanding, but when I start to have any feelings for her I feel guilty."

"Sounds perfectly normal to me. I haven't encountered anyone that could take the place of Mary since I lost Mary and I may never. I am so aware though of the blessings I received over the years she was here. I grieve, but I also feel so lucky and blessed to have all we did have. Michael continued, "Adrian, I want you to know that as you work through your grieving that it is okay to spend time with Rachel as a friend if not more. She is a big help to us all, but it is clear to me she has a strong affinity for you."

"Thanks Michael, that will help me with my guilt complex. However, I know it will take some time and I told Rachel that."

"What did she say to that?"

"Well, she understands and she is willing to wait."

"Rachel is quite the girl!"

Michael said, "Okay, last question. Are you okay with the idea of having Rachel along for the trip to Israel?"

"Absolutely, she is a big help."

"Sorry, one more question!" Michael could see lunch was almost ready. "Would you be interested in prefacing the Israel trip with a week in Egypt since the Hebrew people were exiled there for so long? This would be you and Rachel alone. I can't be gone that long, so I will join you in Tel Aviv for the start of the Israel trip."

"That would be fine," Adrian said suspiciously.

"Okay, let's eat."

After lunch the group gathered for the afternoon session.

"I must admit, I don't know if we can top the session we had this morning. I got so inspired by what all of you said. It is so refreshing," Michael smiled. "Let us turn our attention this afternoon to some of the work Nancy has done for us. Rachel pitched in to help and what I've seen before today will help all of us as we move forward with our biblical research. Nancy will take us through a history lesson involving a timeline of key biblical events dating back to Adam."

Adrian couldn't help it and had to ask, "Nancy did you actually witness all these events?"

"Adrian, you keep your mouth shut," she said as she glared at him.

Still keeping her eye on Adrian, she smiled and said, "Fortunately, a lot of people have developed time-lines like the one I am going to show you. Rachel and I looked at many of these and built one based on what we saw as a consensus as to when events occurred. Michael told us that exact dates were not necessary and to use them only when there was overwhelming consensus. Michael wants us to focus on the broader scope of the history leading up to Jesus so we all have the same relative understanding of what occurred and what the sequence might tell us about God's plan."

Michael interjected, "What we are going to see is to look back 6,000 years. Keep in mind the description Moses gives us in Genesis was written approximately 3,500 years ago. So much of what Moses wrote about had to have been passed down by word of mouth. Also, people then largely thought the earth was flat and had very little, if any, scientific understanding. With that said, Moses' writings are masterful and, perhaps divinely inspired. Moses is likely the first of many prophets as well as a great leader of the Hebrew people. Sorry to interrupt, Nancy, please continue."

"No, thank you Michael. Without your guidance I know Rachel and I wouldn't have the product we have. Continuing on, using the genealogy outlined in the books of Genesis and Matthew as well as Moses' description of events, we have prepared an abridged version of key events leading up to Jesus' birth."

Nancy passed out a two-page outline. "On the first page we highlighted the major events from Adam to Abraham. On the second page we highlighted the major events from Abraham to Jesus. So let's go through each page and discuss the highlights."

Adrian piped up, "Already I like what I see. Having read bits and pieces of the Old Testament over the years this will really help me understand the flow over time."

Nancy responded, "Okay hold your approval until we explain the whole two pages."

"Please pardon the interruption," Adrian politely said.

"Interestingly, we have a good time-line from Adam to Abraham based on Moses accounting of each generation up to Abraham. We have two lists of generations from Abraham to Jesus. One is from Matthew, and one is from Luke. Both relate Jesus directly to David, but understanding the years between generations is not available for either list. Matthew's list goes from Jesus' father, Joseph, to his father and on to David and ultimately to Abraham. Luke's list goes through Mary's family to David and on to Abraham."

"At any rate, no one seems to be certain as to when Abraham was born and when he died. There are multiple estimates in publications and we are not in a position to be specific about the dates this important figure in Hebrew history actually lived. We know he lived 175 years according to Moses and for our purposes we estimate Abraham died approximately 4,000 years ago. With these as the basis for our time-line, you can follow from the top of the page to the bottom. Adam was born roughly 6,000 years ago. Based on our belief that Adam was the first man born with a soul in the 'image' of God, and Eve was the first woman born with a soul in the 'image' of God, we have the start of God's plan for mankind."

"The next major timeline event we list is the great flood. Based on Moses' writings in Chapter 18 of Genesis we can see that Noah was alive and involved in surviving the two-year flood about 4,900 years ago. That too is when God struck a covenant with Noah promising to never destroy mankind again with a flood. Continuing on to the next major event is the construction of, and then God's destruction of the tower of Babel in what we now call Babylon. God had become unhappy with the fact that people were not spreading throughout the earth as he had intended. Instead, people had settled in the fertile region of Babylon and simply built a huge tower trying to reach God. God, seeing the utter futility of this, decided to confuse the speech of those in the region with multiple languages. This led to the division and dispersing of the people. All this occurred about 4,200 years ago."

"God then found someone he admired and wanted to bless as the patriarch for generations to come. That person was Abraham. Importantly, God loved Abraham and blessed him. At an old age of 100 years Abraham and his wife Sarah had a child named Isaac. A few years later God challenged Abraham with a mandate that Abraham build an altar and sacrifice his beloved son to show his commitment to God. God stopped the sacrifice when Abraham was prepared to carry out God's request - because Abraham had shown his faith in God. God followed this with a covenant that Abraham would become the patriarch of a great family and have the rights to the land of Israel."

"On the second page we start with Abraham's grandson, Jacob, who moves his family to Egypt when their lands are suffering famine. This all takes place 3,900 years ago and is followed by Moses who enters the picture 3,500 years ago and leads the Hebrew people from bondage in Egypt. As the Hebrew people settle the lands of Israel, they go through a period of being led by Judges. The prophet Samuel is noteworthy in the later stages of this time and helps guide the leaders who would listen."

"This era is followed by a time of Kings starting about 3,050 years ago with Saul and leading to David and Solomon. As the kingdoms within Israel began to divide 2,900 years ago, the first of many prophets entered the scene in Israel starting with Elijah. These prophets provide us with 500 years of interesting testimony on what God had in mind for His people to know. Buried in many of these prophetic messages are clues to God's plans for the Hebrew people, and mankind in general."

"The next major event in the Old Testament is the exile of the Hebrew people following the Babylonian conquest and utter destruction of Jerusalem 2,600 years ago in 586 BCE. As the Hebrew people return to their homeland following the Persian armies conquering the Babylonian empire, Jerusalem was rebuilt starting about 2,450 years ago. As restoration continued, the 400 years leading up to the coming of Christ Jesus ended with the Roman Empire largely in control of the entire region."

"Jesus' birthdate is not entirely clear. It is highlighted in the Book of Luke in Chapter 2 as having occurred while Israel was under Roman rule, and during the time Caesar Augustus issued a decree for a census to be taken. The passage mentions that Quirinius was governor of the region at the time of the decree. Since he was in that post first from the years 6-4 BCE and later from 6-9 AD, it is not certain as to which time period Joseph and Mary travelled to Bethlehem to register."

"Michael read up on the different theories and concluded we should adopt a birth year of 4 or 5 BCE since King Herod was still alive, and there are other references to Herod being involved in having Hebrew babies killed to remove the threat of a messiah rising from the population. This seems to be well collaborated by many other studies. With that assumption, we have a paternal family tree from Adam to Jesus. I hope this helps."

Everyone clapped and Nancy smiled, albeit a sheepish smile. Lots of questions and answers followed. Everyone was pleased to have a common timeline to help with their work.

"Thank you again Nancy. I appreciate you stepping out to do this work and I believe we have just what we need to put into context what we read in the Old Testament. We have a lot of work to do in covering the Old Testament and the gospels to better understand Jesus. Everyone should read Genesis and Exodus before we meet next. More on our next meeting in a minute or two."

Michael continued, "I do want to place one other frame of reference out there for us to keep in mind. It is sort of like the scientific information we dug up on evolution versus creation. In this case it has to do with the earth and mankind being created in six days. Now I am sure some believers are of the mindset that the world was created in six days. Perhaps the days were slightly different than what we think of as far as a day goes, but they believe the words in Genesis just as written."

"Science on the other hand, tells us something totally different. Science tells us that the universe was created nearly 14 billion years ago. Our Milky Way galaxy was created nearly 10 billion years ago. Our sun, our moon, and our planet were created 4-5 billion years ago. Of those that lived on the earth in the time of Moses there were few to none who even contemplated that the earth was spherical, much less, understood what makes up the universe. Hence, Moses had to write in a way that people would understand creation, and he did so in an appropriate manner. Whether he understood more than he wrote it is reasonable to believe he needed to communicate in a manner people of his day could understand."

"I want us to reflect these facts in our final report. They need to be part of our acknowledgement that once again we need to balance literal facts with scientific reason. God's word and science do coexist! God, as creator, has given us a creation with a balance of Divine Design and natural science. Hence, we should seek a balance in reading the words of those who preceded us with the facts we have been able to see since those words were written."

Adrian added, "Michael, I agree. The work on the origin of the human species opened my eyes to the fact that the Bible is correct, but sometimes we *interpret* it differently. We do need to remember to take the time to search for other meanings in the words we read from the Bible. We often may be interpreting them incorrectly. Searching for the 'balance' you mentioned is something that can help us look for the true meaning in the Bible."

Rachel said, "I know I am guilty of reading something and interpreting it my way. Still, all of us should be up to the challenge of considering other meanings."

Michael thanked the group for the meeting and told the group they would next meet at a different location. He told everyone to pack their bags next Monday for a three-day trip to the coast. He wanted to surprise them but he did have to ask them to bring a raincoat and a waterproof hat, as well as a pair of hiking shoes. He then concluded the meeting with a prayer.

25

Lake Quinault, Washington

Earlier in the day Michael received a call from Nancy who was suffering from a bad cold and asked to skip the trip. She said she would cover the office for a few hours but needed to get some rest. Michael assured her that would not be a problem and to take it easy for a few days.

Michael, Rachel and Adrian then left Mercer Island in Michael's car and headed for the Washington coast. They drove down Interstate 405 to Interstate 5 and headed west to Aberdeen. Continuing on their journey, they passed through to Hoquiam and north on Highway 101 for about 35 miles. Had they kept driving north they would have driven along the Pacific beaches south of Forks and then on to the north end of the Olympic Peninsula. As it was, they turned east near the south side of Lake Quinault. From there the road winds eastward into the Olympic National Park and through one of the prettiest valleys in the entire U.S., where large conifer trees of many species grow in this wet region that classifies as a rain forest.

Stopping a short distance off of Highway 101, Michael parked at a beautiful lodge situated on the lake. Michael had rooms for each of them and a meeting room reserved. Everyone unloaded and moved into their respective rooms and then gathered near the massive stone fireplace situated on the north side of the building. The windows and doorways of this lodge provided spectacular views across the lake.

When all three were together and they had taken in the view for some moments, Michael took them outside. Although this had been a mild winter, the rain gauge just outside the lobby door on the back deck removed any doubt about the fact this was a very rainy location. The outside rain gauge measured over 17 feet in height. Enough to track rainfall up to 200 inches per year.

Situated in a virtual rainforest, the wettest of years brings rainfall totals close to topping out the gauge. Winter months require close attention on a near daily basis to keep up with the rainfall when the "pineapple express" brings heavy rain from the southwest. These rain-laden cold fronts originate near the Hawaiian Islands and carry large amounts of water until they hit the coastline of the northwestern states as well as British Columbia. Besides watering a rich diversity of forest lands, the rains turn to snow in the higher elevations along the coastal mountains and particularly in the Cascades mountain range. Glaciers, although receding at a fairly rapid rate, are numerous in these mountain ranges with some as low as 4,000 feet above sea level, while others grace the higher slopes of Mt. Rainier as well as other peaks in the Cascades.

At lunch Michael explained his enchantment with this location. Years ago he had backpacked across the Olympic mountains from the east side near Brinnon, Washington to a national park campground called Graves Creek located less than 20 miles east of the lodge. The hike was about 30 miles in length and took them from sea level to over 4,000 feet at Anderson Pass where there is a small glacier. From Anderson Pass, a steep trail leads down the west side through old growth timber to the Quinault River. He also had fond memories of bringing his family to the lodge each summer.

Mary and Lisa loved to spend time at the lake. Michael became pensive and withdrawn as he fell into his memories.

Adrian looked at Michael with concern. "Michael, is everything okay?"

Wishing to be alone with his thoughts, Michael answered. "Why don't you and Rachel check out the boat-house and see if a canoe is available to take out on the lake? The weather is exceptional for this time of year, however but might not be this way tomorrow. Let's regroup at 4:00 p.m. in the meeting room."

Adrian took the hint that their company wasn't wanted at the moment and did as Michael suggested. They were told there was an available canoe down at the dock, including paddles and life vests which they placed in the canoe before they discovered that neither one had ever been in a canoe. Adrian didn't mind and he was game to head out across the lake. However, Rachel wasn't quite so adventurous.

First, Rachel tested the water and found it to be pretty cold. Freezing was the word she used and she did not want to tip over in a canoe and have to start swimming, with or without a life vest. So after a brief moment, she looked Adrian straight in the eye and said, "I am not paddling across this lake with someone else who has never been in a canoe before."

"Oh come on, don't you trust me?" Adrian laughed.

"Absolutely, I trust you to find our way out of museums in France. I trust you to rush through them…"

Adrian used his paddle to flick some lake water at Rachel.

"Hey!" Rachel laughed as she wiped away the cold water.

In an appeasing way Adrian said, "Okay we'll hug the shoreline and not venture beyond a reasonable swimming distance from the shore. How's that?"

"Sounds great!"

They had a mildly pleasant time managing to zigzag their way a half mile along the shore and back. They were both worn out from the excursion and retired to their respective rooms before the 4:00 p.m. meeting.

Michael opened the meeting with a prayer. "Oh, Lord God Almighty, who has brought us on this journey, thank you for the grace and wisdom that has brought us to this point. Direct our thoughts, words and works so they may be directed to the fulfillment of your will. We petition to you that you restore Nancy's health again. We place our worries in your hands knowing whatsoever you do, you do for the love of us. Lord, we request that with you we will gain a greater understanding of your plan for mankind, specifically now, to better understand Jesus' role in your plan."

Michael explained, "While I was gone for three weeks, I spent time reviewing reference notes from a couple different Bible editions. I collected a lengthy list of passages that I thought would give insight into Jesus and His role in God's plan. However, I want to make it abundantly clear that I believe not all of God's plan is understandable. There simply is no good way to completely understand the fallout in heaven that took place with the angel Lucifer who ultimately becomes the evil one we call Satan."

Michael characterized this point as being one that God, for good reason, has not chosen to divulge to us. "We could speculate on what is not understandable, but we should trust in God and concentrate on what we have been told."

Likewise, Michael reminded the group of the issue as to whether the group should engage in a comparison of other religions. The group had agreed earlier to not do comparative work. They understood that divisiveness would result, and agreed that with love as a central theme in Christianity they should respect anyone's decision to believe as they wished. The group was dedicated to building a stronger case for Christianity and not attempting, in any way, to tear down someone's beliefs.

"Okay, here is what I prepared for us today. Let's look at our questions again."

1. *Is there a God? Is he knowable and believable?*
2. *What is the origin of the human species? Why did God make humans?*
3. *Did God send Jesus as a prophet or as His Divine Son?*
4. *Is there a plan for Jesus' return? If so, what is the plan?*

"We all agree that we have answered 'yes' to the first question. We have concluded that in answer to the second question, based on the preponderance of the evidence available today, the only rational explanation for the origin of humankind is Divine Design. This is predicated on the deficiencies in Darwin's theory of evolution and the overwhelming evidence that humankind originated in a very complex form from a divine source."

"That brings us to the third question. Did God send Jesus as a prophet/teacher only or was he also the messiah? Embedded in the question, of course, is whether Jesus was more than a man. I have gone through hundreds of reference notes and targeted those that dealt with Jesus' birth and baptism, the deity of Jesus, his humility, his priesthood, his incarnation, his ascension, his name as Lord, his obedience, his transfiguration, his similarity to the expected Messiah, and his role in the Second Coming. I suggest we take these references into consideration and build a picture of Jesus' role in God's plan."

Adrian questioned, "So, we are not going to go through the entire Bible starting with page one?"

"Adrian, I really think that would be a waste of time and needlessly drag this answer out for far too many months. It would be very difficult to do that and not get side-tracked every time we turned a page. Keep in mind, the Bible is not a story in chronological order. It is a composition of many books and somewhat subjectively arranged. Fortunately, others have cataloged the Bible in ways that make it easier for us to search out what we need."

Adrian countered, "It seems to me we might miss something in taking this approach."

Michael smiled, "Believe me, having started down the path you suggested, I quickly found myself bogged down in more information than I could handle. I felt my time would be better spent writing computer code for a program to extract what I needed. As I said, fortunately, others have done this well enough to meet my needs. Of course, anywhere we feel the need to delve further into a particular topic we can do it."

"Okay, if you think it will save time and still get to the key points, I am in," Adrian acknowledged.

"I think we should give it a go, and then see at the end of the day if we like the method or not." Rachel added.

"Fair enough," Michael agreed.

Continuing, Michael started, "Okay, we need to deal with Jesus' birth and the prophetic messages leading up to the birth. Let's go to Isaiah 7:14 which was written about 2,700 years ago. Isaiah calls for the house of David to deliver up a child from virgin birth named Immanuel. Reading on in Isaiah, he elaborates that this child will be a *'wonderful counselor and a powerful king'*."

"In the Book of Luke, much like Matthew, Luke describes how Jesus' birth was foretold and how John the Baptist was born before Jesus to proclaim the coming of the Lord. Later in Chapter 2, Luke mentions that a devout man in Jerusalem meets Jesus' parents as they enter the temple and he proclaims the destiny of Jesus to be a *'light for the Gentiles'* and that he will bring glory to the people of Israel."

"Luke does a beautiful job of detailing the way in which John the Baptist paved the way for Jesus. Chapter 3 covers this beautifully. Later in that same chapter Luke gives an important clue that helps us estimate Jesus' birth year and to understand that as a rabbi, Jesus was prepared to begin his ministry at the age of 30. Based on our expectation that Jesus was born near 4 or 5 BCE, we can estimate Jesus' ministry to have begun around 26 AD."

"Just as importantly, we all need to read the Book of John. It is beautifully written, as Adrian has previously noted, and it includes a self-confession from Jesus about his divine nature and his relationship with the Father."

"Any questions so far?" Michael asked.

"You are on a roll. Keep going,'" Adrian chimed in. Rachel nodded.

"Okay, let's shift briefly to Jesus' baptism. Matthew's description of the baptism in Chapter 3 is short and to the point. John the Baptist recognizes Jesus and tells Jesus that he, John the Baptist, should be baptized by Jesus - not the other way around. Jesus corrects John in this, and John the Baptist does indeed baptize Jesus in the spirit of God. The description of John baptizing Jesus is beautiful in that the heavens opened and the Spirit of God descended upon Jesus. Mark, Luke, and John give similar accounts in their respective gospels. All note similarly that the Holy Spirit descended on Jesus like a dove."

"The baptism of Jesus is at the heart of his incarnation as the Son of God. There are a number of related biblical references I want to discuss that address Jesus' incarnation and I see them as important references to his divinity. First, in Chapter 1, John states again that John the Baptist makes it clear that he is not the light but simply the witness to the 'true light.' He goes on to profess that a man was coming who would be the *'true light.'*"

"Later when Jesus is confronted by others he takes on the question of who he is. In John Chapter 8:54-56 he says:

'If I glorify myself, my glory means nothing. My Father whom you claim as your God, is the one who glorifies me. I know him. If I said I did not, I would be a liar like you, but I do know him and keep his word. Your father Abraham rejoiced at the thought of seeing my day; he saw it and was glad'."

"Then in Romans, Chapter 8 Paul tells us the reason God sent Jesus. It reads starting at verse 3:

'For what the law was powerless to do in that it was weakened by the sinful nature, God did by sending his own Son in the likeness of sinful man to be a sin offering. And so he condemned sin in sinful man, in order that the righteous requirements of the law might be fully met in us, who do not live according to the sinful nature but according to the Spirit'."

"Later in Romans Paul says something quite interesting about God's plan. He says in Chapter 11 verse 25:

'I do not want you to be ignorant of this mystery, brothers, so that you may not be conceited: Israel has experienced a hardening in part until the full number of Gentiles has come in. And so Israel will be saved, as it is written'."

"All the accounts I reviewed this evening set a very dramatic stage for Jesus' entry into his role as the Son of God. His teachings, miracles, love, humility, sacrifice, and ascension will further testify to his role as man with God's divinity, and God's blessing as the only Son of God. Lastly, I believe the testimonies and promises we will study regarding a second coming of Christ Jesus, will further convince us of God's plan to use His Son to judge the world and bring heaven to earth."

"Paul also teaches us to respect the mystery of God's presence to us in what Jesus did. He expresses it in his first letter to Timothy in Chapter 3 verse 16 saying:

'Beyond all question, the mystery of godliness is great: He appeared in a body, was vindicated by the spirit, was seen by angels, was preached among the nations, was believed on in the world, was taken up in glory'."

"According to the Book of Hebrews, Paul introduces us in his letter to the Hebrews with a very pointed outline of God's purpose in sending us Jesus. He says in Hebrews, Chapter 1 verses 1-4:

'In the past God spoke to our forefathers through the prophets at many times and in various ways, but in these last days he has spoken to us by his Son, whom he appointed heir of all things, and through whom he made the universe. The Son is the radiance of God's glory and the exact representation of his being, sustaining all things by his powerful word. After he had provided purification for sins, he sat down at the right hand of the Majesty in heaven. So he became much superior to the angels as the name he has inherited is superior to theirs'."

After a lengthy discussion Michael said, "Let's take a break for now and start back in the morning. In the morning after breakfast we will gather back here and finish our discussion on what I've covered this evening. And if tomorrow afternoon looks good we can go for a hike. I know a couple of interesting hikes we can do depending on the weather. Have a good night!"

After breakfast the following day, the group reconvened. Adrian asked if he could interject a few words. Having slept on the topics covered the day before he was moved to mention a few new thoughts.

Rachel asked for another minute or two while she got the recorder up and running for this session. "Okay, we are good to go," she said.

Michael responded, "Adrian, take as long as you need."

"If I may add a few comments relative to our second question on the origin of humankind. All these passages help me fill in a few of the gaps we have in answering the earlier question about man's creation."

Adrian went on, "For example, we may want to note that God may, in fact, have endowed Adam with more than a soul. He may have provided Adam with enough intellect to enable him to rise above other species to 'subdue' the earth. I know the Jewish faith includes that element in their creation picture. I think we should be open to that possibility."

Michael said, "On that point I agree. How about you Rachel?"

Rachel nodded, "I think it is quite likely that God did just what Adrian said, so, yes I agree."

Adrian continued, "Secondly, we have not adequately defined why we think the Christian God is the same as the Jewish God. I believe we all see that to be the case, but we need to show that obedience to laws and tradition are more prominent in the Jewish faith. Likewise, the emphasis on love is greater in the Christian faith. Still, Jesus was a Jewish rabbi reaching out to Gentiles and he certainly felt we should serve the same God. He never said anything to invite the belief that there was a difference. He did everything in his power to teach about the Father and the expectations the Father has for us all."

"We know that prophesies tell us that God is sending to the world a messiah from the family of David and from Jesse's tree. Notably, these prophesies do not name Abraham or Isaac or Jacob. In fact, they mention David and his father, Jesse. I know Christians and Jews may see God slightly different; and, hence, we have different traditions and practices. Yet, the God of Christianity has always been the God of the Jewish people. Thanks be to God for being so loving as to include Gentiles!"

"Well spoken, Adrian. I agree and seeing Rachel nodding I think she agrees, as well. Let's include it in our final report. You both know how I fully expect us to continue to come up with important thoughts and concepts. We just need to work them in as best we can. We'll change or add anything up to the time we finalize and even thereafter. So, keep with the inspired work," Michael concluded. "Do we have any other thoughts that should be discussed before we move on?"

Rachel said she had one. "Do you remember the other day when Nancy spoke up about God's plan for mankind being based partly on His desire to have a family?"

"Of course," they all said.

Rachel continued, "Well, last night I could not get that thought out of my mind. I think it is such a real and wonderful concept that we should make it a major reason for his creation of us. I think we need to elaborate on some of the evidence that points to that conclusion."

"What kind of evidence?" Michael inquired.

Rachel picked up a list, "Mostly a myriad of simple facts. I got up in the night and wrote these down knowing you would ask.

- *First, God is referred to as the Father.*
- *Second, Jesus is referred to as the Son.*
- *Third, Jesus showed great affinity to children in his ministry. In fact, he told us that we had to come in faith like children.*
- *Fourth, Jesus considers his followers to be 'brothers and sisters in Christ.'*
- *Fifth, God set the standards for obedience like a father would in giving his commandments.*

> *Sixth, Jesus emphasizes throughout his ministry that love of the Father and love of others is paramount to God, that is, the first two commandments.*
> *Seventh, God has given us 'free will' and a set of individual gifts just like what we see in children who grow up and express their lives in unique ways."*

After a short pause Rachel continued, "Since doing this yesterday I have one more thought I would like to interject. One change I would make to my family portrayal, is that the Father comes across as both Father and Mother. The love that emanates from the Father is so maternal at times. The soft side of God makes me want to believe he is both the Father and the Mother of all creation."

"Another wow!" Michael crowed. "Yes, wonderful! What do you think Adrian?"

"Listening to you, Rachel, made me think of my own family. Not just the blessings of family at home, but also the blessings of relatives and friends. I do see that love for family in God. Throughout his creation I can see God's interest in wanting to be a part of a family. Even though family is not always perfect, it is something special in our creation, and I have no doubt God's purpose in creation is for him to expand his family to include us. And yes, God comes across with the nurturing love of a mother, as well as the stricter obedience love of a father. I can see your point. Thanks for elaborating on Nancy's concept."

Michael continued, "Okay, that leads us right into the concept of obedience to God and to the example Jesus set. Of course we are all aware of God's desire that we be obedient to the commandments. We know that Jesus reaffirmed that desire. There are several passages in the Bible that add to the concept of obedience and, of course, Jesus' life is testimony enough on the subject, but let's look at a few of these passages. In First Peter, Chapter 2 - Peter describes Jesus as the cornerstone of God's spiritual house containing all believers. Later in the chapter Peter makes it abundantly clear that as believers we are to respect authority and do good deeds that glorify God. Submitting to authority is expected of God's people, even though it leads to suffering as it did with Jesus. For by enduring that suffering, we surrender to God and we are seen favorably in God's eyes."

"In Paul's letter to the Philippians in Chapter 2 verse 8 he says:

'...and being found in appearance as a man, he humbled himself and became obedient to death – even death on a cross'."

"In Hebrews Chapter 5 verse 8 Paul tells us, *'although he was a son, he learned obedience from what he suffered.'* We see that God rewarded him for his suffering by raising him to sit at his right hand."

"Any comments on this morning's passages?" Michael asked.

"I never really thought of suffering as part of being close to God. However, this got me thinking more about why Jesus went to the cross and why we have to surrender to Jesus to be a part of his reconciling sacrifice," Rachel said.

"Like Rachel, I never really thought much about how suffering is tied to forgiveness. I thought, like most, that suffering is something we should avoid. I knew that Paul suffered many pains in his life and he was elated in having to deal with them," Adrian added.

"I believe the Bible is full of men and women sacrificing because of their belief. Much of that suffering comes from a failure to have followed the Lord. Take the suffering the Hebrew people have endured when they have strayed from God. It all emphasizes that God places a very high value on obedience," Michael said.

Continuing, Michael said, "At this point I would like us to take a break. I am getting to a point where I feel I am somewhat over my head. When we reconvene this evening we will have a guest join us, The Reverend John Osgood, who is on vacation this week. He is staying just north of here at Kaloch Beach and has agreed to spend this evening with us and help us get through this important discussion of Christ. In the meantime let's take a drive. It is not raining and the drive should be pretty. Adrian, you grab lunches in the dining room. I ordered them to be ready now. Let's meet in front in 20 minutes. I'll get the car."

They drove to the upper end of Lake Quinault and stopped to see the world's largest Sitka Spruce tree. The tree is enormous and they got someone to take their picture in front of the tree. The sign next to the tree tells the viewer that the age of the tree is estimated to be 1,000 years old (half the time between Christ and us). It is 191 feet tall, and 58.9 feet in circumference. As they drove farther, the pavement ended and they continued driving on a gravel road east, along the south side of the Quinault River. After 15-20 minutes they reached Graves Creek Campground. Parking at the trailhead, they took a break for lunch. Michael assured them that they were here on an exceptional day, as he had fully expected a deluge of rain.

Taking advantage of the good weather, they hiked into the forest on a well-maintained trail for two miles. Large Douglas fir trees dominated the forest along with Western Hemlock and Western Red Cedar trees scattered throughout. Eerie moss hung from many of the trees and the deep soils were soaked from recent heavy rains. Besides being surrounded by this beautiful old-growth forest, a stream ran parallel to the trail a short distance away. They passed a few campsites that looked more inviting as a summer campsite than they did this time of year.

The return hike was quicker than the outgoing one but they all enjoyed the chance to get some exercise. Rachel thought it would be great to hike across the Olympics, although the thought of carrying everything on her back for that kind of lengthy hike, didn't seem quite so exciting.

They returned to the lodge and showered before dinner. Reverend Osgood was a favorite of the group and they all looked forward to the evening session with him. Dinner was extra special. Everyone had salmon, the featured menu item. After dinner they took a 30-minute break and joined in the meeting room for their session with the Reverend. Michael introduced John Osgood who insisted everyone in the room simply call him John.

John opened the meeting with a prayer and said Michael had brought him up to speed on their work thus far that day and he hoped he could carry them through a meaningful session tonight.

"Michael, asked me to do this a week ago before I left on vacation. He helped me understand where he hoped you would be by the time I got here. So, as I understand it, he assures me the group is where he expected you to be and you are ready to press forward. So let me frame where I believe you are and where you are headed. You are wrestling with the question of whether Jesus came as a prophet or a messiah. Essentially, you are searching for the reason or the reasons God sent Jesus. You have covered part of the answer to this question by discussing Jesus' special virgin birth, his baptism, and corresponding incarnation, his role as the 'cornerstone' of the church on earth, his God-given divinity, and his role reinforcing God's demand for obedience. I hope I have that right."

The group nodded.

"My discussion is sandwiched between the work you have already done and what Michael has outlined for future sessions. As I understand it, this will include discussions and conclusions regarding subjects like the messianic messages in the Bible and God's role for Jesus in the prophetic second coming. Is this correct?"

Everyone looked at Michael. "Yes, and I am hoping you can help us with those as well."

Adrian asked, "Sounds good John, and I too would love for you to help us with the rest of our work of understanding Jesus better. But we will need a lesson as to what Jesus did that convinces us and others that he is The Christ. Is your talk going to get us there?"

"Perceptive question, Adrian. I hope my discussion with you frames a clearer picture of who Jesus is. Paired with tomorrow's session where Michael is going to lead you into a review of the miracles that Jesus performed, yes, I think you will be very close. If that does not get you there, then the discussion of Jesus' resurrection is bound to stir your soul. In truth, when your heart and your soul fill with the joy of knowing that Jesus is the true Christ, then you will know. Hopefully, the mind will follow the spirit, not the other way around."

Adrian smiled and said, "Sounds good! Thank you!"

John carried on, "The first point I want to make is that the tradition in the Hebrew faith that relates reconciling sin is through a sacrifice. Please join me and read in Leviticus Chapter 4 verses 1-12." John paused, "Sounds gruesome doesn't it? Not exactly something we see today. Yet, these are the words of God to Moses. Basically, what God is telling us is that He expects there to be sacrifice for sin. In the days of the Old Testament the sacrifice required by God was something of value like a young bull. Still, God is saying that a price must be paid to undo the sin that has been committed. Sin cannot go away without some act of sacrifice. Period."

John then asked, "Why is this important today?"

Rachel piped up, "Obviously, a sinful mankind needed a sacrifice to redeem itself from sin."

"Excellent, my dear. You win the prize!"

"Now go to Paul's letter to the Hebrews and look at Chapter 2 and read the verses 14 to 18." John paused while the group read. "Sounds familiar to what you read in the Old Testament a minute ago. Yes it does! It tells us that Jesus needed to be sacrificed for us. He was tempted like us and he was free of sin, therefore he has been given the power to redeem our sins. Period!"

"Next, let us understand that Jesus serves as our high priest. Again in Hebrews Chapter 4 read verses 14-16." After another pause John continued, "God placed Jesus in the lofty position of high priest so that he could show us the ultimate mercy in his saving grace. Jesus was one of us, and he too was tempted in the same ways we are tempted. Therefore, we have an understanding high priest in heaven."

"Also read Chapter 5 verses 4 through 10." Again John paused. "See how beautiful God's plan fits together and how consistent God remains throughout the ages. He gave us His Son so that he could live amongst us and experience what we on earth experience, and having done that, Jesus will serve as the judge over all souls and will reconcile unto the Father all who believe in him. His reconciliation will be through his own blood shed for our sins."

"Likewise, now read with me Chapter 7 verses 24 through 28. They say:

'...but because Jesus lives forever, he has a permanent priesthood. Therefore he is able to save completely those who come to God through him, because he always lives to intercede for them. Such a high priest meets our need – one who is holy, blameless, pure, set apart from sinners, exalted above the heavens. Unlike the other high priests, he does not need to offer sacrifices day after day, first for his own sins, and then for the sins of the people. He sacrificed for their sins once for all when he offered himself. For the law appoints as high priests men who are weak; but the oath, which came after the law, appointed the Son who has been made perfect forever.'

Here we see again the work of God enabling Jesus to step up as the highest of high priests. This is beautiful in its meaning and it tells us we can count on Jesus to intercede for all believers. This concludes the first of two parts for tonight."

Michael asked for a short break before proceeding. After returning, they entered into a lengthy discussion of what they had heard from John. The session had gone on to the point where Michael asked

John if he could return the next morning to finish. He said he would prefer that and he might bring his wife along. They agreed on a time to meet for breakfast and bid each other good night.

The next morning John and his wife Alice arrived to have breakfast with Michael, Rachel and Adrian. Alice had been to the lodge many times in the past and considered it a favorite spot. She loved the view and especially sitting on the back deck during the summer on a clear day. This time of year she loved sitting by the fireplace reading a good novel.

After breakfast, Michael and Adrian loaded the car with their bags and checked out of the lodge even though they had the meeting room reserved till noon. They met the rest of the group in the meeting room to finish what they had worked on the previous evening. Alice pulled up a chair near the table and pulled out her knitting. She was happy to listen and knit she said.

Michael asked John to open the meeting with a prayer and he graciously did. Michael thanked both John and Alice for being available and told the group that John would try and make one or two of the future meetings involving their planned biblical work.

John said he had enjoyed the session they had the prior evening and hoped this mornings' session would be as helpful. He then asked the group to turn to the book of Matthew Chapter 2. "I want to take you through eight different passages this morning that I feel are important to cover as part of your effort to understand Jesus' role as Lord. These passages come from different witnesses/writers and from different times and they help define the position Jesus was given by God."

"The passage in Chapter 2 is a familiar one about the three kings. But it is important to note that Bethlehem, which is located four or five miles south of Jerusalem, had long been believed by the Jews to be the town from which the messiah would come. Paired with the fact that Jews believed the messiah would rise from the house of David, Jesus' birth in Bethlehem was clearly foretold. Combined with the visit from the Magi looking for the future king of the Jews, King Herod decided to search for the child and kill him. Of course, Joseph and Mary had been warned by God to take their son and escape to Egypt, and they did so. This story shows that God's plan from at least 1,000 years earlier included bringing Jesus to earth as a child. The timing was God's choice and, no doubt, part of God's plan as well."

"Continuing on, let's look at Luke Chapter 2. Here Luke tells us of another separate event that foretells of the birth of the Christ and points directly to Jesus. This is the story of shepherds in the field who are approached by an angel from heaven. In verses 10-12 the angel tells them,

'I bring good news of great joy that will be for all the people. Today in the town of David a Savior has been born to you; he is Christ the Lord. This will be a sign to you: You will find a baby wrapped in cloths and lying in a manger.'"

"Ultimately the shepherds went to Bethlehem and found Jesus. Later in that same chapter there is a story about a devout man called Simeon who spent much of his time in the temple in Jerusalem. This man had been told by God that before he died he would see the Christ. When Mary and Joseph brought Jesus to the temple to be consecrated Simeon took the baby in his arms and praised God. Later in verses 30-32 Simeon says,

'For my eyes have seen your salvation, which you have prepared in the sight of all the people, a light for revelation to the Gentiles and for the glory to your people Israel'."

"Through Simeon, God tells us that Jesus is Lord over both the Jews and the Gentiles. This helps us tie the two faiths to the same God and realize that we are all brothers and sisters in Christ, who is in The Father."

"Now let's go to the book of John and look at Chapter 1 verses 17-18. John says,

'For the law was given through Moses; grace and truth came through Jesus Christ. No one has ever seen God, but God the One and Only, who is at the Father's side, has made him known'."

"Therefore, one of the major reasons for Jesus to have come amongst mankind was *to make God known to us*. Up till that point in time God had not revealed himself so fully to the Gentiles as he had to the Jewish people. Jesus made this possible and he did it." Following some good discussion, John moved on. "I want you now to turn to Paul's letter to the Romans and go to Chapter 10. First read verse 4 where it says,

'Christ is the end of the law so that there may be righteousness for everyone who believes.'

This tends to lead us to an understanding that Jesus ushers in an entirely new era. He opens God's redemptive love to anyone who believes in the Lord and, hence, in the Father. Another emphatic reason for his coming!"

At this point the group needed a break and took a good long one with small discussions going on amongst all.

John started again, "Okay the last verse provoked a lot of comments. I think the next few verses will help narrow some of the concerns you have about the broad nature of the previous verse. So bear with me as we jump ahead in that same Chapter to verses 9 through 13." They read,

'That if you confess with your mouth, Jesus is Lord, and believe in your heart that God raised him from the dead, you will be saved. For it is with your heart that you believe and are justified, and it is with your mouth that you confess and are saved. As the Scripture says, 'Anyone who trusts in him will never be put to shame. For there is no difference between Jew and Gentile – the same Lord is Lord of all and richly blesses all who call on him, for everyone who calls on the name of the Lord will be saved'."

"Now don't you see how Jesus brings together both Jew and Gentile? This is undoubtedly one of Jesus' primary goals."

Rachel jumped in, "Wow, Paul makes that so clear. I had not thought of it quite that way. I have always felt the Jewish faith was a separate faith with the same God, but this sounds more like we as Christians are, in fact, brothers and sisters with our Jewish believers."

"Well, many of our Jewish brothers and sisters have not accepted Jesus yet. In fact, the Jewish world suffers every bit as much as our Christian world does with increased secularism," John added. "Okay, carrying on, Paul helps us understand how God has given each person unique gifts. He tells us that it is the combination of all these gifts where we really find the body of believers. In Chapter 12 he makes the case that each function of the body is as important as any other. So too is the body of Christian believers."

"Later in Chapter 13 Paul tells us that of three gifts including faith, hope and love, love is the greatest. It is what God the Father and God the Son have shown to us from creation to salvation. This virtue in Jesus is part and parcel of the package Jesus brought to us. It is at the center of his relationship with the father and his relationship with us."

"In Paul's letter to the Philippians he makes note also of the genuine humility that Jesus had in his ministry and the fact that we should adopt a similar demeanor. In Chapter 2 verses 3 and 4 Paul tells us,

'Do nothing out of selfish ambition or vain conceit, but in humility consider others better than yourselves. Each of you should look not only to your own interests, but also to the interests of others'."

"We could go on and on if we had the time, but I think it best that we move along. I have one more passage to share and then I will be done. Is everyone okay with that?" Seeing no objection, John continued. "Let's turn our attention to Paul's letter to Titus, and, specifically, Chapter 2 verses 11 and 12. They read,

"For the grace of God that brings salvation has appeared to all men. It teaches us to say no to ungodliness and worldly passions, and to live self-controlled, upright and godly lives in this present age, while we wait for the blessed hope - the glorious appearance of our great God and Savior, Jesus Christ'."

"These passages, in combination, help us understand that Jesus is the Lord from God the Father. He possesses traits that make us want to be like him and he encourages us to do so. Our individual nature and gifts are well regarded by the Lord and he sees each of us as equally important to the full body of believers. These passages are intended to be instructive to all believers, and fully inclusive, as well. Also, they raise hope for the time ahead when God returns Christ Jesus to the world."

Michael stood up and thanked John for being so helpful. He thanked Alice for letting the group share some valuable time with the two of them today. He asked Rachel to send a copy of the meeting transcript to John so he could review what was recorded for accuracy and proper context. Lastly, he presented Alice with a two-pound box of her favorite chocolates. She was thrilled!

26

Leavenworth, Washington

A week and a half later on a Sunday the group headed north on Interstate 405. Nancy was back with the others and glad to be feeling better. She had read the meetings notes that Rachel had transcribed and was impressed with the work they had done. She was happy to join them for this excursion.

Finishing his worship service schedule in a couple of hours, Reverend John Osgood had agreed to join them for their Sunday evening session and the Monday sessions, but would have to return home late Monday. Alice was not going to be able to join John on the trip as she had a couple of welcoming visits to make, to greet two older ladies who were joining the church.

John had enjoyed his visit with the group at the Quinault lodge so much that he told Michael that he would be happy to lead the first two or three sessions at Leavenworth. Michael was even more thrilled!

The drive for the group of four took just over two hours. Leaving Interstate 405 north of Redmond, Washington they drove northeast on Highway 522 to Monroe. There they turned east on Highway 2 and enjoyed the mountain scenery for the next 85 miles, at which point they reached Leavenworth.

Leavenworth is a site originally populated by Native Americans. Members of the Yakima, Chinook, and Wenatchee tribes originally settled, hunted, and fished in the area. In 1890, the original town was built when the Great Northern Railway constructed and operated a rail line to the area for logging products. When the logging business slowed, the rail company closed the line and rerouted train traffic. The town all but died.

Then in the 1960s, civic leaders in the town decided to make a dramatic change to the town by converting it to a Bavarian motif. They embarked on a campaign to get business owners to embrace the conversion of the town to look like a Bavarian Village. The result is a thriving tourist trade. And, the alpine setting of the town is a perfect backdrop to the architecture of the relatively new town.

After checking into the hotel near Front Street, Michael invited everyone to an early dinner at a nearby German restaurant. Beforehand, everyone had time on their own to walk the streets and do a bit of shopping. Michael told everyone to join him in the meeting room at the hotel at 7:00 p.m. and that John would join them and lead the session.

Nancy decided to take a rest, so she stayed in the hotel. Michael wanted to get ready for the session, so it was Rachel and Adrian who struck out to see the sights. Both had been to Leavenworth before and they knew their way around pretty well. They both seemed to enjoy browsing. In fact, increasingly they were enjoying each other's company, but still avoided speaking much about it.

After everyone returned from dinner, they met and commented on what wonderful German food they had just eaten. The sauerbraten had been one of the favorites. Michael asked Nancy to open the meeting with a prayer. She included a petition for the Lord to watch over the grandkids while she was gone. Everyone smiled at that.

Michael explained that the meetings they were going to have on this trip were to highlight many of the remarkable things Jesus did that distinguish him not only as a teacher, priest, and prophet but as someone who truly has godly powers. John was going to use this first session to highlight many of the miracles Jesus performed. The following sessions on Monday and Tuesday morning would highlight the transfiguration of Jesus, Jesus' appearances after his crucifixion and resurrection, and Jesus' ascension to heaven. He hoped this collection of facts would reinforce anyone's belief in Jesus being The Christ.

John asked the group, "Tell me how many of Jesus' miracles are recorded in the Bible?"

"I can think of a half dozen or so right off, so I'll say 12," Rachel guessed.

Adrian thought for a minute and said, "I'll guess 10, but I bet Jesus performed hundreds that never made it in the Bible."

Nancy, said "I know he did a lot. And I bet he did a lot that aren't in the Bible too. So I'll guess 15."

Michael said, "I've read the Bible more in the last few months than I did in all the years leading up to this past year. I'll say two dozen."

John responded, "Good guesses, all of you. I actually have a list from my old seminary days and it shows a total of over 30. So, Michael you win! Your prize is a tasty Bavarian cream doughnut from the German bakery down the block. Enjoy!"

Michael enthusiastically accepted the pastry and grabbed a cup of coffee to enjoy with it.

"Okay Rachel, you said you thought of some right away. Why don't you tell us a miracle that resonates with you," continued John.

"Well, if I had to pick one, I would say the paralytic man who was lowered by his friends to Jesus. The faith and determination these four men showed is amazing. I can just see them approaching the house where Jesus was preaching and the dismay they first felt when they saw how crowded it was. There was no way they could get their friend through the front door. Instead of waiting outside they found a way to get the paralyzed man on the roof. They had to dig a hole through the tiles right over Jesus! I mean, it had to be raining dirt on the people in the house. Then these friends found a way to lower the immobile man on a mat through the hole and down to Jesus. Their faith was so strong to have done all that, and Jesus recognized this. He healed the man right there."

"Very good Rachel. The account of this story is found in all of the gospels, if I recall correctly. It shows the great faith these men put into action. Still, after Jesus heals the man, the Pharisees and teachers considered Jesus' words to be blasphemy because only God could forgive sins. Jesus rebukes them and says he is the Son of Man, and God gave him authority to forgive sins."

John then asked Nancy, "Do you have any miracles that stand out to you?"

"Yes, but I believe Jesus performed this miracle more than once. Healing the blind has always struck me as particularly beautiful. I have a niece who became blind early in life. She was just a baby really. I see her struggle and know that the things we take for granted every day are a challenge for her. So many times I have wished and prayed for her sight to be restored. I cannot imagine the joy experienced by those people Jesus touched. Still, Debbie, my niece, is the most seeing person I know. She senses more in people than people who have their sight. She is amazing in her faith. She is a constant reminder to me that we are all blind in some way and through Jesus we can be healed."

"Absolutely, thank you for sharing that Nancy." John continued addressing the group. "Nancy is correct in that there are instances where Jesus is witnessed healing the blind. I have three accounts on the list I brought today, which is not a comprehensive list, but includes those that were well witnessed. I will pass this around now, and reference the accounts Nancy mentioned."

RECORDED MIRACLES OF HEALING

Mark 1:40-42	*Heals leper*
Matthew 8	*Heals paralytic*
Luke 4	*Heals fever*
Luke 5	*Heals paralytic*
Matthew 9:27	*Heals the blind*
Mark 3	*Heals lame hand*
Mark 7:24	*Removes demon*
Luke 18:35	*Heals blind man*
Mark 8:22	*Heals blind man*
Luke 13:10	*Heals crippled woman*
Luke 17:11	*Heals lepers*
John 5	*Heals invalid*
Luke 22:47	*Restores severed ear*
John 2	*Turns water to wine*

"We can find the first accounting where Jesus heals the blind in Matthew Chapter 9 starting with verse 27. This account tells us two blind men were following Jesus. Because they believed he could heal them Jesus did just that. Likewise, he goes on to heal a man who was demon-possessed and could not speak. Jesus drives out the demon and the man begins to speak. All in the presence of witnesses!"

"The next accounting is found in Mark Chapter 8 starting with verse 22. In the town of Bethsaida a blind man was brought to Jesus and begged Jesus to simply touch the man. Jesus took the man out of the village, spat on the man's eyes and touched his eyes. The blind man was no longer blind. He could see people. Jesus continued to put his hands on the man's eyes until he could see clearly. Again, he did not want to draw attention to what he had done and he asked the man not to return to the village."

"Finally we'll look at Luke Chapter 18 starting with verse 35. Here Jesus nears the Galilean city of Jericho and finds a blind man sitting by the road. The man calls out to Jesus and finally gets his attention. So Jesus asks what the man wants. The man simply says 'Lord I want to see.' Jesus says to the man "Receive your sight, your faith has healed you.' The man and those around him praised God!"

John glanced toward Adrian, "Adrian, do any of the miracles on the list touch you?"

"Of course, they all do on some level, but the healing of the lepers is rather poignant. While I can't really relate to having leprosy in those days, I certainly have felt alone and abandoned, which I imagine they did as well. When Jesus heals them it isn't just their physical ailments that are healed, He is giving them their life back, the ability to rejoin society as a productive and accepted member. That gives hope to people who are recovering from substance abuse or people, like me, who have suffered great loss and depression. There is comfort knowing that with Jesus we can be healed and feel whole again." Rachel reached over and gave Adrian's hand a squeeze.

"Thank you for that personal testimony, Adrian," said John. "As you can see there are two witnessed accounts of Jesus healing lepers."

"Let's now look at Mark 1:40-42 where Mark tells us,

'A man with leprosy came to him and begged on his knees, 'If you are willing, you can make me clean.' Filled with compassion, Jesus reached out his hand and touched the man, 'I am willing,' he said. 'Be clean!' Immediately the leprosy left him and he was cured'."

"Interestingly, Jesus told the man to not tell anyone, but to go to the priest of the temple so that he could make sacrifices at the temple according to Moses' commands. He did not do that. He told many and the numbers of people who began showing up were so numerous that Jesus had to leave the town."

"The second is in Luke Chapter 17. Jesus was headed to Jerusalem and 10 men with leprosy met him. They called to him and he responded by telling them to go see the priest. Of course they were clean! Yet, only the Samaritan out of the group of 10 returned to Jesus to praise God for the healing. Michael, do any of the miracles here grab your attention?"

"The last one on the list certainly does. It is a popular one and it tells the story of when Jesus turns water into wine. I've heard it mentioned numerous times over the years, even when I wasn't active in church. It honestly didn't mean much to me until I heard Mary's Bible study group discussing it one day. They talked how important wine was in society, especially at a wedding, and the tradition of serving the best wine first and the cheap wine later. When Jesus turned the water to wine it was better than the good wine served earlier in the day. The guests were very impressed!"

John nodded. "Well put, Michael. This is actually Jesus' first miracle and the only one on the list that isn't healing. Let's look at John Chapter 2. Jesus is with his mother in Cana where a wedding takes place. His disciples are with him at the wedding and after all the wine was gone Jesus' mother implores Jesus to solve the predicament. This is one instance where Jesus calls his mother 'woman', which does not denote respect. He is showing that he doesn't take instruction from her. He does, however, turn six large stone jars filled with water into six stone jars with the best wine of the event."

"In performing this miracle Jesus displays the first sign of his power and his glory. The result was an immediate increase in 'faith' of those who were with him. This also displayed Jesus' generosity and his obedience to his mother. I think this is a good time to take a break. Let's take 10 minutes to stretch our legs and then we'll cover the remaining miracles on the list."

Michael refilled his coffee cup and noticed Rachel and Adrian huddled together in deep discussion. He worried about them. He knew they were still grief-stricken over the loss of Lisa and Catherine. A pang of sadness overcame him. He wished more than anything that it was Lisa sitting with Adrian, but he would keep that to himself. He was glad that Adrian was showing signs of being happy again.

John called the meeting back together. "Let's continue our discussion. Does anyone have questions about the miracles covered so far?"

Everyone indicated they had no questions, so John continued. "We discussed one healing of a paralytic, so let's look at the other incident. In Matthew Chapter 8, after entering the town of Capernaum, a Roman centurion comes to see Jesus. He pleads with Jesus to simply give the word that would heal his servant who is paralyzed and suffering. Jesus offers to go and heal the servant. However, the centurion tells Jesus that he is not worthy to have Jesus under his roof, but he knows that if Jesus simply says the servant is cured it will be so. Jesus, pleasantly surprised at such faith, does as requested, and the centurion returns home to find the servant cured just as he knew he would."

"Now go to Luke Chapter 4. This takes place on the heels of the healing just mentioned in Capernaum. Simon Peter lived there and his mother-in-law was ill with a fever. Jesus removed the fever and at once she was up waiting on Jesus and his fellow disciples. Next. We have three miracles that occur on the Sabbath, which angers the Pharisees, for in doing so Jesus is seen as claiming to be equal to God and calling their laws into question. Go to Mark Chapter 3. Here Jesus is, in a synagogue on a Sunday. He finds a man with a shriveled hand. The Pharisees were watching Jesus to see if he would heal the man on the Sabbath, which would be a break with custom and tradition. The Sabbath was not for man to do deeds. Jesus had the man stand in the synagogue and he was healed. Jesus rebuked those who thought he should not heal on the Sabbath, letting them know that the commandment should not be misinterpreted to where it would deprive a person from helping another in need."

"In Luke Chapter 13, starting with verse 10, Jesus heals someone on the Sabbath and is, again, rebuked by those in authority in the synagogue. A crippled woman is healed by Jesus and he confronts those who want to have him refrain from good works on the Sabbath. The crowds of people love him for doing it, however."

"The last miracle on the list is when Peter struck the ear of a servant of the high priest with a sword while Jesus was being arrested. Jesus touched the ear and it was restored. This story is told in Luke Chapter 22 starting with verse 47. It not only shows Jesus' power to heal, but it shows his willingness to avoid conflict as he journeys towards the suffering he must endure to complete the perfect sacrifice for mankind."

"I know that was a lot to take in, but I sincerely hope that helped you understand Jesus' life a little better. I'm happy we got to cover these healing miracles today and I hope it will lead to some good discussion and allow you to make progress on framing the answer to the third question."

The group spent roughly 30 minutes doing just that. And Michael closed the meeting until the next day.

The next morning Adrian led the group in prayer and John picked up where he had left off. "I want to focus this morning on three cases where Jesus actually returned someone from the dead. The last of the three I will discuss is the best known. It is the very public raising of Lazarus. But first, let us turn our Bibles to Luke Chapter 7. This follows Luke's account of Jesus healing from afar, for the centurion's servant. Jesus has travelled to the small town of Nain. He was accompanied by his disciples and a rather large group of followers. As Jesus nears the town gate, he spots a dead person being carried out of the town. The dead man is the only son of a widowed mother and the mother was crying. Jesus felt compassion for the mother and tells her not to cry. He walks over to the coffin and touches it saying *'Young man, I say to you, get up!'* The young man sat up talking and was returned to his mother. The crowd proclaimed Jesus as a prophet and the news of what Jesus had done spread throughout the area."

"It is miracles such as this that made Jesus unique to all that witnessed his works. He possessed power that only could come from God and people knew it. Fortunately, those who recorded these events make it possible for people like us to join them in praising the Father for bringing the Son to earth to teach, prophesize, love and help us believe in the Father as well as the Son."

"Now go to Chapter 8 in Luke and let's look at the scripture starting with verse 40. This story occurs right after Jesus had calmed the seas while crossing the Sea of Galilee to the eastside. A man named Jairus came to Jesus, falling at his feet and pleading for Jesus to come to his house, as Jairus' daughter was dying. She was a young girl of only 12 years and Jairus, who was the head of the local synagogue, desperately wanted Jesus to help her. A messenger shows up before Jesus gets to the house and informs Jairus that his daughter has died. Jesus comforted Jairus and told him to continue believing and that his daughter would be fine."

"Interestingly, Jesus allowed only three disciples and the mother and father to accompany him into the house. Everyone else gathering at the house stood together mourning the girls' death. Jesus tells them to stop crying. He tells them that the girl is not dead and that she is but 'asleep'. The group gathered at the house laugh at Jesus. They know she is dead. However, Jesus proceeds to touch the girl and tells the girl *'My child, get up!'* and she does. Again, Jesus commands the parents not to divulge what has happened."

"Certainly, Jesus knows the story will be told. I believe Jesus preferred that the disciples tell the story later. He certainly wanted the parents to reflect on their faith and not on the notoriety that would surely come if they boasted about what they had experienced."

"Finally, we get to the last miracle involving raising the dead. As I promised, this miracle involves Lazarus. Let's move to the book of John and go to Chapter 11. Besides Lazarus, the main characters in this story are Mary and Martha. Mary and Martha are sisters living in the town of Bethany. You may recall latter in Luke, Jesus returns to Bethany where both sisters attend to Jesus before he makes his triumphant entry into Jerusalem. Mary is known for using perfume on Jesus' feet, and Martha is known for doing all the kitchen work while Mary sits and listens to what Jesus has to say. At any rate, Mary's brother is Lazarus and he is dying at home. The sisters send word to Jesus that Lazarus is terribly sick. However, Jesus knows this is a situation that will help reveal God's glory. He decides to wait a couple more days. Then he returns to Bethany."

"Jesus explains to his disciples that *'Lazarus has fallen asleep but I am going there to wake him up.'* Jesus had to explain that Lazarus was dead. Once they got to Bethany Jesus tells the sisters that *'Lazarus will rise again'*. The rest of the story you know well. Jesus calls for Lazarus to rise and come out of the cave where he had been laid. After a prayer to the Father, Jesus called to Lazarus to come out and he did."

"This ends my discussion of the miracles that Jesus performed. There were many witnesses to these miracles and they have stood the scrutiny of time. No one has ever been credited with so many miracles as Jesus. He stands alone as the one true Lord, the Son of God."

"Still, let me add one important footnote here. Besides the many miracles that Jesus did we should not forget that he empowered his disciples to do miracles in His name. Just as Jesus raised Lazarus from the dead in the spectacular miracle I just mentioned, it should be noted that Peter did the same thing in Jesus' name for a woman in Joppa. Please listen to this account as I read from Acts Chapter 9 verses 32-43:

'In Joppa there was a disciple named Tabitha (which, when translated, is Dorcas) who was always doing good and helping the poor. About that time she became sick and died, and her body was washed and placed in an upstairs room. Lydda was near Joppa; so when the disciples heard that Peter was in Lydda, they sent two men to him and urged him, 'Please come at once!' Peter went with them, and when he arrived he was taken upstairs to the room. All the widows stood around crying and showing him the robes and other clothing that Dorcas had made while she was still with them. Peter sent them all out of the room; then he got down on his knees and prayed. Turning toward the dead woman, he said, 'Tabitha, get up.' She opened her eyes, and seeing Peter she sat up. He took her by the hand and helped her to her feet. Then he called the believers and the widows and presented her to them alive. This became known all over Joppa, and many people believed in the Lord'."

"Miracles performed by Jesus and those performed in his name like the one I just read from the Book of Acts testifies to the fact that Jesus was and is divine. Simply stated, Jesus is the real thing!"

John told everyone that he needed to return home immediately. Alice had called his cell phone and left a message saying there had been a death in the congregation that needed his attention. Everyone thanked John for his help. Michael walked out with John and asked if there was anything he could do. John told Michael who had died and they both knew the lady had been confined to a nursing home for the last couple of years. John said things were well in hand and that he needed to contact the family regarding funeral arrangements. Michael thanked John again and wished him a safe drive home.

The three still in the meeting room had a good discussion of how powerful it was to hear so many of Jesus' miracles back to back as John covered them. It raised their spirits and reinforced their faith in their Lord.

Michael told the group that he had arranged for a tour of the Rocky Reach Dam for the afternoon. He said the tour was his idea to do something fun and that it had absolutely nothing to do with the work they were doing. The tour was to begin at 2:00 p.m. and that they should leave at 1:00 p.m. He left lunch to everyone on their own, but asked that they all plan on meeting together for dinner at 6:00 p.m. and again for a short session afterward at 8:00 p.m. Michael told everyone that he would have the car out front at 1:00 p.m. He asked Rachel to stay for a few minutes. Adrian and Nancy left for the lobby and waited for Rachel.

Michael asked, "Rachel, I've spoken to Adrian about our trip to Israel. I suggested that you and he travel to Egypt for a tour before we meet in Tel Aviv. Is that something you would consider doing?"

"Well, part of me wants to say absolutely, but tell me why would you want us both to go to Egypt? It is not the safest place to go, so why send us there?"

"Good question! The Hebrew people spent hundreds of years in Egypt following a famine that caused them to seek refuge in Egypt. While there, they performed slave work in building the pyramids and other massive stone structures. They performed amazing feats in stone work and stone carvings during these years. All of this preceded their exodus from Egypt led by Moses. So, I would like you to be able to relate what you see in Egypt with what you see in Israel. If nothing else there is a huge historical tie and we should see it."

"Why aren't you coming to Egypt?" Rachel inquired.

"I want to stop in Athens on the way to meeting you in Tel Aviv. If you two cover Egypt I do not feel I need to go."

Rachel added, "As long as the trip looks to be safe, I am in. What did Adrian say? I assume he said yes. Otherwise, I doubt you would send me alone."

"Right on both accounts," Michael smiled. "In fact, you two can decide right up to the last minute on whether you feel safe doing the Egypt tour. If not, then cancel."

"When do we go?"

Michael suggested to Rachel that she line up the Israel tour first, as they previously discussed, for early summer or late spring, and then look for a safe tour group to join to see Egypt. Michael felt seeing the Nile River sights, Cairo and Alexandria would be sufficient exposure to what he would like them to see.

After lunch with Nancy, Rachel and Adrian took a walk around town. Across the street from the stores on Front Street is a city park area. They sat for a while and Rachel and Adrian talked through plans for the trip to Egypt and Israel. Skeptical at first and a bit shocked, Rachel was getting more comfortable with the idea. Although a little paranoid about safety, Rachel felt good that Michael had assured her that they could cancel up to the last minute.

Adrian, having travelled to Ethiopia, said he did not think there would be a problem. As long as there weren't riots in the streets of Cairo, Adrian was convinced that the tour idea was a safe one. He knew the tourism business in that part of the world was a big part of the economy and a country like Egypt would not want to tarnish its own appeal by enabling anyone to harm the tourist dollar flow.

"Wow this will be a bigger adventure than I first thought," Rachel said.

"I am glad Michael is okay with the whole idea of us going to Israel," Adrian added. "I wasn't sure he wanted to do it. It is a good thing he now plans to be there. By then we will have done a whole lot of our Bible work and we will be well into the biblical prophesies about the future. I think it'll be great."

"I didn't think about that," said Rachel. "I have been so engrossed in thinking about Jesus and all he did. Seeing the countryside where he walked. Seeing the Sea of Galilee and the Dead Sea! Then walking the streets of Jerusalem. It is more like a dream to me. Adding Egypt into the itinerary is great too!"

"Rachel, we've been working together for months. I have to admit I am developing feelings for you. Sometimes I feel guilty about those feelings and other times I do not. Being alone at home lately just stirs a lot of emotion in me. I just want you to know how I am feeling."

"Wow, thanks for telling me. I honestly thought you were getting a little more distant lately, so this is a pleasant shock to me. I know you need time to grieve and I admire that you are doing that. I'll be honest with you too. My old boyfriend wants us to get back together, but I've said no. Telling me what you just told me makes me feel better about that decision. Let's just give it all more time and see where it takes us."

"Super, Rachel, you are so understanding. Thanks."

"Adrian, understand I am going through a lesser form of grieving. I really miss Lisa." As she said this she began to cry. Adrian put his arm around Rachel and they sat there comforting each other.

At 1:00 p.m. Michael drove to the hotel's front door and the other three climbed into the car. They drove east on Highway 2 and north on alternate Highway 97 that parallels the Columbia River. After about 25 miles of driving, Michael pulled into the parking area for visitors to the dam.

Michael again explained that the visit had nothing whatsoever to do with their work, but he knew none of the group had been to tour the dam and he thought it would be a fun diversion for them all. The weather was nice and everyone was happy to do something new. They walked around the grounds for a few minutes before their tour was scheduled to start. The dam offers private group tours with an advance reservation. Michael had made the tour reservation a week ahead, so they were locked in. Checking in at 2:00 p.m., they met their guide who was expecting them and the tour turned out to be a personal tour just for the four of them. They were impressed.

The guide explained that the dam was built in the late 1950s and originally included seven generators. An expansion project 10 years later added four more generators. The dam sits on the Columbia River along with many other dams and is located 215 miles downriver from the Canadian border. It is also located 473 miles upstream from where the Columbia River empties into the Pacific Ocean. One of the unique things about this dam is its juvenile fish by-pass system. Built in 2003, the system came on-line to assist the juvenile fish to by-pass the large turbines in the dam, thereby reducing losses of these migrating fish. The group was impressed with the system that can be seen near the east bank of the river.

The group toured the dam seeing the power generators and even seeing right down to fish counters peering through glass windows into a fish passage that guides spawning fish through the dam. Everyone stopped in the gift shop to get their own remembrance of the visit. Then they drove back to Leavenworth, only stopping in the small town of Cashmere to buy the locally-made fruit candy and to sit for a while at the soda counter in the local drugstore.

After a good dinner together, the group reconvened in the meeting room. Michael asked Nancy to start the meeting with a prayer. Again she asked for blessings on her grandchildren. It was pure and honest Nancy.

"Thanks, Nancy," Michael smiled. "Tonight we will carry on with our discussion of Jesus, concentrating our look on Jesus' transfiguration. I'll lead the discussion and review using the biblical references that Reverend Osgood provided. Tomorrow morning I would like Rachel to handle the subject of Jesus' appearance after his resurrection. Here is a list of John's biblical references for you to use. Likewise, I would like Adrian to lead our last subject covering Jesus' ascension into heaven, and here are John's references for that as well. Is that okay with everyone?" Everyone nodded. "Okay, I trust we will be done by 9:00 p.m. tonight, and if we start at 8:30 a.m. tomorrow we should be able to leave here by 10:00 – 11:00 a.m."

Hearing no objections, "Let's turn to Matthew Chapter 17. This chapter follows Matthew's description of Jesus' admission that he will be killed. So Jesus the prophet follows that with an incredible mountaintop experience just six days later."

"Jesus and three of his disciples climb a mountain and find themselves alone high on the mountain. In their presence, Jesus is transfigured with his face and his garments shining brightly. Suddenly Moses and Elijah appear with Jesus and they are speaking. Peter makes a bit of a mess of things by offering to build a shelter for each of the three, but God's voice sounds out instructing the disciples that it is Jesus who is God's son and they simply need to listen to him."

"Interestingly, Jesus, as he often did, gave the disciples instructions not to speak of what they had seen until Jesus is raised from the dead. This so baffled the disciples that they had to ask Jesus about the widely held belief amongst the Jews that Elijah must return before the messiah comes. Jesus straightens their thinking out by telling the disciples that people simply did not recognize Elijah when he came as 'John the Baptist'. He explains to them that the authorities did what they wished to John the Baptist. Furthermore, Jesus explains in verse 12, *'In the same way the Son of Man is going to suffer at their hands'*."

Rachel said, "Another WOW! I am lifted to a new level of faith just listening to that story. It seems like part of God's plan, doesn't it?"

"Absolutely, Rachel, and it is telling me that we are seeing, hearing and believing more and more of a divine plan being played out on the stage of earth," Michael added.

"I'm loving it." Adrian exclaimed.

"Isn't the correct response these days to say 'and the beat goes on.' I love to see you all putting things together in a way that even I can understand. We must be going in the right direction." Nancy was on board with the enthusiasm around the table.

Michael added, "Everyone should keep in mind the fact that Rachel has our discussion recorded and we'll get all these sessions transcribed. Rachel, if you and Nancy need help we can get a 'temp' in to help with all this."

"We might want to do that," Rachel suggested. "We have some trip planning to do rather quickly."

"Fine, then do it," Michael approved. "Now, let's break so we can reconvene in the morning and pick up on the subject of the resurrection. Rachel you will be up."

"Right, I'll be up late tonight!"

Adrian laughed saying, "I'll trade topics with you, if you like."

"Not a chance," she smiled back. Nancy and Michael looked at each other and just smiled.

The next morning it was raining and the wind from the northeast made it cold. Winter was not yet gone. Perhaps snow was falling at the upper elevations and the drive home might be a little longer than the trip to get here. At any rate, the group settled in for their last get-together on this outing.

Rachel started the session with a prayer and then settled into the morning's agenda. "Last night I read scripture in all four gospels dealing with the resurrection of Jesus. Although there are a few differences, the gospels tend to corroborate each other. Basically, the accounts in the gospels depict the discovery that Jesus was missing from the tomb; Jesus' encounter with Mary Magdalene after she discovered his body was gone; Jesus' encounter with two men on the road to Emmaus; and Jesus' later appearances to the disciples."

"So let's take them one at a time, keeping in mind there was no doubt in anyone's mind that Jesus had died on the cross. First, let's go to John Chapter 20 where we find Peter and John at the tomb, having been alerted by Mary Magdalene that Jesus was gone. Peter and John saw the linen and cloth that had been on Jesus and they returned home. Meanwhile Mary stays at the tomb crying. Then Jesus appears to Mary and tells her not to cry. She recognizes Jesus, and Jesus has to tell her not to touch him as he has yet to return to the Father."

"Luke tells us in Chapter 24 that after Mary goes to tell the disciples that she had seen Jesus and what he had said, Jesus is in the company of two men walking to Emmaus. He asks about what they are discussing. Not recognizing Jesus they told him about Jesus being handed over to be crucified. Many were sad because they thought Jesus was the messiah they have waited to see. He told them they should know better and understand the scriptures. He stayed with them overnight and when they finally recognized him the next morning, he vanished."

"Back to John Chapter 20 starting with verse 19, we see Jesus meeting with the disciples. Thomas, however, is missing. Jesus greets the disciples and tells them they must go and spread the word God has given them through the Son. Notably the disciple Thomas was not present at this meeting and a week later Thomas has an encounter with Jesus at a meeting in the same house. The doubting Thomas becomes a full believer during this encounter!"

"Finally, Jesus calls on Peter to lead the way for Jesus by *'feeding my sheep.'* Jesus asks Peter three times if Peter loves him. Three times he affirms that he loves Jesus. This ends the gospel according to John."

Rachel continued by saying, "These miraculous events following Jesus' death were witnessed by many and add to the large list of miraculous acts in which Jesus is shown to be of divine nature. Truly, the Son is in the Father and the Father is in the Son."

The room was quiet and the group took a short break.

Once everyone gathered again, Michael told them that he had checked with the desk and they had reports that Stevens pass had wet snow falling and that it should not be a problem getting over the pass this afternoon. He turned the meeting over to Adrian to carry on with their discussion of Jesus' ascension.

Adrian asked everyone to join him in prayer. Obviously, he had been deeply touched by Rachel's discussion of the resurrection and his preparation to discuss the ascension. "Thanks for allowing me to present this topic. I have never spoken about the ascension before. I have heard it in church but never dwelt on it very long. It was a subject that I tended to catalog with 'make-believe' stories. Yes, I have always believed it occurred, but I did not place it in the same context as I have after studying Jesus intensely as we have during this time together."

"With that said, let's go to Luke Chapter 24 starting with verse 45. Now realize the ascension occurs shortly after Jesus' visit with the disciples following his resurrection. At the end of the visit Jesus informs his disciples that scriptures predict that Christ will suffer death and rise from the dead. This is in Psalms 22 and Isaiah 53. Jesus goes on to say,

'...repentance and forgiveness will be preached in his name to all nations beginning in Jerusalem.'

Then in verse 49 he essentially tells the disciples to stay in the city and receive the Holy Spirit that God will send upon them."

"In verse 50-53 Luke tells us,

'When he had led them out to the vicinity of Bethany, he lifted up his hands and blessed them. While he was blessing them, he left them

and was taken up into heaven. Then they worshipped him and returned to Jerusalem with great joy. And they stayed continually at the temple, praising God'."

"Next, let's go to John Chapter 16 verses 7-11. I want to read these verses because there is a profound message for us in these verses. These are Jesus' words as witnessed by John and they say,

But, I tell you the truth: It is for your good that I am going away. Unless I go away, the Counselor will not come to you; but if I go, I will send him to you. When he comes, he will convict the world of guilt in regard to sin and righteousness and judgment: in regard to sin, because men do not believe in me; in regard to righteousness, because I am going to the Father, where you can see me no longer; in regard to judgment, because the prince of this world now stands condemned'."

"If I may reflect a moment. All these verses that I have read this morning really strike me that God has a very intricate plan that he is working through. Jesus has given us insight into the plan in what I have covered so far. First, as prophesized, Jesus must return to the Father. Second, the Holy Spirit can now enter the world and raise the consciousness of people. Third, men need to believe in Jesus. Fourth, Jesus' sacrifice, resurrection and ascension will lead to the condemnation of Satan."

"I know this may be my interpretation, but boy is it meaningful to me that we actually are seeing parts of a master plan that God is working through."

The group had a good discussion on Adrian's remarks and then he continued. "We've heard from Luke and John so far, so now let's look at what Paul has to say. To read his letter to the Philippians, go to Chapter 3 where Paul tells of the many people who are centered on earthly things. Then in verse 20 he tells us,

'But our citizenship is in heaven. And we eagerly await a Savior from there, the Lord Jesus Christ, who by the power that enables

him to bring everything under his control, will transform our lowly bodies so that they will be like his glorious body'."

"Perhaps this tells us definitively that in heaven we will have a transfigured body as Christ had on earth. Perhaps our look will be much like a pure image of the glory in each of us. Sorry for the editorial notes, but I could not resist. I hope I haven't gone too far with my interpretations?"

Michael said, "Not a problem, Adrian. We are going to have to draw inferences from what we read and what we hear. As long as what we do is backed up with logic and does not run in the face of the written word, I think we will be okay."

Everyone in the group had something to say about the subject of Jesus' ascension. Rachel pointed out that she recently had been in church and one of the Old Testament readings reminded her of Jesus' ascension. She looked it up and asked the group to look at 2 Kings Chapter 2. She read from verse 11,

'As they were walking along and talking together, suddenly a chariot of fire and horses of fire appeared and separated the two of them, and Elijah went up to heaven in a whirlwind'."

Rachel continued, "The images of such an ascension are so dramatic, and I can only imagine the impact it had on Elisha and the company of men who witnessed it. In Jesus' case the disciples are bound to have been in awe as Jesus rose to heaven in their very presence."

After another discussion, Michael closed the meeting with a prayer of thanksgiving for the spirit and knowledge they have gained by studying God's word together. They checked out of their rooms, packed the car and headed home.

27

Victoria, British Columbia

It was three weeks later. Lots of administrative work had been done in the intervening weeks along with one pleasant surprise. John Watson, a friend from the recent past, had heard from Joyce Hillary that Michael had started a non-profit foundation. Michael had played racket ball for a couple of years with John before Mary's passing, but he had largely lost touch with John since then. So when John called, Michael was glad to get together.

The two met at a restaurant in downtown Bellevue and they covered what each had been up to in the past two years. At the end of the meal Michael was surprised when John asked if the Foundation was taking donations. Michael acknowledged they were positioned to take donations, and, in fact, had taken a few. He explained they still had a good ways to go before they were going to have enough information to present potential donors with a prospectus covering the future plans of the Foundation.

Michael had known John since they had each sold their respective businesses in lucrative deals to the same large technology firm. John had done very well in the transaction and that was the first thing they had in common. After they began playing racket ball twice a week, they had a number of opportunities to share their lives, until Michael lost Mary. After Mary's death Michael lost interest in the sport and did not see John often.

Surprisingly, John was very impressed with the verbal report Michael gave. The report confirmed what little he was hearing from others and sparked a keen interest. As it turned out, John had recently been to a three-day event with his church, which left him so energized that he had been looking for a non-profit group to help support. Here he found one. He promised that a check for $500,000 would be in the mail the following week. He wanted to be the first contributor to reach $1,000,000 in donations, and pledged the second $500,000 would be available when the group's prospectus came out, assuming it looked as good as he knew it would. Sure enough, the next week the first check for $500,000 was delivered and seemed to inspire the whole group with the thought that this whole foundation idea may actually work.

For the next group meeting all four of them rode in Rachel's car to Seattle and down to Pier 69 where they caught a private ferry to Victoria, British Columbia. After a two and-a-half hour boat ride, the ferry rounded the seawall and entered the Inner Harbor. The weather was cloudy and cool but no rain. They checked in at a well-known hotel with its majestic view over the harbor. They made it there in time for afternoon tea at 2:30 p.m. This was a genuine British tradition and a real treat. Nancy had been to the same hotel years ago, however the others had never been and they were impressed.

After dinner they met in a very nice conference room reserved for them for the balance of their stay. Michael inquired whether or not the guest rooms were satisfactory and everyone seemed pleased with the old, yet elegant hotel style. Michael opened the meeting with a prayer. He then asked if anyone had any business that needed discussion before starting in on the subject matter.

Rachel addressed the donation they received from John Watson. "Why would anyone give us that sum of money at this stage of our work? I cannot quite fathom why."

Everyone looked at Michael. "I take it the rest of you have the same question?" Nancy and Adrian nodded.

Michael continued, "First, let me say that the amount of money is a relative thing. Just as is the amount of money different people give to the church when they all tithe. Second, John made nearly as much money on the sale of his business as I did on the sale of my business. Third, lots of people need money and lots of people ask for money, so it would not take very long to give any amount away. Fourth, people such as John like to know what people are going to do with the money they give. They want to make a positive difference in lives when they do give money. Basically, they carefully earned the money and they carefully want to know that it is a worthy cause when they give it away. Now that may not be the pure Christian way to look at giving, but it is often the case with the wealthy. In fact, I would say that many people who are wealthy want to have a say in how the money is used. I will not accept money that way. It must be given essentially without conditions. Asking for a copy of our work is not a condition in my mind. It is more of a courtesy."

"So, John goes to an area-wide church for a three-day event. He is inspired to do something and he makes an offer of $1,000,000. It is our obligation to accept it and to use it wisely, so as to reinforce his faith in God. Plus, keep in mind, there are many others like John we will meet later this year or more likely next year, who are just as interested in finding a worthwhile cause to financially support. Giving them the chance to be part of the Foundation's mission is an important part of why I am doing this. It is a chance for me to do this with the wealth God has blessed me with. Likewise, we need to challenge others with an opportunity to support the Foundation in the future as we look to expand its operation."

"Thanks, Michael. The rest of us are not wealthy and we are learning from your insights into the minds and hearts of those who are. If we can unlock the secret of offering what they know they need, namely to be part of our mission, I can see this helping people who I had previously thought didn't need help."

"Good thoughts, Adrian. Just remember I was one of those people not long ago. I am changing and others need the chance to change too. Not all will, but some will. Anything else?"

Not hearing anything, Michael moved on, "We are here for three nights and I hope we can meet in the morning each day; do something fun in the afternoon and then meet after dinner. We return three days from now on the ferry, just in time for the weekend. Tonight we'll simply introduce the subject for the stay here in beautiful Victoria, and we'll read a few verses from the Bible. Thanks to Rachel and Nancy we have great notes from our previous meetings. As you all know, John Osgood will not be joining us on this trip. I did ask him if he could come, but he said looking to the future was not his strong suit, and he wanted us to press on without him. He assured me he would begin each morning with a prayer for us."

Michael said he would lead tonight's talk. He also had made up listings of topics and biblical verses for all the sessions with John's help. He passed out the assignments. Adrian and Rachel got two each and Nancy got one and hers was a shared one with Michael. Nancy was thrilled.

"Let's get started. I posted a summary of our four questions, as they are currently stated, on the wall to remind us where we are on our journey."

    1) *Does God exist, and if so, is God knowable?*

    2) *What is the origin of humankind? Why are we here?*

    3) *Is Jesus a prophet or God's divine Son?*

4) Is there a plan for Jesus' return? If so, what does the return look like and when does it happen?

"So far, we have answered the first two questions and lately we have been dealing with question three by studying Jesus' first coming. Now the Bible doesn't seem to flat out say that God's plan is to have Jesus come to earth twice. Old Testament believers were waiting in expectation of a Messiah. The Hebrew people hoped Jesus would fulfill that role, but their understanding was that the Messiah would lead them into glory. Many had expected the Messiah would come in glory and deliver the people of Israel from Roman oppression."

"Even early Christians believed Jesus would return later in the first century following his resurrection to restore glory to the Hebrew people. Here we are nearly 2,000 years after Jesus' death still reading about the likelihood of a second coming. So I don't think in this week's study work we should be concerned with the 'when' part of the question although we will read hints in various passages. We should study the second coming passages in the Bible and see what they tell us. If we conclude there is strong evidence that there will be a second coming, then our upcoming review of prophesy for question four may render a clue or two on the timing, but that is for another day."

"Thanks for clearing that up. I was concerned we might get overwhelmed this week if we tackled the 'when' portion of the question. I agree, we are not ready for that. In fact, I hope we don't get too far in prophecies till after we come back from Israel." Adrian commented.

"I agree Adrian. Let's go to Paul's first letter to the Thessalonians in Chapter 1. Starting with verse nine where Paul recognizes that others in the region see the faith the Thessalonians have and Paul says:

'...for they themselves report what kind of reception you gave us. They tell how you turned to God from idols to serve the living and

true God, and to wait for his Son from heaven, whom he raised from the dead – Jesus, who rescues us from the coming wrath.' This confirms that expectations were high in the first century following Christ's resurrection."

Michael continued, "In 1 John Chapter 2, let's look at verse 18. John says, *'Dear children, this is the last hour; and as you have heard that the antichrist is coming, even now many antichrists have come.'* Again, this kind of first century language, along with other scriptures we'll read soon, raised the expectation that Christ as the Messiah would come soon to conquer the Antichrist which was believed to be Rome!"

"I do want you to go to the very last chapter of the last book of the Bible. This is Chapter 22 of John's book called Revelation. It has a very important message for us about this entire subject of the second coming. We need to heed what is said here and be very careful to avoid saying or writing anything on God's prophesy that is not written in the prophesy. The language used here is purposely very strict in its tone for reasons we might not totally understand, but God was emphatic about maintaining the integrity of every word prophesied through John."

"In verse six an angel speaks to John saying, *'These words are trustworthy and true. The Lord, the God of the spirits of the prophets, sent his angel to show his servants the things that must soon take place.'* Continuing, the angel passes on the Lord's message, *'Behold, I am coming soon! Blessed is he who keeps the words of the prophecy in his book.'*"

"John continues in verse 8 saying, *'I, John, am the one who heard and saw these things. And when I had heard and seen them, I fell down to worship at the feet of the angel who had been showing them to me. But he said to me, 'Do not do it! I am a fellow servant with you and with your brothers the prophets and of all who keep the words of this book, Worship God!'*"

"In verses 12 and 13 the angel quotes the Lord, *'Behold, I am coming soon! My reward is with me, and I will give to everyone according to what he has done. I am the Alpha and the Omega, the First and the Last, the Beginning and the End."*

"In verse 16 the angel tells John, *'I, Jesus, have sent my angel to give you this testimony for the churches. I am the Root and the Offspring of David, and the bright Morning Star."*

Finally in verses 18 and 19 John says, *'I warn everyone who hears the words of the prophecy of this book: If anyone adds anything to them, God will add to him the plagues described in this book. And if anyone takes words away from this book of prophecy, God will take away from him his share in the tree of life and in the holy city, which are described in this book."*

Nancy smiled and said, "Looks like we are treading on sacred ground to me. We better be careful where we tread in the Book of Revelation. I don't need to have to deal with plagues and that kind of thing!"

Adrian spoke up, "I think you are pretty safe, Nancy. I am glad Michael read these verses early on as we look to the future. We stand well warned and now we need to heed the warning. I had never read this chapter before and I might have been tempted to do something horribly wrong without understanding the consequences."

A good lengthy discussion followed on why these words from John were so emphatic. The group also discussed how they need to approach all the prophetic work that lay ahead in a similar manner as they try to understand God's plan for the future.

Michael got the group back on track after a short break and told the group he had a couple more verses he wanted the group to discuss before they broke for the night. He asked everyone to turn to John's gospel. He explained that the 14th Chapter follows Jesus' prediction that Peter would deny him three times that night. Jesus had already predicted that he would be betrayed that night during the last supper. Judas Iscariot had left the building by the time Jesus tried to comfort his disciples.

"Go to verses 3-4 where John quotes Jesus saying, *'And if I go and prepare a place for you, I will come back and take you to be with me that you also may be where I am. You know the way to the place where I am going.'*"

After Thomas challenges Jesus to tell him the way, in verses 6-7 Jesus tells Thomas, *'I am the way and the truth and the life. No one comes to the Father except through me. If you really knew me, you would know my Father as well. From now on, you do know him and have seen him.'*

Again, the group discussed Jesus' words as captured by John. Everyone had a solid understanding that Jesus knew he would return in the future. Again, the 'when' was unclear to the disciples just as it has seemed unclear to others throughout the centuries that have passed. Michael called for closure and everyone headed off for some reading and then sleep.

The next morning was a beautiful spring day. Michael was elated. He told everyone that he had booked an afternoon visit to Butchart Gardens. Nancy and Rachel were thrilled. Adrian did not seem quite as excited.

Rachel first led the group in prayer and then told everyone that this session was dedicated to some of Paul's writings referencing the second coming of Christ. She asked the group to turn to Paul's letter to the Colossians Chapter 3, likely written in the first century after Christ.

"I want you to read and digest a few of Paul's words on how we should live our lives having accepted Christ. Starting with verse 1 and carrying through to verse 4 Paul says, *'Since, then, you have been raised with Christ, set your hearts on things above, where Christ is seated at the right hand of God. Set your minds on things above, not on earthly things. For you have died, and your life is now hidden with Christ in God. When Christ, who is your life, appears, then you also will appear with him in glory."*

"Now go to Paul's second letter to the Thessalonians, and let's start with the first five verses in Chapter 2. Paul says, *'Concerning the coming of our Lord, Jesus Christ and our being gathered to him, we ask you, brothers, not to become easily unsettled or alarmed by some prophecy, report or letter supposed to have come from us, saying that the day of the Lord has already come. Don't let anyone deceive you in any way, for that day will not come until the rebellion occurs and the man of lawlessness is revealed, the man doomed to destruction. He will oppose and exalt himself over everything that is called God or is worshipped, so that he sets himself up in God's temple, proclaiming himself to be God."*

"This reading seems to tell us that Paul's belief is that the 'antichrist' will first come to rule before the glorious day of Jesus' return comes. Hence, once the antichrist is known the day of the Lord will follow."

This led to some discussion as to who and what is the antichrist. Michael assured everyone that they will learn more about the antichrist in due time.

Paul's second letter to Timothy in Chapter 2 verse 8 illustrates an interesting concept that Paul was looking forward to his gift of a righteous crown following his toils and his service to the Lord. He was picturing in his mind how he hopes to have earned salvation through belief in Christ as Lord and through the many years of service he had in Christ's name.

"In Paul's letter to Titus we find in Chapter 2 a good reminder. Paul says in verses 11-13, *'For the grace of God that brings salvation has appeared to all men. It teaches us to say 'No" to ungodliness and worldly passions, and to live self-controlled, upright and godly lives in this present age, while we wait for the blessed hope – the glorious appearing of our great God and Savior, Jesus Christ'."* Rachel paused.

"I have to think like many early Christians that although he believed a number of things needed to happen before Christ returns, Paul may well have thought the wait would not be too long. Hebrews Chapter 10 verse 25 tells us: *'Let us not give up meeting together, as some are in the habit of doing, but let us encourage one another – and all the more as you see the Day approaching.'*"

"My readings today emphasize all the more how many people must have been expecting Jesus to return in his prophesized glory sooner rather than later. It is so easy for us to be sitting here over 1,900 years later saying to ourselves 'why were they thinking Jesus would come so soon'. Apparently, they did not have any real conception of God's plan. It makes me think about whether we are close to Jesus' second coming or whether we, like them, are just anxious for the second coming to occur in our time."

"Good thoughts Rachel," Michael said. "It will be months before we know how we stand on the matter. We need to keep an open mind and see what comes. I just hope through our prayer and discernment we calmly go about the process we embarked on and see where we are led. Based on our individual backgrounds, I doubt we have very many predisposed hardline beliefs regarding the second coming. Let's just keep rowing the boat, so to speak, and see where we are taken."

Nancy added, "I have always felt comfortable not knowing too much about the biblical past or the prophesied future. I don't know if I can be much help."

"Well, Nancy," Michael interjected, "I've been in the same position most of my life. I am a little blind as to where we are headed, but I believe the process is going to be worth the time and effort."

"I am sort of excited to see where this takes us," Rachel said. "I do know I am learning a whole lot, and I want to finish this so we find out what there is to find out. This is like a big puzzle to me. You start putting the pieces together and if you don't have the puzzle box top or a picture to go by you have to wing it till you start seeing the thing come together. It is sort of a kick to do something like this."

"That a girl! Keep us going girl," Nancy smiled again.

Michael had everyone break to the dining room before noon. After a quick lunch they had a private car take them to Butchart Gardens. They walked through the famous gardens, took pictures, and generally enjoyed the afternoon.

After an early dinner at a nearby restaurant, they watched the sun set with flaming shades of red in the western sky beyond the harbor. The group then met in their meeting room for an evening session. Nancy and Michael said they would make this session short and sweet as they only had four passages to cover. The evening was lovely and a stroll down to the harbor and back would serve to be the way the group would later close out the day.

But first they had their meeting. After a short but sweet prayer asking for discernment, Nancy took the first passage. She asked everyone to turn to Paul's first letter to the Thessalonians Chapter 5. She read verses 1-3, *"Now brothers, about times and dates we do not need to write to you, for you know very well that the day of the Lord will come like a thief in the night. While people are saying, 'Peace and safety,' destruction will come on them suddenly, as labor pains on a pregnant woman, and they will not escape."*

Nancy said, "I am a pretty simple person when it comes to this kind of biblical passage. This tells me we might learn a lot about what is going to happen at the second coming, but we won't know it is coming."

Michael said, "I tend to agree with Nancy. I do think there are two things we need to consider, however. This passage is likely to be one amongst many and we should not be too quick to disregard the 'when' question as part of our Question #4. Secondly, this passage was written over 1,900 hundred years ago and to the extent there are any clues regarding the second coming, we should do a thorough search to see if today it is easier to get close to the 'when'. I don't know the answer, but we need to search for clues starting this fall."

"That's why he earned the big bucks!" Nancy laughed. "Let's go to the book of James. This one is a good one and I think we can all accept it. We are looking at verses 7-8 in Chapter 5. James says, *'Be patient then, brothers, until the Lord's coming. See how the farmer waits for the land to yield its valuable crop and how patient he is for the autumn and spring rains.*"

"I think, that to the extent that there will be a second coming, James is calling for everyone to be patient. I like that."

"I agree, Nancy. I also think James is confirming the belief that when Jesus said he will return, they believed him," Adrian added.

Michael was up next, "Okay, let's look at Paul's first letter to Timothy. Let's see, go to Chapter 4, the first three verses. *'The Spirit clearly says that in the later times some will abandon the faith and follow deceiving spirits and things taught by demons. Such teachings come through hypocritical liars, whose consciences have been seared as with a hot iron.*"

"Before we discuss the previous passage, let me get the last one in, and then we can discuss them together. Again, this one is from Paul's second letter to Timothy and we want the third chapter. Paul writes in the first five verses of this chapter, *'But mark this; There will be terrible times in the last days. People will be lovers of themselves, lovers of money, boastful, proud, abusive, disobedient to their parents, ungrateful, unholy, without love, unforgiving, slanderous, without self-control, brutal, not lovers of good, treacherous, rash, conceited, lovers of pleasure rather than lovers of God – having a form of godliness but denying its power. Have nothing to do with them.*"

Adrian commented, "The first passage says that in the end times, spirits will be turned to evil ways. The last passage is by Paul although in his second letter to Timothy. It relates the same message, but it presses the point that those that are turned by evil spirits will behave in all sorts of evil and contemptuous ways. The list is a long one!"

Rachel added, "It is almost like Satan is given a longer leash and expands his influence in the world as God draws an end to his timetable with Jesus' return around the corner."

"Nancy, what do you think?" Michael asked.

"Well, I am older than all of you and it seems to me that much of what Michael read is happening today. When I pick up the morning paper and read about the happenings in our city and in the nation as a whole I find more damning stories about people than I ever remember. The paper used to have lots of good news stories. Not anymore! I don't know if it is the media doing it or not, but there just seems to be a whole lot more violence and unfriendliness than I remember when I was in my twenties and thirties."

After a few more minutes of discussion, Michael called for an end to the meeting. He wished all a good night and said tomorrow's meeting would start at 9:00 a.m., and the afternoon event would be a tour of the Provincial Museum nearby.

The next day Adrian began the morning meeting with a prayer. Rachel gave a quick update on the status of the upcoming trip to Israel. She said final arrangements were completed for the trip. Trip security looked good for the trip to Israel scheduled to begin in one month. She noted that the three of them scheduled for the trip were to meet the same day in Tel Aviv, and she explained they would be joining a church group from Portland, Oregon that had 15 members going on the trip arranged through a specialized Christian trip organizing company in Idaho. The trip organizer had room for 20 in the chartered bus and only 15 confirmed members of the church in Portland were scheduled to go, so with the permission of the church trip leader, Rachel had booked three of the remaining seats. She thought being with a group would be more fun and safer than doing it with a hired guide.

Rachel went on to explain that she and Adrian were scheduled for a one-week tourist trip to Egypt with a British company that does a massive number of trips there. Furthermore, Michael was booked to Athens, Greece for a two-day stay before joining up in Tel Aviv.

Adrian asked everyone to open their bibles to Mark Chapter 13. He said Rachel would be covering this entire chapter in depth in the afternoon but he wanted to mention one verse to help set the stage. He read verses 26-27, *"At that time men will see the Son of Man coming in the clouds with great power and glory. And he will send his angels and gather his elect from the four winds, from the ends of the earth to the ends of the heavens."*

"I find this striking passage gives us a glimpse into an event that is more dramatic than anything ever seen on earth. Referring to Jesus' return at the end of this age, we are told all souls will be rendered from earth and heaven. This is the second coming of Christ Jesus."

Adrian continued, "Now, the remainder of this session's readings have to do with Jesus' judgment of all souls as part of the second coming. I will not use the book of Revelation for this because I am afraid to try. I'll leave the book of Revelation for someone else later." They all laughed! "I'm going to use one passage from the book of Matthew that pretty well covers the subject in detail. All of us have heard it spoken many times and we need to discuss it in detail today, so we can use it properly in our work to define this important aspect of the second coming."

"Let's go to Matthew Chapter 25. There are forty six verses in this Chapter 25 and I suggest you take a few moments to read it for yourselves. I think you should digest it and then we will discuss it." Adrian gave everyone time to read the Chapter and take notes.

After a short break, Adrian said he wanted to place special emphasis on verses 31-46. He suggested everyone follow his reading. He started with verse 31:

"When the Son of Man comes in his glory, and all the angels with him, he will sit on his throne in heavenly glory. All the nations will be gathered before him, and he will separate the people one from another as a shepherd separates the sheep from the goats. He will put the sheep on his right and the goats on his left.

"Then the King will say to those on his right, 'Come, you who are blessed by my Father, take your inheritance, the kingdom prepared for you since the creation of the world. For I was hungry and you gave me something to eat, I was thirsty and you gave me something to drink, I was a stranger and you invited me in, I needed clothes and you clothed me, I was sick and you looked after me, I was in prison and you visited me."

"Then the righteous will answer him, 'Lord, when did we see you hungry and feed you, or thirsty and give you something to drink? When did we see you a stranger and invite you in, or needing clothes and clothe you? When did we see you sick or in prison and go to visit you?'

"The King will reply, 'I tell you the truth, whatever you did for one of the least of these brothers of mine, you did for me.'

"Then he will say to those on his left, 'Depart from me, you who are cursed, into eternal fire prepared for the devil and his angels. For I was hungry and you gave me nothing to eat, I was thirsty and you gave me nothing to drink, I was a stranger and you did not invite me in, I needed clothes and you did not clothe me, I was sick and in prison, and you did not look after me.'

"They also will answer, 'Lord, when did we see you hungry or thirsty or a stranger or needing clothes or sick or in prison, and did not help you?'

"He will reply, 'I tell you the truth, whatever you did not do for the one of the least of these, you did not do for me.'

"Then they will go away to eternal punishment, but the righteous to eternal life."

Following the reading, Adrian started into his points on the passage. "I don't know about you, but this passage strikes a chord with me. Believing in Jesus as the Son of God means I need to follow him. I need to be Christ-centered in my life. Honestly, part of it is that I want to do that and part of it is that I fear the consequences if I do not do that. So, I am motivated by love to follow Jesus' example, and, honestly, I am also motivated by the fear of what will happen if I don't. Once I really absorbed this scripture, I asked myself what is it that I should do to follow Christ. This passage, more than any other, helped me understand that I really need to focus more of my life on helping others not just in understanding and believing in Jesus. It led me to understand that my belief should be manifested in Christian action and driven by Christian love."

"The first time I read this passage I focused on the question of whether or not I am good enough to be amongst the sheep with Jesus, or would I be found lacking and herded away with the goats. Later, after several readings I came to the conclusion that my faith in Jesus would save me, but I was still left with the question of whether or not I have actually made enough effort to demonstrate that faith by doing what Jesus did. I found myself lacking. Since we have been together by the blessing of Michael, taking on the challenge of building a foundation to help others, I have felt like I am on the path to doing something Christ-like. Obviously, I have a long ways to go, but I know it can happen and that it will happen."

"Admittedly, I really look forward to the opportunities that lie ahead for us to help others. I am anxious to get there, but I know this phase of studying the word will benefit us all as we get closer to doing the hands on work of the foundation. Enough about my journey with this passage, what do you three have to say about it?"

Rachel said, "I am so impressed with what you said about your journey with Christ and how this passage has helped you. I think men relate to the passage as one of decision and action, just like you.

I suspect most women, who are more nurturing by nature anyway, tend to see the passage as a natural extension of their nurturing attitude to simply be kind to others when and where the opportunities avail themselves. What Jesus calls for is not much different than what most women like to do, so we don't make quite as big a deal of this whole idea as you do. We sort of expect things to work out this way, if you understand what I am trying to get across?"

"Not exactly, but then again I am a guy. So, I don't agree exactly, but I do understand your point of reference," Adrian answered.

Nancy added, "Adrian, I believe you are very much entitled to carry on with your belief in this passage just as you see fit. It may well be just exactly what the Lord wants you to do. So stick with it. Now, Rachel makes an excellent point and her point of view is closer to mine. God made us all a little different and somewhere in the 'good book' I remember Paul telling us it is like the various members of the body. All parts are important and it takes all to make up the body. So we all need to believe in Jesus, but we all will see things and do things a bit differently. It's all okay!"

After a pause, everyone looked at Michael, as if to say okay what about you. Michael was deliberating. After not saying anything he started tearing up and Nancy passed him a tissue. She had never seen Michael do this. He was always stoic in her presence and this was definitely unusual. Finally, he cleared his throat and said "I apologize, just give me a minute or two." Adrian called for a short break.

After reconvening and regaining his composure Michael said, "You know, I was just sitting there listening to you three talk and I began to wish Mary and Lisa could be here to listen to our discussion today. I imagined they were here and I saw a smile on their faces. That vision just got to me. Sorry about that. I was not expecting it. Thanks for the break, Adrian."

Michael said he really didn't have a lot to add to what had been said. Then added, "The only thing for me is that I now really love this passage, and I wouldn't mind it if the Foundation used it in some special way, so that it would always remind me of what I just experienced."

Adrian said, "I think we can arrange that."

Adrian continued with the session. "I want everyone to go to Paul's first letter to the Corinthians, Chapter 15. Start at verse 20 and read through verse 28. Adrian waited till they finished. "Now doesn't that passage sum up the fact that Jesus needs to destroy death and its hold on earth so he and his can be placed at God's feet for eternity. The imagery and the finality in this passage is awesome. Now go immediately in the same chapter to verses 35 to 58 and read those." Adrian paused a couple of minutes. "You can't imagine how excited I was to read this passage. This fits perfectly with our belief that man was evolved physically and then was given a spirit. This verse confirms that the first person to whom God rendered a spirit was Adam. It also confirms that we, like Adam, possess a spirit. Furthermore, the passage confirms that there are those who are from heaven (presumably Jesus and others). Lastly, the passage tells us we all are relatively similar in appearance."

This passage prompted a good discussion which Adrian cut short so they could finish their morning work and make it to an early 'High Tea'. He asked the group to proceed to Paul's second letter to the Corinthians. In Chapter 4 verse 4 Paul says, *'The god of this age (the devil) has blinded the minds of unbelievers, so that they cannot see the light of the gospel of the glory of Christ, who is the image of God.'*"

Adrian explained this passage is included to remind us of the heavenly battle with Satan. Furthermore, it helps set the stage for what is to come in the second coming when Jesus binds Satan and removes him from the picture."

"Now go to the Book of Revelation Chapter 14 and read verse 15. Here John tells us that during the seven year period preceding Christ's return that an angel *came out of the temple (in heaven) and called in a loud voice to him who was sitting on the cloud, 'Take your sickle and reap, because the time to reap has come, for the harvest of the earth is ripe.*"

"To me this signifies that God's plan includes a huge harvest of souls at one time. I won't speculate whether these are all righteous souls or else souls who need to be separated as 'sheep or goats'." Discussion followed with the realization from all four participants that they needed more reading to get a fair interpretation of the end times. They realized they were just getting into the subject.

After lunch the group spent three hours touring the Royal British Columbia Museum. They watched an IMAX movie and wandered through the various exhibits in the museum. They all agreed they liked the pioneer-era train station with sound effects the best. After 'high tea' in the hotel's main lobby area they decided to rest or go for a walk. Adrian asked Rachel if she wanted to walk a ways up Commercial Street. She agreed and they headed that way.

On their walk, Adrian commented that he had never seen Michael as emotional as he had gotten that morning. Rachel said she understood what Michael was dealing with, in that he was still recovering from not having Mary around and now, as he gets closer to Christ, he wishes she was at his side.

"That I do understand. For me, it is far more helpful that you are here than I think you know."

"Really," she replied.

"Really, Rachel, you must know I would be at a loss if you were not here."

"I appreciate you saying that, but you too are still going through grieving and I understand that."

"Rachel, I have to carry on with not just our work, but I want to carry on with our relationship. Are you still interested? I know I have been a little distant lately, and I haven't asked you out like I said earlier. I just needed more time to think through things. I've done that, and now I want to spend more time with you if you will let me. I mean in terms of actual dates and that kind of thing."

"Okay, if you think it is time. I am not rushing you."

"I know. You've been great and ever so patient with me, but I know I can't drag this out too long. Some guy is going to come along and steal your heart."

"Well, I am ready for a serious relationship. I will say that. I want to be part of a family with kids and all that comes with that. So, yes, if you are willing to give it a go, I admit I have feelings for you and I would like to see where our relationship takes us."

Adrian responded, "We better let Michael know, so he doesn't think he has an office relationship problem."

"I will leave that to you to discuss with Michael," Rachel said.

"Okay, what should we do for our first date?

"How about going to Egypt!"

Adrian laughed. "Yea, how about going to Egypt on an all-expenses paid business trip."

"I think Michael will be supportive, as long as we are enjoying the trip professionally."

"Well, yes, we'll have professional hours, but we do get some time off from the job to enjoy ourselves. We just can't show up in Tel Aviv with lipstick on the collar or whatever."

After dinner the group convened for their next to last meeting on the trip. They were scheduled to meet in the morning for their last meeting and then catch the ferry back to Seattle. Rachel was scheduled to lead this session.

"I have four passages to review with you this evening about the 'end of the age'. Each of the four are action-packed and I hope they come across as meaningful to you as they are to me. Three are chapter length so I will let you have time to read them before I comment on them."

"The first reading comes from Luke Chapter 21 starting with verse 5. Go ahead and read through the balance of the chapter." Rachel waited quietly until everyone looked up indicating they were ready to carry on.

"Jesus got the attention of the disciples early on in this passage by telling them that the temple they were in would be destroyed and none of the stones would remain standing. Naturally, the disciples wanted to know when this would happen. Jesus let them know that false prophets will claim to be Christ and they should not believe. He tells them that wars will come and go, but the end times will not 'come right away'. This call for patience has rung true for nearly 2,000 years. The temple where the disciples stood with Jesus was completely destroyed by the Romans about 40 years later in 70 AD. Wars have raged periodically through the ages since. Starting in verse 10, Jesus tells more of what must happen in the period before his return. Besides many wars, there will be 'earthquakes, famines, and pestilence'. Then he moves back to the present and tells the disciples they will be persecuted on Jesus' behalf, but that Jesus will aid them through their trials. He tells them that by withstanding their trials, including death, they will be saved."

"Jesus foretells that they will see the Roman army surround Jerusalem. He tells them that this will continue until the time of the Gentiles (i.e. non-Jewish) is fulfilled. As hard as it must have been for them to understand, Jesus told them that the end of the age would come with great signs in the heavens and skies above as well as changes on the earth. For people who largely thought the world was flat, the disciples could only hear these things in great wonderment. Then Jesus goes on explaining the vision of what those who witness his coming would experience. In my mind, there is no wonder that once they heard this, they believed they would be alive to see Jesus return. After describing the end of time events that Jesus knew they would struggle to understand, he graciously provided an analogy to bring this mystery into focus for them. His parable of the fig tree had to help them relate to what Jesus was saying."

"The destruction of Jerusalem in the generation of the disciples confirmed Jesus' prophetic message. As for his second coming we do know from verses 25- 28 that *'There will be signs in the sun, moon, and stars. On earth, nations will be in anguish and perplexity at the roaring and tossing of the sea. Men will faint from terror, apprehensive of what is coming on the world, for the heavenly bodies will be shaken. At the time they see the Son of Man coming in a cloud with power and great glory. When these things begin to take place, stand up and lift up your heads, because your redemption is drawing near'*."

After a short discussion, Rachel got the group going again. "I want to carry on with a similar description from Paul about the second coming. Go to Chapter 4 of Paul's first letter to the Thessalonians. Read verses 13 – 18. After everyone had read the scripture, Rachel continued, "This passage helps us understand the relationship of death and the timing of our resurrection to be with Christ. Paul tells us that in death we are asleep. At the coming of Christ we are told *'the dead in Christ will rise first'*. Interestingly, Paul tells us that those who are alive at the time of Christ's return will *'be caught up together with them in the clouds to meet the Lord in the air'*. I do want to mention that in the next chapter Paul tells us in the first two verses, *'Now, brothers, about the times and dates, we do not need to write to you, for you know very well that the day of the Lord will come like a thief in the night'*."

"On this point of knowing when the Lord returns, there is another reference similar to Paul's. I want you to look at Mark Chapter 13 verses 32 – 34. *'No one knows about that day or hour, not even the angels in heaven, nor the Son, but only the Father. Be on guard! Be alert! You do not know when that time will come. It is like a man going away: He leaves his house and puts his servants in charge, each with his assigned task, and tells the one at the door to keep watch'."*

After another short discussion, Rachel finalized this session with the last passage. "Please turn to Luke Chapter 17 verses 20 – 37. Jesus is asked when the kingdom of God will come. Importantly, Jesus addresses the fact that the kingdom of God is already here. He tells them that it resides inside a person. Whether they understood or not is open for conjecture, but his answer should have been instructive. They should have realized that the spirit of God is in anyone who accepts it. However, Jesus knew they wanted to know when the physical kingdom was coming, and he made it clear they would not know."

Rachel said she knew her final two passages infringed on Adrian's discussion the next day, but that these issues were intertwined in passages such that she thought they would be a good lead in to the next discussion. She felt they should break till the next morning and hold any comments until Adrian had a chance to cover his subject first. Adrian said it sounded like a good punt, but he agreed. They all broke for evening after Michael gave them checkout procedures and the departure schedule. After Nancy and Michael left the room, Rachel and Adrian left together for a walk around the Inner Harbor.

The next morning the group met for the last time on this trip to Victoria. Adrian led the meeting and started with a prayer. After the prayer, he told the others that the focus of the meeting was to review various passages that related to the timing of his second coming and the events leading up to the second coming, much like what Rachel began covering the night before. He said these passages did not relate to dates on the calendar, but they would help interpret those signs. He also said their session would be aimed at helping the group understand current and future times as part of

God's overall plan for mankind, and he hoped that is what the group would focus on.

"The first passage this morning is from Luke. Let's go to Chapter 12 verses 49-59. Please read these and then I'll start with some comments." After everyone finished reading, Adrian said, "Jesus tells us in the first five verses you read that his coming has generated division amongst people and that it will continue to do so. He tells us that he wished his upcoming death was finished. He tells us that each person would have to decide whether he or she was a believer in him or not, and this choice would divide the people."

"As I see it, the balance of the passage I gave you confirms Jesus' expectation that the choice of believing in him was a personal one and not something they should let someone else decide for them. They should not rely on the Pharisees or family members. They should rely on their own conscience. Now let's look at the book of John Chapter 16. Starting with verse 5 read through verse 16." Adrian paused while everyone read the passage.

"Having told the disciples that he will die, Jesus is surprised no one asked where he was going, so he tells them he goes to the Father. He tells them that he must go to the Father so that the 'Holy Counselor' will come. In my view, this insinuates that when Jesus is killed, God will send the Holy Spirit to stir the souls of men and women. Their consciences will be stronger and they will have to deal with their choice to follow Christ."

"Jesus also makes an important point that in Jesus' sacrifice Satan will be convicted and condemned. So, it appears to me that in God's plan, Jesus needed to be sacrificed as a man to put Satan on notice that his days were numbered. Although Satan remains in this world, Jesus seems to hint the day will come at Christ's second coming when Satan will be bound and removed. I think we'll read this clearly in Revelation at a later time."

Discussion of the last two passages went on for a few minutes and then Adrian moved on, "Let's do one more passage before we take a break. Go to Paul's first letter to the Thessalonians Chapter 5. Let's read verses 1 – 11." Adrian paused while everyone read. "Paul repeats his analogy that Jesus will return like a *'thief in the night'*. He calls for his Christian brothers and sisters to be vigilant and to be *'self-controlled'*. He reassures the congregation that God does not want to bring wrath on them but rather save them."

"This passage is another where it seems Paul believes Christ's return could be any time. However, Paul's words are as applicable today as they were in the first century. Vigilance in our faith will certainly be rewarded whenever Jesus returns. Okay, this calls for break time."

Everyone checked out of the hotel and brought their bags to the meeting room. A tray of refreshments showed up to cover the fact they might miss lunch by the time they got to the ferry for the return trip. After the four were ready, Adrian continued.

"Let's look at Paul's first letter to Timothy Chapter 4. In the first verse I find something interesting. Paul says *'The Spirit clearly says that in the later times some will abandon the faith and follow the deceiving spirits and things taught by demons'*. I find this interesting because it highlights the fact, as some other passages do as well, that Satan is deceiving many to not believe in Our Lord. This spiritual battle rages on around us even if we do not notice."

"Okay, now go to Paul's second letter to Timothy. Read Chapter 3 where Paul speaks to the increase of rebellion against God in the last days. People will love many things, except God. He tells us that everyone who wants to live in Christ will be persecuted by those who have been deceived."

After a good pause for the others to read the chapter, Adrian continued. "Next, go to the first letter of Peter and focus on Chapter 4 verse 7. *'The end of all things is near. Therefore be clear minded and self-controlled so that you can pray. Above all, love each other deeply, love covers a multitude of sins.'*

"Lastly, in Peter's second letter, please read the third Chapter." Adrian paused and then said 'There are a couple of verses I want to highlight. Verse 8 says, *'But do not forget this one thing, dear friends: With the Lord a day is like a thousand years, and a thousand years are like a day.'* Boy, this is a statement of relative time. It tells me God's timeline is not the same as ours. Where we may think in terms of days, God can think in terms of thousands of years."

"Peter, in verse 10, also mentions that *'the day of the Lord will come like a thief. The heavens will disappear with a roar; the elements will be destroyed with fire, and the earth and everything in it will be laid bare'.* Sounds like the end of the ages!"

With that, the meeting was concluded. Someone asked Michael why he had been so quiet through the morning meetings. He said, "I have been listening and simply trying to put all this in context with what we've got left to cover.

The group left the hotel and boarded the ferry 20 minutes later for their trip home. Adrian sat with Michael and they were talking intently half the way home, then Rachel noticed Michael was laughing. She saw a wink from Adrian's eye and she noticed a warm feeling run through her veins.

28

Cairo, Egypt

Rachel and Adrian had just endured a long flight from Seattle to London, followed by a flight to Cairo, and were tired and anxious to get some good sleep in their hotel rooms. They were met at the Cairo airport by their tour guide, Abdul Jamal, who ushered them to a small van where another couple from Ohio were waiting. Abdul drove them straight to the high-rise hotel where they were staying and all four were checked in and shown to their respective rooms. Adrian suggested a time for breakfast to Rachel and she agreed.

The next morning after breakfast, Adrian and Rachel decided to do some touring on their own as the official tour did not begin until the following day. They hired a taxi to take them to the Citadel of Salah Al-Din, the alabaster mosque built by Mohamed Ali Pasha. It provided a beautiful view over much of Cairo. The city itself is enormous and incredibly crowded with a population of 19,000,000. After an hour at the mosque, they rejoined the taxi driver who took them to the Golan Bazaar. They had never seen such a thing. They wandered and marveled at the size of this very local market. As tourists they were constantly besieged by sellers of spices, fabric, jewelry, perfumes and all sorts of other wares. Although they saw very few tourists at the bazaar, they never really felt threatened in this crowded venue.

The traffic was horrendous, and Adrian wondered who ran the driving schools in Egypt. It was crazy! After a hair-raising taxi ride Rachel and Adrian returned to the hotel in time for a swim in the hotel pool, afterwards they changed clothes and met in the lobby to go out for dinner. They found a small restaurant around the corner from the hotel entrance, where Adrian had a wonderful meal of sea bass and calamari and Rachel had a chicken and lamb meal prepared with carrots and peas. Dessert was a combination of banana and some kind of unique Egyptian pear. And mint tea washed everything down!

Abdul met everyone on the tour the next morning in the hotel lobby. There were only 18 in the tour group. Tourism was definitely down, but that provided for a more comfortable size as far as Adrian and Rachel were concerned. Most everyone was from the United States. One couple came from Great Britain, and one couple with two kids came from Thailand. The first day the group spent touring the Egyptian Museum in the morning. Everyone loved the display of King Tut's treasure. Abdul bought falafels for the group for lunch, and after finishing lunch they went to see one of the "seven wonders of the world," the Great Pyramids at Giza, which were built around 2,600 BC. The largest of these pyramids is called the Great Pyramid of Cheops.

At the second pyramid the tour group stopped to ride camels. Rachel thought that this was great fun and wanted Adrian to take lots of photos. He obliged but got in an argument with the camel owner on the final payment due for Rachel's ride and the photo session. A policeman stepped in and sent the camel owner off in a huff.

The pyramids stood majestically in the desert sand. Apparently, according to Abdul, it took 100,000 workers 20 years to build Cheops. The construction season had been from August to November since the Nile was flooded in those months, and the workers were needed to farm the fertile fields near the Nile during the balance of the year. Later, the group went to the nearby Sphinx, the guardian of the pyramids. Rachel asked Adrian to pinch her, as she could not believe she was actually seeing what she was seeing.

They returned to the hotel and sat in the lobby drinking tea with the British couple. Adrian commented to the husband what an enormous project the Egyptians had undertaken to build the pyramids. The stones at the base of those pyramids were massive. The British fellow told him that the Hebrews had to have been slave laborers to do the work. Of course, during the tour, the guide had denied the assertion by saying the Hebrews chose to do the labor.

Early the next day Abdul got the group loaded in a bus and took everyone to the airport for the flight to Aswan. Having arrived early, Abdul had a full day of activities for the group. They visited the Aswan Dam first. It was built in 1907 and is the principal power source for the region. The Nile flows from Ethiopia north to Egypt, and the lake behind the dam, Lake Nasser, is huge at 500 kilometers long.

The group took a boat ride to a small Island called Philae where the Temple of Isis was built 3,000 years before Christ. The statues and carvings were impressive artwork. After that short tour the group again boarded the boat headed to the mainland and then bussed north to a small ship waiting at dockside in Aswan. Hibiscus drinks were there welcoming everyone, and after dinner and a belly-dance show the group headed to bed early.

The following day the entire tour group headed to the airport for a 30-minute excursion flight to Abu Simbel, a historical site along the western edge of Lake Nasser. Adrian and Rachel hiked up to the mighty Sun Temple of Pharaoh Ramses II. This temple was reclaimed from the area behind the dam and moved to this site for preservation purposes. They also visited the temple of Ramses' wife, Nefertari. This temple took eight years to build back in 1,200 BC.

Once back in Aswan, they boarded the large boat that served as their riverboat and headed north downriver. The afternoon stop at Kom Ombo gave them a chance to see a temple dedicated to the Crocodile God Sobek. It was constructed between 200 BC and 200 AD. Back on the boat, the dinner meal was a feast of Egyptian and European foods, including falafels, stuffed eggplant and tomatoes, macaroni in sauce, veal cutlets, and a variety of pastries. Interestingly, no women seemed to work on the boat. The few women seen in town were wearing caftans and veils. They were never alone either.

The next morning found the boat tied to a dock when the group rose for breakfast. The group toured a cult temple named Edfu dedicated to the falcon god Horus. It was built around the time of Christ with an extremely tall front gate. Typical was the fact that the rooms in the temple got smaller as you approached the back of the temple where it was said the god resided. Curiously, there was a built-in escape route back there that made the whole thing intriguing. The drawings etched in the stone were quite nice.

After a cruise down the Nile, the boat passed through a set of locks before arriving in Luxor. This is the location where the pharaoh and his wife spent three weeks in the summer every year. After bussing through town, the tour group arrived at the temple Luxor. This is a temple destroyed by Christians at one time and which was now being restored. The sphinx-lined road leading to the temple was beyond impressive. The pink marble obelisk with baboon feet was magnificent, and, surprisingly, its twin resides in Paris. Drawings and writings of Egyptian history cover many of the walls of the temple and enormous columns are found in great numbers.

The next day brought the tour group to the *Valley of the Kings*. This is desert landscape, period. It is remote and serves as the place where pharaohs were buried in shafted tombs built into the hillsides. In this way, the pharaohs hoped their graves would not be sacked as the tombs had been of their predecessors buried in the pyramids. Unfortunately, that thought did not prove to be true. Many of the tombs were unfortunately ransacked. Rachel and Adrian paid extra to venture into King Tut's tomb. The entrance had been hidden for years as there was another king buried in front of Tut's tomb. Apparently, 1,000 pounds of gold was discovered in this tomb when it was first opened.

Lastly, the group went to the Karnak Temple complex. Rachel was blown away by the size of the complex. It is believed to be the largest ancient religious site in the world. Construction began in the 16th century BC. It took 2,000 years to build and is dedicated to the sun god Amun-Re. There are over 100 enormous columns. Two huge obelisks capture your attention as soon as you see them. Adrian had to admit that Karnak was something special to see!

The next day the group flew to Cairo from Luxor and boarded a bus for a trip to Alexandria. They passed many beautiful farms in the desert reclamation area north of Cairo. Abdul told the group that it was very expensive to live here. The farms grow citrus, cotton, and sugar cane. They even saw a banana farm where plastic bags surrounded the hanging fruit. Alexandria is the third largest city in Egypt, located on the Mediterranean Sea. It is located where the Nile flows into the sea. Alexander the Great built the original city in 332 BC. It is the birthplace of Cleopatra!

The Corniche area along the sea front is very European-looking. The city population stands at about 4,000,000 people, and the area includes a large port complex as well as an important industrial area. Cultural events are popular in this thriving commercial city.

The following day the group took a morning city tour. Abdul explained that Alexandria would be inundated with people in another month. As summer sets in the population of the city grows to nearly 14,000,000 as many people leave the desert for the seacoast. As one of the oldest cities along the Mediterranean coast, like Nice in France, it is a highly popular destination for people escaping the scorching heat of summer.

They visited a 2,000 year-old Roman amphitheater made with mosaic flooring and marble seating for crowds of up to 800. The acoustics were incredible as Adrian went to the amphitheater floor and could speak normally while Rachel could hear every word spoken plainly while seated near the top. They could see why it had been used for theater and sporting events. From there they toured the El Morsi Abu El Abbas Mosque. Adrian and the other men were welcomed at the front door, while Rachel and the other women were led around to the right side door where they entered the mosque only to discover they were separated from the men by a long partition.

After departing Alexandria, the group stopped at the St. Macarius Monastery, built for an ancient Christian group called Wadi Natrun. The monastery is located south of Alexandria in stark desert, but interestingly has a beautiful tree-lined street leading into it – along with gum trees growing outside the walled monastery and palm trees inside. It was first built in 360 AD and is noted for having the crypt for John the Baptist. Abdul explained that we were not far from the location were Joseph and Mary brought Jesus as a baby, while King Herod of Jerusalem searched for and killed baby boys. This followed Herod learning that three kings from the east had come looking for the king of the Jews. Herod obviously did not relish the thought of someone else being represented as the 'King of the Jews'.

The tour then drove on to Cairo where everyone was taken to the airport. Adrian and Rachel left on a late flight directly to Tel Aviv. Security at the departure gate was incredibly tight. Each passenger was individually interviewed by a security agent. Upon landing at the modern Tel Aviv airport, they waited for their luggage in the baggage claim area. Rachel noted a very large photograph placed high on the wall. It was a picture taken from space of the eastern Mediterranean. Strikingly, it showed much of the eastern portion of Israel with lots of green vegetation, in contrast to the stark brown desert everywhere else. Apparently, they had just arrived in the 'land of milk and honey'!

A taxi ride to Tel Aviv brought Rachel and Adrian to a nice hotel where they were to meet up with Michael the following afternoon. They would have that day to relax and rest before joining the church group the following day to start the Israel tour.

29

Athens, Greece

Several days after Rachel and Adrian left for Egypt, Michael left Seattle for the Mediterranean. He had contacted Nick Dawson, who had spoken with Adrian on his trip to Athens, and Michael asked if they could spend a couple of days together catching up on their lives and discussing the work of the Foundation. Nick was thrilled to have the chance to see Michael again after so many years. In fact, Nick asked Michael to stay with him and his wife at their home for the three nights Michael would be in Athens. Michael accepted the warm invitation, looking forward to getting reacquainted with Nick.

Nick met Michael at the airport and drove him to his home overlooking a large portion of the city. Michael brought a few small gifts for Judith, Nick's wife. They spent the first evening together enjoying good Greek food and sharing a bottle of fine red wine. After a really long day, Michael went to bed early and slept soundly for nine hours.

The next day Nick took Michael on an extended sight-seeing tour of the city. They spent the day talking and catching up on family matters as well as their respective careers. It was a delightful day, and both men sincerely enjoyed the company of the other. It was one of those days when it seemed like they had never really been apart as friends.

Following breakfast on the second day, Nick asked Michael what time he needed to be at the port to catch his four-day excursion aboard a cruise ship sailing in the eastern Mediterranean. Michael apologized for any misunderstanding. He said his tour group was to be at the pier the following morning at 9:00 a.m., and he had every intention of taking a taxi to the port. Nick offered to drive Michael, but Michael, not wanting to infringe on Nick's hospitality, insisted he call a taxi. They called a taxi company and made arrangements for the following day, accordingly.

"So how would you like to proceed with our discussion today?" Nick inquired.

"First, let me again thank you for the hospitality you showed Adrian while he was here. His trip to see you was very productive and I really appreciate what you did for him. In fact, he returned inspired by all he saw and heard on the trip. You did a particularly good job of expanding his understanding of the lines of science and religion relative to creation." Michael continued with a full description of the work the Foundation had done and the conclusions they had developed.

"Michael, I found Adrian to be a very fine young man taking on a rather monumental task with you and the rest of your group. I am particularly interested to see how you deal with answers to your questions. Not many people want to tackle such a colossal and almost mystic question as 'what is God's purpose for mankind'. Many great philosophers have wrestled with that one."

"Well, Nick, we had to deal with the issue of human origin first. You know, biblical literalism versus science! You helped us with that and that help led us to a belief in what we call Divine Design. We have worked with that belief for months now and we are convinced that it is exactly what God did. He designed us in every sense of the word. Coming to that conclusion took a long time. Yet, believing that in the process of creating us, God imprinted in us a soul that possesses our conscience and our ability to be *spiritually* led rather than instinctively led, we can see God's hand in all that we are."

"Michael, you give me far too much credit. I only hypothesized to Adrian that what you just said is a possibility. I don't know if it is what really happened in our final creation or not. It is you and your work that can help tie this hypothesis to a meaningful theory. I do not know it to be true, but I have seen it as a real possibility for years. Do understand that I too have had to struggle with reconciling scientific fact with the mysteries of creation. Honestly Michael, I struggle with understanding why God would create us in the first place. Where was the need and/or the logic in all that?"

"Nick, let me try something on you and see if makes any sense as a possible answer to that question. We've been wrestling with that very question recently."

"I'd be interested in what you've come up with."

"I must say this will not sound very profound to you. In fact, it didn't sound very profound to me when I first heard one member of our team come up with an apparent explanation."

"Okay, tell me."

"Well, I will expand upon the concept a bit to help give it context."

"Fair enough!"

"This is so simplistic that I am having trouble figuring out quite how to present it to such a distinguished professor."

"Try me!"

"Okay, biblically speaking and scientifically speaking, the creation order includes the creation of many plants, fish in the earth's waters and land-based animals. Afterwards, God created man and woman. In the animal world God's creations were based on family units. Likewise, man evolved into family units. Correct?"

"Yes, Michael, it is well documented in scientific work that man and woman were part of family units everywhere they have been found. That is simple enough to say."

"Well then, if God made us in his image he must have wanted us to be part of his family. He may have created us to play a significant role in his larger family."

"Michael, let me think about that." Nick paused and Michael could see him thinking. This went on for a few minutes.

"Michael, that concept is so absurdly simple. Yet, it may be as good an explanation as I've heard. I cannot think of a better reason. Wow, is this your idea?"

"Well no, it was not my idea. In fact, one of our Foundation employees who has worked for me for many years is the one who just popped the answer out in a meeting not long ago. It was a very simple and clear explanation to her. The other three of us in the room were stunned. We all had to admit it was the best answer we had heard. All the other theories about gathering free-will people around God to give him praise just don't seem to hold a candle to this explanation that centers on family love."

"Michael, I must admit we scientists sometimes need a reality fix to balance our fixation of data-proofing everything. Something so simple may strike at the heart of what God did that is so special about our species. We, as a species, have managed to secure dominion over the earth, one of the very things God is said to have assigned us. Yet, we do not seem to live together without strife and conflict."

"Exactly! However, God is not through with his selection process for those who will be his eternal family. That is why we wait for a second coming and final judgment."

"But why wait?" Nick challenged.

"God wants a certain sized family, and only he knows when that will occur. We have to wait till the family is large enough. Also, it is important to remember that several places in scripture tell us that God will create a new order in heaven and on earth. God needs to close the book on Satan and his followers. God will initiate the new order, we believe, with His new family playing a central role in that new order."

"Michael, I must say I am intrigued. I can't argue a different or better explanation today."

"Okay, Nick, let's get Judith and take her out for a nice late lunch or early dinner. I would like to get to sleep early tonight, if that is okay."

"Sounds good."

The next day Michael got to the port pier at 8:30 a.m. He boarded a moderately large vessel and settled in his cabin suite, and later joined the small tour group in the ship's dining room for lunch. Having only six people in an exclusive group made it perfect to accept the invitation to sit at the Captain's table later that evening.

Rachel had arranged the tour with an elite tour company that never booked more than eight in a group. The price reflected the exclusiveness of the group. Michael did not need to spend a lot of time seeing all the sights, but he did want to focus on a few. The idea behind the small group was to allow group members to influence the duration of stays at each location and to allow for in-depth discussions as needed.

Michael wanted to see the island of Patmos and to see the cave where the disciple John had visions that led to the book of Revelations. He had some special places to see on this trip to the eastern Mediterranean, and Patmos was one of the most important for him personally. The tour guide promised Michael he would get a close-up look inside the cave.

Late in the afternoon the ship docked at the Greek island of Mykonos. Michael took the shuttle ride into town and walked to the waterfront area called 'Little Venice.' Later dinner was served on the ship and Michael, along with the others on his tour, were seated at the Captain's table. Michael had Norwegian salmon, and the food was superb. He felt like he was back home.

That evening in the ballroom, Michael and the other passengers were entertained by dancers, singers and a master violinist. It was a delight to relax with new friends and get acquainted, and Michael enjoyed spending time with the group. There was one couple from Paris in the group and another couple from Milan, Italy. The other single person was a very distinguished lady from London. Her husband had planned the trip a year earlier but he had passed away from congestive heart failure four months prior to the trip. She decided to take the trip anyway. Michael surmised that perhaps he had been assigned her husband's spot on the tour.

The next day the ship docked in Rhodes. Michael left the group to spend his time primarily in the historic Suleiman's Mosque. In the afternoon the group of six boarded a small bus with the driver and guide. They visited the town of Lindos and enjoyed walking the winding streets to an ancient temple devoted to honoring the goddess Athena. On the way back to Rhodes, the driver let the group off near the historic part of the town so they could walk through gates and moats to get to the Old City. Here they saw palaces built by the Crusaders from 1,000 years past. After dinner that evening and another entertaining show, the group called it a day. Michael read awhile in John's book of the Revelation.

Early the next morning the ship was anchored offshore from the island of Patmos. After breakfast, the group boarded a small tender boat, motored to the port of Skya, and then boarded a small van that took them up hills covered in pine and Eucalyptus trees. The destination was the Grotto of St. John. The grotto is a cave located just below the *Monastery of Revelation* which serves as a boarding school for high school boys aged 12-18. Many of these boys attend the school hoping to one day become a monk.

Walking into the building near the cave, they descended stairs into the *Cave of the Apocalypse*. A church service was in progress conducted by a priest for the students. The boys were chanting as the group was politely allowed to circle the cave. They saw where John's head rested while he prayed. They saw where his hands were placed. That spot is now outlined in silver. They also saw the three cracks in the cave that are believed to have emerged when God's angel gave John the revelation. The three cracks are believed by some to represent God the Father, God the Son and God the Holy Spirit. Michael was noticeably moved!

Leaving the grotto they drove to the small town of Hora where the 13th century monastery sits with its two to three dozen monks. A 4th century church remains in the town where St. John converted many of the locals in the later part of the first century AD. Returning to the ship for lunch, it was not long before the ship proceeded to its next destination of Kusadasi, Turkey. This was a tourist stop to purchase inexpensive scarves and other wares. Michael picked out a scarf for Rachel and one for Nancy. He also bought one for each of the ladies in the group. He took an inordinate amount of time to pick out the one for the lady from London.

From Kusadasi the group bused to Ephesus. Here they found an amazing number of ruins. The Temple of Diana is considered to be one of the seven ancient wonders of the world. This is also one of the cities where Paul was imprisoned for some time. St. John spent his last days here in the first century AD. By the seventh century AD there were 250,000 people living in Ephesus, yet today the city, which once was on the sea, is many miles from it. Waters have receded from the area because large amounts of sediment have built up over the centuries.

The next day the ship docked at Athens's port, Piraeus, and after exchanging phone numbers with the other group members, Michael went straight to the airport where he caught a flight to Tel Aviv. He arrived the same day as Rachel and Adrian. He didn't expect to see them at the airport, so he got a taxi ride to the hotel where they were to meet for dinner.

30

Tel Aviv, Israel

It was all smiles at dinner. Rachel was beaming from the entire experience of getting to see Egypt. This had been a dream of hers that really came true. She said, "Michael, thank you so much for letting us tour Egypt. It was such a special time. I really felt safe too. I was not expecting that with all the news we've heard about. Our group was small and we all got along just fine. Wow, and the sights were so impressive. I felt like, in some ways, I had gone back in time. Seeing the desert and the crowds really brought to life what Egypt has become. Thank you so much."

"Rachel, you are most welcome. I have never been to Egypt and perhaps one day I will, but for now it is good that you two got to see it for yourselves, as well as for the Foundation. So many of the biblical people we have been reading about have at one time or another been in Egypt. In fact, the Hebrew people spent centuries there from the time of Joseph to the time of Moses. Now you two are our resident experts on Egypt."

Adrian piped up saying, "Well, I don't know about that. We took a whole lot of pictures and we heard a whole lot of 'guide talk,' but I wouldn't call us experts on Egypt. We did, however, see a lot and learn a lot."

"You know, I was wondering whether or not you two would be paying more attention to each other rather than to listening to the guide."

"Oh, no" Rachel said. "Adrian made it clear we were on business time, not personal time." All laughed at that point.

"Tell us about the visit you had with Nick in Athens," Adrian inquired.

"It was great to see an old friend from years gone by. It only took minutes for us to really connect. It was like we remember from days together in Boston, as it was a comfortable and very enjoyable time."

Continuing, Michael said, "Nick was impressed with your visit Adrian and he said so."

"That's because I bought the drinks."

"I know better. He respected your approach to our Question #2. He said you did it right by working both sides of the human origin debate. Furthermore, he is impressed that our Foundation is embracing the thought he inspired in you about Divine Design. You should feel good about that."

Michael continued on for about 20 minutes about how he and Nick had discussed the belief that God's purpose in creating mankind is to adopt a family where the members have free will and have chosen to accept God as their one God. Nick agreed that there was a definite possibility that family was at the center of God's reason to create us and make us the central part of His new heaven and new earth.

"Nick admitted that another purpose seems to be to time our adoption with God's apparent need to clean house in heaven and on earth. However, he felt only God knew these things for certain, and all we could do is to surmise from what scripture tells us."

Adrian responded, "Well, I'm glad Nick did not rule out our origin theory, and I like his idea of adding a statement about God's need to 'clean house'. That sums it up I think."

"I think we all can buy into that, Adrian." Michael continued, "Now, if I may change the subject as we gear up for this tour. I hope we can simply join in the group tomorrow and enjoy the trip as participants and tourists. We should consider this a vacation and a pilgrimage. Lastly, I want you to know that when we get back we will be working on Question #4. We'll tackle that question by studying prophesy and then we'll contemplate specifically what God's plan is for the future. So let's learn all we can to help us in the months ahead."

Michael, Adrian and Rachel realized they were almost late for the evening meeting with the church group and their guide, so they left the dining room and made their way to the meeting room. They signed in and met those that were gathered for the same meeting. Overall, it looked like a fun and lively group with half the group being young adults and the other half being older. The tour guide, Etain, got the group organized, answered questions, got introductions done quickly and gave out instructions for the trip. He asked for everyone to be done with breakfast by 8:00 a.m. the next morning and to be on the bus by 8:30 a.m.

The surprise of the day for Adrian and Rachel was that Michael introduced another tour member that he obviously knew. She was a single lady who happened to have been on the same cruise that Michael was on in Greece. She was infatuated with the idea of going to Israel, as well as the work Michael was doing with the Foundation. Adrian and Rachel were quickly getting the idea there was more to the story. A mutual attraction seemed to be present.

Apparently, Michael had pulled some strings and gotten the last spot on the tour for her. Perhaps a sizable contribution to whomever made it happen. She had returned to London from Athens, made a quick repack of clothes, and had flown straight to Tel Aviv. Her name was Elizabeth Ashley and her husband had passed away 18 months prior. She dressed well and had a very proper British accent, leading Rachel to believe that she held some stature in the city. In fact, she was the widow of an international financier and was very interested in philanthropic work. She seemed more than a bit interested in Michael and Michael in her. Surprise, surprise!

As the group drove through Tel Aviv, Etain explained that the city was only a mere 100 years old. Prior to that time, the area had been just sand, desert, and camels. Today the population of Tel Aviv exceeds 400,000.

Next they passed by Joppa. This was the first settlement in the area following the great flood. Etain related a number of facts to the group to help everyone get their heads around some of Israel's history. He told the group that Israel's creation as a nation took place in 1948 following World War II. While one third of all Jews were killed in the Holocaust, he explained that Israel had been conquered many times over the ages. Conquerors included the Assyrians, Babylonians, Persians, Greeks, Turks, Greeks and Romans.

The tour bus proceeded north to "Caesarea by the Sea." They saw a desalinization plant near Natanya. Etain also told a short story about how the Israelis defeated the Greeks in 185 BC and crowned a royal family, the Maccabees, who constantly fought over power. Finally, in 68 BC, the Romans took control of the region when King Herod, a foe of the Jews, was made the local reigning king.

In Caesarea, King Herod built the largest port in the world and established the area as a major center in the Roman Empire with a population of 250,000 people. Having been built in 22 BC, it was destroyed later by a Muslim army in 690 AD. The city had been huge with two hippodromes, miles of aqueducts made of stone, Pontius Pilate's home, a theatre, and a beautiful waterfront.

Interestingly, today you find a golf course in the area. This is a rarity in Israel!

The tour continued inland to Mt. Carmel where there is a large nature reserve with various pine, carob, eucalyptus, and olive trees planted and growing. This is where Elijah built a fire and God lit it. It is also where the prophets of Baal were slaughtered.

Following lunch, the group moved on to Tel Megiddo, the scene of the future battle of Armageddon. The view over the valley and its flat plains was magnificent. Many Old Testament battles took place in this area, including Gideon's defeat of the Midianites. This is a crossroad with the Mediterranean to the west, Samaria to the east and Damascus to the north.

Crossing the Valley of Jezreel and driving northeast toward Nazareth the group arrived at Mt. Precipice. Armed personnel carriers passed by heading to the northern reaches of the country. The tour proceeded by the road above and around the city to a high overlook.

Mt. Precipice is the location where town residents threatened to toss Jesus off a cliff. The rocky steep hillside was a foreboding location for the encounter and we could just imagine the scene at the top of the mountain in Jesus' day. Nearby stands the *Church of Our Lady's Fear*, on the site where Jesus' mother stood when the town's people were harassing Jesus. The group sat together and prayed together for the blessings and grace of Our Lord.

Modern Nazareth has a population of about 150,000. One third of the population is Christian. Most of the homes in the area had one or two plastic tanks on the roof to serve as water heaters. Jewish households have tanks colored white while Arab families have tanks colored black. Interesting!

The final stop of the day was in Tiberius, a Jewish Holy City where the Talmud was compiled. The city was built originally by Herod Antipas. The region around Tiberius is known as the "Land of the

Public Ministry of Jesus." The city itself sits on the southwest side of the Sea of Galilee and the group's hotel was right on the beach. At dinner Elizabeth and Michael sat together and talked, while Adrian and Rachel had more time to themselves than they had expected.

The tour group was up early the next day and even got to see the sun rise over the Sea of Galilee. This is an area that is 600 feet below sea level and one that has a tropical climate. This is the within central Jordan Valley.

The tour bus drove through the area called "Path of Arbel," which is where Jesus walked along the shore of the Sea of Galilee. The group got out and the guide said they should walk the area so as to walk where Jesus walked and not look for monuments. The group did just that for a short while imagining Jesus at the shore of the sea.

The group then stopped at Tabgha which is the site where Jesus fed the crowd of 5,000. It is also the place where Jesus appeared to the disciples after his resurrection known as the "primacy of Peter." A small church called *Mensa Christi* is located nearby and is believed to be the site of the rock from which Jesus served the meal to the disciples.

From there Etain took the group on to Capernaum. At this point in his life, Jesus considered Capernaum his home and many miracles were performed by Jesus in this area. The group saw Peter's house with the ruins of two churches around it.

Next the tour moved on to the Mount of Beatitudes, west of Capernaum. The group stood on the hillside looking down to where Jesus spoke to the multitudes. The area was a natural amphitheater and everyone could easily imagine Jesus delivering the "Sermon on the Mount". The church's pastor read The Beatitudes and said a very thankful prayer filled with praise. It was a touching and spirit-filled moment for everyone.

Returning to Tiberius, the group cleaned up and then went to dinner. Michael and Elizabeth joined a couple from Portland at a table for four while Adrian and Rachel joined a couple from Lake Oswego.

The next day the tour headed south. The Sea of Galilee was calm, and hot springs just south of town were producing water at 97 degrees (Celsius). The river Jordan continues south out of the Sea of Galilee. The bus passed a kibbutz called Degania Alef. It is a commune for folks who live simply and collectively. There are many of these in the region, according to Etain.

Fifteen miles from the Sea of Galilee the group stopped at Beit She'an. Sitting at the foot of Mount Gilboa is this well-preserved Roman amphitheater. An Egyptian stone tells the story of the death of King Saul here. Canaanite ruins have also been discovered above the site with more Roman ruins below.

Crossing the 'pilgrim road to Mecca' the tour stopped at the Spring of Gideon at Shiloh, and then on to Jericho located a few miles north of the Dead Sea. Many consider Jericho to be the oldest city in the world. There is a stone tower in the town that is believed to be 8,000 years old, making it the oldest building in the world.

The area around Jericho is over 800 feet below sea level. It is very well known for growing dates, bananas, watermelon, and oranges. Nearby is where Elijah parted the Jordan River with his rolled up cloak causing it to open up so he and Elisha could cross the river. This is when God took Elijah to heaven in a "whirlwind" and Elisha then was endowed to perform miracles. It is also the area where Jesus was baptized by John.

Seven miles south of Jericho, the Khirbet Qumran ruins are located on the northwest shore of the Dead Sea. The Dead Sea scrolls were discovered here. Jewish Essenes inhabited the area from the first century BC to 70 AD. The Essenes were a strict Jewish sect committed to the Torah and all scriptural documents. As Romans moved into the area, the Essenes left after hiding the ancient scrolls in clay jars in dry caves on hillsides, and it was only as recently as 1947 that two goat herders discovered the caves and the scrolls.

The group headed for the Dead Sea and their hotel. The Dead Sea is the lowest place on earth, which is situated at 1,300 feet below sea level. The sea water is 33% salt, which means nothing lives in the sea's water.

The area is popular for people with certain ailments. Folks needing treatment for psoriasis, climate therapy, rheumatism, and arthritis go there for treatment. Adrian and Rachel got into bathing suits after arriving at the hotel and walked down to the waterfront. They enjoyed floating around in the water – as the high salt content does not allow a person to sink. In fact, Adrian just sat down in the water and felt like he was sitting in a soft chair. It was a strange sensation.

Dinner was a spectacular buffet. Michael, Elizabeth, Rachel and Adrian all sat at the same table and they had a delightful evening together. Elizabeth was incredibly fun to be with and she had been well-informed and was very interested in the work of the Foundation. In fact, whether her interest was more toward the Foundation or toward Michael came into question during the meal in the minds of both Rachel and Adrian. That changed when Michael asked Elizabeth to take a walk after dinner on the hotel patio. They did seem to enjoy each other's company more and more as each day passed.

Since the next day was the Sabbath, the breakfast did not include any hot cooked food. It was all cold or previously prepared. The orange yogurt was superb!

The major stop for the day was Masada, a UNESCO site. It is a fortress built by King Herod atop a huge mesa in the desert. To get to the top most of the group took the tram, however, a few brave young souls took off hiking up the path. Masada was built atop the mesa 1,300 feet above the valley floor. Essentially, the top of the mesa is at sea level and includes a large palace with 18-foot walls surrounding the top complex.

Famously, Masada is known for the holdout that Jewish zealots made at Masada when the Romans, in their last days of ruling the Holy Land, began a siege of the fortress. It took three years for the Romans to finally break through to the top. Nearly all the Jews died by 73 AD, defending the fortress "to the last man."

The next stop was En Gedi Springs where fresh water flows from the hillside through an oasis-type canyon. This is where David had hidden from Saul when Saul was determined to kill David. It is also in a cave here where Saul and David made peace between themselves. The group took time to find a private spot to read from Psalms and pray. Elizabeth and Michael were seen together shedding a few tears as they sat close holding each other. Both were reflecting on how they had suffered the loss of a spouse. Then they reveled in the fact that now they were in a place so meaningful. It was comfortable to be in this garden with someone who was traveling the same road of grief.

Meanwhile, Rachel and Adrian sat together near a small waterfall holding hands and smiling at each other. They too prayed silently and shared tender moments together.

On the road to Jerusalem Etain pointed out several Bedouin camps near the road. He explained that many of the nomadic ways are still being followed these days. However, these people do not move as often as they did in the past. They still have camels to travel about but they do not farm crops. They have plenty of goats, and in many ways they live like they did in the days of Abraham or Mohammed. As the tour bus approached the city of Jerusalem, they passed a small traditional site. Etain explained that they were passing the "Inn of the Good Samaritan." Everyone on board the bus recalled the story Jesus told.

Jerusalem is the "City of the Lord." It was 4,000 years ago that Abraham was asked by God to sacrifice his son Isaac. At that time the city was known as Salem, Etain noted. The bus parked at the Mt. of Olives and everyone got out and walked to an overlook of the city. In the foreground were thousands of Jewish graves and to the side of the burial sites was the Garden of Gethsemane. Further down below was Jerusalem itself. WOW!

From their elevated vantage point the group could clearly see the walled city, the *Temple Mount* with the *Dome of the Rock*, and many other wondrous sights. Roughly, 750,000 people live in this ancient and historical city where Israelites and Palestinians compete to continue to expand the city.

Aboard the bus, the group was ushered through the tunnel of Mt. Scopus into the modern city. They passed universities and a large hospital before arriving at their hotel. After settling into individual rooms, the group gathered together at long tables for a nice meal in the hotel dining room. The day had been special and Etain promised three more special days ahead before ending the trip.

Starting the next day at the Temple Mount was exciting for the group. The Temple Mount encompasses 45 acres and is surrounded by a thick wall. The Temple area sits just over a rock ridge called Mount Moriah. This is the location where David prepared the site where his son, Solomon, ultimately did build the Temple. Earlier still, it served as the site where Abraham was told to sacrifice Isaac.

The city wall surrounding the old city is very impressive. Etain explained that the walls had been rebuilt many times. The most recent time was 460 years ago when Suleiman the Magnificent of the Ottoman Empire decreed that the walls be rebuilt. Etain also explained that if the group were to walk the outside perimeter of the city they would see all the unique gates of the city. He described the historical significance of many of the gates and the various names of each. Most gates have at least two names. The group entered the South Gate, also known as the Dung Gate.

Crossing into the Temple Mount area Etain pointed out two temples. One is unmistakable. The *Dome of the Rock* has the large golden dome that stands as the world's most famous mosque and is the iconic picture found in any photo of Jerusalem. It is built near or perhaps over the original Jewish temple site. It is a huge structure. Strangely, and perhaps not intentionally, a marble panel near the main doors depict what looks like Satan from the shoulders up. Perhaps just an odd coincidence of construction, but a strange one at that.

When the group passed through the security check at the entrance to the Temple Mount they peered over the side of the wall and could see directly down upon the many people standing at the Western Wall, which is better known as the *Wailing Wall*. It was a sight to behold. They even saw Orthodox Jews hitting the wall with their heads while they prayed. This is a common tradition apparently.

Jews are not allowed on the Temple Mount site for any religious purpose as the site remains Muslim property. Within the *Dome of the Rock,* the group was told that a large rock is located in the center of the temple. This is the cherished sight where Mohammed riding a horse was said to have been raised into heaven. In the Jewish tradition the large rock is the site where Abraham prepared to sacrifice his son Isaac.

As the group departed the Temple area, they were permitted to pass through security at the Western Wall and to hike through the Rabbinical Tunnel. It extends from the Wailing Wall to the site of the Antonia Fortress 50 feet below the present-day surface at the Wailing Wall. Here they saw excavation work being done along the old wall of the Temple Mount. At the bottom of the tunnel where the ancient wall was, 150 feet high Adrian spotted several stones that appeared to be of the same size and shape as those he and Rachel had seen at the base of the pyramids of Giza a week or so earlier. According to Adrian, the stones looked as though the same stone mason had prepared them for construction. They were enormous and they fit perfectly!

In the city on Mt. Zion the group walked through the upstairs room made famous in Da Vinci's painting of the Last Supper. Although the windows in the painting were different it was strange to be standing in what was most likely the space where Jesus held his last meal with his disciples before he was hung on the cross. The group was getting noticeably tired and Etain told everyone that they were headed back to the hotel on French Hill for some leisure time and then dinner. He asked everyone to rest up overnight and be ready to go again after breakfast. Two days to go, he noted.

Leaving the hotel the next morning, the bus headed to King David's City outside the city walls. Once there, they toured Hezekiah's Tunnel, built by King Hezekiah to protect the city's water supply when the city was threatened by the Assyrians. The tunnel consists of a 1,777-foot conduit built through solid rock that brought water from Gideon's spring outside the walls to the inner part of the city. The water flowed into the Pool of Siloam.

Etain led the group through a parallel tunnel called the Canaanite Tunnel to the Pool of Siloam where Jesus healed the blind man. The group paused to read scripture before moving on. The next stop was the Jewish Quarter via the Zion Gate. After entering the gate, they watched as a Bar Mitzvah was in progress. The celebration had men holding a white canopy while the boy and family members danced beneath the canopy. It was a joyful scene.

From the Bar Mitzvah the group was ushered to the local bazaar area where hundreds of shops were selling this, that, and the other. The women were thrilled, so Etain let everyone take an hour to get back to the bus. One couple did not make it back, but showed up later at the hotel having found a taxi after getting very lost.

Following their shopping, the group, minus two, walked to the Lion's Gate and climbed aboard the bus for a trip to the Holocaust museum known locally as the Yad Vashem Museum. Established in 1953 as a memorial in memory of the 6,000,000 Jews who were annihilated during World War II, it was an emotional display and tribute to the Holocaust victims. So many children were lost to the careless acts perpetrated in the name of ethnic cleansing. It was hard not to shed a tear.

The museum was remodeled about 10 years ago, and is a riveting sight to see what is an appalling travesty in mankind's history. There are thousands of trees planted in the area around the museum dedicated to those who helped Jews survive the Holocaust. Of the 6,000,000 lives lost, one quarter were children and the memorial to them is deeply touching. Yes, this *was* a holocaust in any sane person's mind!

After an excellent dinner at the hotel, Michael and Elizabeth moved to the lounge area. They asked Rachel and Adrian to join them, but Rachel wanted to walk around the local vicinity, take in the city view, watch the sunset and find a pharmacy where she could get cold medicine. Adrian offered to walk with Rachel to get a little more exercise and to avoid catching Rachel's cold while indoors.

Elizabeth asked Michael, "Are those two romantically involved? They seem to be, how do you Americans say it, a 'thing'?"

Michael chuckled. "You might say that. After a year of dealing with loss of family and loss of a best friend, they are helping each other through the grief stage."

"Michael, don't be foolish. I think they are getting past that stage and I believe they are smitten with each other, if I may use another slang word you Americans use."

"Well, Adrian recently approached me to ask if I minded them spending time together socially in light of their position with the Foundation. I told Adrian, that as long as it did not disrupt our work it was fine with me."

"Yes, and then you sent them off together to Egypt," Elizabeth replied.

"Guilty as charged, but to make a slight correction, I in fact, set the trip up before Adrian approached me."

"I need to watch out for you, Michael. You are a sly fox. Now what have you told them about me?"

"Well, not much Elizabeth. As a matter of fact, I don't quite know what I would say to them. Any suggestions?"

"You could start by telling them I am interested in learning more about the Foundation as a potential donor."

"Is that all?" Michael replied.

"Well, you tell me."

"Elizabeth, I will admit to two things. First, besides being a potential benefactor to the Foundation, I am beginning to see that your expertise in the international publishing arena would be a good fit to our team. If we end up with a unique product, we may need a publisher with international connections to help get our message out to the world."

"And the second reason?"

"Well, well, aren't you the direct one tonight."

"Again, the second reason?"

"Elizabeth, you and I have both been through difficult times. It is hard to move on with a social life."

"For the third time, the second reason," Elizabeth persisted.

"Okay, I do have feelings for you, but I am a little slow to say it. I have to wait and see."

Elizabeth touched Michael's hand softly and said, "Michael, I just wanted you to say you had feelings for me, if you do, in fact, have feelings for me. That's all. I am not asking for a marriage proposal. If you asked me I would say 'no.' See, Michael, I have feelings for you as well. I admire the grief you are dealing with since your wife's death. Yes, I've been through that same experience. I did not go to Greece, or come here, looking for a husband. I simply want to see more of the world. I've worked long hours over many years, had a great husband and loved every minute of it. But now the work is gone, my spouse is gone and I am anxious to find something that will reinvigorate me. We share a similar journey in some respects. If we have feelings for each other, shouldn't we see where it leads us? If the only place it leads us is to a business relationship with your Foundation, then that is where it is meant to go. But if there is more to the story, don't we owe it to ourselves to at least test it?"

"Wow!" Michael gazed into her eyes for a very long moment. He saw sincerity and a small tear well up in one eye. "Okay, let's formalize our Foundation relationship and add some social time in with it. I'll fly to London and you fly to Seattle once in a while. I'll be up front with my crew at the Foundation that we have interest beyond the Foundation to see each other socially."

"Fair enough. When will I see you next?"

"Why don't you come to Seattle in a few weeks or, perhaps come to Hawaii? In the meantime, draft up some proposals we should consider. Just remember we need an electronic distribution concept at low cost to maximize our distribution to the world market. We need the report to be available to the world in many more languages than English. If a proper low-cost system doesn't exist, then we may need to create one. I can put a team together to do just that, if necessary."

"Fine, but without a completed product we are going to have trouble raising money and publishing interest. Also, I would like to spend time in Seattle learning more about the Foundation's work. I will come prepared to make a sizable donation if I like what I see. Hawaii sounds interesting, you'll have to tell me more about your plans."

"Fair enough. There is no reason we shouldn't mix a little fun in with the Foundation business. I do want to have one of our last group meetings in Hawaii. It would be a great place to have you come for business and pleasure."

"I like the sound of that. Okay, if I like the results of your study and if you want to go international with the report in book form, then I will come prepared to contribute as much as £ 1,000,000. There could be another contribution later if I like what I see!"

Elizabeth continued, "As a matter of fact, why don't you stop in London for a few days on your way back to Seattle and let me show you around? You could meet a few of my friends and we could discuss business or, as you Americans say, 'whatever'."

"That is an intriguing thought. I would be honored. I will break the news to Adrian and Rachel tomorrow. Shall we say I'll stay three days?"

"That would be fine. I will not say anything to Adrian or Rachel until you say you've spoken with them."

The last day of the trip started with everyone in the group packing their bags and getting them to the bus after breakfast. This would be a very special day in the lives of every member of the tour. What they would see and experience would stay with them forever.

Etain and the group exited the bus at the Mt. of Olives and they began the one-mile walk downhill to Jerusalem. As they descended, they passed the huge Jewish cemetery on their left. Other tour groups were filing to the left into the Garden of Gethsemane. Etain's group veered to the right and he explained the group had an appointed time reserved to enter the other half of the Garden for a private visit. Everyone waited patiently and excitedly the few minutes it took to clear out the group ahead.

The gate keeper opened the locked gate and the group filed in as if we were entering a church. The church pastor had everyone sit down for a reading from the Book of Matthew. He ended the short service with everyone joining in saying the Lord's Prayer. Thinking the group would be ushered out of the Garden, everyone was thrilled when Etain announced that everyone could disperse throughout the Garden for 10 minutes of meditation.

Seeing Adrian and Rachel head off to a stand of olive trees and sit beneath a tree, Michael invited Elizabeth to do the same. It was quiet and everyone was touched by the fact that they were now where Jesus spent time with the disciples and where he was captured and taken to a trial that led to his death on the cross. The olive trees in the Garden had sprouted from ancient trees much like redwood trees do. In fact, there was a Mediterranean Redwood tree in the Garden at the time Jesus was there according to Etain. He said it was under that tree that Judas gave up Jesus to the guards. WOW!

Leaving the Garden when time was up found everyone somber, yet filled with the Holy Spirit. The Bible had come to life during the trip, but this experience topped the trip by lifting the spirit to new heights. The group walked into the city through the Lion's Gate. Like other gates, this gate had three names. Besides Lion's Gate it is known as the Sheep Gate and Stephen's Gate. A short ways ahead Etain stopped everyone to explain they would now be walking the Via Dolorosa or otherwise known as the Way of Sorrow. It is the traditional path of Jesus as he was taken to be crucified.

Walking by the Pool of Bethesda, Etain reminded everyone that this is where Jesus healed a man who had spent 38 years as an invalid. The pool was large and deep. It was over 300 feet long and about 200 feet wide with a depth of up to 25 feet. Next, they entered a church. It is a Greek Catholic church called St. Anne's. It stands in honor of Mary's mother who is believed to have been born there. It was built by Crusaders in around 1,100 AD. The acoustics in the church are marvelous. For lunch everyone was on their own. Rachel found a pizzeria where a table for four worked perfectly. Falafels were ordered for the entire group and a bottle of wine made for a good lunch.

The women were thrilled to get to the Jewish Quarter were they could again shop in the bazaar. Scarves were the target for most, but there were many items to draw ones attention. Adrian and Michael each bought beautiful hand-painted silk scarves for a gift.

The house of Caiaphas, the High Priest, was next. Everyone made their way to the basement where Jesus was imprisoned before his trial. It is a deep rocked pit and in Jesus' day the only access was through a hole in the ceiling. Outside is a courtyard and Etain explained that it is where Peter denied Jesus three times. A statue to Peter is located there and a golden rooster sits atop the adjacent church.

The next to last stop was at Golgotha, the 'Place of the Skull.' The rock stands some 45 feet high and is the high ground of Mt. Moriah. It is the traditional sight for stoning and crucifixions. There is no doubt about the fact that while looking at the rock formation it looked like a skull to all members of the group. The group concluded it has an eerie look.

Lastly, the group headed toward one of two sites where it is believed Jesus was buried. One site is located at the Church of the Holy Sepulcher. The group visited the other site where hundreds of people were congregated to either see the tomb or to pray at the site.

Upon entering the tomb, which was cut from solid stone, each person went down two steps. To the right they could peer into a chamber with a stone bench where it is believed Jesus was laid after his death on the cross. In the front of the cave there is a track for a large round stone to be rolled in front of the doorway so as to seal the tomb. What the group saw matched very well with what is written in the Bible about Jesus' burial.

Seeing the suspected burial site of Jesus was an emotional experience. Etain quietly took the group to a private seating area where the church pastor led prayers. It was a moving experience to say the least!

After a group dinner and a bus ride to the airport, Etain expressed his hope that everyone had had a good tour. Folks collected their bags, offered tips to the guide sealed in envelopes and said farewell to one another.

Rachel, Adrian, Elizabeth and Michael caught the same flight to London three hours later. Rachel and Adrian transferred to a flight to Seattle at Heathrow while Michael, having whole-hearted support from Adrian and Rachel, left with Elizabeth for a stay in London.

31

Mercer Island, Washington

It was just over a week before the group was assembled to meet with Michael and wrap up the work done in Jerusalem. Michael had given everyone an assignment to identify the stated purposes for Jesus to come to earth. After an opening prayer and some time to exchange an update on the Foundation, the group got to work on the assignment.

Michael said, "I asked each of you to take a specific book of the Bible and go through that book looking for Jesus' own words describing what he is on earth to do. In other words what is it that Jesus is trying to do while here? Since we accept Jesus' body of teachings along with the miracles he performed as evidence of his divine nature, we need to understand his mission so we can better understand how the years since his death and the years yet to come fit into God's plan for mankind."

"I'll start with the book of Matthew since it is the one I assigned myself. In Chapter 3 Jesus encounters John the Baptist who says their roles should be reversed. Jesus corrected him and said John should baptize him to *'fulfill all righteousness'*. So Jesus came to be baptized."

"Next Jesus was tempted by Satan as noted in Chapter 4. We know this from scripture. Jesus was tempted and he chose God's way, not Satan's way. So Jesus came to be tempted just as we are tempted by the devil. Later in Chapter 4 we know that Jesus came to teach. He beseeched those he taught to repent. He asked his followers to become fishers of men, thereby setting the stage for future evangelism in the name of God. In Chapter 5 Jesus makes it clear he is not here to replace the commandments given by God to Moses, but rather he had come to fulfill both the law and the prophets."

"In Chapter 8 he clearly demonstrates that he is here to heal others and to show mercy and love to all who have faith in him. Later in Chapter 8 when the disciples were in a boat on the Sea of Galilee, Jesus appears at night and brings calmness and encourages faith to those in the boat. Later in Chapter 14 Jesus does the same thing while his disciples are in a boat in a storm."

"Jesus came to deliver warnings as illustrated in Chapter 11. Jesus gives stern warning to cities that fail to repent their sins. Jesus came to teach through parables as evidenced by the many parables recorded in Chapter 13. In Chapter 15, I found it interesting that Jesus' encounter with a Canaanite woman results in him telling her *'I was sent only to the lost sheep of Israel.'*
Her response prompted him to grant her request. Could this chance encounter have helped him begin to focus on the Gentiles as future believers in Jesus and His Father?"

"In Chapters 16 and 17 Jesus announces that he will be killed and he reveals himself to a few of his disciples while in a transfigured state with Moses and Elijah. Again, this shows his divine nature. In Chapter 22 he teaches that we should obey the governing powers as they request but to also give God what he requests. In other words he teaches us to respect earthly authority, as well as heavenly authority. Also in Chapter 22, Jesus clarifies the law by telling us that the law is centered on the first two commandments. He tells us to focus on those. Essentially, he is telling us to focus on love of God and love of others."

"In Chapter 24 Jesus warns us of the signs leading to the end of the age. This is a chapter we need to come back to when we are trying to understand where we are in God's plan and what lies ahead. So mark this chapter down for further discussion. For now Jesus confirms to us that he will return and he will be the judge over all mankind separating those who remain with him from those who are cast to eternal punishment."

"In Chapter 27 Pontius Pilate asks Jesus if he is the king of the Jews and Jesus answers *'Yes, it is as you say'*. Ultimately we see that Jesus came to Jerusalem at the end of his ministry to die for our sins. His resurrection described in Chapter 28 reveals to the disciples that Jesus truly is the Son of God. Jesus further emphasized his divine nature to his disciples by meeting them after his resurrection near Galilee where he spoke with them and commissioned them to serve the Father, the Son and the Holy Spirit by baptizing others."

After a short break, Nancy picked up the discussion with the Book of Mark. "I am glad I drew the shortest of the gospels and I even took my break time to line out everything that Michael covered with his rundown on the Book of Matthew." Everyone laughed.

"Michael clearly spoke of Jesus spending a large amount of his time teaching. The quotes I read in Chapter 1 of Mark describe Jesus' intent to preach. I suppose that is the same thing in a general sense, but I thought it was important that we at least add that word to the list of things he clearly came to do. Likewise in Jesus' healing episodes, Mark points to the fact that Jesus forgives many in addition to the healing he did. That too is an important word or action we should add to the lengthy list we already have."

"In Chapter 2 I found it interesting that Jesus says 'I have not come to call the righteous, but sinners'. This shows his intent to help the lost sheep find their way. He is wanting to find lost souls and reclaim them! In Chapter 3 I found it interesting that Jesus took on the Jewish synagogue crowd and leaders by doing things that were prohibited by synagogue rules. Hence he came to make a few corrections to the way things were being done!"

"At the end of Chapter 3 Jesus makes an interesting point about family. He points out that all the followers are his family. Basically, Jesus is expanding family to include all those who believe in the Lord. I like that he came to emphasize that point. Perhaps it has been covered, but, if not, it needs to be. In Chapter 8 Jesus clearly tells us that if we want to be saved we must take up our cross and follow him. This is a call for action by Jesus, and he certainly came with every intent to tell us that so we understand what it means to believe and to follow."

"In Chapter 9, Jesus makes it clear that he is going to be betrayed, killed, but would rise in three days. Of course, all this came to pass in Jerusalem shortly after saying it. In Chapter 13, Jesus tells us about the signs that lead to the end of the age. I don't fully understand the meaning but Jesus obviously was very clear in having that as part of his mission while he was here."

"In Chapter 14, Jesus clearly claims to be the son of God when asked by the leaders of the synagogue. He even says to them that they will see him coming on the clouds while he is seated at the right hand of God. Like Michael's report, the end of the Book of Mark is focused on Jesus allowing himself to be crucified, buried and then resurrected and given to ascension in the presence of the disciples."

After a short lunch break the group reconvened in the conference room. Rachel asked to speak before Adrian proceeded with the Book of Luke.

"Michael, we haven't heard much from you about your time with Elizabeth in London and whether or not you see her as having an active role in the Foundation. You two seem to have hit it off. Would you fill us in?"

"Thanks for asking Rachel. Sure, I should have volunteered more about our relationship."

Michael went on, "Our relationship is both business-related and personal. On the business side I am convinced Elizabeth can help us in two specific ways. First, she is impressed with our work and our goals. We spent hours discussing what the Foundation has done and what we have plans to do in the months and years ahead. I spent the time to do all that with her while we were on the Greek Island cruise where it became apparent she could be a major financial contributor to the Foundation. That side of things has progressed to where she has committed to a substantial donation."

"There is one very important additional opportunity we may have with Elizabeth from a Foundation perspective. She has spent much of her professional life in the publishing world as you know. We are going to need that expertise before long in a big way."

Adrian asked, "Could you expand on that?"

"Of course. I have no doubt in the course of religious history, Christian history in particular, that we are nearing the end of what is called the era of 'spreading the gospel'. We are still firmly in that era but we aren't finished with it. Furthermore, the journey we are taking together in answering key questions about our faith is clearly the same thing hundreds of millions of people around the world are curious about. We have a chance to produce a book that can help people navigate through all this. We have a chance to significantly help literally millions receive the gospel and strengthen their faith. Jesus clearly calls upon us as Christians to do this very thing. Elizabeth, I believe, can help us with the form that book takes and the publication and distribution of it."

"Wow, what a wonderful thought, but I am not sure I'm qualified to adequately contribute to that, Michael," Rachel exclaimed.

"Sure you are, Rachel. We all are. Think back to how the disciples felt inadequate. Yet, Jesus empowered them in spirit and walked with them through it. We can do the same with the Lord's help," Adrian added.

"Exactly," Michael said. "We all can do this. As a matter of fact, we are doing this. Furthermore, we are blessed with the resources to do this. We are blessed to be in an era of tremendous technological capability to do just this. E-books are here to stay. The internet allows us to put our book in the hands of anyone in the world who has internet access. That is huge!"

"Let me say this. If we have a product worthy of getting to every person on earth we have the ability to do it. We can have the book translated into any language where it is needed. Elizabeth has some excellent connections in that regard. She also is well connected with top-shelf authors who could assemble what we produce and make a book of it. I have friends who can assist us in every possible electronic venue to efficiently distribute and market our book anywhere."

Everyone sat at the table without saying a word for a whole minute.

"Now I'm really scared!" said Rachel.

"You aren't the only one!" said Nancy. "But, I have full faith that if anyone can lead us there Michael can."

"No," Michael corrected her. "We can do this with God's help."

Nancy replied, "Okay, 'we' can do this. I am in. Now tell us about the personal side of this relationship with Elizabeth. I can't believe you two spent all your time in London thinking this up." Everyone laughed.

"No, we did not spend all our time on business. We had a few dinners out, but mostly we talked. It was good for us to open up to each other about our personal losses and to share the conflicted thoughts we have about what it all means for the future when all along we each believed our spouse would be with us till the end. At any rate, we agreed that we had feelings for each other. We agreed to meet periodically in either London or here in Seattle. We believe the Foundation work is something we can share together as we piece our somewhat broken lives back together. Beyond that we don't know where it will lead but we intend to see. I hope that meets with your approval because you are my family."

Adrian piped up, "Michael, you have our full support. We are with you!" Rachel nodded. Nancy said, "Remember, separate rooms is proper." Everyone broke out laughing.

The group broke for the day and reconvened the next morning. Adrian was first up continuing their discussion of things Jesus came to do and did. He started in with the Gospel of Luke.

"First, let me say that after crossing off all that Michael and Nancy covered yesterday I was not left with much. You two did great work and the things you outlined made a huge impact on me as to how comprehensive Jesus' mission was."

"In Chapter 2, after healing a man in verse 10 Jesus says '...*know that the Son of Man has authority on earth to forgive sins'*. I think Nancy mentioned this yesterday. It bears repeating because this is one of the main messages Jesus brings to us. He confirms that he is the only one who will reconcile believers to God! This is a big wow! In Chapter 4 of the Book of Luke, Jesus is in Capernaum at a synagogue where a man possessed by a demon approaches him. The demon in the man recognizes Jesus and Jesus drives the demon away. The crowd is awed by the power of Jesus over demons. Therefore, Jesus came to show his divinity again."

"In Chapter 5, Jesus tells the Pharisees and the teachers of the law that he has the power to forgive sins so that they clearly know that the Son of Man has God's authority on earth. In Chapter 6, when Jesus makes his speech outlining the Beatitudes, Jesus encourages those listening to love their enemies and to not judge others. Love becomes such a foundation of his ministry in the New Testament that we all have to believe that it is a major tenet of what he came to do. His emphasis on loving God and loving others, as we discussed yesterday, is so prominent in his teaching. It must rank right up there as a principal message that he came to demonstrate in his acts and to preach in his teachings."

"Clearly, in Luke as in the other gospels, Jesus performs miracles to show his divinity and his mercy. Such acts reinforce his love for those who showed faith in him. In Chapter 10, Jesus shares an example of a good person in the story of the Samaritan. He makes the point in his journeys that it is not just the Jewish people who can know God, but Gentiles too can know God and show the kind of love God wants us to show to others."

"In Chapter 12, Jesus clearly warns those whom he teaches that they should be wary of the hypocrisies of the leaders in the church. Later in Chapter 12, I found a part of what Jesus came to say fascinating. I had heard it before, but I had forgotten it until I read it for this session. I won't forget it ever again as it has made a real impression on me. Let me quote Jesus in verse 49 thru 52. *'I have come to bring fire on the earth, and how I wish it were already kindled! But I have a baptism to undergo, and how distressed I am until it is completed. Do you think I came to bring peace on this earth? No, I tell you, but division. From now on there will be five in one family divided against each other, three against two and two against three'.*"

"After all the teaching on love it is so different to hear Jesus say he has come to create division. However, it is a major proclamation in two ways. First, Jesus makes it clear either you are with him or you are against him. Secondly, the choice of being with him or not has serious consequences. Although we are told to not be quick to judge others, the fact is that Jesus will divide mankind through judgement in the end. The consequences of which lead to eternal life or eternal death."

"In Chapter 21, Jesus clearly prophesies about the future. He outlines that there will be an end to the time of the Gentiles and then he will return. With that return will come redemption. In Chapter

22 the disciples ask Jesus if he is the Son of God. Jesus replies '*You are right in saying I am*'. So again Jesus did come to confirm his relationship with the Father."

"Lastly, it always deserves repeating, in Chapter 24 Jesus returns from death and meets with his disciples to reassure them that he is with them in their ministry. His ascending to the Father was then done in their presence so that they might know and see that he is with the Father."

The group broke for lunch and reconvened afterwards to hear from Rachel on the Book of John. Rachel started with this comment, "I am awed by the Book of John. It is so beautifully written."

"So much has been said by the three of you I don't have much to add. Please be patient if I repeat a few of your points and add a few new ones."

"In Chapter 2, I thought it noteworthy that Jesus' mother asked Jesus to perform a miracle at the wedding they attended in Cana. Jesus told her that his time had not yet come. Still she insisted he help with an awkward circumstance where the wedding party was low on wine. Jesus complied with his mother's request and made wine from water. To me this showed respect for his mother even when he preferred not to do it. And in Chapter 4, Jesus speaks to the Samaritan woman and then to the townspeople who all come to believe in Jesus as the Savior of the world. This is significant in that it shows Jesus' love and his covenant of salvation would apply to Gentiles."

In Chapter 5, Jesus breaks the Sabbath by teaching. He informs those who are protesting that the Father is always at work and like the Father he is at work. Later, he instructs saying that the Father does not judge anyone, but it is he the Son, Jesus, who will judge all. In verses 24 to 25 Jesus says, *'I tell you the truth, whoever hears my word and believes him who sent me has eternal life and will not be condemned; he has crossed over from death to life. I tell you the truth, a time is coming, and has now come when the dead will hear the voice of the Son of God and those who hear will live'."*

"In Chapter 6 verses 28 and 29 Jesus is asked *'what must we do to do the works God requires? Jesus answered, the work of God is this: to believe in the one he has sent.'* Jesus makes it clear to all of us that the one important thing in our lives is to believe in him as the Son of God. If we do that we will repent and we will have our sins forgiven. Later in verse 35 Jesus says *'I am the bread of life. He who comes to me will never go hungry, and he who believes in me will never be thirsty'."*

"Later in Chapter 6, Jesus makes it clear that one of the disciples is a devil. Clearly he is referring to Judas, but this shows the others that Jesus does, in fact, know our beliefs and our allegiances. Interestingly, in Chapter 8 verse 58 Jesus says *'I tell you the truth,'* Jesus answered, *'before Abraham was born, I am'*. This makes it clear that Jesus was present in heaven before Abraham was born on earth."

"In Chapter 10, Jesus clearly shows that he came to convict the Jews who did not believe in him. Although they attempted to stone him for blasphemy he challenged them as non-believers. Elsewhere in Chapter 10, in verse 7, Jesus says *'I tell you the truth, I am the gate for the sheep'*. And in verse 11 he says *'I am the good shepherd. The good shepherd lays down his life for the sheep'."*

"In Chapter 11, upon his arrival in Bethany to see Lazarus' sisters, Jesus tells Martha *'I am the resurrection and the life. He who believes in me will live, even though he dies; and whoever lives and believes in me will never die. Do you believe this?'* Of course Martha answers yes and Jesus raises Lazarus from the dead in the presence of others."

"In Chapter 14, Jesus clearly outlines to the disciples the way to salvation. In verse 6 he says *'I am the way and the truth and the life. No one comes to the Father except through me. If you really knew me, you would know my Father as well. From now on, you do know him and have seen him."*

"In Chapter 17, Jesus prays for himself as he faces his upcoming crucifixion, but he also prays for the protection of his disciples. Since he needed his disciples he asked the Father to be with them in his absence. What love this showed at what was to be a horrible day for Jesus. Lastly, in Chapter 21, I found it touching that Jesus would ultimately forgive Peter for his denial of Jesus. What a loving gesture following a horrible death for Jesus. He again showed us all his mercy and his love for his followers."

Rachel concluded her work saying again, "I see love in Jesus on every page I turn!"

Michael thanked everyone at the table for their work and presentations. "I can't tell you how important it is to me that we read the Word, that we study the Word, and that we discuss the Word. All of this deepens our faith and brings us in spirit to be with God. Thank you all!"

"We are at the end of our work answering Question #3. We have endeavored to determine whether Jesus came as a prophet or a Messiah. I believe if those were our only choices we might have to say both. As a prophet Jesus instructed us in God's ways.

> *First, he told us of God's expectations to be focused on believing that Jesus was the Son of God.*
> *Second, he told us to repent and place our faith in Jesus to wash away our sin and to reconcile us, in the end, to God.*
> *Third, Jesus taught us the virtues we should aspire to in our endeavor to be more like Him. He taught us about forgiveness, love, hope, faith, humility and how he wants us to treat others.*

> *Fourth, he taught us about his expectation that we should spread the word so that others could share in his love and his offer of salvation.*
> *Last, he said he will return to judge the world and to bring about a new heaven and a new earth."*

"That may not be a complete summary and we certainly can add to it later as we dress up the work we have done. It does however bring us to Question #4. That is: If Jesus is the Messiah what is the plan for his future return?"

"It is pretty evident we are well into the time of the Gentiles. In fact, I believe it is evident we are nearing the end of that period. If that is the case, then we may well be moving towards the end times referred to in both the old and new testaments. Do you all agree?" Everyone nodded.

"I suggest we do a couple of things to get the ball rolling. First, I think we should get a plan together for how we are going to proceed through this task. I would like to work with Adrian over say the next week to put together a draft plan for us to talk about next week. Is that okay?" Everyone signaled that would be good.

"The second thing I would like to do with your agreement is to plan a 10-day trip to work through as much of this as we can."

Rachel asked, "Where do you want to go for this?"

"I was thinking about Hawaii, Maui specifically."

"I'm in!" Rachel said with a big smile on her face and a wink at Adrian.

"I'm in!" Adrian followed in line.

Nancy paused, "Michael could I bring my husband along. Not for meetings, mind you, but that is a long time for us to be apart. Besides we have never been to Hawaii and we have talked about that being a nice anniversary trip someday."

"Nancy, I think that can be arranged. In fact, I am thinking of having Elizabeth come for the last session or two in Hawaii and then possibly stay on there for a few days after we are finished. You can have Larry come anytime. Heck, Adrian and Rachel may want to use some vacation time and stay longer as well. We can work out the details next week when we meet. Sound okay?" Everyone smiled and nodded.

Part Four

The Return

32

Mercer Island, Washington

A week later the group joined together to map out a plan for dealing with the question of Jesus' return. After an opening prayer, Adrian started the discussion with a suggested format.

"Working with Michael during the past week we put together a process that should get us to where we want to be. It involves a fair amount of biblical research and a fair amount of subject matter research. If we divide up the prep work and have time to do a good job researching the topics we've targeted, we should have a fair chance of completing our work in Hawaii over eight days, starting the day after we arrive. That is why we may want to extend the trip to a full two weeks. A little recovery time may well be needed."

"Rachel said that since the group will arrive in May the tourist pressure will be relatively low and there shouldn't be a problem staying four extra nights." Everyone seemed to be smiling at the prospect of staying for some rest and relaxation.

Adrian inquired, "Well then, I take it everyone is in for eight days of work at the front end of a two-week stay?" Everyone concurred.

"Michael and I believe we need two more preparatory sessions here before we travel to Maui. Since we won't fly to Maui for a month yet, we are planning to schedule these a week apart starting two weeks from now. This will give us time to catch up on our current work of getting our report well documented for the first three questions we've been working on."

Rachel piped up, "So will we have a lot of work to get ready for these two sessions? I am swamped with what I've got on my desk right now and I don't have much time to prepare for those meetings."

"I don't think it will be a problem. Let me go through these two meetings and then let's answer your question."

"Sounds fine. Thanks!" Rachel replied.

"The first meeting is one Michael would like to lead, so I'll let him outline the meeting."

"First, let me address Rachel's question. Other than taking the time to attend this half-day session, there will be no work required on anyone's part. My intent is to have no preparation for this meeting. In other words, I plan to have someone outside our group attend this meeting and spend a half-day educating us on a particular subject matter I know we need to learn more about. Especially since we are planning to interpret prophesies in the Bible about the future. The subject matter is the City of Jerusalem, because we need a history lesson on that city. It has been at the center of countless battles, sieges and a couple of complete destructions. It is the center of God's focus in terms of geography, and may well hold the key to interpreting prophesies about the future. So, it is my intent to have an expert come here and take us through a history lesson."

Nancy chimed in, "So do you have an old classmate from back east who knows all this history and who is anxious to come to see you?"

"Nancy, you know me too well. You are close. Although she is not yet confirmed, I do have a friend from Boston who would very much like the honorarium we will provide for a trip to the northwest."

Nancy countered, "Well this all sounds good as long we don't have to take a test on the matter afterwards." Everyone broke down laughing.

"No fear, my dear Nancy. I wouldn't think of such a thing."

"That said, I take it there are no objections?" Adrian queried.

Adrian continued, "None heard, let's move on to the need for a second meeting before we head to Maui. Wow, that really sounds good - going to Maui!"

"The whole purpose of the second meeting is to get answers about how we plan to tackle this question while in Maui. We are going to need to spend some time preparing for that trip prior to going. Let me go through the plan for the days we work in Maui, and I think having time together a full week ahead of going on the trip will help us all in our prep work."

"Since we plan to have eight sessions there, let me break them down for you. Now this might change slightly by the time we get to the meeting a week before leaving here, but it is unlikely. The first two sessions are to be led by Michael and Nancy, and the subject matter is the Old Testament prophesies about the future. This will cover the Old Testament, starting with Genesis and ending with Malachi, and only involve those prophesies Michael and Nancy think we should discuss."

"The third session is dedicated to understanding the prophetic word from Jesus about the end times. Rachel and I will lead that day. The fourth and fifth sessions will be dedicated to understanding the New Testament prophesies about the end times. I will lead the fourth session and cover the Book of Revelation. Rachel will lead the fifth session and cover the balance of the New Testament, excluding what we will have covered in the third session. Session six will be led by Michael and it will deal with current events and situations that may help us establish where we are in the countdown to Jesus' return. He will help us see what might happen in the future to trigger what we are told will happen."

Nancy said, "I am glad he is on his own for that one. I would be a heavy anchor if my name was up there with his." Again, they all laughed.

"The last two sessions will be dedicated to drawing the best conclusions we can about the future and the role Jesus will play in it."

"After what I just said, now, I really do hope my name is not up for leading those discussions either." Nancy smiled again.

"I think Adrian needs to lead those," Michael smiled.

"I accept," Adrian said.

Michael then said he would like to comment on the process. "I think if we do something a bit unique with this process we will get to an answer quicker, so let me make a suggestion and see what you think."

"If Nancy and I approach the Old Testament prophetic word from Genesis to Malachi, I think we can build a good understanding fairly quickly. We will retrace some of the Old Testament history just so we can get things in their proper context. Then we'll focus on some of the key prophetic messages in the Old Testament. This will be the first two sessions. We'll only have one, four-to-six-hour session per day, so we have time to do a little reading and relaxing, as well."

"Next, I suggest Adrian and Rachel proceed first with a focus on Jesus' prophetic words from the gospels. This will focus us on what Jesus says is important for us to know about the future. There is duplication between the writers, so you can pick and choose what we should focus on. That should be the third session."

"The twist in all this is the Book of Revelation. I believe it may serve us best if Adrian starts this session at the back of the book and moves backward through the events that are outlined after Jesus' return. At that point, we will all understand what is outlined for the time of the millennium and beyond."

"Once we review that part of God's plan, Adrian can take us through the tribulation years leading up to the second coming. Otherwise, I assure you, we will all get lost in the chronology and struggle to understand the end state of God's plan. It is far too easy to get lost in all the drama and symbolism if we start at the beginning. Believe me I have already tried it both ways!"

Adrian commented, "Since Michael first hit me with the idea I have come to really like the approach. I want to try it."

Rachel responded, "My first thought is that this seems like a strange way to go about it, but I can certainly go along with the idea."

Michael carried on, "Okay, that will be session number four. Session five will be done by Rachel and she will highlight other prophetic messages in the New Testament that she feels we should discuss. We don't know yet how extensive that might be. We'll have to wait and see what Rachel finds."

"Sessions six and seven will focus first on where we are in the world currently, relative to God's sequence of events. We'll try and relate our present situation to the prophetic words we've studied, to see what is ahead. This will give us something of an idea as to where we are on God's prophetic clock and what the future may hold."

"In our last session I hope we can focus on what it is that we should be doing through the Foundation to do God's work. I trust this exercise will focus on the priorities for the foundation and what we need to do to accomplish those priorities."

Everyone seemed to agree with the process as long as Michael led the last three sessions. Michael agreed and said, "Thanks everybody, let's end in prayer today." They held hands in a circle and each spoke a few words in prayer.

33

Mercer Island, Washington

"Good morning to everyone," Michael announced and then led the group in prayer. "I would like to introduce you to a friend and colleague of a friend of mine. This is Ruth Shalev from the Hebrew University in Jerusalem, where she serves as a Professor of History."

"Currently, Ruth is serving her sabbatical in Boston and she has graciously agreed to join us for today's session and lead us through a history lesson centered on the Holy City of Jerusalem. I have asked that she give us a 'freshman' history lesson this morning, and then this afternoon allow us to get her thoughts on the accuracy of Daniel's prophesy from an Old Testament perspective. Before we turn the session over to Ruth, I would like each of you to tell her about yourself and clue her in on what you are doing with the Foundation."

"Oh, I forgot to mention one thing. Just so we all understand. Ruth is a Jew and she practices Jewish tradition. However, she is a Messianic Jew and she fully believes that Jesus is the Messiah. In Israel and elsewhere, the Jewish community calls Jesus Yeshua. As Christians, we believe in the same God that Ruth and other Jewish people believe in. It is just that most Jewish followers have not yet accepted Yeshua as the Messiah. Well, I hope I have not butchered the introduction too much."

In turn, Adrian, Rachel and Nancy introduced themselves and their individual responsibilities in the Foundation. Nancy got everyone smiling when she said she hoped freshman meant high school not college. That was vintage Nancy!

Ruth started, "Let me give you a short description of my background. I grew up in Jerusalem. My grandparents on my mother's side were living in Poland during the build-up to World War II. They were killed in a German concentration camp. My grandparents on my father's side moved to Jerusalem in 1949. My father served in the Israeli military retiring 20 years ago as an Army general. My mother escaped Poland before her parents were sent to the camp and managed to survive the war in southern France, eventually immigrating to Israel in 1952 where she met and married my father in 1956. I was born in 1958."

"I moved to Jerusalem from Jaffa, 10 years after first entering Israel when I was 19 years old. I studied at the university, worked for the government and then began my teaching career. I currently write books and I teach. So let's get to the history lesson Michael asked me to present. But first, are there any questions about me?"

Adrian asked, "If I may, when did you become a Messianic Jew and how did that come about?"

"In my youth I was like many Jews. I felt marginalized by what had happened to my grandparents and by the hateful discrimination that I saw against Jews. I also liked the comfort of the Jewish faith where Jesus is a prophet and not the Messiah. After all, if he was the Messiah, how could he have died and not led us to our promised salvation?"

"As I grew older, and became more learned and worldly from my extensive travels, I began to open up to the thought that Jesus may well be the Messiah and his sacrifice was a fulfillment of scripture as well as a sacrifice for the whole world, or at least for those who come to believe in him as the Son of God. I was 48 years old when I accepted Yeshua as my Savior. Since doing so, I have never looked back and I have felt closer to God than at any point in my life. I now feel his presence in my life. Also, I am fortunate to have others around me who are also Messianic Jews and we are all growing closer to God. It is comforting to have others in your life who are devoted to the same beliefs."

"Thank you!" Adrian said.

"Okay, let's hit the high points on the history of Jerusalem. Let me power through this and please write down your questions and I will address them at the end of my rundown."

"Jerusalem is one of the most ravaged cities in the world. It is a city that has been attacked over 50 times. It has been besieged over 20 times, and it has been totally destroyed twice. When I say destroyed I mean pretty much levelled! I'll cover the two destructions specifically in a few minutes. First let's go back in time. Nancy, this will be the junior high school version."

"Thanks," Nancy smiled.

"The first settlement is estimated to have been approximately 5,500 years ago. This is just before the Bronze Age. Houses started showing up in the area of the city 1,000 years later around 2500 BCE. The first walls showed up 700 years later around 1800 BCE. It is largely believed the name Jerusalem began to take hold by 1400 BCE."

"Now the people residing in the area called Jerusalem were not of Jewish descent. They were nomads. They were fringe groups of Arab descent. It was not till approximately 1,000 years before Christ, that King David took it upon his army to attack and conquer the site of Jerusalem. After that, the Hebrew people erected what is called Solomon's Temple. This is the first temple constructed on the Temple Mount site which is also noted as the site where Abraham was prepared to sacrifice his son to God."

"The next major event in the history of the city is the Babylonian destruction of the entire city in 586 BCE. This is the first of the two times Jerusalem is completely destroyed. It is a significant event in the history of the Jewish people living in the region, as they were exiled to Babylon, starting in 605 BCE when the city was first besieged by the Babylonians. By 586 BCE the Jewish people were largely gone from the entire region for a period of 70 years. This exile had been foretold in scripture. I am sure you will find it as you study Old Testament prophesy. Next, the Babylonian Empire was conquered by Cyrus the Great and he grants the rights to the Hebrew people for them to return to the city of Jerusalem. Over a number of decades the temple is rebuilt and the walls of the city are rebuilt, as well."

"Then the Romans come and conquer Jerusalem under the command of General Pompey. This takes place in 63 BCE. Of course as you know, when Jesus is born, the city is under Roman control and it stays that way until the Romans decide to completely destroy the entire city in 70 AD. The Romans still controlled the region around Jerusalem and they even reconstructed parts of the city as a Roman city. Later the city falls to the control of Muslims from 638 to 1099. Notably, the Dome of the Rock that sits on the Temple Mount is constructed in 691 AD. The hold on the city by Muslims ranges through many centuries, but is interrupted a few times by Crusaders from Europe capturing the city and parts of the region. By 1250 AD, the Muslims had dismantled much of the city and the population declined significantly. During the time of the Ottoman Empire, Jerusalem was captured in 1517 AD. In the 1530's Suleiman the Magnificent embarked on a major reconstruction of the city's walls and gates. This event may well serve to be significant in your work using Daniel's prophesy about the coming of Christ. I hope you note it in your work ahead."

"By 1917, the British had captured Jerusalem, and after World War II ended both Britain and the U.S struck a deal to allow Israel to be re-established as a nation in its own rights. So, in 1948 Israel became a nation once again. Then in 1967, following a six-day war, the city of Jerusalem joined the country with very specific agreements as to what rights the Muslims have relative to the Temple Mount, and what the Jewish people can and cannot do on the Temple Mount."

"This is a short thumbnail rundown on the city's history, but I do think it is sufficient for what you need. This afternoon we can discuss in more detail some of the interpretations and conclusions you need to consider in your work to see how prophesy relates to the second coming of our Messiah or your Christ."

"Michael, should we break for lunch or do you want me to take questions now?"

"Ruth, I think we should break for lunch now. It is a beautiful spring day and I think our catered lunch is here and set up for us on the outside deck where we can enjoy the view." Everyone agreed.

Michael started the afternoon session with a prayer of thanksgiving and petition. He asked the Lord to be with them in their deliberation of Daniel's words from Chapter 9. He asked for insight and understanding.

"Ruth has a powerful message for us in interpreting the vision that Daniel wrote about in Chapter 9. It is a very personal message, and not necessarily a University or an official one accepted by the church. She hopes this presentation causes us to think about what Daniel's message tells us of the first coming of Christ, but it may also give us a clue about the Second Coming. Ruth, we are happy you are here to share your insight on this fascinating prophesy with us."

"Thank you, Michael. I am not often asked to do this, but I am always ready to do so when an inquiring group wants to have their minds expanded. That is not to say you will use what I am about to say, but I trust it will make you think about the accuracy of prophesy.

"First, a little more history. The Book of Daniel was likely finished around 530 BC. This date puts the writer in an era shortly after the capture of Babylon by the Persian king Cyrus in 539 BC. Cyrus ultimately sees the plight of the Hebrew people and agrees to help them in rebuilding the temple in Jerusalem. The temple is completed in 516 BC, after lots of opposition by Persian authorities. Actual work on the city walls did not begin until Nehemiah arrived in Jerusalem in 445 BC. Let's stop here and I want each of you to read slowly Daniel Chapter 9 from verse 20-27. This is frequently called the *seventy 'sevens' prophesy*." Keep in mind, to the writer of this verse, a day is a year. Therefore, a week is really seven years, and 70 weeks is really 490 years."

Ruth then read Daniel's words in the eight verses, *"While I was speaking and praying, confessing my sin and the sin of my people Israel and making my request to the Lord my God for his holy hill – while I was still in prayer, Gabriel, the man I had seen in the earlier vision, came to me in swift flight about the time of the evening sacrifice. He instructed me and said to me, 'Daniel, I have now come to give you insight and understanding. As soon as you began to pray, an answer was given, which I have come to tell you, for you are highly esteemed. Therefore, consider the message and understand the vision:"*

"Seventy 'sevens' are decreed for your people and your holy city to finish transgression, to put an end to sin, to atone for wickedness, to bring in everlasting righteousness, to seal up vision and prophecy and to anoint the most holy."

"Know and understand this: From the issuing of the decree to restore and rebuild Jerusalem until the Anointed One, the ruler, comes, there will be seven 'sevens,' and sixty-two 'sevens.' It will rebuild with streets and a trench, but in times of trouble. After the sixty-two 'sevens,' the Anointed One will be cutoff and will have nothing. The people of the ruler who will come will destroy the city and the sanctuary. The end will come like a flood: War will continue until the end, and desolations have been decreed. He will

confirm a covenant with many for one 'seven.' In the middle of the 'seven' he will put an end to sacrifice and offering. And on a wing of the temple, he will set up an abomination that causes desolation, until the end that is decreed is poured out on him."

"Let's continue. The accuracy of this prophesy is rather profound. Let me explain. This prophesy provides a timeline for the atonement of Israel's sins. It starts with the issuance of a decree which is widely regarded as the charge given by Artaxerxes I to Nehemiah to rebuild the walls of the city. It goes on to say that 483 years, that is 69 weeks of years, will pass from the decree to the '*cutting off of the anointed one*'."

"Well, the anointed one unquestionably is Jesus and the cutting off means removal or death. Since the announcement is widely believed to have been delivered in either 445 BC or 444 BC, we have the rough starting date for this prophesy."

"Next, we have most experts agreeing to Jesus' death to be between 27 AD and 40 AD. In fact, the majority believe Jesus was crucified very near 30 AD. Now if we believe this prophesy is based on the Babylonian calendar of 360 days per year, the 69 weeks-of-years amounts to 476 years on the Gregorian calendar (i.e. 69 times 360 divided by 365.25). That given, the prophetic message Daniel passed on says that the 'anointed one' would be 'cut off' in or near 30-31 AD. In fact, I have read a very detailed calculation with more precise dates that concluded the decree was given on March 5 in 444 BC, and the 69 weeks of years totaled 173,880 days, resulting in a date of March 30th 33 AD. That day is said to be Palm Sunday, a few days before Jesus was crucified on April 3rd 33 AD."

"In many ways, this prophesy has bolstered my belief in the word of God and in the predictions he has passed on to us about the future. I trust this work you are doing will have the same result this example has had on me. However, it should not take away from the work we all must do to spread the gospel and share God's love with others."

Michael asked, "Help us understand who Artaxerxes is?"

"There were three Persian kings named Artaxerxes. The one I referred to is the first. In fact, there were many delays over the years in allowing the work on the temple and the city. For example, soon after the decree to rebuild the temple and city, Artaxerxes was solicited by commanders in the region who voiced strong opposition in allowing the rebuilding to go on in Jerusalem, due to the troublesome nature of the Hebrew people. The stop and go nature of the rebuild went on for years. The temple was finally completed in 516 BC, and the walls around the city were completed in 444 BC."

Adrian asked, "As we study this prophesy, why should we think this prophesy applies to the future?"

"Adrian, there are a couple of good reasons. First, I mentioned that the city was destroyed twice. Once before Christ was crucified and once after. The second total destruction occurred roughly 40 years after Jesus died. The Romans destroyed Jerusalem in 70 AD. Hence, it needed the walls and everything else rebuilt."

"Okay, I have it. The Ottoman Empire helped rebuild Jerusalem in the 1500's AD," Michael interjected.

"As you say, you got it!"

Michael smiled, "Thank you for your patience and your insight. We are just beginning to catch on, and I think this is going to be as exciting for us as it has been for you."

"Well, as a history professor I have an advantage. If you can get the next puzzle piece figured out, let me know."

Ruth continued, "I do want to make another point relative to your question, Adrian. Have you ever heard the expression that the only thing we learn from history is that we don't learn anything from history?"

"I think we've all heard the expression," Michael noted.

Ruth continued, "Well, over the years I tended to agree with the quote. Today I hope we are smarter and we now can learn from history. Let me tell you there is a lot of what I might call duplicity in Christian history. We just talked about the fact that Jerusalem was destroyed once in the Old Testament era and once in the New Testament era. Now think of another."

Nancy said "I have one."

"Okay tell us, Nancy."

"Tell me if this counts. Abraham was asked by God to sacrifice his son Isaac for glory to God. Jesus was asked to sacrifice himself for the glory of God."

"Very good, Nancy! Anyone else?"

"Jesus came at the end of the Old Testament era and he will come again at the end of the Gentile period."

"Well done. I am impressed."

"I can't be left out," Adrian blushed. "It seems there is a common time line of 2,000 years for the time of the Jewish people and then 2,000 years for the Gentiles, assuming we are nearing the 'end times'."

"Again, well done, that one bears watching, doesn't it? I've done my job Michael, and I think your group is well positioned to continue making strides toward your goal. It has been a pleasure working with you, and now I must go catch some sleep before my return flight to Boston early tomorrow morning. Michael, particular thanks for your hospitality and generous donation to my work. Call if I can help in anyway."

"Come, let me drive you to your hotel," Michael offered.

"Thank you, I appreciate that. Your company will be far better than the cab driver I had this morning."

Ruth and Michael left immediately and the other three sat there looking at each other in a state of wonderment.

Rachel shook her head. "How does Michael find people like Ruth? I can't believe what we just experienced. I thought today was going to be some drab boring lecture like I used to get in sixth grade. I came simply hoping I would not get any homework out of going to class. Then we get this! I don't know what to say."

Nancy smiled, "I've seen it many times. Michael has this incredible array of people he knows and stays in touch with. He makes a few phone calls and comes up with just who he needs for whatever he is doing. I am still amazed by it myself."

Adrian spoke up, "I probably should feel as inferior as anyone could to be doing what I am doing, but I don't. Michael has raised us all to a higher level and inspired us with sessions like this to believe we actually can do what we are trying to do. Just think how far we have come over the past few months. I am so blessed to be in this position. After the losses in my family I had days where I was ready to toss in the towel. Once again I am inspired."

Rachel added, "I could not believe how neat it was to sit here and have Ruth ask a tough question at the end. It was a tough one to answer on the spot, but we all had a sense of what she wanted us to know. We saw it through and came up with some amazing answers. You guys are great, and so is Michael."

Rachel added, "Oh, and I was prepared to daydream today about the upcoming trip to Maui. Well, as the session came to an end I looked back over the day and not once did I daydream. Now I feel like I am really looking forward to our sessions together in Maui even more than the beach."

Nancy interjected, "That may change once you see the beach. Michael has shown me pictures of his trips there over the past ten years and I think you two will love it there. I hope we can keep our heads in the game while we are in work sessions."

Adrian asked if the three of them could pause and pray together for the blessing they had received today." Each person spoke to what was on their heart. They broke for the day. Nancy headed home. Adrian and Rachel went out to dinner together.

34

Mercer Island, Washington

At the beginning of the next day's meeting, Michael asked Nancy to lead the group in prayer. He then outlined the agenda for the day.

"There has been some excellent work done over the past two weeks. Logistical plans for the Hawaiian trip have been made. As it turns out we are going a week later than first thought due to the need for us to have a little more preparatory work done. It seems to fit everyone's schedule okay and that is all good. Nancy's husband Larry will be along for the entire trip although he will not be participating in our meetings. He is looking forward to a lot of hot-tub sessions, beach walking, and reading. Elizabeth will join us for our last two sessions as an observer. She will stay the days following our last session and then plans to spend a week here as my guest."

Rachel asked if anyone had any issue with their itinerary. Adrian was wearing his new Hawaiian shirt and sat there just smiling. No one had a concern. After all, the itinerary included a Hawaiian Luau for the entire group, along with optional snorkeling, diving, or sunset cruises. The sessions seemed a little overwhelming, but the downtime seemed to be well covered.

Rachel mentioned some additional good news. Two contributors recently donated $100,000 dollars each. Michael sat there smiling. The Foundation had far more funds available this day than it did when it was first started. Michael seemed to think this was just the beginning. Rachel asked Michael where he saw the Foundation going, based on the work the group had done to date.

"Rachel, this is a good question. We plan to address this in-depth in one of our last sessions in Hawaii, but you are not asking too soon. First, we need to complete our work in answering the questions before us. We are down to the last. Personally, I believe we have finished the most difficult portion of this endeavor, although I imagine I am the only one that sees it that way. I suspect you feel a little lost and bewildered about how this will all shake out in Hawaii. Will we reach the end with nothing or something that is very special? I tell you, we have come so far from where we started a year ago. I have no doubt we will surprise ourselves with the final product as long as we stay true to the word of God. We are seekers and he is helping us find our way. I believe God wants us to succeed in getting the answers right and I believe he wants us to share them throughout the world. Not everyone has the time, much less the resources, to do this. I know God blessed each of us so we could do this as long as we dedicated ourselves to it for His glory and not for our own. This is part of spreading the gospel and that is what we should be doing at this point in time, on God's clock."

Rachel spoke up, "Thank you, Michael, for saying what you just said. Thanks too, for the extra week to get ready for Hawaii. Sometimes I see the work as a job, but you are right, this is a calling and we need to finish it and share it. Thanks!"

Adrian added, "Michael, you were absolutely on target when you said we are basically privileged to be in the position we are in. Sometimes throughout this past year I know I have felt unworthy to be doing this, much less be paid well to do it. Then I think of the poor fishermen in the boat with Peter who are asked to travel with Jesus, and then to carry on his message to others when Jesus was gone. Just think how inadequate they must have felt. Yet, they gave their lives for the sake of Jesus. Just look at how well off we are. I feel humbled and determined to follow in their footsteps in some small way. I hope and believe that each of you feels the same."

Nancy smiled, "I know we are entering the final phase of laying out a blueprint for the Foundation, and I want to share one observation. It has been an extraordinary experience for me to have watched the three of you grow into such fine Christians. It brings tears to my eyes when I think of the changes I have witnessed. It has been a blessing to see three people take such hardship and heartache and turn it into so much good." She paused. "I need a tissue."

After a short break the group reconvened.

Michael started, "I am so proud of you three. Let's rejoice in the Lord for bringing us together, and let's keep moving ahead for the day of his return is one day closer."

Nancy had a question, "Do we have to read the whole Old Testament in search of prophesy?"

"No, Nancy I plan to develop the list and I'll simply give you your half to discuss. That should keep it simple."

"Perfect, when can I get the list?" Nancy pressed. Rachel could not help chuckling.

"Nancy, you are a taskmaster," Michael said. "How about next week?"

"Fine by me, boss," Nancy smiled.

Adrian had a question, "Any more thoughts on how I should handle the Book of Revelation?"

"Adrian, you have a tough one to deal with. Other than the earlier discussion we had on the sequence of your presentation, I think we all have to stick to the 'word' and avoid too much interpretation. When you make an interpretation, make us aware of it and we will sort it out then, or in sessions seven or eight."

Michael continued, "I have session six on current world events and how some of these events may fit into God's timeline. As you three go through your own workup on prophesy, I would appreciate it if you would jot down any thoughts you come up with that relate to the world as you see it. I could use a little help with the whole subject of relating prophesy to today's world."

"Any more questions?"

"I have one," Rachel spoke up. "Do I need to bring my own snorkel?" Everyone cracked up!

35

Lahaina, Hawaii

After landing at the Kahului airport on the island of Maui, Michael, Nancy, Nancy's husband Larry, Rachel and Adrian were transported by limousine to their hotel on the northwest side of the island of Maui. It took about 40 minutes to get to the hotel, and along the way they could see the massive mountain called Haleakala, which is a dormant volcano. Standing at 10,000 feet above sea level, it is the dominant feature on the entire island. In fact, if you measured the elevation from the seafloor to its peak, you would have a mountain taller than Mt. Everest. As the limousine reached the west side of the island, the Pacific Ocean fanned out to the west, interrupted only by three islands of Hawaii. Most prominent are the islands of Lanai, and to the north, the island of Molokai. Both look impressive from the northwest coastline of Maui.

Proceeding northwest, the driver took them through the town of Lahaina, once a thriving whaling village, to the resort area just north of the town called Kaanapali Beach. This beach is widely reputed to be the best beach in the United States, and is divided in the middle by a massive rock formation called Black Rock. This is a prominent location where a large volcanic rock formation extends into the sea and it separates the north beach from the south beach. The hotel is approximately a mile south of Black Rock, at the end of a modern development on the south beach.

After unpacking, all five strolled north along the beachfront passing other hotels and condominiums before arriving at a popular area caller Whaler's Village. There the group was seated in a nice oceanfront beach-side restaurant for dinner. After a long six-hour flight, they were ready for some relaxation. They stayed till the sun set and returned to the hotel for a good night's rest.

Due to the warm afternoons this time of year and the lack of tan they each confessed to have, the group of four had agreed to try to meet for an early lunch each day, and then meet at 12:00 p.m. for four to five hours in a reserved conference room to do their work together. Following that, they would take the balance of the day off to enjoy the pool, beach, or other activities. The schedule would provide time in the mornings for all of them to read any prepared handouts that were part of the presentations and discussions they were scheduled to have over the course of the eight days they were to have meetings. They all agreed to attend the beachfront church service on the upcoming Sunday.

The next day at 12:00 p.m., Michael started the group meeting with a prayer thanking God for opening the minds and hearts of their group to receive love and understanding. He asked for strength and insight as they moved on with their work together. He expressed how he had been impressed the night before that the group had asked to get an earlier start to the first day.

"Well, good day to everyone. I trust you got a good night's sleep and are prepared for the journey we will take over the next week or so. With God's help, we will get through all that has been lined out for us to do. I trust this will be a very inspiring week or so to cover the key points of God's plan forward."

"Let me first read you portions of an e-mail I received from Ruth. It is something that is insightful and something we should be mindful of as we look to the future. After thanking us for the opportunity to visit with us she says, 'Here is some info you might consider after our discussion. King Cyrus of Persia, being led by God, took Babylon. Suleiman the Great had a dream that inspired him to rebuild the walls around Jerusalem. Therefore, understand that God uses kings and leaders to fulfill scripture.' She goes on to encourage us to stay the course. I offer this up because it is my intent to press the scriptures in Jeremiah and Daniel regarding Jerusalem pretty hard over the next two days. I believe they may tell us a lot about the future."

Michael asked Nancy to review her work on the relative events and dates from Adam to Christ, to get everyone on track with the biblical accounts and their approximate timing over the 4.000-year span leading up to Jesus.

Nancy summarized, "From the fall of Adam to Abraham we had a span of approximately 2,000 years during which we had the great flood, the building and fall of the Tower of Babel, and the early biblical years. Once Abraham is on the scene and is prepared to offer his son Isaac as a sacrifice to God, the Hebrew people become God's chosen people. God makes this known through a divine covenant spoken to Abraham. After moving to Egypt, Moses leads the Hebrew people out of Egypt. After a long delay in the wilderness, the Hebrew people finally arrive in the Holy Land and proceed through three centuries of Judges overseeing the people."

"At the halfway mark of this 2,000-year period, in or around 1,000 BC, David becomes the King of the Hebrew people, and David's family becomes the line from which the Messiah is prophesied to come. Through the following 1,000 years there were many kings and many prophets. Some of the kings were not very good. In fact, a number of them were despicable and God became very angry."

"Ultimately, God had enough of the disobedience, and Jerusalem was attacked in 605 BC, and finally overtaken by the Babylonians in 586 BC. The Hebrew people were taken into exile for 70 years. Thereafter, the return to Jerusalem was interrupted many times, but a notable return was made by Nehemiah in 445 BC when he led the work to rebuild the walls of the city so the citizens could defend the city against intruders. Ultimately, in the Old Testament era, the Romans overran the region and took control of Jerusalem. As we all know, the Romans maintained control through the time of Jesus."

"I think it would be wise to stop here and take a break."

Following a 15-minute break, Nancy continued "I want to thank Michael and Rachel for helping me through this. I could not have done all this on my own."

Michael responded, "Nancy doesn't give herself enough credit. We enjoyed our discussions on this matter and her report reflects more detail than what she shared today. Nancy wanted to present the highlights today and let everyone read her report, if you really want more detail. Oh, and Rachel helped us as well. She has done more with these reports than I think any of us know. Thanks, Rachel."

Following another 10-minute break, Michael took the lead in the discussion of Old Testament prophets. He explained the work he had done focused primarily on the prophets starting with Samuel, continuing with Isaiah in the 8th century BC, and through Malachi in the 5th century BC. However, he said he did want to start with a few comments from an earlier period where Moses helped to set the stage for the prophets that came forth in the 'era of judges,' followed by the 'era of kings' and, finally, the era of Israel's 70-year exile to Babylon."

"Okay, let's set the stage with Moses' account of Noah. First, it needs to be noted that God made covenants through the Old Testament era to the time of Christ. God's covenant with Noah was basically an unconditional guarantee to never destroy **all** earthly life with a natural disaster like the flood. He used the 'rainbow' as a mark of that covenant which shows His long term commitment to people and to his word. Later, God makes another covenant with

Abraham to grant the Holy Lands to Abraham and his ancestors. Still later, God promises to be Abraham's God and to be the God of his descendants. These were divine promises meant to endure the test of time."

"Notably, nearly 1,000 years later during the rule of King David, God made a covenant with David to preserve the lineage of kingship through David's family. Ultimately, having been born in the line of David, Jesus became King of the Jews and brought a new era of God's mercy not only to the Jews, but he extended that love to Gentiles who would follow the way of the Son of God, Jesus. These covenants collectively show how God is not an ambivalent God, nor a passive one. Rather, the nature of God is to require obedience and love, and in return to give love and mercy. Keep these covenants in mind as we go through the Old Testament today and tomorrow."

Following a short break, Michael continued. "I want to emphasize the last point about God foretelling the fact that King David's reign would last forever. Let's take a brief look at the prophet Samuel who lived 3,000 years ago at the beginning of the 'era of kings' when Saul, and then David presided over the people of Israel. In the second book of Samuel in chapters six and seven Samuel gives an account of another prophet named Nathan. He was told by the Lord to tell David to build a house for God and that his kingship would last forever. Ultimately, David's son, Solomon, built the temple in Jerusalem and David's family line led to Jesus."

"David and other psalters provide us with beautiful and instructive prose in the book of Psalms. They tell us that all nations and all people will be accountable to God. They tell us that the proud will fade and the humble will rise. They tell us that those who rely on the Lord will be rewarded. They give us insight into the future, as they understood it, and that in the end peace will overcome all opposition. They tell us that all persons are to acknowledge that they are dependent on and responsible to God. They tell us that Jerusalem is the royal city."

"In Psalms 97-99, the writer describes the Lord's judgement on earth and the need to exalt the Lord over all the earth. This is a forceful testimony of God's presence in the world and God's willingness to display his power and glory to the world. Now please read Psalm 110 to see the wonder of how the writer captures the position Jesus ultimately takes in heaven after his time on earth. Keep in mind this psalm was written roughly 1,000 years before Jesus was born and roughly 3,000 years ago today."

"The book of Ecclesiastes is also a source of insightful personal writing and prose. It was likely written during the time of King Solomon and may, in fact, have been written by King Solomon himself. In it, the writer states that man, even godly men, cannot find out the larger purposes of God or the ultimate meaning of man's existence. Man is viewed as 'chasing the wind.' Life not centered in God is purposeless and meaningless, and without God nothing else can satisfy. With Him all of life's gifts are gratefully received and used and enjoyed. Therefore, reverently trust and obey God."

"This summary of some of what is said in the book of Ecclesiastes made me wonder if what we are doing is even possible. Then I thought again, that this book was likely written 3,000 years ago and so much has happened since. Primarily, we are blessed with having had Jesus among us, and we have had so much of God's plan outlined to us that we are in a far different situation than King Solomon was at the time his book was written. At any rate, these are just a few of the wonderfully written insights into the beliefs at the times of David. Many prophets followed Samuel and David. Notably Elijah, Elisha, Jonah, and Amos, all of whom provided spiritual advice through the years when Israel was a divided kingdom. This led to the time of the great prophet Isaiah who lived 700 years before Jesus. We all need to understand many things spoken and written by this prophet."

"Now turn to Chapter 7 of Isaiah and read verses 13-14. Here Isaiah writes of Ahaz, King of Judah, who is told by the Lord that a virgin birth will yield a son who will be called Immanuel. This is an event that occurs 700 years later. Now look at Chapter 9 verses 6-7 where

Isaiah tells of a son who will be called 'wonderful counselor, mighty God, everlasting father, prince of peace'. He will reign forever. Now go to Chapter 11 where Isaiah tells us that *'a shoot will come up from the stump of Jesse'*. Again, this is a reference to the fact that Jesus would be born from the line of David. In fact, Jesse is David's father."

"Next, look at Chapter 13 where Isaiah tells us of the upcoming defeat of the Babylonians by Cyrus the Persian. This prophesy was 100 years ahead of its happening. In Chapter 14 he tells us that the people of Israel will return later to their land following the defeat of the Babylonians, which is what began to happen in 539 BC."

"Adrian, you will appreciate reading Chapter 24 and relating the imagery in the words to what you are seeing in the Book of Revelation. I believe this is a vision much like what John describes in the Book of Revelation, yet is written 700-800 years before Christ. It tells me God knew all along that there would be a period of utter destruction in the days before the Messiah takes his rightful place as Lord over all on earth. Chapter 34 does much the same thing. In Chapter 41, Isaiah describes a king from the east who obeys God's will to conquer another nation, and this is precisely what happened when Cyrus the Great of Persia conquered Babylon in 539 BC. In Chapter 42 Isaiah raises up the Messiah as the source of hope for all people."

"In Chapter 45 Isaiah clearly tells us that the Lord has anointed kings. In this case, the Lord anointed Cyrus, the King of Persia, to defeat and punish the Babylonians. He goes on in Chapter 49 to outline the future efforts to restore Israel following the Babylonian exile. In Chapter 49 verse 16, Isaiah tells us about the restoration of Israel after the return from exile. He exclaims *'See, I have engraved you on the palms of my hands; your walls are ever before me.*" I mention this verse because the walls of Jerusalem have special meaning in prophesy as we will see again in the Book of Daniel."

"Next, look at Chapter 60 verses 10-14, where it says that Jerusalem is the city of the Lord. It reminds me of what Ruth said about the importance that Jerusalem has been and always will be to God. Lastly, please look at Chapter 65 verses 17-25. This sounds much like what we might expect after judgement day. This may well be an early description of what we'll see in the Book of Revelation when Christ promises a new earth and a new heaven. Adrian will have more for us on that later."

Adrian replied, "You are right in saying there are many prophetic statements in the Old Testament that predate what I've read in the Book of Revelation. It strengthens my belief that God has had a plan in mind for a very long time and he has shared parts of that plan throughout history."

"I agree, and I think it is vital to our work to understand that Isaiah and others predicted the coming of a king descended from David, and this king would reign with righteousness forever. Jesus was and is that king. He leads us in righteousness, he delivers us from sin, and he became the light to the Gentiles. Thanks be to God!"

After their final break, Michael started, "Okay, I've tried to emphasize a lot of points up to this part of the session. I want to cover one more prophet today and then we will be done. I want to talk about the prophet Jeremiah. He lived around 600 BC."

"The reason I bring up this prophet is that he made a profound foretelling of the Jewish exile from Judah, and Jerusalem specifically. In Chapter 25, Jeremiah passes on God's message that the Israelites would be exiled for 70 years. After the 70 years, Jeremiah said the king of Babylon would be punished by God, as would be his lands and his nation. All of this, in fact, happened. Now why do I make a point of this prophesy? Well, the destruction to Jerusalem by the Babylonians was the first, and at that time, the only complete destruction of the city. The walls were torn down. The temple was destroyed along with the city."

"I want you to remember as we progress through the days ahead that God punished the entire nation around Jerusalem in this process, and specifically those living in His Holy city of Jerusalem. He punished them from the time the first siege took place in 605 BC, up to the time the city was completely destroyed in 586 BC, and then punished them for 70 years in exile to Babylon. It was not until 516 BC that the city and notably the temple were restored. In many ways, he took these years away from His people as a price to pay for their sins and lack of faith. He lifted his protection of them for a total of 89 years."

Adrian said, "Thanks for making this important point, Michael. I am dealing with a similar circumstance in the New Testament that relates closely to the one you just covered. After the Romans destroyed the city of Jerusalem in 70 AD, the walls were not rebuilt for nearly 15 centuries. They were rebuilt by the Ottoman Empire, and this fact may serve as a relevant event more than I originally knew. I won't say any more now, as I need to deliberate for a while. Thanks, again!"

"Adrian, that's why we're doing this," Michael responded. "Let me hit on a number of verses in the Book of Jeremiah to fill out some of his prophetic work, and then we'll wrap this session up."

"The Lord was very unhappy with Israel leading up to their occupation and destruction. Years before the destruction takes place Jeremiah prophetically stated in Chapter 25 verse 11, *'This whole country will become desolate wasteland, and these nations will serve the king of Babylon seventy years'.*"

"He goes on to say in the next verse, *'But when the seventy years are fulfilled, I will punish the king of Babylon and his nation, the land of the Babylonians, for their guilt,' declares the Lord, 'and will make it desolate forever'*. In Chapters 27 and 29 Jeremiah tells us of the restoration work that will follow the exile and the faith that will then be shown to the Lord. At this point, I should also mention an interesting scripture reading from 2 Kings, Chapter 25. In verses 8-10, we are told the destruction of the temple in Jerusalem took place in August of 586 BC. In fact, the date of destruction is August 14, 586 BC, and the cause of the destruction was a fire set by the commander of the Babylonian troops. This is significant because it backs up the earlier statement I made that the temple was rebuilt later in 516 BC. This is the same 70 years prophesied by Jeremiah. Okay, that is enough, if not too much for this afternoon. No more group meetings today. We have a dinner reservation in the hotel dining room tonight. I forget the time?"

Rachel responded, "We meet in the dining room at 7:00 p.m."

"Okay, I'll see everyone then. Thanks for listening. We'll be back here tomorrow at 12:00 p.m."

The following day, Rachel showed up to the meeting room with a hint of sunburn. She had stayed out in the sun just a little too long, and it showed. Everyone hinted that she might need to take it a little slow these first days. She just smiled.

Michael started things by asking Adrian to lead the group in prayer. He drew out a long prayer with all the things for which the group should be giving thanks. Then he made a petition. He asked the Lord for a discerning mind and a loving heart as they continued their discussion on God's plan for the future. He admitted that he may have shortcomings in understanding God's plans, but that he was committed to the task at hand, as were all of his partners in the group. It was a touching expression of humility and faith.

Michael stood up and said this would be the final day to cover the Old Testament prophesies, and if anyone had questions to be sure to write them down as there would be time at the end of the session to cover them.

"With that said, let's get started. Today, I want to spend most of our time on one book in the Bible and then follow that with just a few highlights in a couple of other books. However, this first prophet is regarded by many as making one of the most important prophesies for the era before Christ, as well as raising the possibility that this prophesy may apply to the future. This prophesy is from the book of Daniel. Please turn to Chapter nine and read the entire chapter. You will see that Jeremiah is mentioned early in the chapter, so keep that in mind as you read. We are going to be spending our time discussing verses 20-27 in some detail, so read those two or three times."

"I'll need time to read those three or four times, if you don't mind, Michael," said Nancy.

"Take all the time you need!"

When everyone was ready to continue, Michael proceeded, "Moving ahead, the book of Daniel was completed around the time King Cyrus of Persia captured Babylon. This would place the time near 530 BC. The book describes Daniel having visions and interpreting those visions. He also interprets the visions of others including kings, and he lives to see many of them fulfilled. I would like everyone to read the 20 pages or so that cover the entire book. Please read these before we have our last two sessions. You need to appreciate the way God used Daniel to interpret dreams and prophetically describe God's plans."

"Okay, let's see, Chapter 9 starts with Daniel having a vision of the archangel Gabriel coming to Daniel praising him as one highly esteemed in the eyes of the Lord. Gabriel delivers a message and a vision. This vision/message is known as *'the seventy sevens'*. It outlines the fact that there will be sixty-nine 'sevens, before the anointed one (i.e. Christ) is cut off."

"In other words, 483 (i.e. 69x7=483) years after a decree is rendered to rebuild the walls of Jerusalem 'the anointed one' will be cut off (i.e. killed). Again, this prophesy is made near the year 530 BC. The decree Daniel is referring to is not given until 444-445 BC, when King Artaxerxes sends Nehemiah to Jerusalem to rebuild the walls of the city."

"If we accept the fact that the timeline was given in Babylonian years (360-day years), then the actual date prophesied for the cutting off of the anointed one would be 30-31 AD. So, did Jesus die at that time?"

"While three of us were in Jerusalem, Etain, our tour guide, answered that question by telling us there are many theories about when Jesus was crucified. Most all of them say Jesus died between 27 AD and 40 AD, he said. Most chronological listings I have seen in the U.S. show dates very early in the 30 AD range. This is driven from the belief that Jesus was born around 4 BC, during the first of two censuses taken in that era. Paired with Luke's account that Jesus' ministry started when he was 30 and lasted three-and-a-half years, one could conclude that Jesus died in 30-31 AD, making the Daniel prophesy very close if not exact."

Adrian, Rachel and Nancy were amazed. A lively discussion rambled on for 15 minutes. Everyone was excited and wanted to address whether or not this prophesy had an application to the New Testament era, since the group was well aware that the city was destroyed one more time in the 1500's AD. Michael begged off on going that far in this session, but promised to give time to the subject when the New Testament session came up for discussion.

"I will say this, however. In verse 24 of Daniel, in Chapter 9 Gabriel says *'seventy sevens are decreed for your people and your holy city to finish transgression, to put an end to sin, to atone for wickedness, to bring in everlasting righteousness, to seal up vision and prophesy, and to anoint the most holy'*. It would be difficult to say one way or another that all of this has been done. Therefore, it leaves me with the thought that this prophesy may have an application to the future. This is exciting and we will deal with this in a later session."

Rachel commented, "I don't quite see how it could be applicable if we are talking about a date when the anointed one dies again?"

"Excellent point, Rachel. The possibility I raise is that 'cutting off' may not mean death. In fact in Jesus' first coming, Jesus may have died physically, but he was resurrected and simply cut off from our physical world. That would lead to the possibility that in the future perhaps Jesus is cut off from the world while Satan is given a free run. That possibility keeps me interested and I hope you can buy the argument that we should keep exploring that as a possibility."

"That seems reasonable at this point. I'm in."

After a good long break, the group gathered and Michael explained he had two other prophets to mention. "Let's take a quick look at a prophet who wrote around 520 BC named Zechariah. Please read in Zechariah Chapter 14 verses 1-9. I love the last verse where Zechariah says *'The Lord will be king over the whole earth.'* The reading continues and provides a vivid warning to anyone attacking Jerusalem. This is another descriptive account of the commitment Jesus has in defending the Holy City. Now go to the Book of Malachi, a prophet who wrote around 440 BC. Here is another account of Christ's glorious coming in power and might. It follows many of the other descriptions of total defeat of those who oppose Israel."

"So many of these writings from prophets, inspired the Hebrew people to stay loyal to their faith and wait patiently for the day of the Lord. For centuries these people have waited. At times they have drifted into evil and the Lord has been swift to punish them. Yet, redemption has been there for them always. Praise God for His patience and his willingness to open His arms to those of us who are Gentiles as long as we believe in his Son and act on those beliefs."

"This ends Nancy's and my work on the Old Testament. It has been an arduous journey as we have had to read, and then reread so much, but in the process of doing so we have grown in our love of God's plan and his purpose for us. We believe that with so much history behind us we are closer to understanding God's plan and being able to convey it to others. We have no doubt that when we finish our work in the next week we will see well into the future and reconcile God's basic plan in our minds."

There were no questions when Michael asked for them. He knew the group was tired.

"Thanks for enduring the long lectures in these first two sessions. You were great! Let's join in prayer and close this session." Michael asked each person to pray whatever was on their heart at the time. They prayed out loud one at a time holding hands in support of one another. Michael was in tears at the end. He knew Mary was in heaven and looking down upon him and probably also shedding a tear of joy.

That evening everyone was on their own. Nancy and Larry rested and called home to talk with their grandkids. Rachel and Adrian went to dinner together at a lovely restaurant in a neighboring hotel, where they held hands as they watched a couple of swans swim by their waterside table. Michael had room service bring his meal to his room where he ate alone on his lanai overlooking the ocean. Later he phoned Elizabeth who had just gotten up in London. They conversed about Elizabeth's upcoming flight schedule and other things.

The next day after a relaxing breakfast, the group convened at 8:00 a.m. having decided to get started early, have lunch together, and finish in the mid-afternoon. They planned to catch the late afternoon, sunset dinner cruise on one of the many catamaran boats leaving from the beach each evening. Michael wanted to mix in a few activities and change the meeting venue to keep the group fresh while pushing through their agenda.

Rachel started this third session telling everyone that the format today would be a little different. First, she explained the focus would be almost entirely on what Jesus said, through the gospel writers about what we should expect in the future days leading to his return. Secondly, Rachel and Adrian expected to have more discussion to ensure that the group shared a common understanding of the scriptures before they started drawing conclusions about what all this means for the future.

Rachel continued, "To set the stage a bit, let's review a few things. We are blessed with so much more information and history than the early Christians had. Many of the early Christians expected Jesus to return as the powerful messiah king they wished for and deeply wanted to believe he would come soon. Today, 2,000 years later we have Jesus' words and various accounts of his life and his teachings. Meaning, we have nearly 2,000 years of history in which to put those words into context. So we need to study Jesus' teachings to ensure we are grounded in the word. Said in another way, we believe our Lord was born in 4-5 BC. He had a virgin birth in Bethlehem, and by 26 AD he was baptized and begins his public ministry. After approximately four years in his ministry he was tried, crucified, buried resurrected and ascended into heaven. Shortly after his death the Christian church was 120 strong. As a church, they scattered, grew in numbers, reformed again and again until we find ourselves today a church of 2,000,000,000 believers, with one in three on earth claiming Christianity as their faith. Christ Jesus is our Savior and we expect a Second Coming in the future. We also expect that return to end a period of strife in the world that has not been seen before. We expect that return to bring peace to the people who believe in the Lord."

"With that said, we need to take this time to listen to what the Lord has spoken and to what has been recorded in the Bible. I want to take you through a few Bible verses and then we will have a short discussion. Afterwards, Adrian will take us through the balance of what we have for today. Let's read in Luke Chapter 24 verses 36-45. Take your time and read theses verses carefully."

After a while Rachel continued, "Keep in mind these statements from Jesus are after his death, after his resurrection, and after his encounter with two men on the road to Emmaus. Jesus is with his disciples and calming them down from their surprise and their doubts. He goes on and assures them that everything that has been written in scripture must be fulfilled and that they must preach 'in his name to all nations'."

"Okay, what reactions do you have to what Jesus declares in this appearance after his death?"

Nancy piped up, "I think I would have been in tears if I had been there in that room when Jesus appeared. He even showed the group his scars and let them touch him. It must have been so spectacular a scene that it strengthened the disciples' faith and filled them with the spirit to do all of what they did in the years to come."

Michael added, "And to think with all that occurred in the few days leading up to this event, Jesus could keep his focus on seeing that God's word in the scriptures was being fulfilled to the letter."

Adrian said, "Michael, this reaffirms that as Christians we all need to expect God to do what he has always done. That means he will abide by all prophesies and by his word."

Adrian went on, "Rachel and I wanted you to be aware of what Jesus says in John 14 verses 30-31. He says, *'I will not be with you much longer, for the prince of this world is coming. He has no hold on me, but the world must learn that I love the Father and that I do exactly what my Father has commanded me.* Please understand that Jesus refers to Satan as the 'prince of this world' in this particular reading."

"Preceding these two verses Jesus also says in verse 28 *'You heard me say, I am going away and I am coming back to you.'* With all the emphasis by God in seeing that the Word is fulfilled, this assures me that Jesus is going to return. We may not know the hour or the day, but the fact that it will happen is not a question for me."

Nancy concluded, "I don't think it is a question for any of us or anyone who truly studies God's Word."

"Well said," Michael added.

Adrian started again, "Before we get too far into the Second Coming, I would like to take a few moments to let us read Jesus' proclamation on his purpose in returning. Please read with me from the book of John in Chapter 14. I'll read the first four verses."

Adrian read, *"Do not let your hearts be troubled. Trust in God; trust also in me. In my Father's house are many rooms; if it were not so, I would have told you. I am going there to prepare a place for you. And if I go and prepare a place for you, I will come back and take you to be with me that you also may be where I am. You know the way to the place where I am going."*

"A couple of verses later Jesus says, *'I am the way and the truth and the life. No one comes to the Father except through me. If you really knew me, you would know my Father as well. From now on, you do know him and have seen him.'*"

"All of this is said just before Jesus instructs the disciples on the fact that as he departs he will send the Holy Spirit to teach us and remind us of all the things Jesus has spoken. This completes the trinity in God and making God's presence felt by any who believe in the Son and the Father."

After a short break the group reconvened. Adrian asked everyone to turn to Matthew, Chapter 24. "We will proceed together through this important account of the signs of the end of times. Jesus has just left the temple in Jerusalem where he had delivered seven woes to the crowd there. As he left the disciples were told that all of the buildings that they could see before them would be destroyed. Of course, this was a foretelling of the destruction of Jerusalem by the Romans that would come in 70 AD. As Jesus climbed up the Mount of Olives the disciples inquired of him when this destruction would take place and when would he return. He said there would be deception by others claiming to be the Lord. There would be wars, famines and earthquakes, and all this was simply the birth pains of what would come."

"In verses 9-14 he says *'there will be persecution of those who follow him and many will grow 'cold' and fall away. Lastly, he says the gospel will be preached throughout the whole world and 'then the end will come'.*"

"In the verses that follow, Jesus cites a very specific event as being one that was prophesied by Daniel as being 'the abomination that causes desolation'. When this occurs it triggers horrible events for Judea and perhaps the entire world. Jesus tells us, were it not for the 'cutting short' of that time, everyone would die. Furthermore, there will continue to be great deception by those who are evil."

After those terrible days, Jesus says, *"the sun will be darkened, and the moon will not give its light; the stars will fall from the sky, and the heavenly bodies will be shaken."*

"Then read in verses 30-31 the description of the Lord's return." Adrian paused. "Finally, the next four verses provide a parable leading to Jesus' statement that *'heaven and earth will pass away but my words will never pass away'*. Of course, everyone asks when these events will occur, and Jesus continues his words telling us that *'No one knows about the day or the hour, not even the angels in heaven, nor the Son, but only the Father'*. These words from Jesus will help us understand the vision of the end times in John's book of Revelation. That book was written decades after Jesus' death, yet it is very much the same story with more details. We'll see that in the next session."

After a short break the group gathered and Adrian continued. "I want you now to look at the Book of Luke. Go to Chapter 21 starting at verse 5. Read through the entire chapter and see just how close Luke's account is to Matthew's."

After a few minutes Adrian proceeded, "Notably, Jesus warns us of great deception in the world. You will see this again notably when we discuss the Book of Revelation. Elaborate schemes will come to those in the world to convince many that a false messiah is real. Many miracles will be performed to deceive those on earth at the end times. Heeding these warnings will be critical for the lives of those who experience this time leading up to the end of the world as we know it."

"Luke also captures the fact that wars will prevail and many will die. Famine and plagues will spread across the world widely. Earthquakes and pestilences will perpetuate fear and death. Preceding this will be massive persecution of those who believe in Jesus. Luke tells us to expect Jerusalem to be surrounded by armies and trampled upon until the times of the Gentiles are complete. Then we are told that there will be *'signs in the sun, moon, and stars'*. Then Jesus will return in glory."

"Importantly, Jesus states in verse 32 *'I tell you the truth, this generation will certainly not pass away until all these things have happened'*. This passage leads me to wonder when the timeline of a generation has or will start. I certainly cannot answer that today. Perhaps we will have a better idea as we work through other prophesies or perhaps we will never know. Lastly, I could not find much in the Books of Mark and John to add to this topic. However, John has given us more than we may understand in the Book of Revelation. We'll get into that tomorrow and I hope you will have read it at least once before we get to the meeting."

Nancy piped up, "I saved it for tonight's bed time story. I hope that is okay!"

"You might find yourself asleep well before you get to the end! It is an action-packed and lengthy book." Adrian responded.

"Does anyone want to add anything?" Adrian asked.

Michael had a question, "I am curious about the comment Jesus made that all these things will happen in one generation. Any ideas after looking at these gospels?"

"Well, it is a good question, Michael. The only mention is what I covered in Matthew. Let me double check my notes. Here it is in Chapter 24 verse 34 Jesus says *"I tell you the truth, this generation will certainly not pass away until all these things have happened.* The only thing I found interesting was that this statement in both gospels follows the same passage about a fig tree. To me this indicates that either Jesus will return in the spring or perhaps it is an expression signifying that it won't happen till conditions are right. I admit that I struggle trying to interpret any clue as to which generation Jesus is referring. I also assume, but can't be certain, that a generation is 70 years."

Michael responded again, "I find your thoughts provoking. Let's pick up on those as we go through the Book of Revelation and see if we can sort that out."

"Any other comments?"

"Can we go to the pool now?" Rachel seemed anxious.

Michael said, "Sounds good to me. Just a couple of logistical things. I have arranged for us to go to Wailea tomorrow for our fourth session where we will focus on Revelations. We have a conference room at a very nice hotel with great grounds and facilities. We'll leave here at 9:00 a.m. and start our session there at 10:00 a.m. I expect we'll be in session till late in the afternoon, so I made reservations for dinner at a waterfront restaurant on the other side of the island. I know you will enjoy the location, and the fresh fish dinners are excellent. We won't return till 8:00 p.m. or 9:00 p.m. tomorrow night. I trust that is okay with everyone?"

"Seeing no objections, we are done for the day. We'll meet on the beach for the sunset dinner cruise shortly."

After a perfect sunset and a fabulous meal aboard a catamaran, Michael, Nancy and Larry headed for their rooms to read. Rachel and Adrian set off on a walk along the beach. They walked to Black Rock and went to the upper floors of the hotel located there taking in the magnificent view. They held hands all the way back to Whaler's Village. Out on the beach they sat on the sand looking out over the dark ocean and stared at the stars. With a slight chill in the night air Adrian put his arm around Rachel. They kissed and tried to name a few constellations. They were very much at peace with one another. The glint in their eyes was evidence that love was in the air!

36

Wailea, Hawaii

The next morning the four enjoyed a pleasant drive south to Wailea. Had it been whale season they surely would have seen a number of whales breeching and swimming near the surface. Several high vantage points provided great viewing to the west and to the south.

After driving past Kihei they entered the Wailea-McKenna area. This area is dry and requires irrigation to maintain the lush vegetation that is planted throughout the developed area. World-class golf courses meander through nicely developed home sites, hotels and condominiums. This is an up-scale area for certain.

Arriving at the hotel, the group was met by a valet attendant who took the car and parked it for Michael. The group was escorted inside, although the openness of the inside made it look and feel like the outdoors. Lots of open air passageways were possible due to the low rainfall. However, the striking feature of the hotel was its expansive and elegant views across the ocean. Literally captivating!

Michael commented, "Okay, it is not every day we get to meet in luxury like this, so enjoy it while you can. The room we have is for special board meetings, celebrities and high-level dignitaries. We are lucky to get it and I expect our catered lunch to be over the top. All that aside, today we will hear from Adrian on one of the most talked about books in the bible. It is the last book of the Bible and is written by Jesus' closest disciple, John. John is the only disciple who was not killed for his ministry. He was, however, exiled to the Mediterranean island of Patmos. As you know, I was fortunate enough to have toured Patmos and to actually enter the cave where John received visions from heaven and had them written down by a scribe as he recited them."

"Today Adrian will take us through John's writings starting backwards to begin with, to ensure we understand the end-state of what John saw and was told. At some point he will go to the front of the book and proceed forward. I promise you it will be an exciting time. Adrian, I turn the floor over to you."

"Thank you, Michael. You are correct. We are going to take an exciting ride through this very unique and complex book. Michael was definitely right in asking me to start at the back of the book. However, I convinced him that part way into that I needed to return to the beginning of the book and move forward to tie it together with the end. This may sound convoluted but I assure you it will eliminate a lot of confusion. How many of you read the Book of Revelation?"

Rachel said she had read it twice. Michael said he had read it more times than he could count. Nancy looked sheepish and said she had read half last night and it put her to sleep. She apologized as everyone laughed.

"Michael, I know you must have read the book backwards at least once." Michael nodded. "Rachel, how about you?" She shook her head and said she had read it slowly and deliberately twice, but read it from Chapter one to Chapter 22 both times. She said it just didn't seem natural to read it backwards.

Adrian smiled and said, "I bet very few have ever thought to read it in reverse order. Well, guess what? We are going to start with the last chapter and cover a few chapters in reverse order before we go to the beginning. You will catch on quickly and find it relatively easy, I believe."

"Let's start with a stern warning from the Lord. Read from verses 18 to 19 in the last chapter, Chapter 22, where John writes *'I warn everyone who hears the words of the prophecy of this book: If anyone adds anything to them, God will add to him the plagues described in this book. And anyone who takes words away from this book of prophesy, God will take away from him his share in the tree of life and in the holy city, which are described in this book.'* Now, please join me in saying the words in verse 20, *'Yes, I am coming soon. Amen, Come, Lord Jesus.'*."

"Now in verses 12 to 16 Jesus starts with the words, *'Behold, I am coming soon!'* and he ends with *'I, Jesus, have sent my angel to give you this testimony for the churches. I am the Root and the off-spring of David, and the bright Morning Star*. At the beginning of Chapter 22, John writes about an angel's description of the new Jerusalem with its flowing living waters. God and his Son are seated on thrones in a beautiful peaceful scene in the Holy City."

"This last chapter simply depicts a vision of the beautiful glory of God's new creation and provides an affirmation that Jesus will truly return, where heaven is brought to earth. It also presents us with a vision that should encourage us that God's plan for a new order in heaven and on earth will be fulfilled. In Chapter 21, we see the new heaven and the new earth that replaces the old. We see a new Jerusalem and the residence of the Father and the Son, no longer hidden from mankind."

Adrian added, "To me this helps reinforce the fact that in God's plan the 'end state' of the world as we will see it is so wonderful that we should not be blinded by anything that keeps us from the heaven to come. In Chapter 20, at the back-end of the chapter we see that mankind is judged person by person. Those whose names are not written in the Book of Life are condemned. Preceding the day of judgement is the fact that Satan will be given a time to deceive the world, but that time will be cut short and Satan will be cast into the lake of fire where the 'beast' and the 'false prophet' preceded him."

"Satan's doom comes at the end of the millennium when Satan marshals all his forces against God. They congregate to devour God's people near Jerusalem and are consumed by fire from heaven. All those whose names are not in the Book of Life go to their second death in the lake of fire with Satan. Preceding Satan's fate Jesus will rule on earth with those who survived the great tribulation with faith in the Lord. This time is expected to last 1,000 years. This time period is frequently referred to as the millennium! Jesus will have this time with the martyrs to help them become priests. This too is the first resurrection. The second is for all other souls after the millennium."

"Wow!" Nancy says. "I missed some major action last night by not getting to that part. I am anxious to hear more."

Adrian stopped and a short discussion followed to answer questions and clarify what had been covered. Adrian then moved to the beginning of the book having set the context of how the book ends. It now was a matter of getting the rest of the story on how events unfold to get back to where Jesus binds Satan for the millennium.

"Any more questions at this stage?"

Michael spoke up immediately. "No, please continue. Finish. We are listening and we must hear all you have to say first."

Adrian continued, "Now keep in mind that John was a 'beloved' disciple of Jesus. He wrote this book with the help of a scribe while praying to God in a cave on the island of Patmos where he was exiled. God made all that is written in the book of Revelation known to John through visions and spoken word."

"Furthermore, John thought these visions and messages were the foretelling of events that would occur soon. In Chapter 1 this is his stated belief in verse 3. Having received specific accounts on seven churches in his visions, John was very conscientious about seeing that each account was delivered to the specified church. He records the seven churches in Chapter 1 and sends letters to each accordingly. He clearly states that the source of the directives, visions, and words is the Lord and that the Lord told him what to write to each church individually, to make it abundantly clear that they know the Lord is holding them accountable for their actions. The Lord clearly specifies what pleases him and what displeases him."

"These letters to the seven churches comprise the balance of what is written in Chapters 2-3. They are very specific in nature, and some are condemning while others are complimentary. Please bear with me as I finish with Chapters 4 and 5 as these two chapters are a prelude to the story of a scroll with seven seals."

"In Chapter 4, John is given a view of the temple in heaven. The throne in the temple is described so that John can truly see the glory of heaven. Then in Chapter 5, John is treated to a special event. He sees an angel proclaim to those in attendance at the throne *'Who is worthy to remove the seals from the scroll in the hand of God? The Lord is the only one worthy. The elders fall down and worship the Lord and the Father.'* What a glorious scene!"

"Chapter 6 is where Jesus, and only Jesus, opens the seals on this small scroll handed to him by God the Father. Jesus, the Lamb, opens the first seal and out comes a white horse with a rider. The second seal yields a red horse with a rider destined to take peace from the earth. The third seal produces a black horse with its rider holding a pair of scales. The fourth seal yields a pale-colored horse with a rider named Death, and to him is given authority over $1/4^{th}$ of the earth in which to kill *'by sword, famine, and plague'*."

"The fifth seal depicts a scene in heaven where those who were slain because of their belief in God are seen pleading to the Lord, asking how long must they wait for judgement. The Lord gives them white robes and tells them to wait till the necessary number of brothers is reached. Finally, the sixth seal is broken and the result is a great earthquake. There is an eclipse of the sun, the moon is red and stars fall. Mountains and islands are removed from their place! Everyone hides in caves and among rocks for fear of their lives. Chapter 7 ushers in a vision of four angels holding back the wind on the four corners of the earth. Then another angel places a seal on 144,000 from the twelve tribes of Israel. John sees a throng of white robes in front of the Lord. He is told they are from the tribulation and they serve the Lord night and day."

"Chapters 8 and 9 describe the first 'woe.' It is a series of seven angels each sounding a trumpet in heaven. These angels are preceded by a scene at the heavenly altar resulting in fire being hurled to the earth causing thunder, lightning, and an earthquake. This serves as a warning for what is coming. Each of the seven angels sounds their trumpet in advance of a particular malady. The first brings hail, fire, and blood, killing a third of the earth's vegetation. The second angel triggers what sounds like a massive volcanic eruption causing a third of the creatures in the sea to die. The third angel follows with what appears to be a large meteorite striking the earth, causing one third of the water on the earth to turn bitter. The fourth angel triggers a change in the source of light upon the earth. One third of the sun is blocked as is the moon and the stars."

"The fifth angel is preceded by an alarm that the next three trumpets will be more horrible than the others. A star falls from the sky to the earth and opens the Abyss. Out of the Abyss comes smoke and locusts who torture all those who do not have the seal of God on their foreheads. This lasts five months. The sixth angel brings 200,000,000 troops into war. One third of all living on earth are killed by 'fire, smoke, and sulfur.' John tells us that those who survive this do not repent to the Lord and continue to worship idols of various sorts. The seventh angel is the one who starts the second 'woe' in Chapter 10. The angel delivers seven thunders, but John is asked to not write down what he sees. He is told to leave the words bound up. So that is what he does!"

A catered lunch arrived and the group had a little trouble relaxing after what they had just heard. Everyone seemed alert though and interested to see how the rest of the presentation played out. Even Nancy was engaged in the topic.

Carrying on after lunch, Adrian said, "The first part of Chapter 11 tells us that the Gentiles will 'trample' on Jerusalem for three and a half years during which God will provide and protect two witnesses. These two will have great powers and cannot be overcome by any adversary. They will prophesy for 42 months. Ultimately, Satan will come and destroy them. But after three and a half days God will raise them to heaven causing a great earthquake, killing a tenth of the population in the city, more precisely the scripture says 7,000 will die. (Therefore the population of Jerusalem at the time will be a mere 70,000 – compared to a current population of about 800,000). All of this is the second woe!"

"Later in Chapter 11, we see God's seventh trumpet sounding. The angel sounding the trumpet says, 'The kingdom of the world has become the kingdom of our Lord and of his Christ, and he will reign forever and ever.' In heaven, 24 elders fall to the floor and praise God saying that the time has come to judge the dead, reward the righteous, and destroy *'those who destroy the earth'*. A tumultuous event in heaven opens God's heavenly temple and reveals the *'ark of the covenant'*. Chapter 12 reveals details of a war in heaven in which Satan, the dragon, is suddenly hurled to earth. He leads a war against Israel and all other nations. Satan prevails for a period of three and a half years. So, if I read the scripture correctly, I believe there are three and a half years to cover all of what is included in Chapters 13-19. Please check me on that, if you have time."

"Any questions?"

Michael glanced around and saw none. "No, you are on a roll. Please continue."

"Okay, if you say so. In Chapter 12, the woman characterized in the vision seems to be the Jewish state of Israel and seems to tell us that the Jewish people will flee the country for that three and a half year period while the dragon (Satan/antichrist) rules. Most interestingly, this chapter describes a major war in heaven where Satan is attempting to destroy Christ the Lord. Michael, the archangel, triumphs over Satan tossing him to earth along with his angels. Basically, God cleans house in heaven, if I may interpret this in my own words."

"Now, in Chapter 13 we see a false prophet coming out of the earth. He aligns himself with Satan, the antichrist who earlier in the chapter comes from the sea. (I believe Satan as the antichrist leads a group of nations into war against Israel and all who believe in the true Lord Jesus). The false prophet is the one who places an image of the antichrist in Jerusalem's temple and declares he will kill anyone who does not worship the antichrist."

"Chapter 14 ends with a massive rapture of souls. Prior to the rapture of righteous souls God sends angels to warn the people on earth against allying themselves with Satan, and, thereby losing their souls. Chapter 15 brings seven angels who bring plagues upon the people of the earth. Chapter 16 is a description of seven terrible *'bowls of God's wrath'* being poured out on the earth and in the heavens above. It all leads to the final battle at the valley of Armageddon in northern Israel."

"I was perplexed by Chapter 17 and I could not have told you the meaning of this chapter when I first read it. I still am not sure, but I am pretty certain it refers to the antichrist coming out of the sea. The seven heads and the 10 horns may represent a confederation of Islamic states. The woman mentioned appears to be a city that rules over the kings of the earth. Home of the United Nations, in New York City, is the only city that comes to mind. I am sure others more learned than I have studied this passage and this book in much greater detail than I have, but this is the best I can do without reaching out to experts. My conclusion, however, was bolstered and my mind went racing when I read in Chapter 18 that a financial center would be destroyed. The financial center is compared to the city of Babylon in the Old Testament era. Obviously, New York fits the description, and I have relatives there."

"I think I am done, and this was the hardest exercise I have had to do since working here. I prayed for help more times than you will know. I got to the point of utter frustration; to the point of feeling like I was right there with John sometimes. I really want to go to Patmos someday."

Everyone clapped. Each person said they were glad Adrian took on the task to cover the Book of Revelation as no one really wanted to do it. Not even Michael!

Adrian passed out a summary of his presentation, and asked everyone to write down any comments they may have and get them to him so he can finalize his written report. Everyone agreed.

The group took a break and wandered around the premises for a half-hour before leaving. Rachel and Adrian even walked down to check out the wedding chapel on the hotel grounds. What a setting for a wedding! Not that anyone had any bright ideas about having one there.

After loading up in Michael's rental car, he drove the group to a beachside restaurant near Paia noted for good fresh fish meals. The atmosphere was very Hawaiian and they had a wonderful meal. Most of the group had macadamia nut encrusted mahi-mahi. It was mouthwateringly good. Afterwards, Rachel and Nancy picked up a couple of souvenirs at the restaurant's store to take home as a remembrance of the occasion.

They drove back to Lahaina and called it a day.

37

Lahaina, Hawaii

It was one o'clock in the afternoon and Rachel was in charge of the presentation for their fifth session. Her task was to review the other key books of the Bible to see what else there might be that the group needed to consider in preparing an answer to the final question on Jesus' plan to return.

She asked the group to stand and gather in a circle to pray. They held hands and Rachel asked each to say a prayer for their work. Rachel started with a long and passion-filled praise for the Father, the Son, and the Holy Spirit. She led into a petition that the Holy Spirit be with them as they continue their journey of study and discernment. Each person followed with their own expression of gratitude and love.

Rachel began, "Yesterday's journey that Adrian took us on in the Book of Revelation was amazing. I had never really clicked with that book. It always seemed strange and I never knew whether it was talking about things that happened long ago or whether it was all about the future. If it was about the future, I didn't really think it was something that would ever affect me. Now I know it may affect me, as well as the ones in eternity, and it may happen in this lifetime. That's a big wow for me! I am afraid today's session will be shorter and not quite so interesting. I am simply going to supplement what we've heard so far. However, I believe this will reinforce what we heard earlier. Hopefully, you will appreciate all the more what already has been said."

"I want to start with a scripture reading from John 3:16. It is well known and I adore its simplicity. Jesus is quoted as saying, *'God so loved the world that he gave his one and only Son, that whoever believes in him shall not perish but have eternal life'*. This verse instills so much hope for everyone. It reassures believers that they are on the right track and it encourages non-believers to believe since God truly loves them. Even earlier in this same chapter, John makes it abundantly clear that we may be born in the flesh, but we need to be born in the spirit, as well. The spirit comes to us when we truly believe in Jesus the Son, and in God the Father. I love the way John writes."

"Please listen to John's Chapter 6 verse 40 where Jesus is quoted, *'For my Father's will is that everyone who looks to the Son and believes in him shall have eternal life, and I will raise him up at the last day'*. Again, this should comfort believers and encourage non-believers to become believers. Now I am not so naïve as to believe all non-believers will do this, much less even think twice about it, but this is why we need to get the gospel out to everyone and make sure they understand that they need to take a stand on their personal beliefs."

Michael interjected a comment, "Rachel, you make an excellent point. We can't say what you just said too many times. We need to get the word out to everyone in the world and let them know they have a choice to make. Importantly, this needs to be one of the things we include in our list of things to focus on achieving with the Foundation."

The group discussed how this focus point might be accomplished by the Foundation. Michael felt like the work they had done to date and what they were about to finish, could be widely distributed throughout the world in a way to encourage others to read the Word and to make intelligent decisions on what they truly believe about God the Father, God the Son, and the Holy Spirit. Helping people address those beliefs is something worthy of doing. It is as important as showing love to our neighbors since it is the one thing that may save someone's life.

The discussion went on for over 30 minutes. Rachel concluded, "Michael, I am really glad you made this topic a point of discussion. It is something I want to be a part of doing."

"Well, you just might be in charge of that, Rachel," Michael smiled.

"Oh, did I just volunteer for something?"

Adrian chuckled and said, "You got it girl!"

"Moving on, I have one verse that might help with Jesus' ascension into heaven. Let's look at Acts Chapter 1 verses 1-11." Rachel paused till they were done. She went on, "First, the early part of the reading emphasized the importance of having the Holy Spirit dwell in the disciples before they began their ministry. Secondly, two men suddenly show up and ask the disciples why they seem so amazed at Jesus' ascension to heaven. The two explain that Jesus will return the same way he left. This seems to fit with John's description of Jesus' future return in the Book of Revelation."

After a short discussion, the group prepared to break for the remainder of the day.

Michael closed with a prayer and these comments. "Thank you all so much for everything you've done. I want you to take the next two days off and enjoy some time here on Maui. Our next meeting will be here in three days. We'll start at 12:00 p.m. that day and each of the following two days. Tomorrow Elizabeth will arrive. She will not attend our next session, but I did ask her to join us for our last two sessions. She said she will listen and only speak when asked. Of course, just knowing her a short while, I think we may need to give her a pass on that promise two or three times a day. Have a good evening and enjoy Maui."

Michael caught Adrian before he got away. "Adrian, could you hang around for 10-15 minutes, I have something to ask you."

"Absolutely, just give me a minute with Rachel." Adrian told Rachel he would call her room and they could discuss plans.

"What's up boss?"

"Two things. First, I want to thank you for taking on the hardest part of this process so far. I am impressed."

"Thank you, Michael. That means a lot, but you are the one on the hot seat to help us put all this together. I don't envy you, but I am excited about where we are, especially since none of us have ever done anything like this."

"It is amazing to see what the Lord can do with four people who surrender a large part of themselves for the Lord's sake. He is using us. I can see that now."

"I agree."

"Adrian, I could use your help tomorrow for an hour or two. Any chance you would be available?"

"Well, Rachel and I were planning to rent a car and see a bit more of the island. But if you are available early I am sure Rachel would like to sleep in. How about if we meet at 8:00 a.m.? That way Rachel and I can get away by 10:30 a.m."

"Okay let's do it."

"Michael, I am curious. Can you give me a heads-up on what we need to do?"

"Of course, I would like to take Matthew's gospel in order and compare it to the sequence in Revelation and see what it tells us. I want to know whether it fits with a couple of Old Testament timelines I highlighted in my talk earlier."

"Sure, let's give it a try. Your room at 8:00 a.m.?"

"Okay, I'll have breakfast called up to the room."

"See you in the morning."

It only took an hour and a half for Adrian and Michael to do what Michael needed. Of course, Michael had done much of what he needed before Adrian showed up. By 9:30 a.m. Adrian was on the phone with Rachel and they were on the road by 10:00 a.m. They drove to Maui's Upcountry area for lunch. Afterwards they headed to the top of the Haleakala volcano. They parked at the National Park visitor's center. It was cold, and it was windy, so they left after a quick look into the crater.

Meanwhile, Nancy and her husband took a cab to the Maui Aquarium. Nancy was thrilled with the aquarium and wished the grandkids were there. They had an early dinner and went to bed after watching television. They needed to get caught up on Seattle Mariner baseball. Today's game score was not all that good unfortunately.

Michael called Elizabeth and wished her another good flight. The day before she had flown to Seattle, and had a one night layover at a convenient but nice hotel that Michael had arranged. She would leave the following day on a direct flight to Maui. She seemed excited to see Michael and enjoy the beach. Michael had arranged a nice oceanfront suite for her. She would certainly be comfortable, and the view from the suite was stunning.

The following day the whole group met at 8:00 a.m., walked down to the Whaler's Village area and attended a beachfront outdoor church service on the patio of a local restaurant. They enjoyed the music, the Word and the fellowship of other Christians.

Afterwards, Rachel and Adrian headed back to the hotel for a day of relaxation and sun. Nancy and her husband did much the same. Michael did some preparation work for the next three sessions. In the afternoon he drove to the airport to meet Elizabeth. He bought a traditional flower lei near the airport to give her when she got to the baggage claim area.

Elizabeth loved the greeting. Michael gave her a sweet kiss after putting the flower lei over her head. She smiled as Michael said 'Aloha.' They drove back to Lahaina and got Elizabeth settled into her suite. She was truly impressed with the accommodations and the view. Dinner in the main dining room was pretty special and they had plenty of time to talk.

As planned, Elizabeth was going to miss the next day's session which Michael said would not be long. He told her about the shopping that was available within walking distance and she was set to do that while Michael was in session six with the group. She was looking forward to sitting in on sessions seven and eight, if it was still okay with the group? Michael assured her that the group was okay with the idea. He said he had arranged a sunset dinner outdoors the following evening at a neighboring hotel, and that would be a good time to relax with the team and meet Larry, Nancy's husband.

The following morning at 9:00 a.m. Michael, Adrian, Nancy and Rachel met for session six. Michael opened the session with a prayer and followed that with a short outline of what the group needed to do in each of the next three sessions to get them to the end of answering Question #4.

He explained that today's meeting was to simply review where today is on God's clock and what trends they see that may propel the sequence of events leading to Christ's return. He explained that the next day's session would outline the likely progression of events as best they can determine it, with prophesy as the basis. The last session will be to highlight those things the Foundation needs to do to follow Christ's will in light of where we are in God's plan.

"Is everyone onboard with this effort?" asked Michael.

"I don't know how we are going to do all that, but I am looking forward to the ride," Nancy quipped.

"Okay, I think we all feel a little uncertain as to where this will end. That is okay! We just need to see where the process leads us and be mindful that through our prayer we can surrender some of the heavy lifting on this to the Holy Spirit. After all, that is why we've been listening to so much of what is written. Hopefully, we've heard what was intended when it was said. I want each of you to take some time to read some papers I've collected on various subjects I intend to touch on today. Please take 15-20 minutes to read your stack. Take notes and be ready to talk about the highlights of what you read. I'll lead us through all this when you are finished reading and taking notes."

After 20 minutes had gone by, Michael continued. "We know that Jesus ushered in 'the time of the Gentiles'. Adrian told us that in the Book of Revelation John's first visions dealt with seven letters to seven churches. This was part of the beginning of the time of the Gentiles. In 1948 Israel was re-established and Jews from around the world have been returning to the Holy Land in large numbers ever since. Hence, it would seem we are also in the 'era of the Jewish people'. Something is different about this point in time than at any other time in nearly 2.000 years. I'll speak more about this tomorrow. For today I simply want to emphasize this point."

"Back to the Book of Revelation. We see that after the letters to the churches, John's vision in Chapters 4 and 5 focuses on heaven where God hands Jesus a scroll with seven seals. Chapter 6 is where Jesus opens the first four seals unleashing four horses with riders. Notably, anyone reading the description of these four riders might interpret them differently, but the result is that 1/4th of the earth's population is killed. Other than the flood in Noah's time, there has never been an event we know of with such a devastating result. With today's world population well over 6,000,000,000 that means the loss of life will exceed 1,500,000,000 people. Comparatively the loss of life in World War II is estimated at just over 50,000,000. That means the loss John relays to us is 30 times the loss in all of World War II."

"What this also entails is that there will be a conflict of epic proportions, and adding to that calamity John tells us there will be a massive earthquake and celestial changes. Furthermore, this is just the beginning of a series of horrible events cast upon the earth and all its inhabitants. Certainly, no one on earth is going to misunderstand what is happening if this prophesy is communicated around the globe. This event should put everyone on notice that the old is ending and the new is coming, but only after much more happens. Do you think people around the world accept the fact that our destiny has such calamity in its future? I would like Rachel to talk through a few points she has highlighted in the readings I gave her. Rachel, you're up!"

"Michael gave me an article on a study made a couple of years before the year 2000. The article says nearly one in four Christians expect Jesus to arrive in their lifetime. Interestingly, only 66% of Christians believe Jesus will return to earth, and only 40% of Christians in the polling believed Jesus will arrive before the end of the 21st century. I felt those were the main points in the article."

Adrian chimed in, "I am not terribly surprised at the results. Most Christians that I have known do not focus on when Christ will return. Most are happy with the period of spreading the gospel that we're in. They don't look any deeper than that. It is basically more comfortable that way. Plus no one has made a good case that they need to be concerned about the nearing of Jesus' return. Few, if any, have made a good case as to when that is likely to happen so why focus on it."

Nancy spoke up, "I am one of those. Adrian. I want to concentrate on what I can do for my family and others."

Michael followed, "My take on this is that it is okay not to be overly concerned about the possibility of 'end time' events. Yet, it is okay for others to be concerned. As Christians we are all different. Part of that difference is in what we need mentally to help us grow to the strongest Christian we can be. Those that need to have answers to God's plan should be able to get them."

"More and more, as we develop our minds we are going to ask tougher questions. Not everyone, but I know a lot who do. Our traditional church institutions are not good at answering the tough questions that young, or rather any inquiring minds have today. That is why when we finish this whole question and answer quest that we are on, perhaps we can help those people around the world get the answers they need."

Rachel added, "Michael, your point is exactly what drew me to join this effort in the first place. I hope we succeed."

"Good response, Rachel. Okay, let's take a short break."

As the group gathered again, Michael turned the next segment over to Nancy.

Nancy started, "Not too long ago, the New Jersey coast was hit with a freakish storm that did a lot of damage to the homes along the coast. Likewise, remember when Texas and Oklahoma were hit with tornadoes and flooding to the point of shutting down the fourth largest city in the United States. These were terrible events for those who were there. However, what is described in Chapter 6 is at a whole different level. Michael gave me two articles to highlight. The first has to do with earthquakes, and one potential spot where a cataclysmic quake could occur. It is the super-volcano under Yellowstone Park. The article from 2013 indicated the molten rock under the park was two and one half times larger than previously thought. Shockingly, it has the potential for a blast 2,000 times the one that occurred in 1980 at Mt. St. Helens. Scientists say the amount of material below the surface indicates an explosion could match the largest of three eruptions over the past 2,000,000 years. This would be a global event. It is possible that a large earthquake could be triggered by the build-up of molten material under Yellowstone."

"Also, a recent article in a well-known periodical highlighted a known and potentially cataclysmic-type fault near Seattle called the Juan de Fuca Fault. Its potential for destruction is enormous for the northwest coastal region. Of course we are all aware of the San Andreas fault-line in southern California. In fact, many areas throughout the world are known potential earthquake zones. Another article Michael passed along has to do with the fact that even the United States is not well prepared for either a major natural disaster or a nuclear disaster. Having seen FEMA struggle in dealing with Hurricane Katrina as well as with other large events makes it evident that a disaster of the scope of nuclear blasts or massive earthquakes will test our whole response system in a way never seen before."

Michael added, "I think we have to recognize that there are those in the world who have a different agenda than we do as a nation. One of those is Russia. No doubt the Russian President is absorbed with the idea of expanding Russia to encompass the lands previously held under the control of the Soviet Union. He has led a little-known effort worldwide to control as much of the uranium reserves in the world as he can. He has expanded Russia's naval presence in the Black Sea as well as in the eastern Mediterranean. Therefore, he may well have expansionist ideas well beyond what we have seen to date."

"The Russian President's next election will occur in 2018. He will run again for a six-year term. Not being able to run again at the conclusion of that term, which he most likely will win, I would not be surprised to see the Russian army cross many borders to expand Russian influence and control shortly after his next election. Russia has a large nuclear force and the Russian leader may be inclined to use it. This, mind you, is my form of speculation and only a personal one. With that in mind, Adrian has a few articles on Europe. They describe a situation where countries are dealing with aggression from Russia and changing demographics. Please continue, Adrian."

Adrian continued the discussion, "The articles I have on Europe indicate the continent tends to look inward more and more, rather than outward. With rising Muslim populations, a high cost of providing services, and governments prone to socialism, they can only expect less and less of a role in international affairs and more of a focus on the home front. One writer believes the recent past will show Europe fading and counting on the U.S. more and more to be the policeman and leader of world events. Hence, a world leadership void is developing and could get worse. Of significant note, Europe's population trends are astonishing. Birth rates are so low in nearly every country that they are no longer reversible. With the loss in population so evident, the influx of needed laborers has brought in massive numbers of Muslims who are now populating many cities and will soon out-populate traditional Europeans in a number of countries. Christian churches are turning up empty and Muslims are constructing mosques at a fast rate throughout Europe."

"Essentially, Europe has changed so dramatically in the course of a generation, it is not likely that it will return to any image of its past as the population change is destined to continue. Also, the concept of 'freedom of religion' is not accepted by many Muslims and that, ultimately, leads to wars within borders and wars outside borders. The U.S. President says we are not fighting a religious war, but that does not make it so. Calling the aggressive nature of radical Muslims a terrorist event does not make it so, especially when the underlying common cause is religious differences. The reality is that we are all closer to religious war than we may think."

On that note the group broke for lunch. Larry and Elizabeth joined the group and everyone got caught up on each other's lives. After lunch, Larry escorted Elizabeth to Whaler's Village for some additional shopping. They enjoyed the walk and getting to know each other.

Michael continued with the group, "Let's look at two more subjects before we close for the day. First, Adrian will take us through some information on the Middle East. Then I will talk about America and some financial risks on the horizon."

Adrian began, "Nary a week goes by that we are not being bombarded by news in the Middle East. Over 90% of that news is bad news, and Americans at home are basically at a point where they are pretty much numb over it all."

"I saw the same thing earlier in my life when Vietnam dragged on and on,' Nancy said. "Peace in the Middle East seems unlikely to most Americans."

"Iran is not giving up on getting enriched uranium so it can build the bomb. Palestinians continue to wage war with Israelis for land rights. Islamic militants want to have Sharia Law a national requirement everywhere. Islamic extremists want to kill infidels everywhere. Islamic extremists want to kill Muslims of a different sect. Many Muslims want to wipe out Israel. Alliances within the Islamic Middle East are bringing strange bedfellows together to gain control. As these alliances come together, the U.S and its allies will have less to say about how they handle the affairs within these countries. Not as reliant on foreign oil, the U.S in particular will continue to gravitate away from the Middle East fighting. At least until Israel becomes challenged militarily, to where the U.S. will have to decide whether or not it will stand by Israel in combat against a major invasion."

"Turkey and Saudi Arabia appear to be working together more closely, and the head of the Turkish government seems to be moving away from the U.S. and NATO, and more toward being a leader in regional Islamic affairs. Greece, likewise, may leave the European Union and develop stronger ties with Turkey and others in the Middle East. All this bears watching. I will say that after what I have read in the Old Testament, there is absolutely no doubt in my mind that God will direct or allow certain leaders to do certain things. He has done it before and there is little reason why he wouldn't continue to do it. So we must take some of what we see as something the Father will allow to occur, if not even encourage it. Either way, God's will be done! Even Prime Minister Netanyahu has stood in the United Nations and said, 'In our time, the prophesies are being realized' (October 2013)."

After a short discussion, Michael picked up the lead. "Let's talk about the risks to the U.S. that might spur on the events we've been talking about. First, although buoyed by a moderately strong and innovative economy, public policy has resulted in staggering debt. Future generations will likely be smothered by this debt. The insatiable desire for the 'cake and eat it too' of public politicians has burdened the future economy in ways we have never seen. We are far too vulnerable to endure the risk of our own debt. For example, we cannot control what the majority of the world wants as its 'currency reserve'. If the major players of the world were to say America is carrying too much debt they could vote to replace the U.S. dollar as the currency of choice."

"Has this happened before? Yes. After WWII, the pound sterling was replaced with the dollar. Great Britain's economy suffered in the 1970s and it took years to overcome the effects of that change. Inflation and high unemployment are just two of the struggles a country faces with such problems. Having the debt level we are carrying and allowing it to increase is just wrong! What we learn from history is that we don't learn much from history! Not to end on a sour note, we know that the Lord will come and we will join him in a new heaven and a new earth. Praise be to God."

A lively discussion followed before the group broke. Everyone agreed to meet in the dining room at 7:00 p.m. for dinner. Michael had a table reserved which would allow for everyone to enjoy a beautiful sunset at 7:00 p.m. Some nice string music was scheduled as well.

"Tomorrow we'll start at 1:00 p.m. and I think you will enjoy the session Adrian and I have planned. I hope it is an exciting look at how the Old Testament may give us insight into the future. We'll go until we are done. See you at dinner!"

Nancy took advantage of the time between events to call her grandkids. Michael and Elizabeth took a nice walk along the beach. Adrian and Rachel had the same idea but walked in the opposite direction.

The next day started with a beautiful sunny morning. Once up everyone made their way to the pool area or to the spacious lawn area where there was more shade under the palm trees. Everyone was out except for Michael. He had had a restless night.

To Michael the whole idea of wrapping up their discussions on what the future holds, leading into a time of tribulation, and also outlining what the Foundation group should be doing in light of their beliefs, was just too much too soon. He believed they all needed more time to let some of this soak in. They needed to work up reports covering so much of what they had covered. He needed to change the process slightly and make better use of the two remaining sessions he was to lead. Finally, late in the morning after feeling frustrated he sat alone and prayed by himself asking for direction.

After a short prayer Michael opened the session, "Good morning! I hope everyone had a relaxing morning and is ready for today's session. Elizabeth is joining us this morning and this will give her a chance to listen and hear about where we see the Father's plan taking us in the future, and what we should be doing to help spread the gospel. As a major investor in the Foundation, we are honored by your presence and the faith you have in our broader mission to do God's will."

Elizabeth thanked everyone for allowing her to join them. Knowing she was still very much of an outsider to the workings of the group, she said she fully supported the goals of the Foundation and hoped she could help in ways beyond being an investor. Catching up on what the group had accomplished would help her identify areas where she might help, if the group was interested. Otherwise, she hoped everyone was okay with her listening to today's session and tomorrow's as well.

Rachel responded, "Elizabeth, thank you for being here. We have already accepted the fact that one of our greatest needs going forward will be to take what we have done, as well as what we have yet to conclude, and use it to help spread the word. Since we do not have any real experience in the publishing world, your help and insight will prove to be invaluable. Thanks for travelling so far to join us."

"My, my, thank you Rachel. This is one of the most beautiful places in the world. How could I turn down Michael's invitation to join you this week? We will see if my involvement as a working partner is beneficial or not."

Michael interjected, "Just so you know, Elizabeth will return with us to Seattle. She and I will discuss her future involvement while she is there and I want everyone to feel free to offer opinions one way or another on the subject. Elizabeth and I have a personal interest in one another that will continue, irrespective of any decision about whether she should have a major role in the Foundation other than as an investor."

Adrian commented, "Elizabeth, I am sure you realize the family and work backgrounds that we four share. It has already been a long road for us to get to where we are with the work of the Foundation. Yet, from the very outset Michael and the other three of us have been dealing not only with personal loss but with a new and exciting adventure to discover God's plan for the future. We want to help people throughout the world see that they are a part of God's plan and that they can share in God's glory and in His merciful promise of salvation. Michael knows you can help us, so it seems to me that a big part of the decisions about your potential role is whether or not you want to dedicate the same kind of commitment to seeing this through as we do. If you are on board with that then it would be our delight to have you join us. Said another way, this situation from my standpoint is more about whether you want to join us rather than whether we want you to join us."

"I am truly honored by what you say, Adrian. I was not expecting either your remarks or Rachel's. Please let me answer that later." She had a tear rolling down her cheek.

Michael said, "Okay, okay! I need to start out by saying I would like to make a change to the schedule of sessions. This is session seven with one to follow. Coming into today I had planned to deliver a proposed summation to our work and get your input as to what we might add or subtract from that draft. Tomorrow's session was intended to take our summation and generate an outline of what the foundation should do as we go forward. However, it came to me this morning that we would be hard-pressed to do an adequate job of all that. Hence, I propose that we hold off on the topic for tomorrow's session till we return home. We need time to think and rethink what we have done in the past sessions. Furthermore, we need to have adequate time to really think on what I am going to lead you through today and tomorrow."

"Therefore, what I propose we do today is to concentrate on the events that Jesus tells us will happen just before he returns as outlined in the Book of Matthew and the Book of Revelation. Putting these two pieces together from the two books will help us better understand the scope of what is coming at some point in time. Adrian and I worked together doing this and I want to share the view we have with all of you."

Rachel spoke up saying, "I would really love to have time to hear what you two concluded. I have been having trouble with piecing all we've seen in those readings. I know I could use a better perspective on all that."

"That goes double for me," says Nancy.

"Okay, I am prepared to help with that today and Adrian will help too."

"How do you see tomorrow's session going?" Rachel asked.

"Rachel, at some point we need to discuss the 'when' in all of this. Now we all know Jesus said we would not know the hour or the day. He could just as easily have said we would not know the year or the era, but he didn't. Now that doesn't necessarily mean we will know the month or the season or the year, but the prophecies have shown us how many times they proved to be accurate predictions. Perhaps there is a way of getting close, using as much history as has passed since Jesus spoke his answer to the question posed by the disciples about when these things would happen."

"To the point of your question, Rachel, I would like to take you through two Old Testament prophecies that possibly give us a strong hint as to when all these things take place. Now this may be speculation. It may simply be a hypothesis to consider, or it may be a theory with adequate proof to make it a valid standing possibility. At any rate, we need to take a position on timing, and we need to continue to research the issue if we are to be a beacon to others of God's plan. I don't think we can produce a definitive statement of timing until we see more clearly that the events highlighted in scripture are actually happening, but we need to not only highlight what those events are, but we need to put forth the best information available on timing that we can."

Elizabeth raised her hand, "If I may, you have covered so much in a short period of time from what I read, it is overwhelming to think you can actually propose a timeline for these future events. I would love to see what you have to propose, because that is the big question many people have about this somewhat mystical end-times story. Having an answer to the question will be important to the inquiring minds you will be wanting to reach. I think you need to be very careful, but you absolutely need to address it."

Adrian added, "In some respect it is the million-dollar question. I think Elizabeth is right. I just don't think many of us in the group have a good answer. Hence, I would love to hear Michael's take on the question. So, yes Michael, please plan to do that tomorrow."

"Okay, let's take a look at the chart Adrian and I prepared for this session when we took Matthew's work on signs of the end times and paired that with John's Book of Revelation. I think this will help." Michael passed out the outline and left everyone to study it for a few minutes. They took a break and started back 20 minutes later.

During the break, Michael told Elizabeth that if things moved along as he hoped he expected the group would reconvene shortly after they returned to Seattle to talk through the path going forward with the foundation's work. This would include getting the report material written in a form appropriate for publishing and distribution worldwide. Elizabeth felt good about that, and had a few ideas to discuss when the time was right. Michael told her the two of them would cover that after the meeting tomorrow.

As the group came together Nancy said, "Why didn't we have this before we had to go through all those chapters in the Bible?"

Michael smiled, "Well, Nancy if we had had it then, we would have put it out there."

"That's okay, but I still need an interpreter for the chart."

"Okay, let's start there," Michael responded. "You'll see on the left side Adrian and I listed all the major events depicted in Matthew's account of what Jesus said about the days leading up to his return. It starts with the world experiencing much deception. That is followed by war, famine and a massive earthquake. These are the beginning of 'birth pains'. Interestingly, if you look at the right hand column you will see that from Chapter six in the book of Revelation forward, there is a description of the six seals that Jesus opens. They bring war, inflation, and an earthquake. Notably, John's vision includes a statement that a quarter of the earth is controlled by leaders who bring war, famine and plagues. Even wild beasts add to the terror of mankind in that part of the world. There is no clue or spoken word here about when this may happen or how long this will last. Obviously, this could last several years or a great many years. We just don't know at this stage, and we may not know for certain until we see significant deception throughout the world, and that assumes we will recognize it when it occurs."

"One thing I just don't understand is where does this deception come from? Is this from Satan?" Nancy asked.

Michael responded, "That is the logical conclusion, as I see it."

Adrian added, "I think it is definitely from Satan, but also his allies."

"Looking back to Matthew, it appears Jesus is telling us that as all this is going on, there will be significant persecution and hatred of Jews and Christians alike. This appears to be something that is on a scale far greater than what we saw in World War II, but it is very possible that the holocaust was part of this era. Still, Christians are mentioned as a persecuted group and I believe that indicates something significant for the future. To me it is part of a holy war against all infidels, but with particular targeting of Jews and Christians by Muslims. Next, Jesus tells us in the Book of Matthew that as wickedness becomes widespread *'the love of many will become cold'*. Therefore, people without a firm faith will falter and their hearts will *'grow cold'*."

"In some respects, you could say we are seeing the *'growing cold'* part of that taking place today with secularism taking the place of a faithful church population. This scenario also seems to line up as a fair representation of today's society where there is a movement to a 'me' generation rather than a 'we' generation. Lastly, having the gospel spread throughout the world is the necessary final phase before a time of great distress occupies the world. Now, I could make a very strong argument that in the last 100 years you have seen all the events described today as things that have happened. Likewise, you could argue that we have not seen the apparent magnitude of this as described in the scripture. I think it would be a stretch, however, to say we've had the massive earthquake predicted. We have had serious quakes in recent years, but nothing compared to what is described in scripture. In fact we haven't seen anything on the scale of what is coming!"

"Now in Revelation Chapter seven, we have the 144,000 Jews 'sealed'. These are those who are given God's grace and ultimately God's salvation as they receive a forehead seal protecting them as God carries out his judgments on the world and in heaven. Now from the start of sealing the Jews up, to the time of the two witnesses in Jerusalem (i.e. Chapter 11) we really aren't given any clear clues as to how long that might take. But as Adrian described them, these are horrible times. He told us to expect massive fires, loss of life in the sea, polluting of fresh water bodies, celestial changes, locusts, war involving 200,000,000 troops, and $1/3^{rd}$ of mankind killed."

"We don't know how many years this will take, but it should be safe to say it will take years for this devastation to take place as described. We are told there will be a period of three and a half years where Gentiles will trample on the holy city. Later, two witnesses for God will have great powers and will speak of God's grace for three and a half years under God's protection. Importantly, Jesus will have had the responsibility to initiate the opening of the seals and calling for the trumpets. It seems to me God takes over in Chapter 11, when the witnesses come to the scene. This also seems to be at the point when the seven-year tribulation begins. I say that because in Chapter 11 John's words specify a time of 1,260 days for these two witnesses. This is the first half of the tribulation."

"The second half of the tribulation begins after Satan kills the two in Jerusalem and God resurrects them to heaven. During this last three and a half years Satan dominates the earthly scene. Chapters 12 through 18 depict a string of sobering plights that the earth and its inhabitants must endure. Adrian covered them well in his presentation and his draft report. All of this precedes Christ's return; Christ's handling of Satan; the millennium; judgement day; and the presence of a new earth and a new heaven. Listen, let's take a break for 15 minutes and then get back together for questions."

Everyone sat still for a few minutes looking at the chart Adrian and Michael had put together. They were a bit overwhelmed seeing all the mystery of the 'end times' put on one page. It seemed a little hard to believe. Once back, Rachel asked if they had any clues from the work they had done as to how long the whole sequence would take to play out.

Adrian said, "Both of us pressed hard to look for clues, but all we found were the references to the three and a half year periods and Jesus' statement that all the things Matthew recorded would be done in a generation. I think Michael has some ideas for all of us tomorrow that might shed light on your question, Rachel."

Michael added, "There have been a number of folks who have tried to pin down that answer. I haven't read many of those, as I felt we shouldn't be biased by anyone else's work and or conclusions. That is why tomorrow I am going to present something to you that you may find very interesting. Perhaps others have come to a similar or better conclusion, but I am unaware of them if they are out there. Again, that is why we will dedicate tomorrow's final session to your question."

Nancy quipped, "Well, the whole thing is a mystery to me!"

Michael chuckled, "Nancy, you are not the only one. People from the first century thought Jesus' return was right around the corner. Even Paul seemed to think the time would be sooner rather than later."

Rachel asked, "Part of why I ask is that if Jesus' return is a long way off, then our work at the Foundation needs to be based in spreading the gospel and helping others. If it is soon, then some of our work may need to help people prepare. That's all I was thinking when I asked the question."

Adrian responded, "I think your thoughts mirror those of us all. It is part of why we really need to see if there is a hint of the timing question. Still, if we don't have a clue, then we know we have our hands full just helping others with the Word and with their walk with the Lord."

Michael asked Elizabeth to close the session with a prayer. She didn't seem surprised and she definitely felt comfortable in praying with and for the group. Michael told everyone to enjoy the rest of the day on their own. He told the group that he had reserved a different venue for tomorrow's session, and everyone needed to be ready to go at 9:00 a.m.

Michael had a quiet dinner with Elizabeth at a neighboring hotel. It was a beautiful spot where they could hear the surf and see the moonlight reflecting off the ocean. A gentle breeze was enough for Elizabeth to wear a shawl over her shoulders and she looked absolutely stunning. The flickering light from the gas-lit torches surrounding the outdoor dining area danced across her face, and her smile was most becoming.

"Michael, why are you so driven to do what you are doing?" She asked. "You've explained how you dealt with the tragedy of the car accident and your desire to seek out a Christian life, but I see a driven, no let me rephrase that - I see a man obsessed with discovering something no one else has found. Am I wrong about that?"

"What makes you think I am obsessed?"

"Well, it is not that you are trying to get answers to a few questions that no one seems to have found. No, it is not that. It is the unbridled determination you have and the intensity of that determination that I want to understand. You see from a person who has lost her partner, her husband, her confidant and her friend I understand the strain you bear from your loss. I understand how you need to grab hold of something because you have lost so much, but you can't keep driving yourself so hard. Health-wise you just can't bear up under that kind of strain forever. I had not seen so much of that in London, but after being here a couple of days, I really do see it in your eyes."

"Elizabeth, I hate to admit it, but you're right. For someone who hasn't known me long you seem to understand me pretty well."

"Well, Michael, I don't claim to know you well. I consider myself a good judge of character, and I was impressed with you from the first dinner we had together on the cruise. Now don't get me wrong. I admire a man who is determined. I like that quality in a man."

"Likewise, Elizabeth, you struck me as a wonderful person that evening. You are smart and determined in your own right. You aren't a bad dancer either." They laughed.

After a few moments of silence Michael confided, "Elizabeth, I am trying to make up for lost time. I have not had the right priorities in my life and when I suffered the loss of my immediate family I wanted to quickly turn my life around. Like others with secular leanings, I had questions about my faith as a Christian. This work has forced me to stand up to those doubts and resolve them. I have become more committed to doing what God needs me to do than at any point in my life. That may not be saying much, but it is what has driven me. Can you understand that?"

"Of course, I can. All I am saying is that now you need to not just think about your Foundation, but you need to trust others more to do the work while you enjoy the ride a little more. Don't put so much of the strain on yourself. It is obvious to me as an observer that you are strung too tight and you need to delegate more. Think you might be able to do that?"

"Let's talk more about that after tomorrow. I am still wound tight to get through tomorrow. Bear with me one more day and then let's talk more. I appreciate what you are saying and I have a feeling you are right."

"Sounds fair enough. Now let's have another glass of wine if that is okay. We still have half a bottle!"

38

Kapalua, Hawaii

At 9:00 a.m. the next morning the group met in the hotel lobby, and Michael had a shuttle van pick them up. Michael asked the driver to take the Lower Honoapialani Highway to the hotel where session eight was to be held. The drive was scenic along the beach as they continued driving north. Lots of condominiums, apartments and private residences dotted the highway until they reached a large development area with a beautiful golf course. Turning right at a small quaint church they proceeded to the hotel where Michael had reserved a conference room with a great view northward.

From the balcony area next to the conference room, the group stood looking out over DT Fleming beach, and in the distance they could see the well-known surfing spot called Honolua Bay. Today the surf was small and only a handful of surfers were out. However, in the winter when a large northwest swell hits the islands, this spot 'goes off' as they say in the islands. Wave heights rival some of the spots on Oahu's famous North Shore.

After settling into comfortable chairs around the conference table, Michael asked Adrian to start the session with a prayer. Adrian agreed and took his time contemplating before speaking. Adrian reached deep and said one of the most powerful personal prayers anyone had heard. He was obviously moved by the fact that this was the last session on this trip and one that, after studying the Book of Revelation, was close to his heart.

"Wow, thank you, Adrian," Michael said. "I think each of us feels the same. Thank you for bringing us to a point of being Christ-centered for this important session, and pointing out our need to be Christ-centered in all we do."

Rachel spoke up. "I believe Adrian's prayer on being Christ-centered is so very important. We may not have all the answers to things we question, but if we are open to what the Holy Spirit wants us to know, then we'll know what we should know. Then it is just a matter of following that and doing the best we can for the sake of the Lord."

Michael added, "Well said, Rachel, I hope that is what we are doing. It is all part of 'let thy will be done, not let my will be done'. Don't you think?"

"Absolutely!"

Nancy added, "I really relate to the comments all of you are making. Adrian, the phrase 'being Christ-centered' is a bit new to me, but it rings true to me. Furthermore, I believe we have been doing that from the beginning. Something in Michael's soul was moved to get this Foundation off the ground and moving in the direction to help others in their walk with the Lord. I think the Holy Spirit spoke to Michael's soul. He listened and we have been together with him for over a year now. We are all dedicated to doing the work of the Lord. All of that is good as long as we stick with the word and don't start making up stuff."

"Nancy your comments are well taken and more appropriate than you know for this session, in particular. Shall we get started?"

Elizabeth spoke up, "If I may! Let me simply say I am so incredibly impressed as to how each of you are searching for what the Lord wants you to do. Not once in the time I have been around you, has one of you taken off on a tangent pushing a personal agenda. You are to be commended for that. Thank you, again!"

Michael glanced around the room and saw that everyone was ready for him to proceed, "Thank you for your comments, Elizabeth. We plan to continue doing what you have observed. If we ever get off track on doing that I trust someone will raise the issue."

"Okay, I have a fair amount of information to cover today. First, I do want you to be mindful of the comment I made yesterday. Today's subject about when the Lord will return is one I believe cannot be answered precisely. Therefore, we need to be aware of speculation, hypothesis and theory. You need to judge my comments and as far as the report I write, I would like to omit anything that is speculation and call anything that is left for what it is, either a hypothesis or a theory."

"Let's start with why I don't think we can be precise about the date of Jesus' return. First, Jesus told us we would not know the *'day or the hour'*. Secondly, Adrian told us in Chapter 10 of the Book of Revelation that 'the mystery of God will be accomplished' at a point in time just before the seven-year tribulation begins. Since we are not there yet, we can't know just yet. Basically, Christians have seen a lot of things happen over the past 2,000 years. There has been speculation from the very first century after Christ, as to when the Lord will return. Most of it has been speculation. Early on the speculation was based mostly on hope. However, after this much time we may well be getting close enough to start seeing signs that precede the events highlighted in the 'end times' scriptural references."

"Let me propose a theory and the facts that I believe back it up. Then let's judge the validity of the theory. If the theory does not stand up to a reasonable test then at best the so-called theory is a hypothesis that needs more work to determine if it is a theory or if it should be tossed out. Now keep in mind, Jesus' return precedes a lot of action and a number of events. Adrian outlined those events in his presentation on the Book of Revelation. Jesus' return precedes the defeat of Satan, Jesus' binding of Satan for the millennium, Satan's doom, judgement day and the new earth and the new heaven."

Adrian spoke, "Don't keep us in suspense much longer. Let's hear your theory!"

Michael laughed, "Okay! Based on the evidence I have read I believe there is a strong possibility that Our Lord's return will occur in 2037 or slightly sooner. The sooner is only because God may well be waiting for a certain number of earthly saints before He sends Jesus to close out Satan. Well, that is the theory and now we must hear the facts that potentially substantiate the theory. So here goes. Bear with me as I go through a number of things that drive me to believe this is a theory worth considering in our work. Notably, I will say that our future work should include work leading to the best answer we can find on this question of 'when'."

"Importantly, we have discussed before that there seems to be a pattern to God's plan for mankind. From our creation there seems to be a sequence of events that depict a plan in the mind of God. Recall our discussion that God may well have a 7,000-year plan in mind for mankind as we know it. If we say Adam was the first man with a soul, then God's clock started roughly 6,000 years ago. There was a time between Adam and Abraham that lasted 2,000 years in which mankind went through many trials to disperse and obey God. Abraham brought about a new era and God made covenants with Abraham regarding his people. This was the time of the Hebrew people and it lasted 2,000 years up until the time of Christ. Today we are nearly 2,000 years past the death of Jesus, Our Lord and Savior. That is a total of 6,000 years or using Peter's mention of the fact that to God a day is like 1,000 years or like 'six days'. The 'seventh day' or the 7,000-year period is the period described in the Book of Revelation as the 'millennium'."

"Now, keep in mind, if Jesus died for our sins in 30 AD, then the time of the gentiles would likely end in 2030, with a seven-year tribulation period to follow. This is one way of getting to Jesus's return being 2037. The above case for the time of the Hebrew people and the time for the Gentiles is that Abraham was the one who was asked by God to sacrifice his son, Isaac. Interestingly, although God stopped Abraham from making that sacrifice, just over 2,000 years later God went through with the sacrifice of His Son."

"The next step I want to take you through is the possibility that Old Testament prophesy may well foretell events in the New Testament era. Some of these prophesies may lead us to a closer understanding of God's plan. The first one I want to discuss is Daniel's prophesy of the 'seventy sevens' that I mentioned in our discussion of Old Testament prophesy. We covered much of this, but let me refresh you on it."

Michael continued, "Daniel's prophesy correctly predicted the 'cutting off' (i.e. the death) of Jesus. Daniel prophesized that from the issuing of the decree to rebuild the walls of Jerusalem (about 444 BC) to the 'cutting off' of the 'anointed one' (Jesus) the time would be 69 weeks of years (483 years in Babylonian times equals 476 in our time) or 30 AD."

"Daniel's prophesy related directly to the first rebuilding of the walls of Jerusalem following their destruction by the Babylonians in the late 580's BC. This was the first destruction of the walls. The second and only other destruction of the walls came in 70 AD when the Romans destroyed nearly all of Jerusalem. The rebuild of those walls did not take place until the Ottoman Empire controlled Jerusalem. In 1535, Suleiman the Great issued a decree to rebuild the walls of Jerusalem to protect the city from Egyptians. Using Daniel's prophesy, and using the 69-week verbiage to represent todays years (483) we might say the 'anointed one' would again be 'cut off' in 2018."

"All this only makes sense to me if 'cut off' means 'ascended' in the Old Testament version and 'withdrawn' in the New Testament version. I am sure we could find the work of more scholarly folks who have looked into this prophesy. It is intriguing, but certainly not conclusive. Before we take a break, does anyone have any questions? I have one more prophesy to take you through and I find it most intriguing and possibly the best explanation for my theory."

Adrian responded, "Michael, I honestly don't see enough in what you've presented so far to make a strong argument for your theory."

"Well spoken, Adrian. I did not either. However, when I paired the next prophesy with God's apparent inclination to even things out in terms of time given for the era of the Hebrew people with the time given for the era of the Gentiles my interest piqued. Let's see what you say after the next discussion."

"Fair enough!"

After the break, the group reconvened. Michael gave an update on their plans for the balance of the day. "We will have a catered lunch delivered to the room in an hour. That should give me adequate time to cover Jeremiah's prophesy. After lunch we will hold a discussion on this whole matter of just when does Jesus return. Now I want to take you away from the focus that Daniel places on the walls of Jerusalem. Although interesting and perhaps very accurate for the Old Testament, Daniel's prophesy might lead me to believe that Jesus will be 'cut off' in 2011 (using the Babylonian years converted to today's years – 476) or 2018 (using the modern years of 483). Still, this doesn't make perfect sense. There is far too much yet to happen based on the Book of Revelation for the 2018 date to be fathomable for Jesus' return."

"Something that makes more sense to me is the prophesy of Jeremiah, and how God may be using what happened in the Old Testament to balance the timing in the New Testament. First, I believe God has shown throughout history to be willing to adjust to the circumstances. I believe God wants the Hebrew people to have had a fair share of time, like the Gentiles, to get right with His Son. Largely based on that belief, when I read about Jeremiah, I found that God was very anxious to limit the punishment he dealt out to the Hebrew people for not following his commands. For example, God witnessed many years with kings over the Holy Lands doing despicable things and allowing people to disobey His commands."

"From 605 BC, when the Babylonians defeated the Egyptians and took control of the area around Jerusalem until 586 BC, the Babylonians periodically besieged Jerusalem. Remember some of what Ruth told us, if you can. During this 19-year period, Israel was led by kings who were despicable in their own right and allowed despicable things to be done in God's Temple. By 586 BC, the Temple in Jerusalem was destroyed and the Babylonians held control over the city and the region. As prophesied by Jeremiah, the Hebrew people were taken to Babylon and held there in exile for 70 years. In part, this punishment was ordered by God for the disobedience of the people of Israel. Not only were they doing despicable acts, they failed to allow their lands to go fallow for one year out of seven as God had instructed. They had become greedy and harmed the land in the process. God punished them."

"In some ways, God took 89 years away from the 'time of the Hebrew people' by punishing them in this way. Could it be possible that today we are living in an era where God is permitting Israel to regain those years? Let's consider the possibility. Israel was re-established as a nation in 1948. Then 19 years later, the Six-Day War resulted in Israel gaining control of Jerusalem, although they settled the war by an agreement that did not give them full control of the Temple Mount. If God wanted to return lost time to the Hebrew people, then giving them nation status in 1948 placed them on track to recapture that time. Thus, 19 years later they got the Holy City back. Finally!"

"This means that the Jews are recovering those years simultaneously with the Gentiles. In fact, if the Gentile period ends in 2030, which is 2,000 years after Jesus' sacrifice, the Jewish people get the last seven years to themselves. Part of what intrigues me about this scenario is that it provides sufficient time for the many events in the Book of Revelation to be accomplished and it all gets completed in one generation starting with the time the Hebrew people regained control of God's holiest site."

Rachel asked, "Michael, didn't you say in your theory that the return of Christ could be earlier than 2037?"

"Good question, Rachel. Yes, I did. That is because the events Adrian and I put together from the Book of Revelation could take less time than I might imagine. Since this would still fall in the 'generation' comment Jesus makes in the Book of Matthew, I believe that makes it a real possibility. Now Rachel's question gets directly at the handout I am going to give you now. It is the same one Adrian handed out earlier, except this one has years on it. They are estimates only and they deserve lots of scrutiny to perfect them. Some of the events give us times, like the five months the locusts will swarm as depicted in Chapter 8. At least it looks like all these events could happen within this timeframe."

Nancy asks, "So if I read your chart right, starting in 2018 we may see some of the things we have read in the Book of Revelation start happening and by 2037 Jesus would be here. Is that a fair interpretation?"

"Yes, Nancy that's what it says. Personally, I expect things to go well for the next several years before a financial collapse drives the world into a depression that leads to war and all the events outlined in the Book of Revelation."

"I might actually make it into that time period. Not sure I like the thought of what you see, however."

"If it is a plausible explanation, then we better get our act together. We will need to get the word out and help people prepare spiritually," Rachel added.

"Rachel, you are on target. Likewise, we may need to focus on people's physical needs as well as their spiritual needs," Michael confirmed.

The group broke for lunch. There was a buzz about them as they discussed the bombshell Michael had just dropped on them. No one had seemed to think that the events in Revelation would happen in their lifetime. Certainly not Nancy. She wanted more time for rocking her grand kids. She just might have to go and do that anyway, she said.

After lunch they met for an hour discussing the work Michael had done. They asked him for his opinion on whether he was highly confident in the conclusion or not. He told them he felt it was the best answer he had seen, but that he had not come close to doing any serious comparative work with biblical scholars and writers. That needed to be done, yes, but coming to one's own conclusion was important to do first.

"I am sure that with some research and some comparative work this theory can be polished up or torn down. I want to have time to do that before bringing it up for a final thumbs up or thumbs down by the group."

Everyone agreed that would be a worthy cause. In fact, everyone would look to their own work to find either supporting evidence for the theory or contrary evidence. In the end, they agreed that it may be hard to do, however. Also, they agreed that it would serve the Foundation best at this point not to discuss the specifics of Michael's theory with any outsiders to avoid publicity of any sort. That meant not showing anyone the chart Michael had provided with dates. Michael asked for and got permission from the group to make a couple of exceptions, including to allow Michael to show the work to Reverend Osgood and/or his colleague Thomas in Boston.

Michael realized that there would be a backlog of administrative work needing attention when everyone returned home. He told the group to plan on taking some time to get caught up on any important administrative matters, then work on the reports that need to be completed on the work they each had led. After that was done, each of them would need to get all of the information to Rachel so that she can start finalizing the overall report for the Foundation.

Michael told the group that they didn't need to meet for three to four weeks. He told them to prepare a plan for what the Foundation should do with all this work that had been done to date. Basically, Michael wanted everyone to come together and make a plan for going forward.

Back at their hotel, the group took the rest of the day off. In fact, they started their individual vacations that afternoon. Nancy and her husband enjoyed their time together. Adrian and Rachel had a wonderful time doing all the tourist things to do on Maui. They drove to Hana for an ultralight airplane ride. The views were spectacular. They went on a trip to the small island of Molokini and loved the clear water snorkeling. They even saw green turtles while snorkeling off the boat on the return trip to the harbor.

Meanwhile, Elizabeth and Michael had a delightful time. The first couple of days they simply stayed near the pool and beach. Later, they went out a couple of nights. First, Michael took her to a luau. The next night they went for a nice dinner on Front Street in Lahaina. They did have a long talk about Michael's approach to delegating more work to the others and the need for him to focus on the larger issues. Elizabeth felt Michael should take more time off and he was receptive to the idea.

Michael commented, "Elizabeth, I thought a lot since our talk last night and I agree I need to disengage more. I will do that. I plan to announce some position changes soon." He summarized the major changes he had in mind and Elizabeth was impressed."

Elizabeth responded, "I didn't know if you could do that yet. I am impressed with your decisions and I believe you will never regret the moves you've explained to me. Now what about us?"

Part Five

Looking Ahead

39

Mercer Island, Washington

The group gathered for their first meeting in over a month. Michael had a first class meal catered with fresh salmon from Alaska as the main course. Everyone enjoyed the luncheon, and they even indulged in a glass or two of a fine red wine from Washington State's Columbia River region.

Michael opened the gathering with a prayer and commented on just how blessed he felt after all the hard work everyone rendered over the past year plus.

"I want to get one important formality covered upfront. Actually, I am a little late in doing this. I have been so deeply involved in our quest to answer Question #4 that I let this matter slip my mind for a month or so longer than I should have. While this past year has taken us to new heights in our quest to better understand our faith and to help the Foundation move forward, there is the practical matter of your bonuses. I am so very pleased with each of you. You have all contributed more than I expected in your first year."

Rachel interrupted, "Michael, you told us that our bonus would be at the end of our second year. We still have a ways to go for that."

"You are correct, Rachel. However, we've done more than I expected in the time we've been together. I want you to have half the money now. The remainder will come to you at the end of the two years."

Each person at the table was given their first pay bonus in an envelope with a personal letter tailored to thank each member of the group for his or her contribution.

"Although the initiation of our endeavor was prompted by tragedy, I hope each one of you are glad that you made the choice to join me in what we have done. I know I am very grateful to have had the pleasure of working with each of you and I am very excited about where we are right now, and where we are headed. On a more personal note, I love you three more than you will ever know. Along with the Lord, you have carried me when I needed carrying. You manifest a Christian love I admire and cherish. I hope we can carry on to new heights with Jesus as our leader."

Adrian jumped in, "Michael, I think I can speak for everyone on the team in saying that this has been a remarkable experience. Each of us had our own reasons for joining you on this quest to lay out the fundamental reasons for our faith. Each one of us has been dealing with changes in our home life. To have the opportunity to come together as a team and to do something this important is a dream come true." Adrian continued, "We all appreciate the bonuses we are receiving today and they may have been an inducement for signing on in the beginning. However, what we have learned and done together is the reward you have given us and we are all so very appreciative. Thank you!"

Michael smiled and said, "The bonuses have been well earned. I look forward to paying the balance next year."

Again, Adrian responded, "Michael, your leadership is what got us through all of what we have done. There is no way we would be where we are without you."

Rachel jumped in, "Michael, I agree with everything Adrian has said. For me, I am a different person today because of this past year. All the intense study work we have done has made my faith so real. It is now not just a part of me. It is central to who I am. I am so excited to see how we wrap this all together in the months ahead and start really helping people see what we see." Rachel continued, "We have a huge opportunity ahead of us to enable others to walk the path we've walked and to explore the things we have seen. Our work in this next year will enable so many others to strengthen their faith. For others who have not been believers, we have a chance with God's help to open their eyes to God's plan for them."

Nancy joined in with her grandmotherly way. "Michael, I agree with the comments from Adrian and Rachel, but I am not going to get too emotional. Thank you for this bonus. Although I do plan to deposit the check today, I am so looking forward to what we are headed to do. But, I honestly am equally excited about working a little less and seeing my grandkids more. I have had my faith in God reaffirmed by all we have done and I am so glad you youngsters are catching on. Honestly, I don't need to know as much as you all want to know. I am happy to be a bit surprised as things unfold in the future. However, I will help as much as I can as long as I get more time in with those grandkids."

Everyone laughed and toasted Nancy for her wonderful perspective on life. Michael shared the following, "One day we will all remember those words and relax in the peace and comfort those words are meant to deliver. Thank you Nancy for all you've done. You have helped in so many ways and we will take whatever time you can devote to our work ahead. Do understand we want you to press on with spending more time at home. We support you in that endeavor. We will, however, continue to cherish your presence for the time you can work with us. Let us reconvene tomorrow at 9:00 a.m. to outline how we intend to plan for the future of the

Foundation. Pray for discernment and careful attention to God's intent. We want the Foundation to be Christ-centered, as Rachel and Adrian so aptly have encouraged. This should be a challenging task, but certainly no more difficult than the challenges we have already faced. Praise be to God and to His Son Jesus."

The next morning Michael started by asking Nancy to lead the prayer. She said a child's prayer. It was so classic Nancy.

"Nancy," Michael said, "Your prayer this morning reminds me of Jesus' advice to his followers, that in order to get into heaven we would need to be like children in committing our faith to him. It is so easy for children and often so difficult for adults." Michael continued, "I would like to hear from each of you about my last presentation on God's plan for Jesus to return. I want to hear from each of you as to what you honestly believe our position should be on 'when' Jesus will return. Adrian, would you please start."

Adrian started, "I would be happy to do that. Let's see. Where to start? You asked whether the position you offered was speculation or a hypothesis or a theory. That question takes me back to my science classes. I guess I felt the evidence you offered was sufficient to throw speculation out, but I was not certain that you proved the conclusion was fact. Therefore, I know your idea is at least a hypothesis and it may be a solid theory. I have not researched opinions and studies on the subject enough to either be critical or to heap on accolades. Sorry, but that is where I am today."

"Nancy, how about you?"

"Michael I have known you a long time. I've seen you pull off some amazing things. I don't know anyone that I would trust to decipher this cloud of prophesy more than you. So I am sold on the theory concept."

Nancy continued, "With that said, let me say that my answer is my head talking. It is what I believe the Bible tells us. However, my heart springs with the hope that the world has already seen the time of tribulation. For example, the two World Wars this nation endured along with many others in the 1900's was enough for many to think they were the wars to end wars. My hope is that my grandchildren will grow up in a millennium led by Christ."

Michael responded, "Nancy, I think we all would love to embrace that for which your heart longs. I do know there are some well-regarded religious scholars who believe exactly what you described is happening. They are a group of 'post-millennialists.' I think I have that right. Nancy, we could study that theory as an alternative to our stricter biblical view, if we wish to do so. Personally, unless it is rooted in the Bible I would prefer to recognize it but not endorse it as something to expect."

Everyone agreed with Michael for the time being. Michael called on Rachel.

"I love you Nancy! My heart shares your hope. Yet, when it comes to the question on Michael's theory I find myself in a cloud regarding whether we are speculating, or getting close to the true interpretation of the Bible's message. I have to say the theory Michael presented may need some work to fully validate itself, but it is certainly one worth continuing to refine. I hope I am not the deciding vote on the matter. Speaking of a cloud, I think my head is still in a cloud regarding all we've heard on the subject. I am not in a position to make a clear decision. I know what you presented is more than speculation."

Michael said, "I respect the frank and heartfelt opinions of each of you. Thank you! This will continue to be a topic for discussion and one worthy of more research. Any other thoughts we should discuss?"

Adrian raised his hand like a reluctant student. "Michael, I might offer a suggestion. I crossed paths with an interesting individual who lives just a couple of hours south of here that I think you would find interesting to talk to about this hypothesis or theory. He has written a book that I read on the 'end times' from a family perspective. He concluded that Jesus may well return in 2018. He did a good job of outlining the happenings before Jesus' return. His book was written in 2003, I believe, and he now recognizes that he made an error in the return date by not considering the importance of the capture of Jerusalem in 1967. He had felt the 1948 date was key. I think we should talk to him and see what he thinks about your theory. Also, he has some interesting skills as an engineer that might play well in some of our plans to have a modern visitor center that educates people on this subject. That's how I got to know him in the first place."

"Okay Adrian, if you think we should do that, then set it up. We can discuss ideas on both subjects."

Early the next morning Adrian and Rachel joined Michael for three short conference calls. They spoke with Nick Dawson in Athens, Joel Goldstein in Munich and Thomas Carr in Boston. Michael promised each of them a copy of the group's final report and thanked them for their help.

The following morning everyone gathered for the follow-up meeting. Adrian started the session with a prayer.

Michael outlined the purpose of the meeting. "Let's make a list of the things we would like to see the Foundation do in the next three years. I want this to be a brain-storming list. From it we will prioritize the things we think are most appropriate and most realistic. Who wants to start?"

Rachel spoke up immediately. "We have been dedicated to answering four questions from the beginning. We have always driven ourselves to answer the questions as completely as we could but realizing we could spend our lives working on any one of them. Of course, we wouldn't do much good for anyone other than ourselves if we just kept working on one draft after another. We need to get the questions and answers we have out to others, so our work can help others get over the hurdles that mentally block many potential Christians. So I think our first priority is to complete our work as thoroughly as we can in a short period of time so that it is ready to go out to where it can do some good." She continued, "That being said, we must also find the best means by which to get the story out to people. It needs to be in a form that people will read and not just some research paper that only a few will want to read."

Adrian concurred, "We've discussed what Rachel just said before and I believe those two priorities have to be number one and two. Hopefully, in two to three months we should be done with the reports and we should make plans for distribution in some form thereafter. Elizabeth seemed to have a personal interest in helping us on this work. Is that still the case?"

Nancy replied, "I spoke with Elizabeth several times at the end of our stay in Hawaii. She came across as someone who has lots of ideas and is ready to explode on the scene to help us in getting the message out. Michael, I know you and Elizabeth must have spoken a lot about this."

"Yes we did, and I am happy to share those thoughts with you, but first I want to be very clear that we have complete agreement on the first two priorities for the Foundation work."

Adrian interjected, "There is no question in our minds. With the belief that the world may see major occurrences any time starting in 2018 we better make this a priority."

Michael asked Nancy if she was on board with this. Nancy replied, "By all means! I think we all agree on that." Everyone nodded approval.

"Okay then!" Michael continued, "So let me give you a brief rundown on what Elizabeth brings to the table regarding the publication of our work. She is impressed with our work and she said to me that our work is helping her just like it has helped us in our walk with Jesus. In fact, she is reassessing her beliefs and seeing where she needs to be dedicating more of her time, talent and treasure."

"Her suggestion to us is to contract with a professional writer to write a novel for us. The publication market is constantly looking for good novels that have a truer meaning woven into the story. Basically, she has offered to find the appropriate author and contract with the author on behalf of the Foundation. The author would speak with each of us about the journey we have taken over the past year and weave our findings into a fictional characterization of what we have done to discover our answers. In other words, the book would be a long parable-like story to involve readers in a journey of discovery much like the one we have undertaken."

The second part of her proposed plan is to line up someone to assist in the electronic publication of the novel, so that it can be widely distributed through the internet and translated where necessary. This should get us maximum coverage throughout the world."

"Paired with this idea of mass-marketing she believes we need to access interpreters who can translate the book into many different languages. Selling the book, perhaps with a complimentary Bible, to the far reaches of the globe may help spread the Word and the Gospels throughout the world just as Christ would do."

Rachel said, "Now we are talking about something totally impressive. Getting out our work, along with Bibles, to remote locations in their own language is beyond anything I imagined. This would be fantastic, but it might also be expensive."

Michael picked up on Rachel's point, "If we use funds generated from the sale of the novel in North America and Europe to finance the distribution worldwide, we really might have a dynamic situation that is self-supporting. There has been enormous progress in Africa and China in expanding the number of Christians. We need to help them as they find others searching for faith."

Nancy added, "Michael, I can see you are already envisioning how this might come together. I've seen it before and you are doing the same thing. You see an opportunity and then you dream up these amazing ways to make it reality. Like always, I am in on all of this!"

Adrian asked, "Michael, I agree with Nancy and Rachel. We do not know Elizabeth well enough yet, but we trust your judgement."

"Perhaps, this will help." Michael, showed the group a check made out to the Foundation for £250,000.00 that Elizabeth had given Michael before she flew home to London. "This is another donation to the Foundation from her and it is not contingent on the group agreeing to move ahead with her ideas. She simply believes in what the group has done and what the Foundation will do in the future. She simply is making an offer to help if we want the help."

Adrian reacted, "Wow, Elizabeth is placing her treasure in the Lord and the work we are doing for the Lord. I am in just like Nancy and Rachel."

Michael responded, "Elizabeth is a wonderful woman and one who is passionate about what we are doing. She has not seen anyone in the United Kingdom contemplate anything as ambitious as what we are doing. That is why she is so willing to help. I think we should embrace the opportunity she suggests and see if she can lead us there. I take it that we are unanimous in that feeling?"

Everyone nodded.

After a short break, Michael and Adrian explained Adrian's request to meet with Ken Duncan from Longview, Washington. After a short debate on whether it was a good idea to involve another person, the group agreed it would be a good idea, if for no other reason than the Foundation may need someone like Ken.

Adrian explained, "I would like for Michael to meet with Ken, not just because he wrote a book on one of the major issues we have on our list, but Ken also has skills that may be necessary for another Foundation priority."

Michael followed Adrian's lead, "If we want to truly spread the gospel we may choose to use missionaries across the globe to help carry the message of what we have learned. We may want to provide a central education center in our area for missionaries to study what we have learned. We may want to offer travel expenses and/or accommodations while missionaries stay here for classes. Yes, this will cost, but it may well serve our desire to get the word out."

Adrian added, "It also fits with another priority Michael and I have discussed. That is housing a modern visually interactive education facility in downtown Seattle where people from around the world can walk through a time tunnel from Adam to the time of Jesus' return and beyond. Michael and a few of his friends own a well-located building near Pikes Place Market where the Foundation could lease enough space to house a modern attraction to educate people. The facility would also serve as the learning center for missionaries and a place for advanced studies on what we have yet to discover."

Rachel, "You two have been thinking about some big plans. I like the ideas. Help me understand where does Ken fit in with this last idea?"

"Sorry, Ken is an electrical engineer with extensive experience in designing and managing large entertainment projects. Somewhere I have the list of major projects, like the large music center in downtown Seattle. He has travelled all over the U.S. doing the kind of thing we are envisioning for the Foundation."

"Sounds expensive!" said Rachel. "I'm sure Michael has a plan, though."

"I do, but it's too early to talk about it. What I will add at this point is the fact that I have had discussions with a locally based non-profit company that provides aid throughout the world. They have a remarkable arrangement with suppliers who provide medicine, food, building supplies, school supplies, and even farm animals at cost. It is a company that could use our financial support to expand their support of the poor world-wide, but more on that later."

Nancy had a question. "First, I love what you just mentioned Michael. Secondly, I have a suggestion; if we are going to go to such lengths on several projects, how would you feel about establishing a monthly or quarterly periodical, in print and on-line, that gives people an update on world events, Foundation news, and the latest vision ahead?"

"If we adopt all we have talked about to this point, I would think your suggestion is appropriate. Do you have anyone in mind who would lead such an effort?" Michael inquired.

"Michael, I know better than to bring up something new like this and not be willing to do it. I've been around you long enough to know most of what you are thinking. Yes, I would do that as long as Adrian agrees to review each edition before it is published."

"Why me?"

"Adrian, I simply expect Michael to be travelling to London a lot in the future and he won't be around as much as you. I also know Rachel will be a large contributor to the publication, so that leaves you to do the review."

Adrian smiled, "I think the idea is great!"

Michael wrapped up this session, "Well, well! I am not going to ask if anyone else has a pet project they want to add to our growing list of priorities for the Foundation. We seem to have a full plate at this stage and I like it. If there are no objections, then I suggest we meet back here in three days. Meanwhile Adrian and I will meet with Ken Duncan and report back at our next gathering. Nancy, would you close us in prayer?"

The following day Michael and Adrian drove south on Interstate 5 to Longview, Washington. They found Ken's home across the street from Lake Sacajawea on a nice shady lot with tall Douglas fir trees. The setting was tranquil for a town with heavy industry all along the Columbia River.

Ken Duncan had lived in Longview for 25 years. He had been interested in prophesy for 40 years, and in those years he has been fascinated by the question of when Christ will return. Like the Christians of the first century AD he believes we are close to "the return." Unlike the Christians of the first century, he has had the chance to see much of the world that has an additional 2,000 years of history.

Lots of people have read the tea leaves and been wrong. Ken even acknowledges he has been wrong in the past, but he believes God has made it almost impossible for anyone to decipher prophesy correctly until several important events actually occurred. He had believed the last piece of that puzzle had been made clear and there was but one conclusion. He had thought Jesus would return in 2018 based on the belief that 70 years after Israel became a nation Jesus would return. Basically, he based his belief on the concept that Jesus would return one generation after the Jews regained their country.

"Ken, it is a pleasure to meet you. Adrian said we should meet, and I appreciate you taking your time to meet with us."

"Michael, Adrian told me a little of what you are doing and I admire your undertaking. The subject matter has been a passion of mine for 40 years. So, if there is anything I can do for you to help you I will be glad to try and do it," commented Ken.

"So, Adrian, where do you want to start?" Michael asked.

"Michael, I think it would be appropriate to start with a prayer and then we should ask Ken to explain his theory on when Christ will return." Adrian led the group in prayer.

Following the prayer Michael said, "Okay, I am all ears."

Ken proceeded, "Michael, you and your team have done an impressive job of taking on the questions you are answering. Adrian, gave me a little insight into the approach you are taking. I am amazed with your intent and the objectiveness with which you are tackling such difficult questions. Yet, I understand your work is now at the point of addressing the fundamental question as to when Christ will return."

"That is one of the main ones we are dealing with currently, yes."

"I have experienced some frustration over the 40 years I have pondered on that question. First, let me say that 12 years ago I concluded that Christ would return in 2018. Since the tribulation has yet to start, it is clear I was interpreting the scriptures incorrectly. Until 2011 passed, it was not clear to me how we should interpret what I believed was the one key prophesy that hints at Christ's return. Sure, there are many events yet to occur that will make it clear when the tribulation has started. Those events are largely noted in the book of Revelation. Also, it is abundantly clear that the return of Jesus will be preceded by a seven-year tribulation. Are we in agreement with that?"

"Yes, so far, so good!" Michael responded.

"Time is a relative thing to God. Peter tells us that 1,000 years to us is like a day to God"

"We are on board with that concept, as well. In fact, has Adrian mentioned our conclusion that God is working through a 7,000-year period?"

"Yes Michael, he did, and I agree with that concept. That is largely what convinced me that your thinking process is on track. But don't think you are alone in that belief. Many people of the Jewish faith have also concluded that to be the case. In fact, some of those folks of the Jewish faith believe that the 7,000-year period is tied to the Jewish calendar. Those folks, in turn, believe the period has over 200 years to go before the Messiah returns in that we are only in the year 5777 on their calendar. In many respects, I hope they are correct, at least for the sake of my children and grandkids. However, I do not see that to be the case."

Michael interjected, "Okay, I understand the 6,000-year theories, and I believe God gave us a clue about when Jesus would return. He gave many prophetic messages in the old and new testaments that were clearly meant to reduce fear of the future and to instill hope and assurance for the future. So what prophesy did you misinterpret and what is your updated view as to when Christ will return?"

"In the book of Daniel, Chapter 9, Daniel delivers a prophesy commonly referred to as 'the seventy sevens'."

"I know it Ken, but that prophesy deals with the timeline from the early return of Ezra or Nehemiah until the 'anointed one' is killed. But even that is difficult to prove. What does it have to do with the second coming?"

Adrian smiled.

"Michael, bear with me through this for a few minutes. First, let us address Daniel's prophesy as it relates directly to the Hebrew people in the context of time as it was intended over 2,400 years ago."

"The prophesy declares that from the time a decree is issued to restore and rebuild Jerusalem there will be 'sixty-nine sevens' before the 'anointed one' is cut off. This is universally interpreted as saying that there will be 483 years between the decree and the death of Jesus. Now, it is likely that the decree referred to is the one made by King Artaxerxes in 445 BC. Later he sends Nehemiah to restore the walls and the city of Jerusalem. Keep in mind this follows the complete and utter destruction of Jerusalem by the Babylonians in 586 BC. You can read about this in Second Kings Chapter 25."

"Now, this is the tricky part. This is where I make an assumption because I can look back on the history and see what has happened.

First, I believe that since this prophesy relates to times before Christ's first coming, it must relate to a prophetic year of 360 days. This is also the time John gives in the Book of Revelation when he is told about the three and a half years of the first half of the tribulation being 1,260 days. Therefore, I surmise the 483 years that make-up the 'sixty nine weeks of years' to be equivalent to 476 Georgian calendar years. If that is correct, Daniel's prophesy predicts the death of Jesus to be 31 AD. Most authoritative studies conclude Jesus died on or about 30 AD."

Michael jumps in and says, "Okay, you acknowledge there is some stretch in your assumptions and maybe you are right and maybe you are not. If I could get comfortable with your conclusions, how do I jump to the present and see this prophesy relating to the Second Coming?"

Adrian was still smiling to himself!

"First, let me say that I understand your skepticism. I have been living with those same concerns for a long time, but I am driven to believe that somewhere in scripture God has revealed His plan. Michael, many people feel compelled to say that since Jesus said we would not know the day or the hour of His return, we should not bother ourselves with searching for it. Yet I believe He chose His words carefully and never said we would not know the year or, possibly, the season. That is what has kept me searching. Especially when we look at the events of today throughout the world, it is difficult not to believe we are getting close. Just look at the noted scholars and theologians who are writing about the fact that the times are near. I've been hearing that for 40 years."

"Ken, you are preaching to the choir on your points. We are with you on wanting to accept the best premise on which to answer the question of 'when'. So please proceed and let us hear how this plays out in your mind."

Adrian is at a point of struggling not to breakout in a big grin.

"Well, if we now take the same prophesy and look to the Christian era using the Georgian calendar, we get a very spectacular look at things. The Christian era would use the literal 483 years to calculate the date of the second 'cutting off of the anointed one'. Now keep in mind Jerusalem has been destroyed completely only twice. It has been besieged and conquered many times, but only destroyed twice. The second destruction occurred when the Romans tore the city down stone by stone in 70 AD. Furthermore, there was a decree given in 1535 by the Ottoman Emperor, Suleiman the Magnificent, to rebuild the city of Jerusalem. Keeping with Daniel's prophesy, we would conclude that Jesus would again be cut-off in 2018. Presumably this is the start of the tribulation, and at the conclusion of that seven years tribulation the 'anointed one' will return in 2025 to begin the promised thousand year 'millennium'."

Adrian could not resist and jumped in, "Wait a minute, earlier you made the case that God's intent in Daniel's prophesy was to use a 360-day year and now you want to use a 365-day calendar. I do not follow!"

"Adrian, a dozen years ago I wrote a book for my children explaining many of the things that I wanted them to know about God's plan for us. I answered a number of questions they had about the Second Coming. Two of my kids, who now are young adults, asked when the Second Coming would start. I reluctantly gave them the best answer I could. I wrote of my conclusions concerning the First Coming and carried on thinking that the same rationale would hold for the Second Coming. My conclusion was that in using a 360-day year the second Coming would occur in 2018. However, that was wrong. Obviously the seven-year tribulation did not start in 2011. That is why I have reconsidered what a year is, in terms of the Christian era."

Michael got up from his chair and walked over to his lakeside window. He stood there for a couple of minutes without uttering a word. Finally, he turned and said "Ken, you may be right. In fact, we agree with much of your work. But can you be open-minded enough to hear a slightly different take on the answer to the question of 'when'?"

"I think so. Please proceed."

Michael carefully explained the concerns he had that if in using Daniel's prophesy to predict the time of Jesus' return, the term 'cut off' meant Jesus had to die. "Maybe it works in the first coming, but the idea of Jesus dying in the second coming is inconsistent with any other prophesy of the 'end times'."

Michael then said that his group considered the word 'cut off' in the Old Testament to likely relate to Jesus' death or ascension. However, in the New Testament era, Michael noted that the word 'cutoff' may mean Jesus is removed from the earthly scene to serve God in heaven. Michael continued by noting that since all this is speculative, it is difficult to use Daniel's prophesy for the purpose of accurately predicting Christ's return.

Michael went on to state, "Even if we accepted that Daniel's prophesy should apply, the case is a hard one to make. Using the full 483 years of time as the 'sixty weeks of years' with Suleiman's 1535 declaration, Christ's cutoff would be 2018 and his return would be 2021 0r 2022. That does not work out well since in 2018 the seven-year tribulation has not come close to starting. Hence, it is unlikely Daniel's prophesy is the answer to Christ's return."

"I will need some time to absorb all you've said, Michael. Where did this take you in your search for an answer?"

Michael stated one other point. "Keep in mind most people agree that 'cutting off' means to be put to death. Christ died once and is not expected to ever die again. That makes it hard to believe Daniel's prophesy applies to the New Testament era."

"I can't argue with that point," Ken admitted.

"Ken, Adrian trusts you to keep our conversation confidential. We have reasons for that. With that in mind, I will explain our rationale for using Jeremiah's prophesy instead." Michael spent the next 20 minutes helping Ken understand the approach the group had taken to come up with a reasonable answer. Ken was going to need some time to digest this, as well. The fact that Michael and Adrian put their expectations in an entirely different prophesy than Daniel's was going to take some reflection.

Michael continued, "Would you mind if we changed subjects? We would like to hear from you more about your experience with high-tech light and sound systems for entertainment. We have an idea to discuss with you."

Ken provided Michael and Adrian with a copy of his work resume. He was in the process of looking for a new project having just completed a large project in Atlanta. Ken walked them through his resume and his experiences of late in design and construction.

Michael asked, "Why do you live in Longview? You have worked all over the U.S. and Canada. You could live anywhere you want it seems."

"You are correct. I have needed to live here. My parents are in a nursing home here. I grew up here and my Dad worked in one of the paper mills in town. My wife is from here and she too has older parents who need some attention. We like Longview and we have been blessed to have enough time between my projects to enjoy the area and to travel the world from Portland."

Michael asked Adrian to tell Ken about the project they had in mind for the Foundation. Afterwards, Ken wanted to know how the project would be funded and whether there were sufficient funds to do all the planning. After hearing what funds were on hand and what the fundraising in the future was expected to produce, his interests were piqued. Ken got even more hyped when Michael explained the other priorities that were being worked on and the small staff that were generating all these ideas.

"Ken, is what the Foundation is doing is something that has any personal interest on your part?" Michael squarely asked.

"Michael and Adrian, I can honestly say I would be honored to do what you've outlined. I am getting to where I would prefer to stay closer to home. In fact, I have contemplated retiring. This would likely be my last job, in all honesty. To be able to finish my career doing a Christian-related project is something I would relish doing. There are a few really good people out there that could do a good job for you. I would be happy to recommend a few if you would like to talk with them. They could also serve as references, if I am in the running for the job."

"I see you have a number of references here on your resume. I presume some of these are the ones you just mentioned."

"Michael, I can get you more names of construction engineers from around the country that you can talk with. Most of those references are people I worked directly for on major projects and only a few that I actually worked with. In the industry, you get to know who is good after all the years I've put in."

"Okay, yes, please send me a list of three or four of the best folks you know. I will contact them and ask them about you as well as check them out. We will be back to you in a couple of weeks."

"Terrific, thank you gentlemen for making the trip to Longview. I look forward to hearing from you."

Adrian said, "Thanks for the hospitality and God Bless!"

After they had left the house, Michael and Adrian looked at each other and Adrian said, "I don't know whether I uncovered a potential team member or not. I like Ken and I hope you felt the time was worth it?"

"Adrian, I am more convinced that God does have a plan. I believe He wants us to have faith in Him. I believe He puts people in our lives who are wanting to do the same thing He wants done. Ken may well be the right person for the job. If you want to hire him for the job, then I want you to check out his references and see if we need to talk with anyone else."

Adrian said, "Let's sleep on it tonight and I'll check with you tomorrow as to where we go from here."

"Okay, thanks Adrian," Michael said as he turned the car into his driveway pausing to take a look at the view over Lake Washington. "By the way, Adrian, I've got one more piece of good news. Remember our earlier discussion with Harold Wilson at Arizona State University?" Adrian nodded. "Well I called him and brought him up to speed on our findings. He was thrilled and even sent us a donation. Praise be to God!"

Adrian responded, "Wow that is very special indeed!"

The next morning around 10:00 a.m. Adrian walked into Michael's office. "Michael, you are not going to believe this. I have been on the phone since 8:00 a.m. this morning. I've spoken with four of the seven on Ken's reference list. I even started at the bottom, not the top. All four said they would hire Ken in a second. They said that if they had any major work where high-tech electrical systems were involved, they would choose Ken over anyone they knew hands-down! I'll call the rest on the list, but it looks like he could be our man."

"Keep me posted!" Michael smiled and looked up. 'Thank you, Lord'."

Later in the day, Adrian reported back to Michael. "I got two more references checked this afternoon and they said the same as the first four from this morning. I see no reason to try to talk to number seven as he is in France on a project."

"Okay, see if Rachel and Nancy can join us in the conference room tomorrow morning. You can make the pitch for Ken, and if everyone agrees to move ahead we'll ask Ken and his wife to come up for a day next week. It is important everyone gets some time with him and vice versa. He needs a little better understanding of where we are headed before we ask him to accept a job with us, plus there is the matter of pay and benefits."

"Adrian, adding staff is an added cost of administration for the Foundation and doing so needs to be done deliberately and with the full knowledge it results in more overhead. Matter of fact, we are looking at adding Elizabeth too. Fortunately, she will not require a salary. She only needs travel expenses and I bet she doesn't ask for all those."

"Wow, Elizabeth's desire to work with us is pretty strong. I trust Ken will be as helpful! Let's sleep on it."

"Okay!" Michael agreed.

Adrian shuffled around a moment before asking a question. "Michael, have you got time for me to discuss something personal?"

"Adrian, you are my right hand here. You get whatever time you want. What's up?"

Adrian sat for a minute collecting his thoughts. "Michael, Rachel and I had dinner last night and I asked her to marry me. She said 'yes'. But we both want to get your blessing before we announce our engagement. We want to get married in six months and we so hope and pray you will be supportive of all this. You have been so wonderful to us. We are deeply indebted to you."

"Well, well, bring me back to earth. Of course, I am supportive and I have to admit I hoped you two would get hitched. I am so happy for you two. Where is Rachel? Get her in here right now!"

It was a 'hug fest' with the three of them and then Nancy was escorted in by Adrian. She started to cry when she was told the latest news. All work was cancelled for the balance of the day and the four of them went to lunch. They took the afternoon off, as well. Adrian and Rachel began calling family. Nancy went home and hugged her husband. Michael returned home and called Elizabeth.

The next day the group tentatively bought off on the idea to interview Ken for the Seattle project. They coordinated work schedules for the following week and came up with two days they would all be in the office. Adrian was to coordinate with Ken and see that he and his wife could come up one of the two days available.

When Ken and his wife Karen came to visit the following week they had a wonderful day. Individually, Michael, Adrian, Rachel and Nancy spent a half hour with Ken and Karen speaking openly about all the work they had done to date. Ken was amazed at how much they had done.

Karen impressed everyone on the team. She was humble, charming and quite funny. Everyone thought she could be Nancy's sister. They even looked alike and their mannerisms were similar. The whole morning felt warm and comfortable. After lunch, Nancy spent time with Karen and they talked about family matters. Karen confided to Nancy that she had never seen her husband so excited about the prospects of a job like this one. She hoped the opportunity might come to pass as this would likely be Ken's last major project. They were close to retiring.

Nancy related to the retirement idea as she too was getting close. Nancy explained the unique nature of working for Michael, and the fun and energy that Rachel and Adrian bring to the workplace. She told Karen that it is more like a family business where everyone wants to contribute to something they see as important.

Karen also confided that if Ken got the job they may want to move closer to his work. She indicated that both their parents were moving to a retirement home in Longview and that would reduce the workload Karen had undertaken. It would still allow them to get to Longview on the weekends when necessary.

Nancy said that looking ahead her workload was going to be less and she planned to spend more time with her family. She told Karen that the whole group was more interested in getting results and not really hung up on work schedules other than meetings to coordinate all the work of the Foundation. She told Karen that most decisions are made by the group and they all respect that practice.

Meanwhile, Ken passed on his gratitude for being considered for the construction manager position. He also greatly appreciated the fact that the position meant that he could follow his passion of working with others to better understand God's plan and to educate others on that plan.

Adrian asked Ken what it would take salary-wise to get him to work for the Foundation. Ken's reply was, "Normally those of us who do this kind of work get a set contract term of employment and a set level of pay and benefits. However, I am at the end of my working career and this would be my last job. Karen and I will either move closer to Seattle or lease a home in the area with the idea they would return to their Longview home when the job was completed. So relocation is a concern."

Ken continued, "Since the project you have in mind will take approximately two years to complete, I would like a contract for that time. I would hope to get $20,000 up front for relocation costs. Lastly, since you expect your employees to pay for their own benefits, I would need an annual salary of $150,000."

"What about transportation?" Adrian asked.

"I will provide my own vehicle as long as I can get paid a mileage fee to reimburse me for the travel time as it relates to the job."

"Ken, what about your work hours?"

"Adrian, in my kind of work you work however many hours you need to work to get the work done properly and on time. That means some long days and some 'comp' time if there is a window to get it. I will average 50 hours a week with some weeks running as high as 80 hours. Basically, I get paid to do the job, not for the hours I put in."

Ken stepped out of the room for a few minutes. Michael made a short phone call to Nancy.

"Nancy says she is on board with Karen. How do you two see things relative to Ken?"

"With the reviews I got over the phone I doubt we could find a better fit if we spent six months searching," said Adrian.

Michael looked across to Rachel.

"When it comes to engineering and construction matters I have to rely on you two. As far as a personal fit, I am totally in. Ken is direct, yet compassionate. He is fair, yet firm. He is a gentleman and still fun to be around. Most importantly to me, he is a Christian with deep interest in the things we are doing. He will work hard, I believe, to help us achieve what we want to achieve. So, I am on board."

"Adrian, how do you feel about the salary, travel, and relocation costs?"

"Michael, I see someone who is very sure of his capabilities and his value. He is not trying to stick it to us with his salary. I think he makes a fair offer for the talent he brings."

"Okay, I say we hire him and he reports to Adrian. You make the offer as he requested. Do it now and in our presence. Tell him he will work for you. Ask him if that is okay, but insist that it is not negotiable."

"You are certain you want him to work for me?"

"I insist."

"Okay, that is fine with me."

Rachel spoke up, "I know this might be unusual, but how about asking Karen and Nancy to join us when we make the offer."

Michael replied, "I like it if Adrian likes it."

Adrian said, "Let's do this!"

Ken and Karen joined the four in the conference room. Adrian led the meeting with a prayer. He then told Ken and Karen that the Foundation staff would love to have Ken join the staff. Adrian's offer was formally made and immediately accepted. Hugs around the room erupted.

Michael told the group that he had a catered lunch in the refrigerator and with Nancy's help the six of them should be able to eat out on the deck in short order. Ken made it clear that he could start work whenever Adrian needed him. Adrian suggested a start date two weeks out and all agreed. Michael even had a bottle of champagne in the refrigerator just in case. The group enjoyed the lunch together and Ken and Karen departed shortly thereafter.

40

Bellevue, Washington

A week later, the group of five were meeting at ten in the morning at a location Michael designated in downtown Bellevue. The location was on the 24th floor of a new building in town. The view across Lake Washington was simply spectacular. There were a half dozen offices, a reception area, a storage area, a kitchen, and a first-class conference room. No one quite understood why they were meeting at that location.

An hour before this scheduled meeting, Adrian had been asked to meet with Michael. Adrian showed up on time and was met at the door by Michael. They sat in the reception area and Adrian was somewhat mystified by the location. Michael had not said anything to either Rachel or him about why they were meeting here.

After a prayer, Michael asked, "Adrian, have you ever read the book in the Bible written by Solomon called the Song of Song by Solomon? It is not in all Bibles. In mine it follows the Book of Ecclesiastes and it precedes the Book of Isaiah."

"Honestly, since you and Nancy covered the Old Testament all I can say is that I know it is there and I did skim it."

"Well, I only read it once and it was late last year when I read the entire Bible from cover to cover. The fascinating thing about this particular book is that after a very successful life in leading the Hebrew nation and gaining incredible wealth, Solomon writes about how foolish everything had been, including his motivation to do all he had done. He basically reviews his own doings and says it and almost everything people do is absolute foolishness."

"Late in his life he comes to the stark realization that the only important thing in life is one's relationship with God. Nothing else really matters, and all the time spent chasing human goals is foolish. He literally goes on and on in prose describing how foolish we are and how foolish he has been."

Adrian recalled, "After losing my wife and my daughter I too had some of those same feelings. I was living the American dream one day and then the 'unexpected' happened and I felt so bad and so foolish for not having loved them so much more. It is like the one thing I do remember from Solomon. Our lives are like 'chasing the wind'."

Michael responded, "Exactly. That is what drove us to start this endeavor in the first place. Day by day we should be working to get our spirit right with God. That is what this is all about. Thank you for pointing that out and I can't tell you how proud I am of your growth and progress. You are a continuing inspiration to me, and I am forever grateful that you are part of this journey with me and the others."

Michael continued, "Adrian, I am going to take a vacation. I want to spend some time with Elizabeth in New York and London. She has found an author of some renown who is interested in hearing more about what we are doing. He may be interested in our offer to commission his services. He is available to discuss the details of what we want done and he has an open block of time between finishing his current book and writing his next book. Anyway, he is willing to discuss doing what we need."

"That doesn't sound like a vacation. That sounds more like Foundation work."

"Well, that part of the trip will be Foundation work, but if that part of the trip goes as well as expected, Elizabeth and I will go to London for a couple of weeks. We may raise funds for the Foundation, but mainly she will show me around the United Kingdom. I am really looking forward to that. After time in London, Elizabeth and I are going to take another tour of the Holy Land much like we did earlier this year. Some quiet time in the Garden of Gethsemane is what I need. When I return let's have a celebration dinner for completing the study phase and the initiation of our action phase.

"Michael, how long will you be gone?"

"Don't hold me to it, but I would guess five weeks. That is what my flight reservations say."

"Do you think we can get along without you for that long?"

"I have no doubt about that. Matter of fact, that is the rest of what I wanted to discuss with you before the others get here. This office is the new Foundation office. I've agreed to a lease for the next three years. This should serve us well for the foreseeable future and we have the option to stay longer if we want. The paperwork is on your new desk. Please sign it and get it to Rachel when she gets here."

"Okay, but this is all rather sudden. Are you going to tell the rest of the group when they show up?"

"No, I am leaving that to you."

"Okay!"

"A couple more things, Adrian. I want you to hold an impromptu staff meeting today when everyone gets here. I've written down a number of things I want you to cover. Here is the list. First, tell everyone I am thrilled with the work we have done to date. Once the report work is done we will start looking outward to help others with their walk with the Lord. Secondly, I want you to take on the role and duties of the President of the Foundation immediately. I trust you will accept?"

"Really?"

"Really."

"Wow, as long as you remain CEO and Chairman I'll do it!"

"Yes, I will do that. Congratulations!"

"Third, I want you to promote Rachel to Vice President and CFO of the Foundation. Oh, by the way you each will get a 10% raise. I trust Rachel will accept?"

"Most definitely!"

"Bless you Adrian! Tell Rachel I have come to love her like my own daughter. I can't tell you how happy I am for you two. May the Lord bless you! Keep me apprised of your wedding plans. Michael continued, "Just a couple of other items of interest. I am going to sell my house on Mercer Island and donate the proceeds to the Foundation. Including the house proceeds, I will pledge a total of $50,000,000 to the Foundation over the next three years. I also plan to raise an equal amount from others over the next three years, resulting in $100,000,000 available to the Foundation's work in the years ahead. My next to last note on the list, is for you to pass along this statement to Rachel, Nancy and Ken. It reads,

'Let us all know that although many of us have suffered tragedy in our lives, we have grown in love for one another and for Jesus.

Moreover, we are committed to following Jesus each day of our lives. Praise the Father, The Son and The Holy Spirit. May thy will be done'!"

"The last note is a letter from one of our benefactors. Rachel received it in the mail and gave it to me, but I want you to have it. The note reads, *'Dear Mr. Channing, my mommy new Lisa and said I should rite u and send 5 dolars to help som 1. Lov Susie'.*"

Both men had tears in their eyes as Michael left for his flight to New York.

#######

Made in the USA
Coppell, TX
26 June 2020